BEYOND THE RIVER

BEYOND THE RIVER

A NOVEL BY

MICHAEL FILLERUP

Signature Books • Salt Lake City • 1995

Cover photo illustration and design by
K.C. Muscolino

∞ *Beyond the River*
was printed on acid-free paper and was composed,
printed, and bound in the United States.

99   98   97   96   95   6   5   4   3   2   1

Library of Congress Cataloging-in-Publication Data
Fillerup, Michael
Beyond the river : a novel / Michael Fillerup.
         p.   cm.
ISBN 1-56085-068-X
I. Title.
PS3556.I429B49   1995
813' .54—dc20   94-37246
                                          CIP

CHAPTER 1

Keith is gaining on the Las Plumas runner coming out of the final turn. One lap, I remind myself. Just once around. No holding back.

Coach Ramirez is on the sidelines yelling through cupped hands: "It's up to you, Jon! All up to you now!"

I glance down at the chalkline, smeared to obscurity, and shake my arms loose, trying to relax, trying to blot out the brown giant in the powder blue jersey waiting on my inside shoulder.

Clichés: Run your own race. He's invisible. Don't wait for the breaks, make them!

The crowd explodes into modulated thunder: Keith has trimmed the lead to five yards. That's not enough, though. I need three more—at least three.

I get them. Halfway down the straight, rigor mortis strikes the Las Plumas runner who staggers into the exchange lane, extending his baton like a stick of dynamite he wants to get rid of. Then Keith, converging on me phantasmagorically, his mouth open wide enough to swallow me whole: "Gooooo!"

It's a good, clean pass, and I quickly pull within three yards. I'm flying effortlessly down the track, floating, but at an incredible speed. I'm Mercury, wings on my heels! I can barely hear the other runners panting a comfortable distance behind. By the time I hit the first curve, they are inaudible, and it is strictly a two-man race, Harry the Horse and me.

I chase him out of the smoky fieldlights and into the dark silence of the turn. The effect is theatrical, as if the lights have been dimmed and the volume turned down, then off. We're in a giant echo chamber, the only sounds our syncopated breathing and sprinting feet. Angling into the turn, I match him stride for stride, the chipping of our spikes like the ticking of twin clocks.

Relax. Stay loose. Don't lose him now.

The volume rises as we race out of the darkness and down the backstretch. My legs are gone—ghost-like appendages, an amputee's —yet they're spinning like a roadrunner's. I haven't gained ground but haven't forfeited any either.

The home crowd has returned, stomping, hollering, chanting: "Go! Go! Go!" "Reeves! Reeves! Reeves!" The fieldlights begin playing tricks on me, multiplying like Viking shields along the pine tree horizon.

Focus now. Concentrate. This is where you lose him.

I zero in on my focal point: Harry's shiny blue trunks, his blue behind. All the way down the backstretch I glare at it like a target, an enemy, while he kicks cinders in my eyes.

We enter the final turn, back into the tunnel, the echo chamber. No Man's Land. The volume fades again. Spikes, hearts, breaths. I feel absolutely no fatigue, no lactic slag. I'm still flying, legless. A spirit. An angel.

Then I do something stupid. I close my eyes for a moment and, opening them, observe the scene through *her* eyes: the fieldlights like translucent suns colliding above the steepled silhouette, the full moon clinging to one tall tip like a big white balloon waiting to be released.

More reminders: You're in control here. You can do whatever you really want to. Maybe.

The whisper becomes a roar. I've gained another yard on him.

Charging out of the final turn, caught in the centrifugal body lean, like two horses harnessed, I can feel his oily shoulder rubbing against mine. And then it happens. My shoulder edges an inch beyond his. I'm taking him! I'm passing Harry the Unpassable!

It is frighteningly easy. One, two, three strides and he's gone, out of my peripheral view. My legs are like a thoroughbred's, gobbling up ground. I'm thinking: school record, meet record, league record. My heart is banging against my ribcage like it wants to jump out. I can see Keith, Annette, Coach Ramirez—they're all there, screaming, cheering. My mother and father. Streamers. Colliding lights. I'm breaking the tape, falling into eager, admiring arms, my blood bubbling like champagne as they hoist me up and chair me off to bloat myself on Cokes and kisses.

Then I hit the wall. No: it hits me. Plows into me, like a flashflood, like a river. I fight it. Arms and legs churning, going nowhere, I wrestle the invisible current until my thighs catch fire, then go numb. The aluminum baton turns to iron in my hand. I lunge for the tape, grasping frantically, but it's hopeless. The current is dragging me back, five, ten, twenty yards. Bound in the water's harness, I watch impotently as flashbulbs envelope Harry in clouds of glory as the twin tails of the broken ribbon encircle his big blue behind.

Then silence. When I finally look up, the stands are empty except for her. She's sitting halfway up the bleachers laughing her horsey laugh.

"Damn you!" I scream. "Damn you *and* Harry the Horse!"

She looks at me sadly and then grows thin and pale, as if dissolving before my eyes.

"Nancy!" I yell, but too late.

Then I'm going under. Her sinewy arms wrap around my legs like tentacles, pulling me down. I kick, slap, pry, twist, trying to wrench myself free. But her fingers are teeth buried deep in my thighs. I can't breathe. My eyes go black.

Somehow I manage to pop my head above the surface and take a bite of air, expecting to go under again, but suddenly I'm free. She has let go. My arms and legs—my whole body—are shaking, the bones glowing through my hands like an X-ray. I look around for her—there! To my left! Tall, pale, translucent, wavering like a great white flame. I call her back but once again I'm too late. Already she has melted into the raging white-water rushing downstream.

CHAPTER 2

Great men and nations have fallen for the sake of a beautiful woman: Troy had Helen; David, Bathsheba; Samson, his Delilah; Antony, Cleopatra. In my mind this was understandable, if not wholly redeemable. A pretty face, I reasoned, pays dividends in passion and prestige. What I couldn't understand was how someone like Nancy Von Kleinsmid did me under. I felt like Robert Cohn in *The Sun Also Rises*. Poor Cohn, the minute he falls in love his tennis game goes to pot. I didn't fall in love with Nancy, but after meeting her I couldn't catch a pass or win a race. My once graceful body ignored my simplest commands. I said, "Leap!" and instead my legs crossed themselves and sent me sprawling on the grass. I said, "Relax, wait, concentrate," but my hands slapped crudely at the spiraling pigskin. Had I been bewitched by envious classmates? Had I contracted some rare disease? One thing was certain, it wasn't Nancy's beauty that blurred my concentration or turned my legs to sponge-cake when I crouched down in the starting blocks. Frankly, Nancy wasn't much to look at.

Keith called her "The Albino Watusi." Except for her hair, the metaphor was perfect. Tall and gangly, she was all arms, legs, and Adam's apple, a skeleton in Salvation Army hand-me-downs two decades out-of-style: plain white blouses and dark wool skirts, thick as kilts, that reached below her knobby knees. White gym socks sagged around her ankles and giant saddle shoes bound size thirteen feet. While her female classmates sheathed their nubile legs in pantyhose or fishnet stockings, she left hers bare—shapeless, sexless, a little girl's. She was aloof. If Ponderosa High had a popularity contest, she wouldn't have garnered a single vote. Yet everyone knew Nancy Von Kleinsmid. You couldn't miss her: the coltish clatter of her oxfords as she marched down the hall with books pressed to her chest, her bushy head bobbing above the crowd . . .

But she was a mystery. When she moved into our little pine tree town shortly after the Christmas holidays, rumors spread. She looked like a refugee. Maybe her father was a Nazi war criminal. The name fit, didn't it? Keith's explanation was more astute. "She's a freak," he proclaimed on more than one occasion. In a way, he had a point. Her feathered mop combined blond tones and textures in such a bizarre way that with a little imagination, abstracting the bush from her head to her pointy hips, she could have passed for a Picasso rendition of an ostrich.

I met her in mid-March of my senior year. I had just been notified that if I did not raise my grade in Calculus from an F to a D, I would be ineligible for the league track finals in May. This is not to say I was your typical dumb jock. True, I was numbered among the student athletes and was even considered something of a prodigy, especially after plucking a Hail Mary pass out of the hands of four defenders to give Ponderosa High its first league title in twenty-two years. As a result, I got a fat head. My teammates said Riddell didn't stock a helmet big enough for Jon Reeves.

But dumb? My cumulative grade point average was 3.6, including Senior Composition and Chemistry. But Calculus was another matter. I simply couldn't listen to Mr. Gilbert, the ex-stormtrooper, ramble on about parachutes and parabolas for an hour every afternoon, not with the obliging spring weather and the River only a few miles away. Plus I was lazy. What didn't come naturally took a back seat in my life. So that afternoon when I checked into the Student Tutoring Center I was desperate. Coach Ramirez had banned me from the track until I brought my grade up. No meets, no practices, *nada*. I had unwittingly secured for myself an indefinite string of free afternoons, giving further credence to the Sunday school axiom, "God works in mysterious ways."

I was the lone client, a relief in some ways, humiliating in others. Mrs. Larson, the grandmotherly program sponsor, directed me to a tall, gawky girl with her face buried in a book. Grinning like a lucky matchmaker, she leaned my way and whispered, as if we two were privy to some intimate secret, "That's Nancy Von Kleinsmid. She's a straight-A student. I'm sure she'll be able to help you."

The introduction was unnecessary. I recognized her immediately: the tugboat shoes, the dowel-like legs . . . Who but Nancy Von K?

Though my instincts screamed, "Run!" I had no choice. It was fourth-and-goal. D-Day. Do-or-die. Also, I felt sorry for her, sitting at that big deserted table, like a traveler lost in time. I took a seat and waited patiently for her to explain limits and derivatives, continuity, composite functions, the precarious alchemy of numbers.

At first she continued reading, oblivious to my presence. Her book was as fat as *Webster's Unabridged*. I noted the title: *Finnegan's Wake.* Five minutes passed.

"Excuse me," I said.

The book dropped, her back stiffened. Snatching the returned test paper from my hand (fifty-two was the score), she cracked open my Calculus text and, without introducing herself or asking my name, zeroed in on the topic for the day: curve sketching techniques.

"Okay," she ordered, "take out a sheet of paper and draw a grid!"

Before I could open my loose-leaf binder, she was drilling me like a Marine Corps sergeant. "How do you find the relative extrema of the absolute value of four minus X squared?"

"What's the second derivative of the function?"

"How do you use this to find concavity?"

"What are the inflection points?"

"Are these oblique or horizontal asymptotes?"

As I labored over problem one, she barked more orders. "Come on! Faster! Faster!"

Yanking the paper out from under my pencil, she scribbled out the answers and thrust it back at me. "There! Now try the next one! Quick pronto fast!" I made a feeble attempt at problem number two.

"Too slow!" Her bony fist hammered the table. "Just like yesterday in the mile relay!"

Surprised, I stopped my work. "You mean—"

"How could you let that blunder-butt from Las Plumas catch you from behind? And on the anchor leg!"

"That blunder-butt," I said, squaring my shoulders, "just happens to be Harold Williams, alias Harry the Horse, who holds the Mid-Valley League record for the quarter-mile."

"I don't care if he holds Tricky Dick Nixon by the g-string. He caught you from behind."

"Well, yesterday wasn't one of my better performances."

"Better performances! I've seen old coots in the convalescent home put on a better show than that. Reeves, you ran like you had six corn cobs up your butt!" (She enumerated each corn cob with a bony finger.)

I was stunned to silence. Other girls teased me about fumbles and mishaps on the field, but other girls had shapely thighs and Pepsodent smiles. Where did this Nancy Von Nobody get off criticizing me? Still in shock, my only counter was a meek, "How do you figure six?"

"Look at the films. You'll see." She slammed the textbook shut and, glaring at me with incriminating blue eyes, asked—no, *accused*: "Tell me, do you enjoy putting on a helmet and tromping around beating the mucous out of your fellow human beings every Friday? I mean, is this your idea of personal achievement?"

I hemmed and hawed while she pontificated on the morality of contact sports and the immorality of me playing them. And for some bizarre reason I was sufficiently intrigued to stick around for a full fifty-five minutes of verbal abuse.

There are points in time when you make split-second decisions that have lifelong consequences. I would make at least four such decisions in Nancy's company, but this first one started the ball rolling, so to speak. Because otherwise I would have walked out of that room and never returned, leaving my fate in Calculus to my own devices and Nancy Von Kleinsmid to hers. Instead, I turned to her and said, "Let's get something to eat!"

She shrugged and sighed condescendingly, "Oh, all right..." Seconds later the bell rang and Nancy leaped to her feet. With one swoop she gathered up her books and mine, grabbed my wrist with her free hand, and dragged me out the door.

"Whoa!" I cried. "Where's the fire?"

She gave my arm another tug. "Kick it in gear, Reeves, or we won't beat the stampede!"

I looked down the hall at the mass of sweaty, urgent bodies rushing to lockers, busses, choir practice, the baseball field. The "stampede" had never bothered me before, but Nancy made it seem as if the entire student body were a converging mob.

"Reeeeeves!" she shouted, giving my arm another yank.

I shadowed her lanky body across the grassy quad to the parking lot, where she paused, hands on narrow hips, breathing deeply, the grin of victory on her face as she watched the student exodus moseying along like a human traffic jam. Standing beside her, I realized how tall she truly was. I stood a shade under six-four but tilted my eyes upward to meet hers.

"Okay," she said, glancing around, "so where's your jalopy?"

"My *jalopy?*" I laughed. "Over there," I said, pointing to the giant ruby shining in the far corner of the parking lot.

Nancy shrugged. "A Ford, eh?"

"No, a Corvette Stingray."

"Ford, Corvette—what's the diff?"

Was she trying to rattle my cage again, or was she simply naive? I couldn't tell. She was wearing an indifferent smirk that annoyed me, but I think I was beginning to like her. She was so unlike the drooling beauties who stroked the red enamel of my car as if it were a pet.

Five feet short of the car she stopped and eyed my prize skeptically. "You know what Ralph Nader says about Corvettes?"

"Sorry, I'm not hep on consumer reports."

She shook her head. "'Death traps.' Real 'death traps.'"

"More power to Ralph," I said. "Get in."

We drove down Terrace Road and onto the Skyway, north past the oak-shaded cemetery and the felt-green lawns of Veteran's Memorial Park where old men in suspenders pitched horseshoes as miniskirted teenyboppers paraded by en route to the A&W. Then on past the dead daylight neon of the Silver Buckle Bar and the ominous escutcheon of the Moose Lodge; left on Star Route, past Mel's A-frame barber shop and the buzzing machinery of Moonbeam Construction, then a long green wall of pines abruptly broken by a red desert studded with tree stumps. COMING SOON! PONDEROSA SHOPPING CENTER! read the billboard.

"All those beautiful trees," Nancy muttered.

"It's progress," I said, baiting her.

"Or regress. It looks like a graveyard. All those little headstones . . ." We drove a ways in silence.

"Where are we headed?"

"The Double-Eagle," I said, noting her expression. There was no change. Either she had never heard of it (highly unlikely) or it made no difference. Double-Eagle, Foster Freeze, what's the diff? I don't know what good spirit prompted me to choose the Double-Eagle. In retrospect, though, Nancy deserved the best because, in her mind, "the best" was no big deal.

And the Double-Eagle aspired to more than hospital walls and salt and pepper table settings. The exterior resembled a splintering old shack from Gold Rush days: hitching rails and wagon wheels. A wooden Indian met you grimly at the door. Inside, you walked on sawdust past hefty tables of lacquered pine surrounded by wood-paneled walls covered with chaps, spurs, branding irons, WANTED posters, Winchesters, lariats. Suntanned students from Chico State drained pitchers of beer as Iron Butterfly and Ten Years After blasted from the jukebox. Fat beef patties sizzled on an open grill; smoke swirled delectably into the dim-lit rafters. It was a status symbol to come here. But weaving through the half-naked bodies (cut-off jeans, halter tops, hirachi sandals), Nancy looked thoroughly unimpressed.

I ordered my usual junk food special: double-deluxe cheeseburger on an onion roll, large fries, and jumbo Coke. Nancy ordered a tuna salad sandwich on twelve-grain bread ("hold the mayonnaise") and a glass of milk.

"You forgot the wheat germ and sprouts," I said.

She waited until we were seated and then proceeded to explain the nutritional value of our respective orders, comparing caloric intake, carbohydrate and protein gram ratios, and U.S.R.D.A. vitamin surpluses.

"What you have there," she said, gesturing to my junk food tray, "is the Triple-Bypass Special!"

"Amen!" I cried, raising my burger as if for a toast. "No sprouts or sunflower seeds for this José! Long live the double-deluxe cheeseburger!"

"On an onion roll," she murmured.

"Definitely an onion roll."

Nancy sprinkled a pinch of salt on her sandwich while I gobbed extra mustard and mayonnaise on my double-beef patties.

"Easy on the salt," I said. "It causes hemorrhoids."

"Just steer clear of the sugar." She aimed an accusing finger at my jumbo Coke.

"You don't eat sugar?"

"Not if I can avoid it."

I was impressed but appalled. "What do you do . . . for fun? I mean, what is life without an occasional sugar fix?" I said it jokingly but I was serious. What *did* someone like Nancy Von Kleinsmid do for enjoyment? She wasn't into sports; she had no friends, no car.

"Try honey," she said.

"Honey?"

She then expounded on the virtues of honey in curtailing diabetes, high blood pressure, cancer, sterility, baldness, impotency . . .

Here I grew bold and challenged her. "Excuse me, but if diet is the key to health and happiness, how come someone like Annette Plikta, who lives on cafeteria casseroles and Milk Duds, looks like Miss Universe?"

"She'd *be* Miss Universe if she ate right!" Case closed. But this made me wonder what this Albino Watusi would look like if she ate more than whole-wheat and honey. Several images flashed through my mind; all made me shiver.

I wolfed down my meal, while she picked at hers, nibbling like a squirrel. Every bite, every swallow, was slow, exact, disciplined. Her lips made none of the smacking sounds typical of after-school snacking. Even the crisp lettuce remained silent to the calculated incisions of her teeth.

A quarter of her sandwich remained when she dabbed her napkin to her lips and neatly folded it up for good. "Waste not, want not," I said, pointing to her uneaten portion. "Kids are starving in Biafra."

"Of course they are. But how would my over-eating help them?"

"I don't follow."

"Your body's not a trash receptacle!" she said, gathering up our used napkins, paper cups, and plastic utensils. I watched as her rangy body glided towards the trash barrel with the hyperextended grace of a basketball player. My teenage brain couldn't help evaluating her on the 1-10 scale Keith and I had devised our junior year. According to this criteria, only one girl at Ponderosa High earned a perfect 10: Annette Plikta, the future Miss Universe. I rated Nancy 1.5.

"Thanks," she said, retaking her seat. "That was good." She smiled—a warm smile this time, genuine. Give her a 2.2. She had beautiful teeth and a nice face, with freckles lightly sprinkled across her narrow nose.

"Ready?" I asked.

"Let's go!"

As we drove east on Star Route, Nancy sat low in the bucket seat, the window down, her eyes almost shut, the wind blowing her hair straight back in a raging Beethoven mane. Her small mouth was clamped tight, almost haughtily, her deprived nostrils sucking in the warm March air. Her eyebrows were pale etchings resisting the force of the wind. Something about the way she sat there, arms folded, eyes closed, hair blowing back, gave her the confident, self-possessed look of a movie star. Her expression said, This is nothing out of the ordinary, driving through the mountains in a red sports car with the captain of the football team. Why, she looked bored. I was beginning to feel self-conscious.

"So what does your father do?" I asked, trying to make conversation, but curious as well.

One blue eye popped open, then the other. "Sleeps," she said.

I laughed. "Mine too. Not much, though. He's an M.D."

"Permanently," she said.

"Oh . . . I'm sorry."

"Somewhere," she added.

If she was teasing, I couldn't tell. She remained perfectly poker-faced. "How about your mother, what does she do?"

"Everything."

I nodded. "Cooks, sews, cleans, washes . . ."

"No. Not that."

"You said everything."

"Everything but that."

This was getting nowhere. When I asked where she was from, her eyes got big and round. "A galaxy far, far away," she said in a quavering outerspace voice.

"Any brothers or sisters?" I asked—a last ditch try for a straight answer.

"More than one, less than a dozen. Nine's fine but ten's the end." She looked at me and smiled. "I'm quoting Cervantes—or Mother Goose—I can't remember. What about you—no, don't tell me: you're an only child."

"How did you—"

"Pampered, egocentric . . . You've got all the symptoms."

"And I suppose you're the oldest?"

She cringed. "Does it show that badly?"

I mulled this over. Her face was no longer coiled to strike but had softened. She looked nice even with that rigid German jaw. Her lips were meek and reticent, a lamb's. Try 3.4. "Not at all," I said.

"Not at all or not at all badly?"

"Both."

Her head flew back with a laugh. "Both! Reeves, you ought to be a politician!"

"Me?"

"Sure! You've got the mind and the face for it!" Her voice lowered a decibel to a tone of pseudo-seriousness. Adding a nasal twang, she mimicked perfectly Mrs. Barsumian, the Girls Vice Principal. "And just what do you plan to do with your life, Mr. Reeves?"

Thus commenced the first of many mock interviews. I played along. "Seriously? My secret ambition is to be a fireman or a cowboy or maybe a lazy degenerate beachcomber."

"And next year, Mr. Reeves? College?"

"If I like it, yes. With a jumbo Coke, of course."

"I understand you've been offered a football scholarship to Brigham Young University."

"Yes. That higher institution of lower athletics has made me an offer. They wined and dined me—"

"*Wined* you, Mr. Reeves? At a Mormon school?"

"Okay, milked me—*milked* me? That sounds . . ."

"Somewhat obscene, Mr. Reeves?"

"Obscene! That's the word!" Nancy had a way of bringing out a dormant part of my brain. Later she would take me to far more dangerous depths.

"Begging your pardon, Mr. Reeves, but do you have any earthly idea where we're headed?"

As a matter of fact, I did. At first we were just going, driving. But partway through our little interview I had made another of those split-second decisions and turned off the main highway. We were winding down the chuck-holed dirt road leading to the River. The sun was low in the west, melting like butter on the horizon. Its glow had a wavering effect on the pines, which appeared as tall dark flames reaching into the sky. A tiny flock of clouds blushed overhead. "So what about you?" I asked. "College?"

Her voice shifted back to normal. "Nope. I'm a victim of Von Kleinsmid's First Law of Economics: no dough, no can go."

I tried to look sympathetic, but this was not news. Most Ponderosans took a job right out of high school. College was a low-priority frill except for rich doctors' kids. "No college. Well, maybe someday."

She shrugged. "No big deal." But then it grew quiet in my Corvette, the only sounds the snapping of twigs and branches as we crawled down the bumpy dirt road. The silence, plus the strobic effect of the sunlight flickering through the pines, made me feel like an extra in a silent movie. This mood persisted until we were fifty yards from the final bend.

"Stop!" Nancy screamed.

I slammed on the brakes. The car screeched to a halt, heaving us forward. I winced as I smelled the burned rubber mingling with the vermilion dust cloud billowing around us like a freed genie. They were brand new radials, and I had just washed and waxed my red gem. "So where's the accident!" I yelled. "Where's the water buffalo I was going to hit?"

Nancy wasn't listening. She was staring quietly across the canyon trying to dissolve the sun with her eyes. She was doing a spectacular job, too, for the only remnant now was a marmalade stain on the horizon. She waited five minutes, until the orange glow had turned flourescent pink, then motioned me on.

At the bottom we were greeted by the sound of distant thunder. We followed the noise down a narrow foot trail, flanked by waist-high ferns, to the edge of a granite cliff. A jungle of trees and plants, many of them exotic, crowded the opposite bank. Directly below us the waters lay still and smooth, black satin. A sweet and sour odor rose from the sandy shore.

Several hundred feet downstream a steel trestle spanned the River. In the twilight it looked like a great metal cage with a dull polish. Just upstream the cliffs curved inward forming a giant horseshoe. Top-dead-center the River squeezed through a narrow gap and plunged twenty feet straight down, crashing between a pair of boulders that angled inward like twin whales surfacing to kiss. This was the Rock. If you had hair on your chest or rocks in your head or both, you could squeeze safely between those two protruding boulders. If you leaped and lived, you were entitled to carve your initials into the trunk of a half-gone ponderosa pine rotting at the base, officially certifying your manhood or your stupidity.

Before long a squadron of bats began zig-zagging above the River. Intermittently one would dive kamikaze-style at the water, pulling out an instant before crash-landing, its leather wings fluttering frenetically as it rejoined the group.

"Do you think they ever misjudge?" Nancy asked.

"And hit the water? I don't know. Maybe once in a while. They're hunting for insects."

"I know."

"Are you afraid? Most girls think bats will get caught in their hair."

She didn't answer. She stood there staring at the bats, not answering.

"If they misjudge, it's not often," I said. "They've got radar, you know. So it's pretty hard for them to misjudge."

Nancy crossed her arms and watched as if she were anticipating an aerial miscue. Then she smiled. "They never miss!" she exclaimed. "Never!"

I looked around anxiously. Directly overhead stars were freckling the sky. The sickle moon was a big white smile, grinning at me no doubt. I gazed up at the towering canyon walls which appeared to be closing like immense jaws that would soon swallow moon, stars, everything.

"You're Mormon, aren't you?"

"Yes." She already knew that: BYU. Football scholarship. "What are you?"

She laughed. "I'm Nancy. Nancy Von Kleinsmid."

"I know *that*. But what *are* you?"

She smiled smugly. "Tell me about God."

"God?" I was cautious.

"Sure! What does God look like?"

"Like a man," I said.

"Oh, does he? Then tell me, Reeves, what kind of a man? Does he have a mustache? Is he a red man? Black? White? Yellow? Or does he change colors to fit the occasion?"

"He's got a body. We're created in his image—two arms, two legs, two eyes, one nose."

I was dreading her next question: "Tell me, Reeves, I'm a woman. If we're all created in *his* image . . ."

"We'd better get going," I said.

Either she didn't hear me or didn't want to. She gazed downstream smiling in her annoyingly omnipotent way. At least she was calling off the dogs on religion—for the time being anyway.

"Why do they call it the River?" she asked. "I mean, doesn't it have a real name? Like Mulligan's River or Red River or some nifty Indian name, like the Watamahogie River?"

"I don't know. Why do you ask?"

"Just curious."

Maybe, but her voice had that mocking edge again. I got defensive. First my running style, then my car, then my diet, then my religion, and now this! The River wasn't exactly a secret, but it had always been special. Ever since my ninth summer when my uncle Steve hiked me down the switchbacks to catch my first rainbow trout, it had been my refuge—a little piece of paradise in the pines. Water nymphs might have bathed here, or the Polynesian beauties you see in paintings by Gauguin. I'd brought Nancy here because I thought she would appreciate it. Had I thrown my pearls to the swine?

"Why should it have a name?" I said, still smarting from our theological repartee.

"*The* River—as if there were no others. Don't you find that a little pretentious?"

"No."

She looked upriver, where the shawl of falling water glistened in the skimpy moonlight. "And that's the infamous Rock?"

"The Rock, yes."

"Have you ever jumped?"

"Sure. Lots of people have . . . Everyone's jumped."

"Excuse me, O Great and Mighty One." She scrutinized the Rock with her all-knowing smirk. "Has anyone ever dived?"

"And lived to tell about it? Only two I know of, and one of them's in a wheelchair."

"Have you?"

A sudden breeze swept through the canyon, chasing off the fallen leaves and ruffling the River's surface like the fur of a frightened animal. "No," I said.

"Will you?"

"Dive?"

"Please."

"Now what kind of question is that, knowing what happened to Steve Valkenburg?"

"A straightforward one, I think."

"Okay, and here's a very straightforward answer. N-O. No."

"Why not?"

"Don't be stupid."

Another breeze came up, this one a bit stiffer, shaking the surrounding oaks and elms. Their porous silhouettes wriggled like schools of black fish. It was an eerie, oriental image.

"Will you jump?" she asked.

"I already have."

"I mean today. Now." She smiled. "For me."

"Are you some kind of screwball?"

"No, I'm Nancy," she whispered. "Nancy Von Kleinsmid. You've done it before."

"I've got my good clothes on," I said, motioning to my polo shirt and corduroy pants.

"So? Take them off."

"Very funny!"

"Mormon boys don't do that?"

Something about her smile—that smirk, that challenge.

"Okay, Mizz Big Shot," I said, "why don't you jump!"

"I can't swim."

Now it was my turn to smirk. "Let's go," I said.

I started back for the Corvette, smiling victoriously as I listened to her footsteps trailing behind. Suddenly they stopped. "Listen!" she said. It took a moment, but soon I could hear the sound of another waterfall, like an echo of the first. But instead of staying constant, it was growing louder, closer.

Nancy's eyes widened. "Come on!" she said, and grabbed my wrist with the same urgency she had shown in the high school parking lot, evading the mob. I was a good runner, a dash man, but I had trouble keeping up. Her ostrich mop was shaking like a pom-pom as her oxfords pounded the dirt. "They say," she panted, "they say there's a good foot of clearance . . . maybe two."

"What?" I yelled. "*What?*"

She stopped at the mouth of the trestle. It protruded out of the tunnel like a piece of complex dental work. "It's like a skeleton!" she said. "The skeleton of the tunnel!"

To me it looked like a giant booby trap. "Nancy," I said, but she was already striding along the ladder of railroad ties, skipping every other one.

"Come on!" she hollered.

And I did. Midway she stopped and lay down lengthwise on the tracks. "What are you doing?" I said. "Are you nuts!"

The noise grew louder, closer. Somewhere upstream a dam had burst and the angry waters were rushing down to bury us. "Hurry, Jon!" She patted the rail impatiently.

"Get up!" I yelled. "It's not funny!"

"Come on, Jon!" The mouth of the tunnel filled with light; the steel cage trembled. "Jonathan!" she screamed. "You're going to miss it!" Such urgency. I could see the veins gripping her throat like a skinny strangling hand. "Jon!"

I laid my body back-flat on the tracks, my head at her feet. "This is crazy!" I screamed.

"Shhhh!"

Were those my bones rattling, or the wooden ties underneath me? I closed my eyes and said a quick and desperate prayer. Then: "A foot—are you sure?"

She laughed. "Just keep your head down!" She yelled something else, but her voice was smothered by the thunder.

Then I did something even more stupid than lying on the tracks. I raised my head and looked back: the cyclops eye was hurtling towards us, splashing yellow light all over the steel cage. Panicking, I rolled over the rail, off the track. Eyes clenched, I hugged the metal bar, riding the earthquake tremors as the hissing, pounding monster roared past. I began counting to myself and didn't stop until the very last echoes had faded and nothing remained but the perfect silence you might expect after a bomb has fallen and the smoke has cleared.

I opened my eyes and sat up, but suddenly I felt very cold. My hands were shaking. "Nancy?"

She was lying perfectly still, ghost-white in the moonlight, her hands cupped restfully on her concave belly, a mortician's perfect pose. "Nancy!"

I scrambled over and, kneeling, lifted her head onto my lap. Her eyes opened slowly, then her mouth, although nothing came out at first. She gazed up at me dreamily, as if she were the beauty in the fairy tale awakening from her hundred years' sleep. Then with a look of extreme sadness and disappointment, she whispered, "You missed it, Jon. You missed the train."

I held those words for several moments, echoing back and forth between the canyon walls which became the sides of my head. I was furious. I think I started yelling at her. Or maybe I just got up and stomped off. I forget.

She ran after me. "Hey! Wait up! I'm sorry!" she said, grabbing my arm. "I guess I get a little carried away sometimes."

I spun around, fists clenched. I felt like punching her. I felt as if I were standing stark naked in front of her. "A little carried away? A little?"

"Okay, a lot carried away. A whole big bunch stupid idiotic carried away. I'm sorry, Jon. Really." She was pleading with her hands.

"Some joke! I hope you proved whatever the hell it was you were trying to prove because what you did . . . Just who do you think you are?" Then I realized I was shaking my finger, just like an adult. "That was *really* stupid!"

"I know," she said, looking penitently at her feet. "I'm really really *really* sorry."

I thought she was being sarcastic, but then I noticed she was about to cry. She was trying to hide it, but I could tell she wanted to. Then I felt rotten. "Look," I said, "it's getting late. Let's get the hell out of here."

We walked back to the Corvette side by side, almost touching. She seemed her old chatty, sassy self again, telling me about the stories she was writing and how she was going to win the Nobel Prize for literature someday. I said that was pretty ambitious.

"'Shoot for the stars!' Robert Browning said!" and she aimed a quickfinger at the white buckshot powdering the night. Then it grew quiet again. The perpetual thunder had softened to the roar of a distant crowd. I remember the pine needles crackling underneath her giant shoes, the night sighs of the River, and the friction of her pleated skirt swishing across her skinny, sexless thighs.

CHAPTER 3

I met with Nancy regularly after that, every afternoon, Monday through Friday, in the Student Tutoring Center. She quickly brushed aside the Intermediate Value Theorem to tackle heftier issues, introducing topics with theatrical statements like, "Did you know that in 1968 the government spent over $800 million testing—not developing, testing!—nuclear warheads?" She prodded until I took a stand. Quoting everyone from Milton to Ann Landers, Nancy would race me around her intellectual big top until I was the proverbial dog chasing its tail. She knew everything.

I never knew how she felt about an issue because she always stood in direct opposition to me. If on Monday I was a hawk, she was a dove; if Tuesday I said give peace a chance, she clamored for war. If I was a Republican, she was a Democrat. When I spoke for ecology and environmental protection, she argued for more nuclear power plants and freedom from foreign oil. Because I was "always" Mormon, she had a field day with religion.

"I thought God loved everyone."

"He does."

"Then how come your church won't let blacks have the priesthood? Why can't women have the priesthood?"

Brother Crumb had prepared me for these questions, or so I'd thought. "We don't know why, exactly."

"Don't know? That's an interesting piece of doctrine. Clever—but not very original."

"Some people say it's because blacks were less valiant in the preexistence."

"Less valiant? I rest my case. You're a racist church!"

"*I* didn't say that. I said some Mormons think that. I mean it's not doctrine."

"Then what is doctrine, besides the 'Don't Know'? And what about women? Were they bad too?"

"Women don't need the priesthood."

"Women don't but men do?"

"Men and women have different roles."

"That's for sure! Master and slave!"

"No, that's not what I meant. Women can have babies."

"Babies for women, priesthood for men. And what if a woman can't have children—is she left in Outer Darkness?"

"Women receive the priesthood through their husbands."

"And if a woman doesn't marry?"

I didn't know. I had never been seriously challenged about my religious beliefs, even though in my own way I had liked raising questions. I suppose I was known as something of a Mormon bad boy, which was okay because I was an insider stirring a complacent pot. But Nancy's attacks were direct. Instinctively, I found myself taking the defensive.

"Racist *and* sexist!" Nancy continued. "Your God doesn't consider blacks and women people."

"Let me check up on what we believe," I said, which meant that I would consult with Brother Crumb or my father.

"You do that, Reeves. And while you're at it, ask your friendly bishop what Joseph Smith meant when he said there's no such thing as immaterial matter. Isn't that fairly obvious? I mean, how profound!"

Earlier I had wondered what Nancy did for enjoyment. Now I knew. She took pleasure in attacking my faith. She worked overtime on it, researching what I was supposed to believe, plotting our next encounter. Her cheeks would flush, her eyes dilate, her mind and tongue engage.

"Are you telling me you really believe that nonsense about Adam and Eve and the snake and the ark and golden plates and the heavens opening like something from the Land of Oz and here comes the Father and his boy saying, 'Stop the music, kiddo! A hundred zillion people can be wrong! Scrap the unholy mess and let's start all over again, from scratch!' Do you honestly think you and your wifey-to-be will live forever as gods populating worlds? Do you really swallow all that?"

What could I say? Should I square my shoulders and boldly proclaim: "Yes! Without a shadow of a doubt!" Or, with the goggle-eyed self-righteousness of Tim Huber, the senior class dork, reply: "Yes, I know! The Holy Ghost has revealed this to me personally!" My response was somewhat less affirmative: "Yeah."

"'Yeah'? You're talking about the most significant commitment of your life—and all you can say is 'yeah'?"

"Well, yeah—I mean, I really do . . . believe."

"Why, Jon? Just tell me that? Why?"

"I just do, that's all. It's a feeling I have."

"A feeling. Like indigestion?"

"No, a good feeling. A . . . warm . . . comforting . . ."

"Oh, comforting. I see."

I could tell by her expression—that know-it-all smirk—that she was circling for the kill. I was desperate.

"If the Mormon church isn't true," I argued weakly, "why would my great-great-grandfather have traveled half way around the world to settle in a desert like Salt Lake? Why would good honest people like my bishop deliberately lie to me?"

Although fervid, my reply was subjective and hence "unacceptable, Reeves, unacceptable." Nancy demanded logic, objectively verifiable evidence, none of this borrowed light.

"If what you say is true," she countered, "then how do you account for all the non-Mormons who died for their God? Does that make their faith true? Custer was a martyr, so was Hitler. Does that make them right?"

"That's not the same thing!"

"It's not? Please, enlighten me."

"You're impossible! This whole discussion's impossible! Can't you get it through your thick head that the *why* isn't nearly as important as the *what*? It's what you do that matters."

Nancy wasn't listening. She was busy purporting her next position. "One more thing, Bishop Reeves. Believe it or not, parents lie. They lie to you about different things. They want to protect you, so they lie. Karl Marx was right when he called religion the great opiate. Religion eases the terror. Remember Hamlet? 'To be or not to be—that's the question'!"

Nancy paused, waiting for my reply, but I had none. It was humiliating. The simple arguments that had flowed so convincingly from my father and Brother Crumb tumbled ludicrously from my mouth. I felt like a fool.

I had raised questions before to aggravate my Sunday school teachers and priesthood advisors. Why, for instance, was it necessary to sit in a brick chapel all day every Sunday to worship God? Couldn't you do this just as well on a mountaintop, or at the River, amid the trees and flowers? If Nature manifests God's creative glory, aren't the forests and beaches as sacred as a building? Also, why all the channels and hierarchies, the super-structure? Why the tedious bookkeeping, the ordinances, if religion is charity and love? Was I really going to interrupt my schooling and football career for two years to dress up in black and white and go door-to-door like a Fuller Brush Man peddling religion in Australia, Japan, or wherever? Why all of the certificate-saturated programs that seemed bent on turning youth into a mass-produced army of hand-shaking, scripture-chasing robots? Did I sincerely believe or was this the convenient, socially acceptable thing to do? Was the church a crutch? Or did I have the guts to crack the granite mold?

These were questions that occupied my private thoughts, though I avoided discussing them with Nancy because I suffered such an awful beating when I did. Only once did I score any points on a theological issue.

"And how do you know God isn't a woman?" Nancy sneered one afternoon in the tutoring room.

Summoning up some rhetoric from a recent semantics unit in Senior Composition, I stood up, cleared my throat like Chanticleer, and exclaimed, "Because, along with the distinguishing features of omnipotence, omnipresence, and omniscience, God also has to have the feature maleness; otherwise, by definition, he'd be a she, not a god but a goddess."

"Bravo!" Nancy cried. "Bra-a-a-vo!" Rising to her feet, applauding, genuinely pleased. "Two points for the polygamist! The kid's got brains as well as brawn!"

That was Nancy. She amused and abused me, entertained and profaned me. She criticized my car ("the red deathtrap"), my clothes ("drip-dry sta-prest preppy firsts from the *Sears Catalog*"), my hair ("old hayhead!"), my brains ("headpiece filled with straw"), my running style ("Frankenstein in slo-mo! Concrete feet!"), my family, my friends. Nothing was exempt.

"So what's it like living in the Versailles Palace?" She was referring to our ranch-style home nestled in the pines at the end of Drayer Drive.

"Sixteen bedrooms?"

"Five—but who's counting, right?"

"And a redwood deck?"

"Yes, I confess."

"Overlooking the canyon? Breakfast with the sun?"

"Guilty."

"And a swimming pool?"

"Yes, but no Jacuzzi—not yet anyway."

"Reeves, remember the starving people in Biafra?"

"How would my living in a shack help them?"

"Touché, Reeves! Touché!"

Although we seldom worked on Calculus during the tutoring sessions, I was soon able to raise my grade out of the red zone as if she'd supercharged my brain via some kind of intellectual osmosis. Coach Ramirez welcomed me back onto the track, but every few days I would ditch practice to take Nancy to Mac's Foster Freeze for an after-school snack (she pooh-poohed the Double-Eagle—"too loud, too sweaty!" Sweaty?) As we sat at a formica table, Nancy nibbling a tuna salad on rye and me slurping a chocolate shake, she would interrogate me about less bookish matters.

"So where were you during lunch today? Out chasing Thunder Thighs?"

"You mean Annette Plikta? Yes, you might say that."

"Might I? When are you going to wise up, Reeves? You think you're irresistible, but it's your red jalopy they're after. Have you ever wondered if maybe even one of your little princesses liked you because you're you—without the Corvette and letterman's jacket and rich daddy? How many of them would give you the time of day if you were stripped to the bare naked, Jonathan?"

I pushed aside my milkshake and laughed, as if everything she had said was utterly absurd, although in truth I'd wondered this myself. "I don't know about me," I chortled, "but I'd give them more than the time of day if they were stripped bare naked."

Nancy wadded up her napkin and crammed it into my half-empty cup. "'Tis not a year or two shows us a man; they are all but stomachs, and we all but food; they eat us hungerly, and when they are full, they belch us.'"

"Shakespeare?"

"*Othello.*"

Like most young men, I indulged in sexual fantasies, and I suppose mine were as inventive as the next guy's, although perhaps dampered by a lack of experience and excessive guilt. While I never committed adultery in my heart, I fornicated in that manner, and my favorite partner was the voluptuous, gypsy-haired Miss Plikta (at the River, on a beach, by firelight in a rustic cabin in the Sierras). It is worth noting that Nancy Von K. never approached the most remote margins of my fantasies. In fact, she was as far removed as a sister or my mother or grandmother.

Nancy must have sensed this, for whenever she caught my eyes trailing the long legs of Miss Plikta she would shake her head with a kind of maternal tolerance. Other times: "A man's brains are in his crotch!" she would sigh.

"Shakespeare?"

"Von Kleinsmid. Chapter fifteen, verse eleven."

In some ways our relationship reminded me of Herod and John the Baptist. I took some masochistic pleasure in having her perforate my egotistical soul. I spent more and more time with her, made time. I found myself taking her questions and jibes to heart—not too much to heart, though: I wasn't about to junk my Corvette, shave my head, and spend the rest of my life picketing Standard Oil. However, in time, when Nancy put on her Barsumian airs and asked what I was going to be if and when I ever grew up, I no longer replied, "A beachcomber or the King of Siam."

"I want to play pro," I confessed one afternoon at Mac's. Leaning forward secretively: "I want to be the greatest receiver in the history of the game—better than Lance Alworth."

Nancy sipped her milk a thoughtful moment, then slowly parted her lips, releasing the straw, and eyed me sternly. "Then do it, Jon! I wouldn't know Lance Alworth from Lancelot of the Round Table, but if that's what you really want, do it! You know how I feel about jocks, but do it! Be the best!" Her fist hit the table like a gavel; the final word.

At moments like this, when she dropped the façade and spoke straight, she launched me into clouds of great expectations: I could do it! I had the strength, the size, the speed, the hands, the opportunities. Keith would say I even had the luck. So why not? I could–no, I would do it!

"Right on!" I said, but my palm slapped the table and catapulted my strawberry sundae smack into my chest. Nancy laughed.

She was wonderful. At her best she could hype me up like ten squads of cheerleaders. At her worst–or, rather, my worst . . .

"So are you going to disgrace town, school, God, country, and the sweet-little-girl-next-door again, or are you going to beat that guy this time?"

"You mean Harry the Horse?"

"Harry the Fairy–whatever. Are you going to run Saturday, or are you going on sabbatical again?"

She was rough on me but protective. "Watch out for Bernhard. I wouldn't be surprised if he's popping."

"Keith? Popping pills?"

"He's been a space-case all semester. Don't mess with that stuff, Jon. It'll screw you up. You've got too much going for you."

"Nancy, who told you this?"

"Bernhard's been doing this all semester and he'll try to mess you up because he's jealous, Jon. They all are. They joke around with you and slap you on the back and call you 'Sundance' and 'Big J,' but they're jealous. You've got a ticket out of here, they don't."

In Nancy's mind the whole town was out to get me. She was paranoid. Was she sinister as well? She made me consider the inconsiderable.

One afternoon in the tutoring room she shoved my Calculus text aside. "All right," she said, "let's try something." Closing her eyes, she pressed her fingertips to her temples like a clairvoyant on the verge of a great revelation. "Okay. I want you to clear your mind for a minute. Throw everything out. Is it clear? Blank? *Tabula rasa?* Okay. Now I'm going to say a word and I want you to describe the first thing that pops into your head. Ready?" She opened her eyes to check. I nodded solemnly. "Okay. Here's the word: love."

"Love? I don't–"

"Come on, come on! Don't think! Just close your eyes and look!"

I shut my eyes and searched for an image. It took awhile. "Okay. I'm six or seven. It's a summer night—late. Midnight, maybe later. I'm wakened by giggling and splashing. I look out my bedroom window and there's my mother in the shallow end. All I can see is her head because she's kind of crouching down in the water. Her eyes are closed and she's just slicked her hair back, and I'm thinking: she looks like a fashion model or a movie star, with her eyes closed and her hair slicked back like that. Then all of a sudden there's this explosion of water, and it's my father rising up like King Neptune with his black beard and sidehair plastered to his chest. He wraps his big arms around my mother from behind, and then she rises out of the water, turning into him. Then I realize she's naked, and so is he. I mean completely naked. No trunks, no anything. Then he grabs her and she laughs and they kiss and the light in the pool is a weird underwater yellowish-blue. Like a dream or a fairy tale."

For once Nancy was absolutely silent. When I opened my eyes, she looked the other way and whispered something, a little sadly I think. Then: "Okay. Another image!"

I had several more like the first, but I was afraid to share them. It almost seemed like gloating. She appeared genuinely depressed. To make her feel better, I closed my eyes again and related something a little more doleful. "This time I'm eight—I know because I was just baptized. It's November, almost Thanksgiving. Rain. My mother had lit a fire but now she wants me to clean out the grate. I take the little shovel and scoop the hot ashes into a metal bucket. But when I try to carry it outside, the heat seeps through the hot pads. I put the bucket down and try again—same thing. Then I get mad and start yelling at her. 'I'm not going to do this! It's too hot! You do it if you're such an expert!' Just then my father walks in and I know I've only got a few seconds to live. I've just committed the unpardonable sin. I've raised my voice to my mother.

"But Dad doesn't say a word. For one deadly moment he glares into my heart. Then he kneels by the fireplace, grabs the searing hot bucket with his bare hands—I think I can smell his fingers melting—and carries it outside to cool in the rain. I look at my mother, then bolt from the room crying."

This time Nancy smiled. "A macho man."

"In some ways."

"If the shoe fits."

"I said in some ways."

"And what does Poppa Reeves think of your ambition to play pro football?"

"Dad?" I chuckled amiably, hoping to defuse her. "He's got it all mapped out. The three M's: mission, marriage, med. school—preferably Stanford, his alma mater."

"No football?"

"College ball's okay, but pro? Dad hopes I'll come to my senses and grow out of it."

"Will you?"

"I hope not."

"It seems to me that's a lot like being a writer. It's something you ought to grow into, not out of. Do you resent his attitude?"

"Dad? Nah. He's just trying to do what's best for me."

"Is he?"

"Isn't he? Pro football, you've got five years, ten if you're lucky. One fluke injury and you're out. Dad's just trying to look ahead."

"Or leading you into a role you don't want to play. It's your life, Jon. Think about it."

Everyone was suspect in Nancy's mind. One afternoon, walking through the woods near the high school, she asked about my mother. It was idyllic: sunlight slanting through the pines, the meadowlarks in full spring song, the resinous smell of pine sap. I let my guard down and started rambling. She was homecoming queen at Stanford; the fifth of nine children; her father was a holy man, a stake patriarch. She'd always dreamed of having a large family. When she couldn't, she felt like a failure. "Being Mormon, you know. Motherhood is a woman's greatest calling." So I was her Isaac, the miracle child, and she spoiled me. Over-protective? I suppose. My father was gone a lot, so she and I became a twosome. My first day at kindergarten she cried and couldn't stop. Possessive? No. Well, maybe a little.

Nancy whirled around, her pleated wool skirt lifting a bit, revealing her knobby knees. "Have you read *Sons and Lovers*? D. H. Lawrence?"

I shook my head, wondering what that book had to do with my mother.

Nancy's bony hands gripped mine with startling power as she bent deep in the knees, as if preparing to spring over the surrounding pines. "Jon, you've *got* to read that book—you've *got* to!"

"Why? Is it polluted with sleazy sex and graphic violence?"

"Sorry. Nothing to taint your pure little mind."

"Then I'm not interested."

"Oh you big dumb jerk from Albekirk! It's about relationships—a mother who can't let go and her son who can't escape her. It's . . ." She reached down in midstride and grabbed a handful of yellow honeysuckle. "There's this one scene where Paul—he's the son—he and his would-be girlfriend are walking along and she starts picking flowers. He's not sure why, but he gets really mad and starts yelling at her, 'Why do you always have to possess them? Why can't you just leave them be—to flourish!' It's a great book. Every Mormon boy should read it."

"Sure. The Bible, the Book of Mormon, and *Sons and Lovers*."

"Read it, Jon!"

I told her I'd try, although I knew I wouldn't. But the next morning when we met at school, first thing, before saying, "Hello, nincompoop!" or asking my position on gun control, she handed me a weathered, hard-bound copy of *Sons and Lovers*.

"Take, read, ponder . . ."

I read that book, then another she recommended. Soon she introduced me to a whole gallery of new friends who were not on Ponderosa's reading list: Joyce, Woolf, Lawrence, Ellison, Pound, Eliot. Later she discussed each work at depths that left me gasping. A highlight was her summation of the writers. She spoke as if she knew each one personally. They were Jimmy Joyce and Ernie Hemingway and Katie Ann Porter.

By mid-April, about six weeks after our first encounter, I was cutting practice so often that Coach Ramirez threatened to drop me from the squad. I knew he wouldn't, since I was by far his fastest sprinter, with or without practice, and his only hope to beat Harry the Horse and Las Plumas in the league finals. My teammates resented it, meaning me and my prima donna attitude, especially Keith, but I was so brain drunk in my fantasies with Nancy that I hardly noticed, or simply didn't care.

Besides, Keith and I had had a falling out several months earlier, and he was looking for any excuse to throw dirt on me.

It was about this time Nancy launched her most ambitious (and preposterous) project: she tried to turn me into a poet. She picked her moment perfectly, when I was most vulnerable, the day after Harry burned me in a dual meet the second time that season. Humiliated by my shabby performance, during the noon hour I exiled myself to a scraggly patch of grass on the outskirts of the schoolgrounds near an old Quonset hut (formerly the auto shop), hoping no one would find me there, knowing full well Nancy would.

I should have known she was up to something when she didn't greet me with an insult. Instead, she sat down beside me, her skinny legs extended and crossed girlishly at the ankles, her stick arms stiff and slanted, supporting her flimsy upper half like tent poles. She carefully smoothed her woolen skirt but said nothing, and I was glad. I didn't feel like talking. I didn't feel like anything except staring at the dry, cracked, red earth and the sun-fried weeds pushing through as the April warmth pressed through the fabric of my cotton pullover. Inevitably, though, she spoke.

"Jon—"

"I don't want to talk about it!"

"What?"

"The stupid idiotic race! I lost and that's all there is to it!"

"Right. You lost. You got creamed, Jon. Smoked. Poof! So what? Is the moon turning to blood? Is Barbra Streisand getting a nose job? No! What's the big deal?"

"*What's the big deal?* I was humiliated in front of everyone and you sit there like a lump. So what . . . big deal . . . *it's only a silly race* . . . You may think jocks run around on four legs grunting once for 'yes' and twice for 'no,' and sports are some invention from the Stone Age, but I care. This town cares. Me and Keith and the others work hard for it. We sacrifice. Have you ever run a 440? You blast out of the blocks and pray you don't die before the finish line. You run until your lungs burn and your legs turn to lead and your body ties itself into a knot—but you keep running. We run to win. And when we lose, it's as tragic to us as when . . . as—ah, hell, as when King Lear loses his kingdom to a couple of snake-in-the-grass daughters. *We* feel it, Nancy. I know it's hard for you to understand."

Nancy leaped to her feet applauding. "Bravo, Jon! Bra-a-a-vo!"

"Quit joking! I'm serious!"

"And I'm serious. Here—" She tore a sheet of paper from the spiral notebook she carried with her everywhere, like a life-support system. "Okay," she said. "Now write!"

"Write?"

"Your feelings. Forget about grammar and spelling or making sense. That comes later. For now, just get your guts on paper."

"Why?"

"Just do it, Jon. Trust me."

I folded my arms defiantly and looked away like a pouting child. "I'm not doing anything until you tell me why."

"Look, Jon, reason not the need."

"No! I want to know why. You're the one who's always railing about blind obedience and not following the mob. So just tell me."

"Why?" She looked positively stumped, baffled. It was wonderful. "Well, because . . ."

"Yes? I'm waiting."

"Because art is life. It's eternal. It teaches us who we are. It makes us strive to be better. Science and history and math give us the facts about life, but art, literature, music make us care about the facts, make us feel. They shoot an arrow to the heart so we don't blow ourselves to kingdom come. Art captures human truth, the summa cum—"

"Nancy, what the hell are you talking about?"

She was silent a moment. Then she turned to me with a look of regret equalled only by that first evening at the River when I missed the train. "You don't understand, do you?"

I was surprised how much this disappointed me.

"Write!" she commanded. "Write! Anything that pops into that peanut brain of yours—the race, Harry the Fairy, Mom, apple pie, me . . . Just write!"

So I wrote. Reluctantly, sheepishly at first, but soon I was scrawling my rage on paper. I called myself a gut-out, a showboat with no show. I'd let my teammates down. I didn't give a damn about anyone but myself.

"The Great and Almighty I." I was a phoney, a hypocrite. In a crowd I flirted with the cheerleaders, but one-on-one I was bashful. I poked fun at religion, called the River the only true and living water. I prayed three times a day, paid tithing, never missed a Sabbath meeting, but I did it all because Mom and Dad said so, because it was the thing to do, because I always had. Because I had never really questioned, never taken a hard look at my religion or myself or anything of substance. Born with a silver spoon, I was crippled by comfort and complacency. Don't rock the red Corvette. I had a dick for brains and a marshmallow heart. I was an idiot for flattery, a sucker for a pretty face. After annihilating myself, I turned my anger on Nancy, the intellectual seductress. She was Salome, the Queen of Sheba, Lady Macbeth, Jezebel.

Finished, I hurled my pen at the Quonset hut. She snatched the paper, skimmed it over. Her face turned to stone.

"What's the matter? What's wrong?"

She re-read my scribble, silently mouthing each word.

"Well?"

She replied coolly: "Embryonic." But she folded the paper into fourths and carefully tucked it away for safekeeping. Then, with her old bravado: "Good! Tomorrow we'll do another!"

And we did. The next day and the next day and the next, until it became routine. Everyday at noon she compelled me to scribble out a few pages. Sports, girls, grades, parents, church, sex—the topic didn't matter, as long as I was writing. When I complained that what I wrote seemed trivial, she agreed.

"Then why bother writing it down?"

"Don't fret about significance," she said. "First you develop the habit, then the obsession. You've got to learn to love writing."

"Love it or leave it. Right?"

"Wrong. You love it when you hate it. I assume it's the same with running. Nothing's trivial except perception. Read Emily Dickinson and William Carlos Williams."

"Right," I said, nodding mechanically.

When Nancy played the literary coach, I followed along as best I could—which wasn't very well. I was a jock at heart. I had no poetic aspirations. That was her trip. But misery loves company, I supposed, so she was always ordering me to write things down—things I'd seen, interesting people I'd met, bits of conversation I'd overheard, dreams, thoughts, ideas, images, moonlight on the River, dogs howling in the night—anything and everything! No matter how "trivial," it had to be recorded. If I related an anecdote about Keith or Coach Ramirez, she'd get after me: "Did you write that down? Write it down, Jon, or it's lost! It's lost!" She was obsessed.

Before long I too was toting around a spiral notebook, even on trips to the River. One day she sat me on a rock, pointed to the water and announced, "Okay, today we're going to write haiku!"

"Hi-who?"

"Don't play the idiot. Three lines with set syllables. Five, seven, five." She opened my spiral notebook and wrote:

> What I thought to be
> Flowers soaring to their boughs
> Were bright butterflies.

"That's Moritake. When Japanese poets write haiku, they try to enter the soul of the thing they're writing about—bird, butterfly, tree, flower. They try to see from their perspective. Got it?" She tapped my notebook. "You try."

Enough was enough. Scribbling down my thoughts and perceptions was one thing, writing oriental poetry was quite another. I handed my notebook to her. "I quit."

"Oh come on, you big sissy!" She handed it right back to me. "What are you so afraid of?"

I could tell by her expression there was no use resisting. Nancy would have her way. I looked around self-consciously to see if any of my football buddies were lurking nearby. I could hear a pack of them carousing upstream.

"All right, but can we go downriver a bit?"

"You really are a gutless wonder, aren't you? Come on!" We hiked a quarter-mile downstream to a secluded beach where I spent the afternoon writing three-line poems about water skimmers and dragonflies. In this way Nancy taught me how to take a deeper look at the little things in life, to smell the muddy banks and hear the sighs in the River's thunder.

Yet no matter how closely I observed, it was never adequate for her. I always missed some critical little detail. One day exactly three weeks before my final showdown with Harry the Horse, she commenced by asking what I had seen on arriving at school that morning. I was ready for her. "Okay, all right. . . I saw the A.M. swarm, the manic masses—kids, I mean. In Levis, sneakers, t-shirts. Also, Keith and company in cut-offs and hirachi sandals with black armbands, mourning who knows what this time? I saw some loud-mouthed juniors playing Frisbee football on the lawn and Cindy Cadman looking very . . . well, very *very* in a skin-tight tanktop and bell-bottom jeans with a red peace sign on her left cheek. Mr. Smith sneaking glimpses of her as he patrolled the quad, grinning his rabbity grin. I saw Gary Jackson flaunting his letterman's sweater in the heat of April, still losing ground with Carla Wheeler who was making eyes at Jerry Richfield in fluorescent orange tennis shoes and no socks and a holey t-shirt with MAKE LOVE, NOT WAR felt-tip-markered across his chest. I saw the Jesus freaks sitting in a circle singing sweet hallelujahs while Janie Stevens strummed a Joan Baez song. I saw—"

"All right, you've got the overall picture. Good. But did you notice the little freshman sitting alone by the flagpole feeding corn chips from his sack lunch to a blue jay?"

I was stopped cold. "Hunh?"

Nancy shook her head in despair. "Sorry, Jon, but you still have not yet arrived."

I knew what she meant, but I tried to laugh it off. "Arrived? I didn't know I was going anywhere."

"I thought you might be. I hoped so. But evidently not. Oh well, your time will come, I suppose." With that, she got up, brushed the bits of grass from her pleated skirt, and sauntered into the woods.

She remained a mystery. I never set foot inside her home, and I met her mother only once, when it was too late. This was not entirely my fault, since Nancy refused to let me drive her home. Day or night, she always insisted I drop her off by the four old mailboxes at the top of the gravel road off the highway. Pressing a load of books to her chest, she would march down the lane, glancing back periodically to make sure I wasn't cheating. I watched from my idling Corvette until her lanky figure vanished in the green oblivion of the gambel oaks. I was never comfortable with this arrangement, especially after dark. But whenever I offered to drive her to her doorstep, she politely declined. If I pressed the issue, she became adamant. And if I took the initiative? I made that mistake only once. Instead of stopping at the four mailboxes, I turned defiantly down the lane.

"Reeves!" she screamed. "What are you doing?"

"Taking you home. My treat."

The passenger door flew open. If I hadn't braked, her spindly body would have been airborne.

"Nancy! What are you doing?"

Gaining her balance, she glared at me through the thin mushroom of dust. "You think you can get whatever you want whenever you want it, don't you?"

"What are you talking about?"

"You know very well what I'm talking about."

"Nancy, get in the car!"

"See! See what I mean?"

"Just get in, will you?" She spun around and started up the hill, her long skinny legs gobbling up ground like a giraffe's. Muttering soft core curses, I shoved the stick into reverse, my tires spitting gravel as I backed up the lane. "Nancy!" I snarled through gritted teeth. What was her hang up anyway? What was she trying to hide? Did she honestly believe there was anything at the end of that gravel road that would shock or surprise me? Give me a break, Von K.! Give me a little credit!

"Nancy!" I hollered, steering my Corvette even with her. "You nut! Get in here!" She never broke stride.

"Okay, okay! Have it your way! But I don't see what the big deal is." She stopped, the irritating grin of victory on her face, and waited until I had backed all the way up to the highway before proceeding down the hill.

But I didn't drive home as promised. I parked by the four old mailboxes and waited until dark to sneak down the gravel lane on foot. There was a barbed wire fence on one side, with knee-high weeds and giant sunflowers dipping their coronaed heads. The smell of alfalfa was strong. Passing through the grove of oaks, I found four homes, all of the same clapboard design, with dim-lit windows glowing like jack-o-lanterns. I knocked at the first door. A tall, long-faced man in a holey t-shirt and Levis answered. His balding forehead protruded like the Bride of Frankenstein's.

I asked if this was the Von Kleinsmid residence? He answered with dead brown eyes. I asked if he knew of any Von Kleinsmids? Same reply. I thanked him and left.

I searched the other three yards until I found tell-tale signs: tricycles, dolls, Tonka trucks, a table setting with plastic plates and utensils. The humble abode of Mother Goose, nine's fine but ten's the end.

Straddling the low picket fence, I crept towards the front porch. Disaster almost struck when my sneaker tipped a plastic bowl, spilling a dark pasty mix (earmarked for tomorrow's mud pies?). I was more careful crossing the porch, freezing at each creak that issued from the ancient planks, waiting for it to fade completely before risking another step.

My luck, all of the windows were covered with translucent plastic sheets (for energy efficiency or secrecy?). It was like peering into a thick fog. Several dark blurs were clustered together—at the dinner table, I assumed—while another drifted back and forth, perpetually in motion. A baby was crying. No, two. Two distinct cries. The other voices were low and garbled. I pressed my ear to the plastic, straining to hear. Then I grew bold and pinched a corner of the plastic sheet where it had been stapled. I felt guilty. I was snooping, I'd given her my word, sort of. But my curiosity won out. I peeled back the corner and crouched down to look. But pressing my eye to the triangular peephole, I was stopped by a ferocious bark. Following a short silence, more barks, louder, closer, joined by the unmistakable scrabbling of paws. I hopped off the porch, hurdled the picket fence, and streaked up the lane at a velocity that would have left even Harry the Unpassable frozen in his tracks.

Driving home, I began second guessing myself. Had my flight been premature? Was the dog really that close, that big, that dangerous? Had I secretly been hoping for a convenient out? Up until now it had been fun and games mostly—child's play. But if I had looked, I would have been compelled to go to the front door and knock. And once that door opened, I would never be able to close it again. I had come this far with her, but now I was entering a different wilderness, an unknown more intimidating than the ubiquitous "X" of our Calculus sessions. I fled.

The next morning I didn't see her on campus, which had me wondering because she never missed school—perfect attendance—which maybe said something else about her home life. I went to the tutoring room sixth hour and struggled through my math assignment, a long fifty-five minutes.

When the bell rang and I got up, she was blocking the doorway. I had never seen that expression on her before: dagger eyes, skinny lips sealed tight, like an incision. Her face looked as if it had been chiseled out of ice. "Don't ever do that again," she seethed.

"Do what?" I said, playing innocent.

"Ever," she said, and left.

Thursday she was back at school carrying on like her sassy old self, as if nothing contrary had ever occurred. I was cautious at first, but after her first dozen insults, I too fell back into old form. At the bell I invited her to Mac's for an after-school snack. She smiled cunningly. "With your track record?" She was referring to my four recent losses—not to Harry the Horse but to farmtown nobodies I should have easily clipped by ten yards. My teammates were spreading more rumors, especially Keith.

"So how about Mac's?"

"You'd better go to practice, don't you think?"

I was a little shocked by that. A little hurt, too. Betrayed even. What did she care about my sports record? Or had she begun viewing me more and more through the eyes of the other fawning females? Had I become a different kind of feather in her cap? Or was she playing games again? Trying to cross an invisible boundary of her own? From the beginning we had shared a tacit understanding. I walked with her, talked with her, joked with her, fought with her. We discussed art, life, literature. We went to the River and to Mac's Foster Freeze. I even went shopping with her. We spent almost all of our free time together, yet I never considered going out with her. Not on an "official date." Not as boyfriend and girlfriend. So shock number two. Cupping her hands to her heart, eyelids fluttering, she asked in a Scarlett O'Hara drawl,

"Mistuh Jonathun, would you please do the 'onuh of escorting this young bay-ell to the Pray-france Day-ance?"

What shocked me even more was when I squared my shoulders, clicked my heels together, and, with a magnanimous bow, replied, "Why suh-tainly, Mizz Nancy! Ah'd be dee-lighted!"

Three days later I got my first real glimpse into her private world. My opportunity came the day I finally asked if I could read some of her stories. At first she balked.

"Well?" I prodded, sensing her anxiety. "Do you practice what you preach?"

"They're not really, umm . . . it's just that, well . . ."

"Well? Come on, Von Kraut, hem and haw, hem and haw."

"They're not quite . . ."

"Just answer the question, please. A simple yes or no will do."

We eyed one another across the tutoring table like bitter chess rivals. She stroked her chin slowly, as if contemplating her next move. Lizard-quick her tongue moistened the faint blond hairs on her upper lip. "All right," she muttered. "I'll bring them tomorrow."

"Great! I can't wait! I'm really looking forward to this, Nancy!"

I smiled. So did she. And that worried me.

The next day she handed me two bloated ten-by-twelve envelopes. "Enjoy," she said.

"Thanks," I said. "I think." Checkmate.

I skipped track practice and our customary trip to Mac's and went straight home after school to read Nancy's tome in private. Page one, volume one began:

ANY CHARACTERS, PLACES, OR EVENTS HEREIN ARE ENTIRELY FICTI-
TIOUS. ANY RESEMBLANCE BETWEEN THESE AND AUTHENTIC PERSONS
OR EVENTS IS STRICTLY COINCIDENTAL.

I smiled at her presumptuous disclaimer and launched into the first story, entitled "Genesis."

He was a big, strong, handsome Mormon boy perpetually trying to flaunt his virility without jeopardizing his virginity. He was supposed to be good, but he wanted to be a little bad. As a result, he often did crazy, although relatively harmless, things.

I felt a jolt. This was me. I continued, reading apprehensively but thoroughly hooked. Derek Scott, the seventeen-year-old nose-thumbing anti-hero, inhabited my sun-bronzed body, wore my corduroy slacks, drove my red Corvette, used my slang to scoff at teachers, and caught my touchdown passes. The disclaimer should have echoed the Dragnet TV series: THE STORIES YOU ARE ABOUT TO READ ARE TRUE; THE NAMES HAVE BEEN CHANGED TO PROTECT THE INNOCENT.

The first six stories won chuckles and a few guffaws. Derek and his friend are arrested for skinny-dipping at the River; Derek hangs his TUCK THE TRESHMEN sign in the school cafeteria. The last story, however, "Third Time's Not Hardly a Charm," was about an obese girl, Sarah, who attempts to catch Derek's eye, a comic start with an ugly finish.

Sarah entered by the back door and dropped her books on the kitchen table. The twins were whining loudly in the living room, which meant that her mother had not had time to feed and change them before leaving for work—that would be Sarah's job. Again. The kitchen was a mess—plates stacked in the sink, bread crumbs, crinkled cellophane, spilled milk drying to a white crust on the counter. The stench of spoiled cantaloupe rinds was attracting a convoy of fruit flies.

The twins' wailing persisted, but Sarah momentarily ignored them and yanked open the freezer and removed a half-gallon of Rocky Road. She took the little bucket and a spoon into the living room and flopped down on the ragged sofa. She stared at the gloomy gray skies. The intermittent showers had left a sparkling sheen on the weedy backyard, but she saw nothing pleasant, nothing but gray.

She had failed again. And she knew she would fail again and again and again. He was holding hands today. Tomorrow he would slip his arm around the girl's waist the way lovers do and escort her from class to class. Today she had almost spoken to him. At the Coke machine. She had sneaked in line behind him, hoping something might happen. It did. She accidentally dropped her change on the floor and her colossal buttocks won a devoted audience—the football goons crowding around their private table, hooting and howling, one of them singing, "No one's gettin' fat 'cept Mama Cass!" While she stood there, stuck in that bent-over posture, her medicine ball belly pressing against her immense thighs, she did not actually cry until his hand slid charitably under her nose, the quarter shining between his pinched fingers, a look of irredeemable pity in his eyes as he mumbled, "I think you dropped this." She had almost spoken to him; had almost mumbled thank you. Almost.

The twins were still screaming. Outside, rain was falling hard and fast. The sky looked charcoal-smudged. She could smell dirty diapers fermenting by the washing machine. She uncapped the lid and buried her spoon deeply into the dark chocolate and began gorging herself, angrily. Again.

CHAPTER 4

My mother never met Nancy face-to-face, yet she became well acquainted with her that spring of 1970. Every night she heard Nancy's exhortations at our dinner table. "Brother Crumb says not to delve into the mysteries," I said. "But where would we be today if people hadn't questioned the status quo? If questioning is of the devil, then the church was founded on two horns and a pitchfork."

"Joseph Smith was seeking the truth," my mother would counter gently over dinner. She would set a formal table for the two of us: china, silver, cloth napkins, wine glasses (with cranberry juice).

"So am I! Am I supposed to believe just because you do? I have to find out for myself."

"That's fine, Jon." Initially my mother seemed amused, as if my intellectual ventures were a teenage whim to be politely tolerated until I outgrew them, like acne. But as I grew bolder, she became anxious. One night I overstepped my bounds.

"You act like everything's universally assumed. You quote the Book of Mormon like it's straight from God's mouth."

My mother's face clouded. "Well, it is, isn't it? The word of God?"

"Maybe not," I said. "Maybe we ought to be talking about that instead of putting the cart before the horse."

"Cart? Horse? Jon?"

"Maybe we ought to discuss something a little more fundamental first—like is there really a God?"

"Jonathan!" The flat of her hand swept across the wide oak dining table and struck my cheek. She recoiled momentarily but quickly recomposed herself. I looked away, angry at myself for provoking her, angry at her for having struck me. And I was ashamed of the thought. Deep down I knew better.

"So much for freedom of thought," I muttered.

My soft-spoken mother, who wore her frosted hair in a bun, had suddenly turned into a raging Valkyrie. "That's not you talking, Jonathan!" she insisted, shaking her finger at me. "That's not you at all!

Who's been putting these crazy ideas in your head? Is it that girl?" She had heard about Nancy through the Relief Society grapevine.

"Why do you say that? Because I'm not toeing the line? Everything's fine and dandy as long as I nod and smile and play the game by your rules, isn't it? As long as I go to church and score a few touchdowns, I get my little sports car and everybody's happy. But as soon as I rock the boat a little—the minute I voice an original thought . . ."

My mother straightened her slender frame, set her white teeth, and roared: "That was not an original thought!"

She was right, to a point. Yes, I was parroting Nancy, but wasn't she articulating doubts and questions I'd secretly entertained for some time? The seed was planted and was bearing a peculiar fruit. Instead of swaggering down the halls at school flexing my muscles, I was beginning to bully people a bit with my brains, especially at church. After listening to one of my diatribes, Steve Powell, a short, sullen convert, began second-guessing his recent baptism. Later, when Bishop Freeman intimated this in a private interview, I answered belligerently: "He's got to swim on his own."

"We all know that, Jon, but why not let him grow some gills first, okay?"

And where was my father during all of this? Out. Gone. Delivering babies. I was resentful. "He cares more about his practice than about us!"

"It's his job, Jon. Mothers don't go into labor after breakfast and finish up before dinner. You know that."

"It's just his excuse."

"Excuse? What's gotten into you, Jon? What's wrong?"

Everything. Everything was wrong now. One night I read her a story I'd written about two men who convince a third to join them in an assassination. Their target? A so-called benevolent dictator. "He was kind and loving as long as his subjects did exactly as he said."

My mother listened dutifully until the end when the conspirators fell upon the dictator with knives. Her fine-lined eyebrows perked up as I read the closing sentence: "And God dropped dead on the marble floor." She remained silent but her expression said enough was enough.

Late that night my father called me into his study and confronted me across the expanse of his desk. "Did you write this?" The ceiling light reflected off his half-bald dome like an omnipotent eye.

I'd told myself to be tough. I tried to look him in the eye, but it was like staring into the sun. I glanced at the wood-paneled walls, the scarlet carpeting, Hippocrates' bronze bust on the shelf. My body trembled, sweat streamed down my armpits. I was burning with shame, although I wasn't sure if it was because I had betrayed my faith for the flighty ideas of a noodle-necked woman or because, once again, I was shriveling in the overpowering presence of my father. Either way, I lost courage again.

My voice cracked. "Yes, sir," I whimpered.

He dropped the manuscript on the desk, the paper-clipped pages fluttering loose. "You know better," he said. It was a statement and a question.

I looked at my hands, humiliated. At that instant I hated my cowardly self even more than I hated him.

"All right then. Let's get back on track here." He nodded with finality. Then he circled around his giant desk and embraced me with his bear-strong arms, a traditional demonstration of love after having thoroughly chewed me up and spit me out.

After that I confined my free-thinking to my afternoon sessions with Nancy and to my journal. But there was an irony at work. In losing my voice in front of my father, I found it on paper. From that day on I wrote without Nancy's poking and prodding. The words no longer spilled out in the self-conscious, premeditated tongue of my mentor but finally in the language of Jon Reeves. Losing, I won. Departing, I was finally arriving—or at least I was moving in the general direction of wherever I was headed.

Nancy remained unimpressed with my literary efforts. My assasination story was lukewarm. She acknowledged its inventiveness but also called it stilted and self-conscious. "Like Ray Bradbury miming Milton," she said, tapping my precious manuscript with the tip of her red felt-marker. I was devastated. She red-inked my story until it looked as if it was hemorrhaging.

"You're writing about ideas, Jon, not people. All head, no heart." She struck her fist against her plyboard chest. "Here, Jon! Here! e. e.

cummings: since feeling is first, who gives a damn about syntax? Just tell the story straight."

It was Nancy who kept me in line when I was staggering like a drunkard trying to find my way. In a silent show of rebellion, I'd allowed my blond locks to creep over my collar and ears. "Time for a haircut, isn't it?" my mother hinted. Coach Ramirez was more forthright: "Cut that damn mop or you're off the team!" When I proudly refused, Nancy chastised me. "Just cut it, Jon. Don't fight the superfluous. Don't ape those smoking jokers who sew a peace sign on their derriere and proclaim, suddenly, 'Behold, I'm an individual!' It's the inner stuff that counts."

Meanwhile, my former friends and teammates grew more vicious. The day after I lost the 440 to some gawky freshman from Orland, I found a little surprise in my locker: two golf balls in a mesh pouch with a note attached: LOST SOMETHING? Keith knew I would recognize his chicken scrawl. Someone else had added: SHE'S GOT HIM BY THE BALLS.

What was wrong with Jon Reeves? My parents, my teachers, Bishop Freeman, my friends—everyone wanted to know. Keith thought he had the answer. So did Brother Crumb. Every Sunday morning now he cautioned me and my peers to beware women with tinkling feet. He warned us about dating non-members and marrying outside the covenant. "Even Solomon was led down the primrose path by strange women. And it's a subtle fall, brethren. They'll use all their craft and artifice: flattery, beauty, secret delights . . ."

Brother Crumb was no simpleton. A huge six-footer with arms the size of tree trunks, he used to play bit parts in gladiator films. For forty-five minutes every Sunday morning he taught me and seven other young men the holy scriptures mingled with the philosophies of men and lurid tales from his hometown, which he called, disaffectionately, "The City of Fallen Angels." He always dressed conservatively—white shirt and solid tie—perhaps to counterbalance his wild hair and goatee and the fact that he was over forty and single, a combination tantamount to cultism in our provincial little town.

I'd always liked Brother Crumb. He never minced words, although he did adorn them quite a bit. We would listen like Boy Scouts mesmerized around a campfire as he related tales of teenage prostitutes, pimps, and pushers. Lately, however, he seemed to be aiming his hellfire directly at me.

"They'll baste you," he whispered, crouching down inside our intimate semi-circle of folding chairs, his barrel chest testing the buttons of his black blazer. "Slowly leading you by the nose like donkeys. They'll fatten your egos and bellies and turn your tough spirits to lard, and then when you're soft and plump and pliable, they'll wave their magic wands and turn you into spiritual swine!"

I would leave Brother Crumb's class sorely humbled. Swine! Led by the nose! That's what had happened to me! I'd grown fat, plump, pliable. I couldn't even win a race anymore. Well, enough! I was going to tell her off. Get thee hence, Woman! What kind of fool was she playing me for? A poet. A writer. Ha!

But Monday morning when I watched her long, lanky body crossing the grassy quad, I grew warm and wobbly inside. It was not hormonal heat but another variety. My resolutions turned to vapor. Nancy and I were friends, and where in the scriptures is friendship condemned? Love thy neighbor as thyself. Wasn't she my neighbor?

Whenever I tried to share these feelings with Nancy, she tore me to shreds. "Jon, it's not like we're hopping into bed together. Or is talking the same as fornication now? The illicit mixing of brain waves? How do you Mormons propose to convert the poor benighted rest of us if you never exchange an idea now and then? Is discourse anathema, like coffee and tobacco? What is it you're so afraid of? The brain God gave you? Or big bad spooky me?" Pressing her nose to mine, she would bulge her eyes, stick her thumbs in her ears, wriggle her fingers, and cry, "Boooo!" I would try my best not to flinch.

"Do those church people in inquisitional black and white scare you? Hey, call it quits right now! Football, writing—whatever your unicorn, forget it! Genius rides on the nose cone, Jon. It can't wait around for the brethren's holy stamp of approval."

She was right. I could feel it deep down. But Brother Crumb rebutted Sunday morning. Satan was the Father of All Lies, he said. The subtlest beast of the field. Beware his secret machinations. He'll smudge the line until good appears evil and evil seems good. Obedience? It robs you of your freedom, he'll say. Repentance? They're using guilt to manipulate you. Sin? A concept to control you through fear.

And so the battle for my soul waged on. Monday through Friday I frolicked in the wisdom of Nancy's world only to be called to repentance Sunday morning when I would regrip the iron rod of faith. But this became more and more difficult as time went by. Brother Crumb's sermons grew stale and scripted. Nancy, on the other hand, kept flourishing. Every day it was some new book, new idea, new insight or metaphor. In priests quorum I played mute, saying nothing unless spoken to, and then my answers were cryptic: yea, nay, suppose so. But privately I countered every word he uttered.

He knew it. He was losing me. The harder he tried, the more stubbornly I resisted. One night, in an act of desperation, he "just happened to be in the neighborhood" and invited me out for ice cream—the oldest trick in the book. Instead of Mac's Foster Freeze he picked the Bonanza Ice Cream Parlour, a "gay nineties" style shop for the old and middle-aged. He'd heard rumors, he said, about a girl. It wasn't his business, of course, wasn't his place to pry—that was the bishop's job. He smiled. I didn't laugh. I stared at the glossy menu, angry and annoyed. Then why are you prying? I thought. Why are you trying to make it your business? Shut up and butt out.

"Except I care about you," he said, cupping his goliath hands on the red-and-white striped tablecloth. His baritone voice, usually thick and rich, sounded froggy and stuffed up. His eyes were red and runny—spring allergies. He kept tripping over his tongue. "You know, Jon, they say . . . they say the best spirits have been saved for the last days. I think . . . I think that's true. Your generation's been sent to earth at this time to usher in the second coming of Jesus Christ. And I think you're . . . well, you're one of those special spirits. You have a special mission here on earth . . ." Brother Crumb's head began arching backwards, his face twisting as if he were in great pain. If he said "special" one more time I was going to scream.

"I don't know what it is—your special mission—and you probably don't know either. Not yet. Your patriarchal blessing can help you out there. But you do. I can see it. When you walk in Sunday morning, the whole room lights up. The other priests look up to you. You're a leader, Jon, and you can use your gift for good or evil. Satan was a brilliant spirit, the Son of the Morning, but he chose—" Brother Crumb's hand flew to his face as if to slap a mosquito. Too late: his head shot forward, releasing a mighty sneeze that sprayed across the table. "Just remember," he said, pulling a handkerchief from his pants pocket and applying it to his nose—honk!—"where all your gifts"—honk!—"came from"—honk!

So what's your point? I thought. At that moment he looked big, silly, oafish. He pocketed his handkerchief, nodding to himself. His eyes closed for several moments, and I wondered if he was praying. Then he told a story. Off the record, he said. He'd never told anyone else, ever. He was twenty-seven, married in the temple, living in North Hollywood. Waiting tables all day and taking an acting class at night. There was this woman, he said, and he began fiddling with one of the little C&H sugar packages in the straw basket. "Women—some of them, you know—they have this way. They'll tell you things. Try to make you think you're something you're not. Not necessarily better than you are, but different. They twist things." His chocolate chip eyes began melting down his cheeks. "I lost her, Jon. Her and the little boy. I've been forgiven—I really believe I have. But it's a helluva price to pay." His giant paw reached across the table and gripped my forearm. "Be careful, Jon. Don't sell your soul for a few cheap thrills. I know. I've been there. I've been to hell and back. And it burns like you can't even imagine."

I tried to remain sour, but I could feel myself softening. I was touched by the fact that he would share such a painful recollection simply to spare me similar suffering. But later, alone, Nancy's voice chimed in: They'll lie to you, Jon. They think it's for your own good, a means to justify the end, but they're still lies—lies so you can sleep at night.

The Mormon in me said Brother Crumb was right. I should set an example. I had responsibilities. But Nancy was right, too. God gave me a brain—use it!

The tug-of-war continued. Not just for my mind but my body also. I couldn't win a race. Exploding out of the starting blocks, my legs turned to mush. I could see the satiated smiles of my teammates. Well, so the hell what? Stupid dumb moron jocks! There were more important things in life. There was literature, art. Who gave a damn about trophies and touchdowns?

Evidently I did. Each failure played over and over in my mind like a slow and mortifying death dream. Nancy had nothing to do with my failures. I was in a slump, that's all. With two weeks left before the league finals, I resolved to prove my critics wrong by beating Harry the Horse. First, I would smoke him in the 440 and then humiliate him on the anchor leg of the mile relay. It would be my swan song kiss-my-grits goodbye to all of them—Keith, Coach Ramirez, Ponderosa High. My final statement in the only language they seemed to comprehend.

I went into crash training. No more chocolate sundaes at Mac's, no more afternoon sessions with Nancy. But no team practices either. I trained solo, after dark, subjecting myself to a grueling regimen of wind sprints: ten 100s, five 220s, four 440s, three 880s, all full out. For two weeks I trained as I never had before. I ran until my legs absolutely refused to move another step, and then I ran a bit more. By the time the league finals arrived, I was in the best physical condition of my life. I was as ready as I could ever possibly be.

But two days before the big meet my teammates tried to sabotage me. They did some cloak-and-dagger business and convinced Coach Ramirez to hold a run-off. All seven of our quarter-milers would race one lap with the first two finishers representing Ponderosa in the 440 and the top four comprising our mile relay team. Never before had there been a cutthroat run-off like that. Entries and relay teams were determined by fastest times. Keith was behind it, no doubt. We didn't even draw for lanes. I was assigned to lane eight. Outer Darkness. Suicide. Keith was playing it cool, wearing spikes with no socks and sunglasses like giant insect eyes. He hammered in his blocks and stood up, shaking his arms and legs loose. I tried to catch his eye but he wouldn't look at me. All right then, be that way! I lowered myself into my blocks and at the sound of Coach Ramirez's whistle broke out like a wild animal. I didn't look back. Anger, hate, resentment, and revenge powered me around the track. Crossing the finish line, I didn't look back either. I snatched my sweats off the infield grass and strutted defiantly towards the lockeroom as my teammmates, bent-double, hands on knees, panted in my dust.

CHAPTER 5

The night before the Preference Dance my mother and I had it out again over dinner. This time it wasn't a dramatic face-slapping but more subtle warfare. My father was absent, as usual, and I was rag-bagging again: I was sick of school, sick of sports. Track—especially track. The league finals had been a disaster. Fifth out of eight in the 440. I wasn't even close. On the anchor leg of the mile relay, I'd passed Harry the Horse on the final turn only to choke coming home. Anyway, who cared? I was never going to run another 440 as long as I lived. The only reason I was even doing football anymore was for the scholarship, so I wouldn't have to sponge off of my parents. I was sick of Keith and all my other fair-weather two-faced back-stabbing friends. Sick of Coach Ramirez and his banal homilies: "Don't wait for the breaks—make them!" "Football is the game of life!" Sick of living at home and getting the third degree every time I flushed the toilet. Every time I sneezed. I wanted out! Thank my lucky stars graduation was only a week away. As soon as I got my hands on that diploma I was off, gone—adiós aloha sayonara good riddance!—to BYU for summer school.

Actually, this was my father's idea. That way I could get a head start on studies, he'd said, and take advantage of the summer conditioning program for freshman football. "You don't want to jeopardize your scholarship." His real motivation was to get me out of Ponderosa and safely anchored in Happy Valley, far from the evil influence of Fräulein Von Kleinsmid. Fine, I thought. Whatever. Anything to get me out of this claustrophobic intellectually suffocating constipating town!

My mother listened patiently to my little tirade, forking dainty bites of rice pilaf into her mouth and chewing slowly, thoughtfully, occasionally sipping water from the wine glasses she always used at suppertime. Shoveling down chunks of braised beef, I got louder, more aggressive. It was all a big joke to her. I was a joke. Noting a strand of frosted hair that drooped down towards her nostril, I thought it looked like a hook reaching down to pick her nose. I hated her poise and patience, her long-fingered elegance, her magenta jumpsuit from Switzer's.

I'm sick of you! I felt like saying. Instead, I said the next worst thing:

"I'm sick of church! I'm sick of all those close-minded imbeciles . . ." For some reason I stopped. Was it her expression—her vacant, uncomprehending eyes? Apathy, indifference? Had she simply given up? I could hear the wind chimes tinkling in the pre-summer breeze. Directly behind her, through the plate-glass window, were the redwood deck where she and I used to share our summer meals and the gingko tree I would dutifully water on her behalf. At that instant everything seemed to freeze in time, or go back to a simpler time when I was her little companion and confidant, playing in the sandbox while she dabbed at canvas, bright yellows, bright reds, sunglasses on her head, sipping lemonade.

As my mother calmly forked more rice pilaf, I noticed something my all-scrutinizing pseudo-writer's eye had overlooked. She was dying. Overnight, it seemed, she had changed from a silver swan into a doddering old woman. Wrinkles cobwebbed her angular face. Her hair had turned to straw. Was I to blame for this? Me and my obstinate behavior? I felt tenderness and sorrow. But then I heard another voice. Don't get sentimental now. Buck up, Jon! Just buck up!

"I'm not going on a mission," I announced. "Why should I? I don't believe a word of that nonsense. And I won't—I will not—be a hypocrite. Not like the others. Not like you!"

My mother quietly folded up her red cloth napkin. Patience, long suffering, kindness, meekness, persuasion—she was going to unload the full arsenal of church weaponry and I was determined not to succumb. She rose slowly, weakly, from the table. "That girl did this to you," she whispered, and carried her plate, glass, and silverware into the kitchen.

What was the matter with her? What was wrong? Why didn't she grab me by my blond mop and slap some sense into me? I yelled after her: "That girl! She has a *name*, you know." She turned on the faucet and began rinsing her plate.

"Well, you'd better get used to her!" I hollered through the louvered doors. "Maybe you'd better even learn her name! Because it just so happens I'm going to marry her! Yes, muth-ther! That girl!"

I was speaking in frustration. I had no such intention. But if my parents thought that putting a few hundred miles of Utah-Nevada desert between me and Nancy was going to terminate our friendship, they were wrong. Dead wrong. Nancy and I would stay in touch: letters, carrier pigeon, smoke signals, whatever it would take. Better yet, why not bring Mohammed to the mountain? Nancy could get a job in Provo to earn enough for food and rent until she established herself in the world of letters. Then she could write full-time. I'd be in the dormitory, but I could smuggle her food from the cafeteria if needed. Basement apartments were cheap. For $20 or $30 a month you could get a bed, refrigerator, bathroom with a shower, and a hotplate. I wasn't allowed to hold a job as a condition of my scholarship, so I couldn't help her with day-to-day expenses. But if things got real tight, I could always sell my Corvette. That would secure ample funds to see us through until I graduated and . . . Yes? Then what? Well, I hadn't thought that far ahead, really. I didn't want to. The main thing was to get her to Provo. If she balked, I'd say, "You're going to miss it, Nancy! You're going to miss the train!"

It was a wild crazy hair-brained out-of-this-world scheme, but it was tailor-made for Nancy, and I would spring it on her tomorrow night, during or after the dance. Of course there were some incidentals to consider such as Nancy's mother and her family, but wasn't she the one who quoted chapter and verse from *Portrait of the Artist*? The real writer must (like Stephen Dedalus) fly above the superficial snares of family, religion, race, culture, to pursue the Priesthood of Art. Well, here was her chance! Freedom! Liberty! And she would even have access to the university library, via me, and if she changed her mind about college education, that would be available in time as well.

But there was another complicating factor clouding my scheme. Would the Spirit perhaps whisper a little more loudly and persuasively in that Mormon town than it had in northern California? Would Nancy's head and heart be softened? The possibility, however hypothetical, warmed me, making me the betrayer again as well.

Nancy was waiting for me by the four old mailboxes at the top of the lane. Like Cinderella, she was transformed from a tall plain girl in Salvation Army rags to a slender princess in a long sleeveless gown, high heels, and white gloves that reached to her elbows. Her short blond hair had been permed and piled high on her head, accentuating her long neck, but tonight she appeared more the graceful swan than Picasso's ostrich.

Ladies' choice, she was supposed to foot all the bills and provide transportation too, but I'd offered the services of my Corvette since she had no driver's license, let alone a car. I also chose Mac's Foster Freeze for dinner, to spare her paying for a meal. She accepted the transportation but insisted on dinner for two at Burton's, a swank coat-and-tie restaurant on the rim of the canyon where they charged ten bucks to peruse the menu. "Just once," she had said, "we will deign to mingle with the eee-leet!" How she scraped together enough money I had no idea, but I pictured her disinterring Mason jars full of nickels and pennies from her basement.

When I stopped the car, she waited for me to get out and open the passenger door, which must have felt as awkward for her as it did for me. In the past she had always refused such courtesies. "I'm not an invalid, Reeves!" What would happen if I tried to hold her hand? Should I hold her hand? It would be an insult not to. And how about a goodnight kiss? Why hadn't I thought through all of these things before? Keep cool, I reminded myself. Play it by ear.

It must have been her first genuine date because she seemed unusually nervous, intermittently tugging at her white gloves and shifting in the bucket seat. Even more telling, she was tongue-tied. An absolute first.

"You look great," I said.

She smiled. "You, too."

The conversation didn't improve much over dinner. Faint circles of blush tinted her cheeks and pinpoints of mascara twinkled darkly around the margins of her eyes. But the white gown was a tourniquet blocking the free flow of ideas to her brain.

I ordered the cheapest entree on the menu, a halibut steak at $19.50, and she asked for the same. No jokes about sprouts or sunflower seeds. We ate in relative silence, as if this meal were our last. I noticed, following dinner, that she stealthily unwrapped a stick of gum and sneaked it into her mouth. Preparing for what? When the waiter brought the check, she placed a $50 bill on it, and we left.

The dance at the high school was so-so. A live band blasted out Credence Clearwater Revival hits so loudly we couldn't talk except in between numbers, which proved to be an unanticipated blessing in disguise. The gym was loud, hot, sweaty, crowded, a far cry from our intimate afternoons at the River and at Mac's Foster Freeze. We were getting looks from some of our classmates, especially Keith who kept pointing and whispering nasty asides.

At 9:30 I asked if she wanted to go outside for a walk. No, she said, let's dance some more! I think she was trying to prove to me, if not to herself, that she could hold her own here. It was a challenge, a test of some kind. She smiled and shook her lanky arms and permed head to the music, a little stiffly and self-consciously, but smiling throughout. I felt sorry for her. She was holding her own maybe, but she wasn't enjoying it. I know I wasn't. The next time I asked her, around 11:00, she agreed.

It was cool outside, the pine scent strong and the sky thickly seeded with stars. The half-moon peered down at us like a sleepy eye trying to decide if it was going to open or close. I took her by her gloved hand. She looked at me and smiled nervously. We weaved through the cars in the parking lot behind the gym and crossed the upper playing field, the smell of fresh-cut grass ambrosial.

The stadium bleachers were built into an escarpment that sloped down to the football field and the oval track surrounding it. We descended the concrete steps, slipped through the open chain link fence, and eventually found ourselves sitting on the big foam rubber mattress in the pole vault pit, the rendezvous of many young Ponderosa lovers. Moonlight frosted the infield, and the pines formed a black barricade around the track. Some prankster had jammed the knob of the nearby drinking faucet. Water drooled over the brim, splattering softly on the grass. Crickets were chirping. You could barely hear the muffled pulsations of the band, like soft little heartbeats.

We carried on another short and strained conversation while I awaited the precise moment to reveal my plan, silently rehearsing how. The literary approach: "Nancy, I'd like to make an Immodest Proposal . . ." Or the Rhett Butler: "Excuse me, Mizz Nancy, . . ." Or play it straight: "Nancy, I need to tell you something . . ." Nothing seemed right. Nothing was right that night. Then why, at that point, did I slip my arm around her narrow waist?

"And what is this?" she asked, smiling.

I smiled back. I remember her eyes—soft and meek and dangerously infatuated. I moved a little closer to her, so our hips pressed together in the sinking softness of the foam pad. My right hand stroked the satin fabric up and down her ribcage. And then I made what would be the gravest mistake of my life. I leaned over and kissed her, tenderly, on the lips.

We drove home in dead silence. I took the long route. In fact I made a big loop around town twice, stalling, buying time, trying to think of some way to repair the damage I'd done. Finally, as I started the third loop, she spoke.

"Where are you going?"

"Home," I said.

"Thanks."

I glanced at her, hoping for reassurance. She was staring straight ahead, solemnly, as if riding in a hearse. The left strap was hanging off her shoulder. She let it hang, like an indictment. I'd never seen her cry before. Tear tracks glistened down her face. Her mascara was a delicate chain of black spittle around reddened eyes.

I was struggling for the right words. She despised clichés, yet I finally settled for the very oldest: "Nancy, I'm sorry." She continued staring out the windshield. "Nancy? I said—"

She cut me off. "So when do you leave for P.U.?"

"P.U.?"

"P.U., BYU—what's the diff?"

"Seven days," I said.

"And counting," she whispered. As we drove along the Skyway, the moon played hide-and-seek with the pines. "That's great," she said. "A university. The big time. And a football scholarship." Her comment rang sincere, no sarcasm or bitterness about me leaving and her staying behind. Suddenly she shot up in the bucket seat, tugging at the hem of her gown as if it were some obtrusion to be disposed of. She turned roughly towards me, with her old spunk and vitality. "Well, don't let them get you, Jon!"

"Get me?"

"Look, I know how these church schools operate. They'll strip you of your you before you can say *amen hallelujah*. First, they'll pare away your character, shred by shred. Potter's clay for their molding. Then they'll start layering you with the somber robes of conformity, all in the name of God and the booster club. Their strategies are devious. Guilt, compassion, threats of eternal sexlessness—anything to break a maverick like you. Remember *Portrait of the Artist?* Jimmy Joyce? Carry it with you like it's your Bible. And careful, Jon. I've seen it happen to the best. The last—"

"Nancy," I said, trying to steer the conversation back where it belonged. Damage had been done and it was my duty to repair it. The Mormon in me said that. But every time I tried to speak, she jumped back in.

"Look, Jon, you may think you're just another pass-catching body-building connoisseur of jock straps, but you're not. The others—Keith Bernhard and Dave Jordan and the rest—they're just your everyday Cro-Magnon blockheads. They're doomed to this godforsaken town just like the rest of us. But you—" She pulled the fallen strap back up onto her shoulder. "You can make it, Jon. You can break the mold. And you're going to. You will. Just don't come back with a crew-cut in dark suit and white shirt trying to make everyone swallow that mythology about gold plates and angels. Jon, don't let us down."

"Us?"

"I understand they've got great skiing in Utah," she said, diverting again.

"So I've heard."

"You ought to take it up. Stay away from the downhill stuff, though. Big crowds, expensive lift tickets, the whole phony ski lodge scene. It's the biggest commercial ripoff since Disneyland. Try cross-country." I nodded obediently. Only a handful of bearded old snowdogs had even heard of cross-country skiing. "And one more thing. Whatever you do, keep writing. Will you promise me that?"

"Me?"

"Yes, you big dumb ignoramus! One of these days you'll snap out of it and trade in your shoulder pads for a typewriter. And when you do . . ." Her voice trailed off and the energy suddenly left her face. For the next few moments she stared wearily into the darkness as if she were bearing the burdens of a troubled planet. Then, slapping the dashboard: "And when you do, be honest! Write what you really truly feel, not what you or your parents or your bishop or some money-hungry publisher says you should feel. Listen to your heart, go with your guts, and you can't miss . . . Next one on the left, in case you've forgotten."

Of course I hadn't forgotten. And this time when I turned down the lane she didn't protest. My tires threw a little gravel as I braked in front of the glorified shack she called home. There was a low picket fence out front, the white paint almost gone. Wagons, Tonka trucks, and other kid toys cluttered the dirt front yard. A blurry silhouette was rocking behind the translucent sheet of plastic in the front window.

I switched off the ignition and turned towards her. "Nancy–" But she had already bolted out the door. "Nancy!" She never looked back.

Clutching the hem of her white dress as she stumbled up the porch steps, she brought to mind Cinderella fleeing the prince's ball at midnight. And I couldn't help wondering what bizarre metamorphosis would come to pass once she slipped through that front door, what odd vegetables would become her spiked slippers, what shabby smock her evening gown, what tragic mask her cool, composed face.

CHAPTER 6

That was my last look at Nancy, her Cinderella exeunt. A week later I loaded up my Corvette and left for BYU and didn't come home until the Christmas holidays when I was shocked to learn that she had married. "No!" I protested. "Not Bill Watson!"

Bill had been Ponderosa's senior linebacker when I was a willowy freshman trying to crack the varsity lineup. He was called "Buffalo" because he was as big as one and twice as ugly. Thick bulldog jowls pitted with acne scars, a prickly pear chin, and fierce brown eyes, one of which was perpetually swollen shut, he looked like the one-eyed, cutlass-bearing brute on the Oakland Raiders logo.

Bill was something of a local legend. I remember one game when a monster fullback from Wheatland ran a 30-dive, up the gut. Buffalo Bill lowered his helmet and filled the hole. It was like two bighorn sheep butting heads. When the gunshot crack finally faded, only Bill was standing. Smelling salts couldn't revive his victim. As they called for the stretcher, Buffalo Bill coolly scratched another notch onto his arm pad with his fingernail.

Another time Coach Ramirez was trying to fire us up for a game we knew we were going to put away in the first quarter. "Boys—men! Football is a game of memories! Why, you'll remember that one block or tackle long after you've forgotten some geometry theorem!"

"What's a theorem?" quipped someone in back.

Everyone, including Ramirez, laughed. But when Buffalo Bill added, "What's geometry?" there was silence. Was Bill joking? Judging by his gorilla gape, no. Big, solid, beer-drinking, slow-thinking . . .

"I can't believe it! Bill Watson! It's surreal!" I was angry. Before leaving for Utah, I'd tried several times to catch Nancy at home, but she was always "gone"—that was all the tallest of the towheads playing in her dirt front yard would say. A lanky boy with bowl-cut hair and aqua eyes, the instant he saw my red car coming he would drop his whiffle ball or squirt gun and rush over to the picket fence, passively blocking the entry.

"Is Nancy home?"

"No."

"Where is she?"

"Gone."

"Gone where?"

"I don't know."

"When are you expecting her?"

"I don't know. She's gone."

"Is your mother here?"

"No."

"Where is she?"

"Gone."

During the exchange, the other children (eight, including two in diapers) would glare at me as if I'd come to take away the farm.

"Thanks. I'll try again later."

My final visit I left a note: I'm leaving Saturday morning–early. Can we talk? No reply. Did she even see the note? I would never know.

My last hope was to see her at graduation. She had declined to give the valedictory address, but surely she would come for her diploma. Wrong again.

At summer school I wrote her at least a dozen times without reciprocation. By mid-July I got fed up: "This is my last letter if I don't hear from you. I MEAN IT!"

In August football practice officially started. Hell Week. Two-a-day, full pads in the ninety-plus heat. This should have helped take my mind off of Nancy, but it did the opposite, which is one reason I performed so miserably. I couldn't concentrate. Couldn't run, couldn't catch, couldn't block. In the huddle, while the quarterback was calling the play, I'd think of something she had said or done. When I ran a pass pattern, the ball in flight became her self-reviling face. No wonder on film it looked as if I'd slapped the ball away intentionally. I had.

Nancy was only one factor. Another was talent. I was a minnow among barracudas. I still might have succeeded had my heart been in the game, but college ball was a different world. Football was the game of life, literally. You had to eat, breathe, and sleep it. All sweat, no smiles. Fun? Who said anything about fun? I found myself pouring far more passion into writing than pass-catching, and it showed on the field: "Come on, Reeves! Where's your grit, man? Where's your want-'em?"

Football-wise things got worse and worse until our second game when an enemy linebacker speared me from behind, destroying my knee as well as my football career. While I silently thanked him, I also wept for having forfeited something that, at one time, I'd desired so ardently. My secret relief was also an admission of defeat.

If I was a washout on the gridiron, in the classroom I was blossoming. My English instructor agreed with Nancy. I had a knack. Reading my personal essay entitled "SNAP! CRACKLE! CRUNCH! Confessions of an Almost College Football Jock," she insisted I enter it in a universitywide writing contest. Thanks to some senior editing, I placed second and shortly after joined the staff of the *Wye*, the campus literary magazine, an unprecedented honor for a freshman. This convinced me that Nancy was correct. I did have a higher calling than entertaining bawdy, boozy crowds with high-five heroics on weekend afternoons. My true destiny was to be a writer.

I started my first novel in November, just before Thanksgiving. About that time I also took up cross-country skiing and healthy foods. I was gorging myself on literature. Except for football and the bitter winter weather, college life was agreeing with me. I was earning A's in all of my classes and making friends easily. In campus literary circles I was well-liked and respected.

I anticipated the Christmas holidays when I could show Nancy my transfiguration. I was also anxious to discuss religion with her. Professor Farnsworth, my religion teacher, had armed me with objective, scientific, quantifiable data to counter Nancy's arguments. For sixteen weeks I had studied the Book of Mormon with a critic's eye and participated in discussions with fellow students who met every Monday night and attended church services together Sunday mornings and afternoons. I was seeing life and religion more clearly now. Nancy's sophistry was just another form of brainwashing. I was ready for her. I didn't view her as an evil agent, as my mother and others had, but I was not going to let her bully me intellectually. I felt confident I could stand up to her now, and standing up to her I would win her respect. Winning her respect was, well, it was the first of many steps leading towards wherever it was she and I were eventually headed. I would take it line upon line.

I also wanted to see my parents whom I had missed much more than I had anticipated. I wanted to show them how much I had matured. I was an adult now, not the whiny pouty spoiled little boy who had roared out of their driveway in June. After an intense semester, I was ready to indulge myself in some old home delights as well. I wanted to sit by the fire and sip eggnog and glut myself at the ward Christmas feast and O.D. on bowl games New Years Day. I wanted all of that. What I didn't want was to explain my football fiasco to everyone or re-open wounds that were perhaps just beginning to heal. I didn't want to become entangled. I had a new life, a new image. I was Jonathan Reeves the writer, not the screwball super-jock. I wanted to keep it that way. What I didn't want was my past. Except for Nancy. Most of it anyway. Her. Us.

With these ambivalent feelings, I returned home for the holidays, where news of Nancy's marriage awaited me. "But why," I asked, showing off some of my literary prowess, "would a girl like Nancy marry a bludgeoning Brobdignagian like Bill Watson?"

My mother, who had wrinkled considerably since I'd last seen her, looked up from her *Ensign* and shrugged. "You know what they say: opposites attract."

"Oh yes! Bill and Nancy! Ponderosa's odd couple! The marriage of true minds!"

"You sound a little upset."

Upset? You bet I was upset! You bet I was mad! I'd been betrayed. All her lofty talk of art and literature, the liberation of the human spirit . . . Hypocrite! Pharisee! Every time I thought about her verbal barbs and pithy put-downs, my anger flared anew. Nancy, who had once called jocks the lowest rung on the evolutionary ladder, had married one. Who was she to criticize me? Don't let them get you, Jon! Don't let us down! Who did she think she was fooling?

Me, that's who! I'd been duped, conned, made an idiot of. Keith and the others had been right. Brother Crumb was right. My parents were right. Everyone had caught on but me. Losing Nancy to another guy was one thing; losing her to Buffalo Bill Watson was insulting. She had done it either to humiliate me or to avenge herself in some bizarre, self-immolating, Nancy Von Kleinsmid way. There was no other explanation.

Was I maybe jealous, too? Just a little bit? I scoffed at the suggestion. "Of her? If she wants to go off and marry some hick town Caliban, let her! What's it to me? She's just like the rest of them. She's no different."

"Oh? The rest of them?"

"You know what I mean. And please don't look at me like that. You of all people know exactly what I mean." I found it very interesting that, now that Nancy was no longer a threat, my mother was sympathetic towards her. I felt betrayed on all fronts.

My mother quietly closed the magazine, set it on the coffee table, and remarked, "I understand she's expecting in March."

I shut up. It doesn't take a genius to calculate the month of conception. I'd last seen Nancy at the beginning of June. Whatever had evolved between her and Bill had been a whirlwind affair which cost her even more respect in my self-righteous eyes. When my mother suggested I pay her a little visit, I threw up my hands: "What's the point? It would be a mockery—a mockery for both of us!" Consequently, the holidays crawled by, and the day after New Year's I returned, rather solemnly, to my beloved books, my literary friends, my cross-country skis.

But it turned out to be a long, dark, cold Utah winter, one of the worst on record, and I was full of gloom. Every time I watched the storm clouds float over the mighty Wasatch Range with the dark foreboding of the Luftwaffe, I felt the same as when I'd learned of Nancy's marriage: betrayed, insulted. I tried to blame it on the weather, but even Eric Swenson, my head-in-the-clouds roommate, knew better. "What's her name?" he said. "S-N-O-W," was my reply.

I tried to lose myself in studies. Day after day I sat in the austere carrels of the BYU library or near the giant hearth in the Wilkinson Center Lounge, coveting the spring visions of Keats, Shelley, Wordsworth, and Hopkins, while outside white confetti fluttered from the sky like a celebration of Melville's all-color atheism. Suddenly nothing mattered anymore—school, writing, church, life. I withdrew from friends and spent more and more time brooding in my cramped little dorm room or taking long, desultory walks to nowhere. One cold, snowy night near the end of February my depression hit rock bottom. Walking along a hilltop on the southwest end of campus, near the Eyring Science Center, I stopped suddenly and let my books drop from my hands. I glared up at the sky, falling in a million little pieces, and said, hopelessly, "What's the point, anyway? What's the whole damn point?" Then I lay down in the snow, closed my eyes, and waited for whatever. I remember praying, or at least thinking aloud: Please get me out of here! A moment later I felt a little nudge—a toe, a hand, I couldn't tell, but it was just stern enough to send me rolling like a log down that hill. I heard a voice at the bottom, laughter. A familiar laugh. I sprang to my feet, looking for the culprit, but saw nothing except the endless curtain of falling snow. I trudged back to my dorm room, wet, cold, and confused. Was this the answer to my prayer? The next day while standing in line at the Cougar-Eat, someone tapped me on the shoulder. I turned around. "Excuse me, but can I borrow a pen?" Her brown eyes could have melted all the ice in Antarctica.

I don't know if it was my desperation, her healing power, or my own brand of reverse revenge, but Vickie Alder helped resurrect me from my dark winter coffin. The snow continued falling, but I had purpose again. To hell with Nancy Von Kleinsmid! She'd made her bed, let her sleep in it with all two hundred-fifty beefy pounds of Buffalo Bill Watson! I had my own life to live.

April 29th of that year would always stand out in my mind for two reasons: it was the first genuine day of spring, and it was the day I received the other news about Nancy Von Kleinsmid. When I drew the blinds that morning, for the first time in five months I saw nothing above the mountains but pure unmitigated blue. The sun rose laboriously, like a winter-stiff athlete out of training.

I was ready. The whole student body was. As the last sheets of snow shriveled to long skeletal fingers to knuckles to nothing, students poured out of their classrooms discarding coats, mittens, mufflers. Coeds, stripping to legal limits, spread their pale bodies on beach towels like the river nymphs back home. Frisbees flew, baseball bats cracked, joggers jogged. To the east, the white tips of the Wasatch blushed hot pink. Westward, Utah Lake was shining like a vast sheet of glass. The fat stacks of Geneva Steel billowed like Moses' pillar of smoke. Tractors rumbled out of hibernation, churning up dark, thawed earth.

Strolling along the sun-warmed path leading to the campus post office, holding Vickie Alder's hand, I was in high spirits. Final exams were over and my term papers were in. A long, relaxing summer of reading and writing awaited me, culminating with a backpacking trip to the Uintas with Vickie. I was happily and indulgently reflecting on the neat little future I'd mapped out for myself: two-year church mission, temple marriage, graduate studies, English Professor/Writer-in-Residence . . . Images of a lakefront home with four kids and a golden retriever prancing across a big grassy yard passed through my mind as I started turning the combination knob on my post office box.

It was a typical letter from home. Dad was dropping his practice in Chico so he wouldn't have to commute. Sister Stanwyck had another set of twins. Bob Gilliam was back from his mission to Japan. Love, Mother. Except at the bottom she had written in tiny but precise cursive: P.S. NANCY VON KLEINSMID PASSED AWAY LAST WEDNESDAY.

My face must have belied my feelings because Vickie slipped her arm consolingly around my waist and leaned her head against my shoulder. Although her soft blond hair felt like silk on my bare arm, it irritated me. "What's the matter, Jonathan?"

"Nothing," I said, folding up the letter and tucking it in my hip pocket. She stopped. "Jon?"

"Some news about an old friend," I said.

"A close friend?"

"Yes."

Her arm tightened around my waist. "Jonathan, what is it? What happened?" Her soft, concerned voice, usually so mollifying, was an annoyance. Suddenly everything about her was annoying. Her potent perfume replicated the hyper-sweet stench of the letter.

"Nothing," I said firmly.

Her arm dropped from my waist, and she assumed an exasperated, put-upon look, her hands akimbo. Then she spewed out some lingo from one of her Family Relations classes. "Jonathan, if we're going to be serious about this relationship we've got to be completely honest with each other. We can't go around hoarding secrets."

As I looked at her—the peaches 'n cream cheeks, the bevel nose, the streaked blond hair tumbling thickly past her shoulders, I recalled

Nancy's prophecy and the black blessing she had given me that early morning after the Preference Dance. Who was this girl? This slender young Idaho Falls doll who loved bowling, Carol Burnett, Robert Redford, and pepperoni pizza? Who was this girl I was planning to companion throughout all eternity? Had we ever discussed *Sons and Lovers*? Had she read Yeats or Whitman? Did she know a cross-body block from a cross-chest carry? Yes, she was cute, charming, adorable. Everyone thought so. A downhill skier on Saturdays and homemaking leader for the Relief Society on Sundays, she had all of the celestial credentials to make a virtuous, lovely wife and mother.

But who was she really? And what was I? An aspiring writer who hadn't seen or suffered enough to write anything of import, who ran from professor to professor with manuscripts in hand, fishing for compliments; a pseudo-literary intellectual, a big little kid who, borrowing ideas from the inspired leaders of a lofty institution, had become so cocksure about his faith that he thought he had all the answers to life's most bewildering questions as neatly tucked away in his hip pocket as the tragic letter he just received from home. What was I really? A yes-man. A snob. For all my new-found academia, I still didn't think for myself, religiously or otherwise, because I let everyone else think for me. I'd even allowed them to chart out the rest of my life, a very nice life indeed. I looked dapper in my velour shirts and flared slacks, studious with my Viking edition of Faulkner in one hand and my Riverside Shakespeare in the other, dedicated and inspired as I stopped mid-stride to scribble some silly thought in my spiral notebook. I'd become everything Nancy had cautioned me against. I'd been gotten.

I glared at Vickie as if she were somehow to blame. "I'll call you tonight."

Her big little chest rose, her lips puckering as she exhaled a long, impudent breath. "Jonathan . . . I want to talk about it now!"

"Later, all right?"

"Jonathan . . ."

I smiled at her and she smiled back. Then: "Vickie, for such a sweet spirit, you can be a first-class pain in the ass."

"Jonathan!"

"Later," I said, and walked off.

Back in my dorm room I lay on my bed staring at the cross-country skiing poster I'd tacked to the ceiling directly overhead. It was a "scenic" picture featuring a gloved, gaitered, and goggled skier and his little malamute pausing at a rippling snow-banked stream as the sun perched atop a snow-capped peak in the background. At the end of a long day I often flopped down on my bed and took solace in this placid winter scene. But today, in the context of Nancy's death, it looked ludicrous, like another commercial farce.

I pulled down the blinds, killing the spring sunshine, and closed my eyes. The first thing I saw was her long body, cold and ashen in the moonlight, lying like a corpse across the railroad tracks. Then her slit lips curling into a wicked little smile. Was it maybe a joke? April Fool's twenty-nine days late? Another morbid Nancy trick? No, don't even think it. Don't even entertain the notion. She was dead. Gone. Never see, hear, touch her again. But how? Why? Delivery room? Car wreck? Broken heart? Gone. Forever.

Other things passed through my mind, but, like a bad laceration, the deeper pain was temporarily numbed by peripherals. My thoughts blurred and began racing everywhere—everywhere but Nancy. What finally came into sharp focus was something that had occurred many years earlier when I was ten, an incident involving a cat that had lost a leg.

It was a kitten actually. I'd discovered it one Saturday morning hiding in the corner of our car port, whimpering. As I walked by, he turned towards me and rose up on his three good legs, offering a pathetic view of the dog-butchered fourth, a furry little sausage hanging from a bloody stump by three or four scarlet threads. I felt sorry for him, not just due to the injury but also because of the way he'd looked at me, his little head tilting innocently to one side, his green eyes meek and trusting.

I was young and easily influenced. In this case I was probably identifying with the white-hatted heroes of TV westerns who shoot their lame horses to "put the poor critter out of its misery" when I decided to do this mangy gray critter a similar favor. If any animal looked miserable, it was that kitten. So with philanthropic intent, I grabbed my pellet gun from my closet, coaxed the animal into a cardboard box, placed the muzzle on the back of his skull, and slowly squeezed the trigger. I winced at the soft, dull "pop!" Unfortunately, the kitten didn't calmly roll over dead as on TV. He let out a loud, gnashing wail and leaped out of the box with back arched and fangs flashing. I jumped back, the pistol trembling in my hand. Panicking, I cornered him, pinned the muzzle between his eyes, and squeezed again: "Pop!" Again he snarled, leaped, took two quick boxer's swipes at me with his good forepaw, and hobbled away.

"You stupid cat!" I hurled the worthless pistol aside and gazed around our front yard in guilt and shame, afraid someone may have witnessed my impotent performance. With two pellets in his skull, the kitten had to be killed, I knew that. But now my head and heart were pounding like a fastbreak basketball game.

I grabbed a rock, the biggest I could lift, and again cornered the kitten. His green eyes were cold now, tense, suspicious, afraid. Gripping the rock with both hands, I raised it over my head and released a piercing death-cry as I hurled it down. His head sank a half-inch into the soft red earth, and his little body went limp but only for an instant. He writhed and wriggled and twisted and turned until his head, gouged with divots, runneled with blood, wormed out from under the rock. And he limped away Rasputin-like, amazingly agile for a three-legged creature with two pellets in his head.

That was too much for me. I ran into the house, down the air-conditioned hallway, and into my bedroom where I turned on my TV full-volume and tried to lose myself in the Saturday morning cartoons. I lasted through five minutes of a Bugs Bunny episode before sprinting back outside, grabbing a shovel, and once again cornering the kitten. Pinning him down with my bare foot, I aimed the blade perpendicular to his neck. As I raised the shovel for the kill, I could feel the desperate tension rippling through his little body. A chill ran up my leg and exploded in my chest. I closed my eyes and thrust the blade straight down, anticipating blood, shrieks, gore, and death. The cat shrieked but lived. I raised the shovel and thrust it down again. And again and again and again. Viciously. But the blade wouldn't penetrate. The kitten screeched louder and louder—an echo? Was it an echo? Again he squirmed out from under my foot, his tough little ribs pumping like bellows, and limped under the sanctuary of my father's Lincoln Continental.

"Come out of there!" I ordered, desperate, angry, frantically trying to scoop him out into the open with my shovel. "Come out, darn you!"

I knew I'd done something very wrong that couldn't be undone. My father, whose business was bringing human life into the world, had taught me the sanctity of living things. He had told me about Brigham Young chastising the pioneers for killing rattlesnakes on their trek west, and how Great-grandpa Reeves would always trap rather than swat house spiders and tenderly release them outside. Even as a ten-year-old I knew, however noble my intentions, I'd botched up badly. Who was I, after all, to ordain myself mini-god and tamper with the life/death scales? My well-intentioned euthanasia caused the animal more misery in ten minutes than he would have suffered in a lifetime amidst the dogs of Ponderosa.

Desperate, I got down on my knees and tried one last strategy—a soft approach: "Here, kitty kitty kitty! Here, kitty kitty kitty! Nice kitty!" The animal didn't budge. I wheeled around and ran.

It happened to be one of my father's rare days off, and he was down on one knee planting geraniums in the backyard when I rounded the corner. With wild hands and weeping eyes, I blurted out my confession.

A hard-working, self-made American hardened by the Depression and World War II, my father the perfectionist had little tolerance for incompetence of any type, although he did have his tender moments. Fortunately for me, this would be one of them. The veins in his shot-putter's arms were bulging, but his expression reflected concern rather than anger. Rising slowly to his feet, he dropped his trowel and patted my shoulder. "Well, we'd better do something, don't you think, son?" Wiping the gooey tear and mucous mixture from my face, I nodded.

My father owned only one firearm, a black powder rifle the husband of a patient had given him in lieu of obstetric fees. He went into the house and returned with the latter. "Where is it?" he asked.

I pointed to the rear axle of the car. A well-timed meow issued from underneath. My father knelt down and very gently retrieved the kitten from under the vehicle. Stroking him softly, he placed the animal in the cardboard box and pinned his neck down with the pipe-sized muzzle. I backed away a few steps until I couldn't see. I remember my father's left eye squinting shut and the kitten's little paws desperately scratching the walls of the box. I turned away.

There was a long, loud echo, like a miniature cannon. The cloud of dark gray smoke lingered several moments, as did the harsh smell of gunpowder and something even more harsh, like burned rubber. I kept my eyes elsewhere: Mrs. Shaw's summer garden, swelling with squash, melons, cherry tomatoes, corn stalks with golden tassels—cheerful colors to evoke sweet dreams of sky castles, fairy godmothers, dancing bears, not the gory nightmare at hand.

"Jonathan," my father said, gently clasping my hand. I knew my duty. Like a condemned man I slowly turned around and approached the box. His little claws were still scratching the cardboard walls when I peeked inside. There was the severed head with the fang-like teeth and the blank green eyes, frozen, artificial, a taxidermist's handiwork. The body looked less merciful. Gobs of raspberry glistened on the jagged neck as the shoulders, legs, and tail continued jerking as if he were still trying somehow to struggle free. It looked like a ball of bloodied snakes trying to get untangled. I turned away and tried not to hear the frantic scratching in the box.

My father's hand lightly gripped my shoulder. "Have you learned a lesson, son?"

I turned around and looked up slowly. "Yes, Poppa," I sniffled and broke out bawling in his mighty arms.

CHAPTER 7

Six months later I was boarding a 747 for Mexico, having just completed eight weeks' worth of language training in Provo. My parents flew in from California to say goodbye. The mauve knit dress that used to fit my mother so snugly now drooped on her broomstick bones. My father tried to keep a stoic front. Gripping my hand, he looked me in the eye and said, "I'm proud of you, son!" I glared at him defiantly: I'm not doing this for you.

All summer we had butt heads over the mission issue. The climax came the morning after the 4th of July when he slipped into my bedroom and flipped on the light.

"Don't forget your appointment!"

"What appointment?" was my groggy reply.

"For your mission interview. I made you an—"

I flung the bedcovers aside. "Break it!"

He thought I was joking. "Seven sharp," he said with a wink. As he grinned down at me, I saw him sharp and clear: a half-bald little Buddha telling me what to do again. I was furious inside. He had no idea what I was going through. In his mind, Nancy's death was an unfortunate asterisk, a blessing in disguise.

"I'm not going," I said.

"Seven's not good?"

"Not the interview." I looked down at the red bedspread, crumpled in my lap. "A mission."

His hand fell from the light switch. "You don't want to go on a mission?"

"I'm not sure . . . I mean, I'm not . . ."

I was tightrope-walking over a fiery pit of sacrilege which had never smoldered in his presence in our home. His voice had a warning tone: Stop! But there was a pleading edge, too: Please . . . not now. My mother was dying. Although he would not say so out loud, he wore this knowledge on his face in his hangdog jowls and bloodshot eyes.

"How do you know we're the only true church?" I challenged. "Have you ever even been to another church? What do you know about Hinduism? What do you know—"

"Jon!" His voice thundered through my room. "You get your butt to that meeting, do you hear me? Jon!"

"No!" I hollered. I was on my feet now, towering over him. "You don't know any more than I do! The only reason you believe is because your father did and his father and—"

"Jon!"

"I'm right. You know I'm right! How do you know anything about the church? Can you prove it? No! Can you—"

"You get to that meeting!"

"Forget it! Forget you!"

Then I was on the floor, rubbing my jaw, staring acidly up at him. His fists were clenched, his iron jaw locked. As he left I muttered, "Asshole!" but by then he was too fed up and disgusted to care.

This was to be the most confusing, frustrating summer of my life. After undergoing several batteries of routine tests, my mother had gone to visit her sister Mitzi in Klamath Falls. "Resting," my father explained. "She just needs a little R and R." Why couldn't she rest at home? Who was she trying to hide from? Me? Was I to blame for this? Me and my contrary behavior?

"This Plikta girl—she's not LDS, is she?" my mother ventured.

"LDS? No."

"Be careful, Jonathan."

"I'm always careful."

"I know. But you're my only—"

"I know, Mom."

"The first shall be last and the last shall be first . . . You're my first and my last." She spoke to me in scriptures now. It was pathetic, yet I was upset with her, or trying to be. I hardened myself for the inevitable.

"Jonathan?"

"Yes, Mom?"

"The Spirit can be so willing, but the flesh . . . "

"It's okay, Mom. Don't worry."

"I won't. I know. But . . . be careful. Please?"

I decided to settle this mission business once and for all. I accepted

Brother's Crumb's challenge: study it out in your mind and take it to God in prayer. Fast, ponder, and ask. Yes or no? If it's right, you'll get a burning feeling in your breast. If not? Fog in the brain. Ask with real intent; the Spirit will manifest.

I hiked down to the River, determined to pray until I received an answer—two days, three days, whatever it took. I wanted something outstanding, a burning bush, a lunar eclipse, a voice. Proof! I wanted concrete proof!

I endured the first day like any other Sunday fast, with growling gut and dizziness. By day two the hollowness in my belly filled with funny puffy stuff that went straight to my brain. I was in an altered state, helium-headed but bewildered. On the one hand, I was determined not to be had by sophistry. Conversely, I wasn't going to disbelieve simply because Nancy Von Kleinsmid had proscribed belief. Whatever I did, it had to be for the right reason. I had to feel and believe it way down deep. I had to find my own drummer, not Nancy's or my father's or James Joyce's. But who was that, really?

I debated this back and forth, pleading for a sign. At one point, in despair, I stepped out onto the Rock and stared down at the two giant boulders where I had been told that Nancy had crash-landed. Leaning forward, I could feel the River's spray on my face and the gravity grabbing me by the shoulders and pulling me forward, out, over the edge. Then I heard a voice, not in the screaming waters, but a sigh, an echo whispering: Don't.

I climbed down and lay beside a scrub pine under a black-and-blue sky sparkling with all the stars of Abraham. For the next hour I bartered. I would serve a mission, I said, if God would spare my mother's life. Don't take her from us now. Not because of me and all the rotten selfish things I'd said and done . . . The irony seemed to snap like a steel-jawed trap: Don't take her from us . . . from me . . . That was it! All my life it had been that way: tit for tat. I was an exploiter, always looking out for number one. I asked God to erase my proposal. I'll do your will, not mine. I'll do the mission regardless of what happens to my mother.

As I talked with God, the cloud matter in my head grew warm and buoyant. I felt myself floating skyward, starward, as if I were surfacing from the bottom of a pitch black pool. No, the heavens didn't part. But for the first time since hearing of Nancy's death I felt a deep, resounding peace. That in itself was a miracle.

I couldn't undo my past, but I could control my future. I could be good, do right. I couldn't bring Nancy back from the dead, but I could share the gospel of redemption with the living.

When I arrived home early the next morning, my mother called from Aunt Mitzi's and ruined everything. It was a little before dawn and her voice was anxious and quavering, so afraid. "Jonathan, I'm sorry to call so early. But I had the strangest dream. Jonathan? Are you there?"

"Yes. Yes, I'm here."

"Jonathan, I had the strangest dream."

"I know. You said that."

"Well, you know what my patriarchal blessing says—"

"Yes, Mom." Throughout my youth she had reminded me of the part that said she would interpret dreams like Joseph of Egypt.

"Jonathan, promise me you'll go on a mission. Will you do that for me? Please? Your father says . . . Jonathan?"

"Yeah, I'm here."

"Your father says—"

"Who cares what he says!"

"Oh, Jonathan, please don't be like that—"

"Mom, when are you coming home?"

"In another week or so. I just need—"

"It's been a month."

"I know, Jon, but—"

"You're not going to get better, are you?"

"Oh, of course I am."

"Mom . . . Mother . . ."

"Promise me, Jon. Please?"

"Yes," I said, my voice breaking. "Yes. I promise."

"Oh, Jon, I'm so glad! You just don't know how happy . . ."

Then Nancy sneaked in, contesting the lessons of the canyon: Of *course* you're going on a mission. Didn't I tell you? Another prophecy fulfilled.

It was my decision, Nancy.

Oh? On what grounds? Holy confirmation? Hallowed heartburn? You can talk yourself into believing anything. Sorry, Jon. A mother's death-bed wish, how could you refuse?

My decision, Nancy. Mine.

Nineteen years of conditioning, Jon. Mormon brainwash.

Mine.

The other missionaries had said their goodbyes and were boarding the plane when Elder Reed, my flight companion, good-naturedly gestured to his watch. I looked at my father who suddenly seemed small and shriveled, like a little round balloon slowly losing air. His sidehair appeared more white than silver. He pulled in his gut and gave me the thumbs up like he used to before a kickoff. "Give 'em heaven, Jon!" he said. He smiled and I smiled back. It was the best I could do under the circumstances.

Leaning into me, my mother licked her forefinger and brushed the short blond bangs back off my forehead, a maternal habit I had tried to dodge since grade school. But this time I allowed it, without fuss, and when she brushed the lapels of my dark suit coat, I allowed her that also, even with twenty-one other missionaries, four of them young women, looking on. Then she stepped back and smiled at me one last time as she straightened my red tie. I kissed her awkwardly on the cheek and started for the boarding ramp.

"Jon!"

I turned. She was running towards me, her brittle arms outstretched. I dropped my carry-on bags to receive her. Our bodies met, and she hugged and kissed me with all of the passionate finality of a girlfriend sending her lover to war.

CHAPTER 8

After a short orientation at the mission home, I traveled by bus to Socorro, a small fishing village on the western coast. My senior companion, Elder Jenkins, met me at the depot, a shack with a makeshift sign. It was spring weather, blue sea, blue skies. It was hard to believe that forty-eight hours earlier I'd been trudging through a snowstorm in Utah. Along the docks, sun-wrinkled fishermen dragged in their nets. Silver-scaled fish glistened in wooden trays of ice. I remember walking the dusty streets that first day, the *vendedores* selling fresh fruits and sugared pastries, fat flies buzzing about, mangy mutts doing their duty on every corner. One image that will remain with me forever: a living skeleton. She was crouching in front of the bakery, a shawl over her head, a ragged dress half-hiding her toothpick body. As Elder Jenkins and I approached she gazed up at us and smiled pathetically, her mouth a cruel Halloween gag. My face sickened, betraying my parochialism: I had never seen true starvation before. She held out a skinny, vein-rippled hand, her palms black-seamed like a mechanic's, and grunted incomprehensibly. Her eyes were hard-boiled eggs bulging out of cavernous sockets. I heard a faint cry from underneath her rags; then a tiny, shriveled fist reached out. It opened like a little flower, groping, then closed tight.

Elder Jenkins looked aside and walked on, apparently oblivious. I remember thinking: You callous jerk! I stooped and gave the woman an apple I'd just purchased from the fruit vendor. Elder Jenkins glanced back at me through his Poindexter glasses and shook his head. Defiantly, and rather self-righteously, I fished into my pocket and gave the woman a handful of pesos. I got Jenkins' point, though, when rounding the corner we confronted a gauntlet of villagers in similar rags, hands out, gazing up at us with impoverished eyes and toothless smiles. Okay, Elder. *Vale la pena.* I can't feed everyone.

Socorro was tiny. By mid-January Elder Jenkins and I had visited every home a dozen times. No baptisms, a few reluctant encounters. The days were long, the work slow, and the routine tedious: up at six, on with the suit and tie, prayer, scripture study, breakfast (warm multi-colored milk on pseudo-American cereal), hit the streets, knock on doors till noon, prayer, tortillas and beans, companion study, more prayer, a short siesta, more doors, more tortillas and beans (with a little fish or chicken maybe), more doors, more prayers, bed. The rose may have been blossoming in the rest of Mexico, but in Socorro it never formed a bud. Most people politely told us to get lost. A few swore at us in Spanish. Every day I was feeling less and less like an emissary of Jesus and more and more like a salesman, the only difference being that I was trying to peddle religion instead of insurance. When I confessed my feelings to Elder Jenkins, he shrugged: "You'll get used to it. You just haven't caught the vision yet." It was easy for him to say. In four months he would be flying home to Vernal, Utah. He was incontrovertibly "trunky." His bags were packed, he was counting the days.

I tried to catch the vision but caught the Revenge instead. As I lay in bed, pale, febrile, my once muscular body shrinking as my insides leaked out both ends, I kept asking myself, What am I doing here? Why am I trying to sell these people something they obviously don't want? If I could offer them something tangible—food, money, a better shot at life . . . But this. Will religion fill the empty belly of that woman squatting in the dirt? Or hush her infant's hungry cry? Does it offer these poor people anything here and now, or am I just dangling carrots to string them endlessly along with empty words? Faith, hope, charity. The Savior offered living water; we let the body wilt and wither.

One night, when my fever was burning like a furnace, I rolled over in bed and pressed my face to the window of our tiny quarters. I saw a fat full moon bleeding apocryphally as the sky darkened in the west. Then a miracle: snow on the streets, shriveling fast. Eggs on a hot griddle. Then I saw myself sprinting for the finish line, racing animals of all sizes, Noah's ark released. Galloping alongside me is a centaur wearing the head of Harry the Horse. I close my eyes and lose him in the dust. I see the Swiss flag, the Red Cross backwards, and standing underneath, arms folded, the Fuhrer with a ten-gallon hat, chaps, and a goatee. Who does he think he's fooling, smiling and shaking hands like that? He puts his arm around me and asks for my temple recommend. Who does he think he's fooling? He directs me to a sign: MORMONS, in six languages. Something is burning, barbecued. Black clouds mushroom over Vesuvius. A door opens and my father walks out on his hands. His legs are bloody stumps. Seeing me, he nods and hollers: "Don't tell them anything, Jon! Not a damn thing!" I have nothing to tell. A Purple Heart shines on his naked chest. His head is shaved bald save a scalplock. "Not a damn thing, Jon!" I follow the flock. Looking up, I see a hole in the sky slowly widening. A huge hand reaches down and gently scoops up the wounded, like baby chicks. I rush over, hoping to be included, but the hand artfully avoids me. Like radar. A soul detector. I note the dirt under the fingernails. Cracks, scabs, calluses. When I crouch down and look up, checking for the sure sign, the hand clenches shut.

"Jon?" "Jonathan?" "Jon?" I woke up shivering—an inner blizzard. The sweat that had drenched me turned to frost. There were voices. Soft and dirgelike. First thought, I'm dead. Second, Good. Then a face loomed overhead, big and bloated, like a head stuffed in a bottle. Its mouth opened, a ring of fangs. I raised my right arm to the square and screamed: "No! Buzz off, Satan!" Talons gripped my shoulder. "Elder! It's okay! *El médico está aquí!*"

The doctor? Yes. *Sí. Muchas gracias.*

Missions are supposed to strengthen your faith, but after a month in Socorro, mine had dwindled to a token vestige. I had naively assumed that once I donned the black-and-white uniform I would magically be converted into God's agent on Earth. My college-educated mind knew better, but still I was hoping. Miracles, conversions, healings at my hands . . . Instead I was anxious, frustrated, and carrying guilt like a mad jockey on my back. I could feel him kicking my ribs and lashing my backside as Elder Jenkins and I walked the sandy streets, when we knelt in prayer morning and night, as we gobbled down tortillas and beans. After a month I wanted out. I wanted to go home. But that only added to the guilt I'd dragged down south with me. Nevertheless, in my heart I was hoping for a swift but honorable release.

The answer to my prayer came my sixth week in the field when President Adams drove 300 miles from the mission home to personally inform me of my mother's death. "Was this expected?" he asked, surprised and bewildered by my stone-faced response. "Elder Reeves?"

I shook my head but answered, "*Sí,*" further confusing him. It was like the day I'd learned of Nancy's death, a delayed reaction. After-shock.

President Adams quoted some scriptures to console me. If they live, they live unto me; and if they die, they die unto me. He reassured me that someday I would join my mother in the hereafter.

"Soon?" I asked, with a half-hope that visibly disturbed him. He didn't realize that now I had two deaths on my head. Those were my thoughts at the time. Death as the dark deliverer, a punishment for my selfishness. My mother's blood-money. Jon, you've done it again!

"Elder? Elder, why don't you sit down a moment—you look . . . you don't look too good." I liked and trusted President Adams, perhaps because he lacked the polished, well-fed look that seemed to characterize mission presidents. Short, slight, and shifty-eyed, with a five o'clock shadow, he looked more like a fugitive cowboy than the local mouthpiece of God. After expressing his condolences for the third time, he explained that although missionaries were prohibited from calling home, in special cases like this . . .

The connection was bad. My father's voice crackled over the phone. "Jon?" he said, weakly. "Are we going to make it?"

I sucked in a deep breath, ran a hand underneath my dripping nose. "Sure, Dad. We'll make it."

President Adams then informed me that, under the circumstances, I would have the option of going home now or completing the rest of my mission.

Home? My mother was gone, Nancy was gone. "*Mi casa está aquí*," I said, and President Adams smiled, mistaking irony for godly dedication.

My father put in his two cents worth: "Finish your mission, Jon. It's what your mother would have wanted."

Tiene rázon, I thought. He's got a point.

After my mother died, the jockey on my back went crazy. I couldn't eat, couldn't sleep, couldn't anything. I finally met with President Adams and confessed a whole litany of sins, hoping this might purge the gunk from my soul: a Milky Way bar I'd stolen from the 7-Eleven when I was eight; the kitten I'd murdered in the name of philanthropy; a roommate at BYU I'd bullied intellectually; the hell I'd caused my mother, hastening her demise. And Nancy. I told him everything—the Preference Dance, the pole vault pit, her marriage and its tragic aftermath. It was the first time I'd shared this with anyone.

President Adams eyed me gravely. "Elder," he said, "you did not murder that girl! Do you understand that?"

I bowed my head and whispered, "Yes," but not very convincingly.

"Do you believe that, Elder?"

I shook my head. No, President.

"You say there was a cliff by a river with some big rocks at the bottom and she jumped—"

"Dived," I corrected.

"Jumped, dived—how can you be so sure it was intentional?"

"She couldn't swim, President! What was she doing up there if she wasn't . . . she had no business otherwise . . ."

"Regardless, Elder, regardless. Accident or intentional, you've got to stop blaming yourself. The only person guilty of anything is that girl, who—"

"Then she'll be damned?"

President Adams's quick little eyes peered into mine, searching for the core. "The Lord doesn't damn anyone, Elder. There is no hell in his plan."

"But what's going to happen to her?"

"Do you believe the Savior suffered and paid for the sins of the world?"

I paused only a moment. "Yes, President."

His ranch-tanned hand reached across the burnished desk and gripped mine awkwardly by the fingers. "Elder, the Lord forgives you for any part in this. Now, please, you've got to forgive yourself."

"But what about—"

"The Lord's just, but he's merciful too."

"This was different," I said, pleading, appealing. "She was different. Totally."

"Well, obviously there were extenuating circumstances. Can we leave it in the Lord's hands?"

He rose from his padded chair, but instead of the customary handshake across the desk, he walked around it and met me face-to-face. I looked down at the carpet, fire-red. "Does this mean . . . she'll go to the Lowest-Low, with liars and thieves and whoremongers? Because if she does, I belong down there with her!"

"Elder!"

"No! I do!" I said.

I don't remember whose arms went out first, but as we stood there locked in one another's embrace, my chin resting on his short shoulder, my tears splashing on his crisp, dark suit, a terrible wonderful warmth rippled through my body. He patted my back tenderly. "I know," he whispered. "I know. Be strong, Elder. The Lord loves you. We're not accountable for knowledge we haven't received. Your friend will have a chance to hear the gospel and be baptized. Her sins can be washed away."

I looked up a moment, hopeful. "Baptized?"

"Of course!"

My chin dropped back onto his shoulder. "I know," I said, still clinging to him. "But that's . . ."

"Yes, Elder?"

"That's partly what I'm afraid of."

I returned to Socorro determined to "stick it out" but not thrilled with my prospects. Then two events transpired that totally changed the course of my mission.

The first occurred at the end of January, my third month in Socorro. One night as Elder Jenkins and I knelt for companion prayer, in a sudden flash of inspiration or masochism I suggested we seek out the good people of La Fonda, an even tinier village forty miles from Socorro. To my surprise, Elder Jenkins agreed. He, too, was tired of knocking on the same old doors. As senior companion, he should have been more suspect, for President Adams had neither encouraged nor discouraged us from proselyting there, although he expressly directed us to actively tract in the other surrounding towns, some of which were half again the distance from Socorro.

We took the bus early the next morning, heading into the rising sun. The sky looked like doomsday, black and red, a sailor's omen. When the bus broke down a mile out of town, we should have taken the hint and turned back. But a little adversity made me more determined. So did the flock of buzzards circling the horizon like black ashes spiraling down a grimy drain. Elder Jenkins began losing enthusiasm, so I bolstered him up with Sunday school homilies: "Shoulder to the wheel, Elder! Oh Babylon, we bid thee farewell!" But it was not duty or honor that was pricking me on. I was in a state of reckless abandon. I simply did not care anymore what happened to me.

We arrived in La Fonda about noon and went straight to the plaza. We set up our portable flannel boards and delivered our pitch. *"Hermanos y hermanas, vengan por aca! Tenemos un mensaje muy importante . . ."*

Customarily, there must not have been much action in little La Fonda, for the sudden appearance of two tall, blond gringos hollering in the plaza instantly summoned a large crowd of men, women, and children. Everything was fine until Elder Jenkins started the Joseph Smith story. Then someone asked a question, and I said the fatal "M" word. A hush filled the plaza. Then curses, through gritted teeth: *"Mormones! Mormones!"* The crowd of curious onlookers transformed into an angry mob, screaming and hollering and shaking fists. On the outer perimeter I noticed the local Catholic priest, a wizened, white-haired man, watching with folded arms. In his dark cassock, he looked like a death figure from an Ingmar Bergman film.

Elder Jenkins grabbed his flannel board and converted the metal fold-up frame into a truncated staff which he brandished in self-defense. I stood in front of him, ostensibly valiant, and confronted the crowd. Elder Jenkins urged me to flee. "Elder Reeves! *Vamanos!"* But I stood my ground, fanatically baiting them: *"Yo sé que Jose Smith fue un profeta de Dios! Yo sé que la iglésia mormona es la verdadera! Yo sé que . . ."*

At that moment I was not frightened. The adrenaline rushed through me like high voltage, sending strange vibrations to my milquetoast parts, but I honestly was not afraid. Nor was I courageous. I secretly hoped the crowd would surge forward, rip me to shreds, and toss me into the fiery furnace so I could die a martyr, missionary sticks in hand. In this way I would at least partly expiate my sins and join my mother in the wild blue forever.

But God was not going to let me off the hook so easily.

The Book of Mormon tells of three days of earthquakes, tornados, smoke, and darkness so thick and suffocating that people can't even light a candle, after which a voice speaks from the sky, neither loud nor angry but "penetrating." The voice of the Catholic priest conveyed such resonance when he said, simply: "*Déjalos!*" Let them go.

Instantly the people backed off, mumbling and murmuring. It took several minutes, but the crowd gradually dispersed. Elder Jenkins raised his blue eyes to the sky and whispered a prayer of thanksgiving. The priest came forward and invited us to dine with him. We accepted but tactfully avoided any discussion of religion. When he offered us lodging for the night, we politely declined. He did not tell us never to come back. I suppose he assumed that even two wet-behind-the-ears gringos had more sense than that.

For the most part, Catholics in Mexico were apathetic towards the missionaries. If they didn't want to talk to us, they simply wouldn't answer the door. The incident in La Fonda was an aberration prompted by the fact that several years earlier a misguided missionary had seduced the mayor's daughter. Elder Jenkins and I had reaped the bitter consequences. We learned this after reporting to President Adams at the mission home. He instructed us to steer clear of La Fonda, to my disappointment. I was hoping for a second crack at martyrdom. Not Elder Jenkins. He was so happy not to have been ordered back to Ninevah that he took me straight to Maria's, the best fresh fruit drink stand in town, and treated me to a piña colada whipped in crushed ice (virgin, of course).

Although my motives were impure, that experience had a profound effect on me. I'd played the lion of God and had enjoyed it. Soon after I would play his lamb as well, baptizing my first of many converts.

After four months in Socorro, I was transferred to San Miguel, another little fishing village on the coast, for six months, and then to the city of Guadalupe. During my first year in the field, I met people from all walks and stations. I sat in homes on the outskirts of garbage dumps and in lavish hacienda-style homes on flowered hilltops. I shared my message with beggars, fishermen, farmers, teachers, doctors, attorneys, politicians, executives. I saw wealth and poverty. I saw humility and faith and courage; deceit, hypocrisy, vanity, greed. I saw life's varied faces for the first time.

I saw things that defied logic or science. At a youth conference in midsummer, hundreds of young Mexican Saints traveled by bus to a vast, grassy plain in the countryside to hear a local church authority speak.

The conference was scheduled to begin at 1:00 p.m., but all morning black clouds gathered overhead—huge, swollen udders that any moment would burst. The four horizons rumbled ominously. Then, at 1:00 sharp, the first fork of lightening split the sky.

One of the leaders stood up, a young branch president only a year or two older than I. I watched in awe as he nervously fingered the black bangs from his eyes, bowed his head, and, in humble Spanish, asked God to stay the storm until his servants had spoken. His voice didn't shake the earth, it was barely audible, in fact. But there was utter silence in that country place. It wasn't half a minute before a blue chink appeared in the filthy sky, and an arrow of sunlight shot down exactly on the wooden platform, spotlighting President Guillermo. The blue crack widened to a chasm, and widened still, until the sky was a vast blue lake with a dark donut around its perimeter. The sun sat dead-center, a glorious bullseye. President Guillermo spoke. The horizons bellowed, and lightning flashed like menacing Ninja swords, but not one drop fell, and the blue center remained clear until the final amen. Then, as the crowd gathered up their shawls and blankets and commenced the long trek home, the dark donut swelled and fattened, blotting out the sun. As my companion and I mounted our bicycles, the first drops of a three-day deluge pelleted down.

"*Fue un milagro, no?*" my companion said, smiling as the fat beads plastered his brown bangs to his forehead.

A miracle? "*Por seguro,*" I replied.

But I continued to struggle with guilt and uncertainty. In my head I thought God had forgiven me, but inside I still ached. Every night after my companion fell asleep I would slip outside and empty out my heart. I did not pray in formulaic thees and thous. I spoke as if God were standing beside me, or sitting rather, patiently listening, perhaps in the way a psychotherapist listens to a patient unload his troubled soul. And each time, gradually, a familiar peace rippled through me. The desolation would pass—not permanently, but I knew I was not utterly alone in this. Still, I grieved, I buried myself in activity, bowing to the great God of Paradox, losing myself to find myself.

It was during this time that writing became my second savior. I was constantly writing letters and scribbling in my journal, hitting the highlights—conversions, healings, the miracle on the plains—but also jotting down thoughts, images, flashes of insight, descriptions of peculiar people I met, bits of dialogue I overheard, spats with my companions, their odd habits and idiosyncrasies, the old storytellers in the plaza, the gossiping señoras in their homes. Anything, everything, I wrote it down before it was lost. I never carried a camera, as most missionaries did. In fact, I took no snapshots at all. My mission was recorded wholly in print. I went nowhere without one of the spiral notebooks that quickly piled up in my cramped quarters. For me, writing was not simply therapeutic. As I scribbled down thoughts and perceptions, I could feel the ink speeding through the narrow plastic tube and onto the paper like my life's blood.

My journals were private. I made that clear to my companions. As a result, some of them grew paranoid. Whenever I took up my pen I was a gunslinger drawing a six-shooter. They would fidget nervously or conceal their faces behind their scriptures, wondering, no doubt, if I was recording for posterity some cloddish thing they had said or describing in unforgivable detail the overnight appearance of a pimple and the subsequent eruption, at fingertip point—splat!—of a white smear on the little tin mirror I'd nailed to the wall underneath a paper sign: VANITY, SAITH THE PREACHER . . .

After initiating an underground newsletter featuring anecdotes, editorials, and "Conversion Stories Your Mission President Never Told You," I gained a little notoriety among fellow missionaries. "*El Autor*" they called me. The Writer. Or *El Poeta*, although poetry wasn't my forte. Everyday I gained strength and confidence in my unofficial calling.

"Why do you do it?" Elder Riley asked one day. "I mean, I *hate* writing!"

"Why do fish swim?" I tossed my head back and laughed, but I couldn't account for this frenzy, this obsession, this—sin?

My zone leader, Elder Martin, thought so. One day he grew fed up or emboldened or both, and asked me to read him an excerpt. I did—a rather sensuous description of a young woman I'd seen in the marketplace. Elder Martin eyed me accusatively. "You shouldn't write things like that in your missionary journal! You're supposed to write spiritual things!"

I begged to differ, paraphrasing scriptures in my defense: "Everything is spiritual to God!" "By little things I make big things come to pass."

"Say what?"

Someone once said a mission is not all good or all bad, but a mixture. I suppose that depends on your definition of good and bad. If we're here on earth to learn about life, then the parameters of goodness are more broadly defined. Exposure to the blood and crud of the world isn't bad. In fact, it's essential. To quote my father: "It'll put hair on your chest!" But that is a philosophical point, and I prefer to leave philosophy to the philosophers. I will say that every mission assumes its own texture and character, as unique as the missionary himself or herself. And every mission has its peaks and valleys and turning points. In my case, it was my last ten months that were the most pivotal.

It started with my transfer from Guadalupe to the little town of Esperanza, in the heart of the Sonora Desert, where I served the balance of my mission. Here I met poverty in its most elementary form. Tortillas were the staple. Beans, a luxury. Cars were eyebrow-raisers, futuristic. The people traveled by burro or on foot. The average home had a dozen kids, a couple of chickens, a goat, and, like it or not, three or four anemic dogs that slinked around waiting for scraps. The people earned their bread by dry farming shriveled stalks of dwarf corn. The harvests were scanty, the sun punishing. It blazed and beat down like a curse. Scorching days, chilly nights. Bleak. Bare. A few patches of sagebrush, some cactus, and, on the north end of town, a lone cottonwood tree whose gnarled, twisted trunk looked as if it were the victim of some unforgiving torture: a daily reenactment of Gethsemane. Otherwise, looking out in any direction, your eyes would glide uninterrupted to the horizon, pausing only for an occasional craggy butte that in the chalky mist and hallucinogenic haze appeared as a shipwreck in a sea of burning sand.

My heart went out to these people. They were dirt poor but industrious, humble, happy, and proud. They wore rags but they were clean. Their homes were old plywood boxes, but they swept the dirt floors a dozen times daily. Young and old, everyone worked except Hermano Vasquez who hobbled from house to house with a fake limp, begging pesos and earning his keep via his comic antics in the plaza.

For Elder Clark and me, it was an austere but enlightening existence. We lived and ate like paupers. Roosters were our alarm clock. Every morning when their voices scratched the pre-dawn dark, I would peek through the window of our upstairs room and watch the first trace of sun like a drop of blood spreading on the horizon. Then the silhouettes of the villagers marching to the fields, tools like rifles on their shoulders, whistling and singing Mexican folk songs. Sometimes Elder Clark and I would join them, in blue jeans, T-shirts, and sneakers. By sunup we would be sweating double thanks to our underlayer of priesthood garments. A six-six basketball star and a six-three would-be football star, Elder Clark and I were giants among these people, yet we could barely keep pace. They called us lazy *bolillus*. We called them *animales*. There was camaraderie; there was spirit. When someone died, the whole village suffered. We worked with them; we laughed and cried with them. But we never converted any of them. They converted us. By that I mean they taught us far more about simple Christian living than we could ever have hoped to teach them. Although we didn't share the same faith, we shared the same humanity. It was true community.

The individual who most typified this lifestyle was the widow Rodriguez. She lived in a pastel-colored house at the end of a box canyon where she, like everyone else in that desert town, relied upon God's mercy to create the miracle of corn without water. The day we met her she was working in her field, a small, spindly woman in a long dark skirt and peasant blouse with puffy short sleeves the color of the clouds that perpetually lingered on the horizon, forever promising rain but never delivering. From a distance she looked thin and frail, but up close I noted the tough muscles in her skinny forearms as she clubbed the stubborn soil with her primitive tool. Her hair was bound in back, thick and dark with a silver skunk streak down the center. She looked about sixty although she may have been much younger. But I also noticed a subtle hauteur in her wrinkled old face. Perhaps it was the dark eyes or the aquiline nose, avatar of some ancient Spanish blueblood.

We greeted her. *"Buenas, Señora."* Did she have time to talk? We had a very important message . . .

"Soy Católica," she said. Catholic. Okay. *Vale.* Who wasn't in this

dinky village? Still, she courteously put aside her tool and invited us into her home.

The floor was clay, the furniture crude, homemade: sticks of wood and branches were artfully lashed together with twine. They would have brought a nice price in a curio shop back home. As Elder Clark and I expounded on the Joseph Smith story and *El Libro de Mormon*, she made us fresh tortillas. To our empty bellies, the smell was tantalizing. As we wolfed down her generous offering, she listened with interest and asked all of the right questions. In the end, though, she restated her position. "*Soy Católica.*"

I was impressed with the Hermana and wanted to stay longer. Motioning towards her half-tilled field, I asked if she could use some help? Her dark little eyes sparkled. "*Ah! Por seguro!*"

I turned to my companion. "Well, Elder?" He was less enthused than I, but we spent the rest of the afternoon hoeing her field in the scorching heat. Later, when I pressed for a follow-up visit, Clark resisted. "You heard her—*soy Católica.*" He warmed up to the idea, however, after discovering the Hermana had five daughters, all beautiful. They were eleven, twelve, fourteen, sixteen, and a buxom, black-haired seventeen-year-old who we privately christened "Miss Mexico."

If my first companion was trunky, my last one was hopelessly horny. Sunday mornings Elder Clark, typically a late riser, would roust me at the crack of dawn, hustle me through breakfast and morning study, and then invent some ludicrous excuse that would position us in front of the Catholic church, a modest structure heralded by a simple wooden cross, at roughly 8:00 a.m., just about the time the *família* Rodriguez was completing its mile walk into town for morning mass. When on the fifth Sunday of these machinations "Miss Mexico" turned and smiled at my companion, or so he thought, claimed, swore by his soul, he was incurably smitten.

"I really think the Hermana needs to hear the third *charla* again, don't you? She's really warming up. I can feel it."

I obliged because I liked the Hermana, and I wasn't exactly adverse to the company of her beautiful daughters either. If I appeared less interested than Clark, it was only because I was still in recovery, i.e., Nancy.

We visited the Hermana three or four times a week. After doing some of the heavier outdoor chores, we would enter her home and repeat yet another of the missionary presentations. Later, as Clark flirted with Miss Mexico over tortillas, I would chat with the Hermana who shared with me the details of her life and her little village. After a year in Mexico, I was quite proficient in the language, and I could not only fully comprehend but also make an intelligent contribution to the conversation. I told her about my life in Ponderosa, where it was perpetually green, and of my parents, the mother I had recently lost and the father who was still recovering.

"*Y el hijo?*" she asked. And the son?

"*El tambien.*" Him, too.

She said she was sorry. "It hurts me," she said in Spanish, beating her fist against her flat chest, "right *here!*" And I could tell by the way her topaz eyes reddened that she was not just paying me hospitable lip service.

She told me about the death of her husband. *El Gripe*, that ubiquitous Mexican disease, grabbed him one day and refused to let go. She told me about the birth of each daughter. She told me how it rained once for ten days and ten nights and the village was almost washed away, a la Noah's flood. And there was the giant cactus that every Easter took on the shape of the sacred Virgin, and the eagle that would perch atop the Catholic cross, and the curse of *Los Borrachos*, the drunkards, who shot the bird over a bet, and the hundred years of drought that followed. Each night, religiously, I added her tales and anecdotes to the curious miscellany cluttering my journals.

The Hermana always fed us prodigiously. For a family of spare means, there was a miraculously steady flow of tortillas in her home. She was like the widow with the eternal hoard of oil and flour feeding the prophet Elijah. Clark and I ate and ate until we had to hoist our swollen bellies off the dirt floor. Our gargantuan appetites amused the Hermana. She seemed tickled by the challenge to fill our bottomless pits.

Oliver Cowdery, referring to the time he spent with Joseph Smith, exulted, "Those were days never to be forgotten!" Such were my feelings about those afternoons with Hermana Rodriguez and my entire stay in Esperanza. I grew to love that old woman, that village, those people, the desert, the heat. Even cockroaches and scorpions took on a fond familiarity. At the end of ten months, I did not want to leave. It was a good, hard, simple life, and a sheltered one as well. If I'd enlisted in the mission force to escape my past, then Esparanza was an answer to prayer. It was as near true utopia as I would ever come. Plus other factors were coming into play. In a recent letter my father casually mentioned he had sold the house and moved to Palo Alto. Ponderosa was no longer home. And Juanita Rodriguez, "Miss Mexico," had begun making eyes in her deliciously intoxicating Mexican way.

But my time was up. I said goodbyes and reported to President Adams at the mission home. He expressed some concern over the dearth of baptisms during my last ten months and gave me some parting counsel. Then I flew back to the states where I encountered the biggest shock yet.

CHAPTER 9

Shortly after my mother's death my Aunt Mitzi wrote me a distress letter. In it she said she had tried to call my father at home but his phone rang unanswered. Whenever she called his office, the receptionist said he wasn't in. She finally drove all the way from Oakland and pounded on the door. A specter answered. "Matthew?" His sidehair had turned death-white and his bear-strong body had shrunken three sizes. A scraggly white beard dripped from his chin. He looked like Rip Van Winkle.

He invited her in but didn't say much, just sat there staring at his hands, picking the lint from his sweat pants and rolling it into little balls. "He even skipped the Christmas Eve party!" Aunt Mitzi wrote, and I could read the alarm in her usually flawless cursive. "He's just like a hermit. I'm so worried about him."

So was I. My missionary mind reasoned that this might be the Lord's way of prompting a reconciliation—not via my mother's death but my father's despair as a result of it. Then I could turn bad into good.

I wrote him several encouraging letters. At first his responses were typically tight-lipped: "Dear Jon, thank you for the nice letter. I am very proud of you." Et cetera. But shortly after my transfer to Esperanza I received a long, rambling letter in which he recapped his forty-five-year relationship with my mother, from their slightly less than love-at-first-sight beginnings to the last chill of her hand at bedside. It was twelve pages of half-coherent stream-of-consciousness, but it was the first time I remember him spilling his heart on paper. "She was a beautiful woman, Jon," he wrote. "She loved you so much." His cryptic postscript brought me to tears: "I do too, Jon. I know I'm not very good at showing it, but I do."

It was several weeks before I heard from him again. By then he had resumed his formal, self-protective prose. But that was fine. He had finally opened his heart, and I knew its true contents. I was ready to mend fences. Or so I had supposed.

The starving derelict of Aunt Mitzi's letter was not the man who met me at the airport in San Francisco. From a distance, he looked trim and sporty in a blue-checked suit, shiny white shoes, and sunglasses with mirror lenses. The scraggly beard was gone and his face was tanned. The biggest shock, though, was his hair: instead of winter-stricken side-tufts, a glossy dark pelt covered his scalp from front to back.

"Dad?" He sauntered forward, trying to disguise his limp. He looked stunningly silly, like John Wayne with love beads. He threw his arms around me, very un-Dad. I was wooden; a fencepost.

"Good to see you, Jon!" he whispered, patting my back.

"Good to see you too."

He grabbed one of my suitcases and proudly led me to his new Jaguar XKE—sleek and silver, with shark-eye headlights. "Like it?"

I nodded. "*Claro.*" Sure.

"Your Corvette's at the house," he said, grinning. "Runs like a top. While you were gone I took it for a little spin once a week just to keep the fluids moving."

"Thanks."

We drove south along the bay in silence. The afternoon sun had just burned through the fog; the green hills looked tropical. Sailboats were cutting across the bay like giant dorsal fins. The white highrises glowed like an outer space city. Soon we were twisting through the heights of Palo Alto. My father tried to make conversation: Stanford football, the mission, college. I was too stunned to speak. Everywhere I looked I saw green, literally and figuratively. Lush rainforests spilled onto narrow streets lined with Cadillacs and BMWs. Every home was a castle: wrought iron gates, circular driveways, nude statues presiding over bubbling fountains. My red Corvette was waiting outside my father's condominium like an odalisque.

"Want to take her for a spin?" my father asked. His hip clichés made me nauseous.

"Maybe later," I said. When I stepped inside my new home, my feet sank into the thick champagne-colored carpeting as if it were quicksand.

"Make yourself at home," he said. He took a huge roast out of the refrigerator—more meat than I had seen in two years—and stuck it in the microwave to thaw. "Too warm, Jon?" He flipped a switch. Some attic ghosts shuddered and blew cool air out the ceiling vents.

He showed me the guest room—"my" room. It was bigger than the entire House of Rodriguez. Then the bathroom: more thick carpeting, brass knobs on the faucets, Jacuzzi jets in the sunken tub. "Relax," he said. "Freshen up. Then we'll talk."

I closed the door. Peace, escape. I turned a knob and the miracle of water poured from the brass spigot. Then the other, and the water grew warm. On the fake marble counter were enough jars of skin cream, moisturizers, and wrinkle-removers to fill an apothecary shop. I opened the cabinet: Grecian Hair Formula, Aloe Vera.

I sat on the wooly floor, head down, eyes closed. A half hour later my father tapped politely on the door. "Jon? You okay?"

"*Sí*—I mean, yeah."

"Why don't you get dressed and we'll go out for a bite. I've got someone I'd like you to meet."

"*Quien?*"

"What?"

"Who?"

"Oh, just a friend of mine." His cautious tone told me it was a female friend. A girlfriend.

"What about the roast?" I asked.

"Wouldn't you rather eat out? To celebrate? After I got thinking about it—"

"*Creo que*—I mean, I think I'll pass."

He didn't push it. "Okay, Jon. I understand."

"You go ahead, Dad."

"Jon?"

"Really, Dad. I ate on the plane. I'm really not very hungry. I think I'd really just like to take a nap."

"You're sure?"

"*Claro.*" I waited for his footsteps to fade, then I curled up in a little ball and rolled over on my side and wept.

The next morning we went to church. Instead of splintered stools and hardwood benches, I sat on velour-cushioned pews that looked as if gemstones, rather than bourgeois behinds, belonged there. The Bishop, a pompadoured young obstetrician, shook my hand firmly and welcomed me home. "Your father tells me you're going into medicine," he said, beaming. At the pulpit, conducting, he was as glib and handsome as a game show host. Everyone in the ward had money. They stank of it. The men shined, the women sparkled. "Mexico!" they said. "How exciting! Did you get many converts?" No, I thought. They converted me.

During the sacrament hymn, I gazed up at the high-beamed ceiling and the long, cylindrical lights suspended from it, and at the rock backdrop mosaically pieced together behind the padded blue theater chairs on the stand, and I thought to myself: This is a long, long way from Esperanza. As the bread and water made the rounds, I tried to get my mind right; I tried to think about the atonement and the Savior's spiritual convulsions in Gethsemane on my behalf. But I was distracted by the plastic cups, the red lipstick stains the women left on the rims, and the clink-clink-clink as they dropped into the metal trays, the inimitable sound of money.

I looked outside, through a slight separation in the side drapes. The sun was bright. On the sidewalk, snail trails glistened like tinsel. The bougainvillea blossoms were magenta ribbons on the fake adobe wall. Perfectly pitted bricks. I began sweating in the air-conditioned chapel. My suitcoat was a straightjacket, my necktie a noose cutting off my oxygen. I started fidgeting, tugging at my tie. My father eyed me circumspectly. "Are you all right?"

I nodded. I managed to simmer down, or at least to give the appearance of having simmered, but the instant the meeting ended I politely wove my way through the claustrophobic crowd and escaped into the sunlight, breathing deeply, hands on knees. A short, tidy brunette in a party-colored dress marched by with a strident clicking of high-heels. She carried a fat black binder under each arm. Braking in mid-stride, she hollered over her shoulder: "And remember the breakfast dishes or no supper when I get home!" Her balding little husband, holding a twin toddler in each hand, nodded obediently.

Arriving back at the condo, I went straight to my room. My father knocked and asked if I wanted to go out for lunch. He knew of a terrific seafood place on Fisherman's Wharf.

"No," I said.

"Pardon? I can't hear you?" He was trying to be patient and accom-modating, but I didn't want that. And what did I want? I don't know. I was angry and frustrated, and I knew I had no right to be. What was my gripe? Everyone at church had been perfectly cordial. The bishop, his counselors, even the crabby fishwife shouting at her husband in the parking lot, they were probably good, honest, hard-working people who paid their tithing and went to the temple regularly and devoted many hours in diligent church service. Just because they had a little money in their pockets, I shouldn't throw stones. I'd grown up with the silver spoon in my mouth, remember? Judge not! Read the Book of Mormon! Money's fine if it's used for good purposes. Your patriarchal blessing tells you the windows of heaven will be opened. Don't turn your nose up at a little metal manna.

I left my room, penitent, intent on apologizing to my father for my behavior. He was in the bathroom. The door was partway open, so I peeked inside and found him smearing make-up on his face. At that point I cracked. "Ah, Dad!" I groaned.

He started, his hands scurrying to cover up the jar. I pushed the door fully open and addressed him as if I were the father and he the son caught ogling *Playboy* centerfolds. "What are you doing, Dad?"

He tried to disguise his embarrassment with a smile. "You gotta keep your looks up, Jon!"

I shook my head, disgusted. "Dad . . . Dad!"

"Look," he said, slapping the make-up pad on the marbled counter. "You just got off your mission. You've been living in the spiritual echelons for two years. You don't know what I've been through." He retrieved the make-up pad and wiped it across his cheek. "You'll understand these things later, after you've . . ."

"After I've what?" He didn't reply, but I knew what he was thinking. Give me a week or two and I would come down. I would adjust, meaning I would be "normal" again, meaning I would forget about dirt floors and adobe and Hermana Rodriguez, and sit very comfortably on my father's leather sofa watching color TV and go back to school and start dating again and taking pre-med classes and meet a nice sweet Mormon girl and marry her in the temple and start a family of my own and an M.D. practice of my own and serve on a bishopric and buy a nice home in a nice neighborhood comparable to this one and generally fulfill the Great American Dream. Just like all the others. "Solly, Cholly! No can do!" I said, slamming the door.

"Jon! Wait! Jon! Someday—" The door opened and his voice chased me down the hall. "I knew it! I knew you'd do that! I knew—"

The next day I sold my Corvette. The low *Blue Book* was $3,600, but I sold it for a thousand just to get rid of it, before I changed my mind. I paid 10 percent to the church and then bought a ticket on Amtrak to Nogales, Arizona. It was a half-day trip. At the border I changed my $857 to pesos and bought a bus ticket. It was a 600-mile journey with a thousand stops, and I rubbed elbows with the peasants, mustachioed men and bulky women. Mommas casually lowered their flour sack blouses and scooped out a breast to suckle their screaming infants. Filled with self-righteous purpose yet trying not to appear so, I gave my seat to an old hunchback with a curly mustache and sat on the jostling floor. The car stank of sweat and urine, the old village smells, but I didn't complain. It was just what I needed to purge myself of the opulent stink of California.

The bus took forever to cover the distance. I threw up twice. By the time it arrived in Esperanza, I felt as if I'd been riding the tempest for a month. My head and stomach were swirling. I walked to the widow Rodriguez's home.

She was in her cornfield, clubbing the earth with her caveman tool. The sun was a sledgehammer, the valley its anvil. When I called to her, the Hermana looked up and smiled, as if she had been expecting me all along. *"Mijo!"* she exclaimed, giving me a big hug. Then, with childlike faith, she explained that her youngest daughter, Alma Rosa, had been running a high fever. She'd prayed all night for help and now—*"Estás aquí!"*

Then it clicked. *"Hermana,"* I said, *"tu eres mormóna?"*

She flashed a yellow smile. *"Por seguro. Todos!"*

I took that to mean her whole family had joined the church, but I soon learned that in my absence almost the entire village had been baptized, Elder Clark doing the honors. He had since been transferred to La Fonda. "We planted the seeds," he would write me later on.

I poured a few drops of consecrated oil from my key chain vial onto young Alma Rosa's head and blessed her with a swift recovery. There was no hesitation in my voice or debate in my mind. Alma Rosa would be healed, pronto! Then we ate. The Hermana added chicken to the beans and tortillas—a special occasion. When I handed her the rest of my money, she looked at me strangely, as if to say, "What am I to do with this?" We need rain, she said, which God will send, and a strong back to help with the harvest, which, she added with a conspiring grin, God has sent as well.

I stayed for eight weeks, hoeing and harvesting. I lived like a peasant again, getting up with the sun and working until dark. I felt at peace; I felt home. Maria's (Miss Mexico's) tortillas grew more delicious every day. But then it was time to go back. School was my reason, although deep down I wondered how long I could live their simple life and remain content? For me it was still a novelty I could abandon anytime. The villagers had no options. I did. And I had plans—big ones.

The Hermana looked at me sadly but nodded. *"La escuela, es bueno, no?"*

School? Good? *"Espero que sí. Ojala."* I promised her I would return someday, when I had more education and something more tangible to offer. For what use was a novice writer in a poor pueblo where strong backs were the order of the day?

She patted my hand and smiled knowingly. Way leads on to way, my son.

I didn't go home, though—or, rather, to my father's home. I hitchhiked to BYU where I'd been awarded an academic scholarship for the spring semester. My father was furious. No note, no phone call, no nothing! Just took off and left! And my car! Yes, Dad, and I gave the money away, too. I was now flat broke.

And on my own, he informed me over the phone. Maybe that would teach me the value of the ever-shrinking dollar. Maybe that would teach me a little gratitude. Maybe that would teach me some common sense! Money doesn't grow on trees, you know?

Fine, I said. Anything to get out from under your bug-smashing thumb! Anything to escape med school!

You're cutting off your nose to spite your face! Don't be stupid!

Look who's talking about being stupid. A face lift, a toupee!

I would pay for my false pride and independence. Returning to BYU, I had to hustle to make ends meet. Basement apartments and hot plate meals. The romance of poverty soon wore off, but at least I was free. I was going to be a writer. Through the magic of language I would stir sleeping spirits, thaw frozen hearts, bring smiles to the lips of the meek and persecuted. In Shelley's words, I would join the unacknowledged legislators of the world. From that point on, I proceeded with an eye single to that glory. Unfortunately, my other eye would shut tight in the process. I would never ask my father for anything again and would refuse everything he tried to offer. By the time I knew better, it would be too late, again. And so I would earn another hole in my heart. I would also get my just comeuppance. My life would not go according to plan, meaning my plan. I would get kicked around by a thousand hobnail boots. But I would never regret selling my car and going south. It was the only truly decent thing I'd ever done in my life.

CHAPTER 10

Pitch black out, the boy barges in at 6:00 sharp and makes a trampoline of our bed: boing! boing! boing! He's bouncy, wired, like a court jester on speed: "Time to get up!" he shrieks. "Time to get up! It's Christmas!" His sisters, standing in the doorway, join in: "Time to get up! Time to—"

No headaches, no excuses this morning of mornings. The usual groans and sour faces as you insist on a kneeling prayer first ("Let's not forget what this is all about, okay?"). Next the systematic unwrapping, littlest gifts first: gym socks, barrettes, electric pencil sharpener, disposable razors. Then the roller blades, the Nordic Track, the stereo. The little jokes in between, oooohing and aaaahing (mock and real), the trashing of ribbons and crisp colored paper ("You can recycle that!" "Tell it to Al Gore!"). Your breakfast special, sausage rolls and eggnog sprinkled with nutmeg, the exotic breads and juices and Santa sculptured chocolates so *verboten* the rest of the year. The balance of the morning is spent assembling train sets, fake baby cribs, plastic mini dishwashers. Playing six rounds of Monopoly and Hero Quest.

By late afternoon they are sprawled in front of the TV watching golden oldies, Jimmy Stewart and Donna Reed trying to unsort their unwonderful life, as I slip outside unnoticed and trudge across the golf course. It's a far cry from Bethlehem. Overnight, magically, it has turned into a meadowland of snow. The white dunes sparkle like giant sugar mounds. Heading nowhere in particular, I notice a pair of fresh tracks which I trace past giraffe palms and Spanish tile rooftops into a sudden forest of ponderosa pines that was a stucco-and-glass highrise a day ago. Weaving through the evergreens, white-frocked friars half-blocking the way, I follow the tracks until they stop at the sandaled feet of a skinny, leathery little woman about my age with ratted red hair and a quilted coat of many colors. She lifts her arms as if spreading her wings to fly. The inside of her coat is lined with pockets. "A thousand and one!" she says, smiling a picket fence. "Go ahead—pick one!"

I smile back. "Sorry, but I'm not a pickpocket."

She titters behind her hand. "Please?"

"Does it matter which one?" I ask.

"Maybe," she says. "There's a story in each pocket. It all depends upon which one." Her little eyes dart around anxiously. Her fingers curl up towards her teeth, as if she is nibbling on a cracker. The premature moon is melting on the mountains, turning them into a delectable dessert. "Hurry!" she says.

Her baggy brown eyes tell me that if I reach into any one of her colored pockets, I'll never be able to go back to where I have come from. Yet if I don't pick one now, this instant, I'll never find my way here again. "Please," she says.

I glance back over my shoulder. Pale columns of smoke are rising from invisible rooftops. I hear a voice that could also be the wind. "I'm sorry."

She looks down at her sandaled feet, wriggles her pink-painted toes, and smiles sadly. Not for her but for me.

I follow the tracks back to my beginnings. That night I break up three family fights. Christmas dinner is splendid, turkey with all the trimmings, and six more rounds of Hero Quest and eggnog by the fire. And that night in bed you whisper in my ear: "Are you ready?"

"Of course. I'm always ready."

"You're sure? You don't—"

"Shhh! Listen!"

"What?"

"Can't you hear it?"

"Hear what?"

Dainty little kerchiefs swiftly, softly fluttering down. Concealing evidence. Second-guessing. Hiding. Healing. Like repentance. "Snow," I say.

"Snow? Oh come on! It never snows in California!"

"Shhhhh!"

CHAPTER 11

"Can you surprise God?"

"Only if he's sleeping on the job."

"There's no difference between foreordination and predestination, is there, if God already knows everything we're going to do before we do it."

"Ah! But we've still got freedom of choice. You could choose not to do what you're foreordained to do. It's not a done deal."

"That's a Sunday school answer, you know. So typical!"

"Can you one-up it?"

"Easy. God's a Know-it-all, right? Otherwise he's not God. It's like he's the director and we're just players on his stage. The difference is he's seen the whole script and we haven't. He knows the ending, we don't."

"We can't ad lib?"

"We may think we can, but a really truly omniscient God would even know the ad libs in advance. There are none, except from maybe our perspective. So time's irrelevant. For all practical purposes, Judgment Day occurred aeons ago, before aeons were invented."

"If that's true, why bother coming to the earth at all, if God already knows the outcome?"

"You tell me. Gloucester had an answer: We're as flies to wanton gods, they kill us for sport."

"Or maybe because we would have challenged the script: 'No, I sure wouldn't have robbed that liquor store on the night of July 16th!' Maybe we have to play out the evidence for or against us."

"What's the point of playing if there's no hope?"

"There's always hope. And there's always freedom to choose."

"Is there? If we've existed since the beginning of time, which has no beginning, then our innate spirit or intelligence or whatever it is you want to call it predetermines whether we'll choose right or wrong. Call it spiritual genetics. Which brings me back to my original question: Can you surprise God? Because if you can't—"

"Remember when the Brother of Jared sees the finger of the Lord? God acts surprised. 'Did you see more?'"

"Yes, but that could be rhetorical, too. 'Did you see more?' Well, of course you did! I showed you more!"

"So we're back to square one."

"Yes, but I've got another can of worms to open."

"You enjoy that, don't you? Opening worm cans?"

"Immensely."

"A chip off the old block?"

"You tell me."

The preceding was not an excerpt from one of my high school conversations with Nancy Von Kleinsmid. It was a postprandial dialogue with my sixteen-year-old daughter Valerie, the kid genius. Val is flunking half her classes because she refuses to submit to boring worksheets that are nothing but mule work and an insult to her intelligence, quote-unquote. Why, for instance, won't her physics teacher simply let her design a nuclear-powered dishwasher or a frictionless V-6 engine and be done with it?

My wife Natalie retorts: "Why can't you just for once in your stubborn little obstinate life play the stupid game? You're slitting your own throat, can't you see that?"

"You said it," she says. "Because it's stooo-pid! A game."

Natalie hollers at her through the bedroom door: "If you don't turn in all those missing assignments, if you don't . . . I'm going to . . ."

"Going to what?" Val snickers.

What, precisely? Ground her? She doesn't drive, doesn't date, doesn't dance, doesn't much of anything except hole up in her room playing her cello and writing scripts for TV sitcoms that are doomed to someday make her rich and famous. And poems—tragic depressing awful horrible nihilistic things, quote-unquote Natalie. "Val, come down for dinner!" she hollers through the wood.

"Leave it outside the door!" Val hollers back. Self-incarceration is a sign of true genius or insanity, the line between the two being very fine indeed.

She tells us she hates church, hates the Book of Mormon, hates Sister Myers her advisor. "All she ever says," Val sneers, "is get married and have babies. Make dumb babies." Val says she hates babies. Would never ever in a million years get married. "Not like that. Not like her." So why are we forcing her to go to church? Doesn't she have free agency? Isn't compulsion Satan's plan? She can't wait until she graduates from high school and is on her own, boy oh boy. "I'll never go to church—*ev*-ver! Just you wait!"

"*If* you graduate," Natalie corrects. Natalie can't understand her attitude. Natalie loved Sunday school, the scriptures, youth conferences. With Val it's always pulling teeth. "What's the matter with her? Why can't she just be a normal kid? Why can't she be like—" Renae Pickett and Jerrilynn Crowley? Obliviously nodding along just because mommy and daddy say so? Natalie makes a sour face. No! Not like them. "It's just that . . . well, when *is* she going to grow up?"

"Just because we believe doesn't mean she will. She wants facts, verifiable data. None of this borrowed light business for her. Believe me, I know her type."

"Oh? And how do you know her type?"

"Take my word for it. I know."

"I don't see how you can just sit there calmly and smugly watching her life go down the tubes?"

"Who's smug? Who's sitting calmly?"

"This is our daughter we're talking about, not some scientific experiment we can redo if it fails."

"What can we do? We've done everything. She can figure it out. It's up to her now."

Am I too indifferent? Am I trying to cover misplaced tracks? Should I give her more time, set a better example, pound the pulpit a little harder, painting life more like a precise checkerboard of blacks and whites instead of pandering to the Great God of Ambivalence?

Val is brilliant yet innocent in a manner wholly different from her younger sister Rachel, whom she used to pick on mercilessly but now simply ignores. "The Null set," Val used to call her, and Rachel would look up naively, smiling her lollipop smile: "What?"

Rachel is the only one who will wake up to discover I have left for the day and weep real tears. "Where's Dad?"

"He took a little trip."

"How come?"

"He needed some time alone."

"You mean like a time-out?" Natalie's cure for backtalk and temper tantrums was ten minutes of solitary in the downstairs bathroom. No books, no toys, no newspapers. Just you, the wash basin, and the toilet bowl.

"Yes. Like a time-out."

Rachel's saucer eyes grow big and fearful. "Is he coming back?"

"Yes, of course he's coming back."

"Is he coming back soon?"

"Yes. Soon. Tonight some time."

"Where did he go?"

Natalie will ponder this briefly before answering, "Home."

"Home?" Rachel's bulbous brow will wrinkle with bewilderment. "Isn't home here?"

She will continue her mawkish questioning until Natalie (wiping the kitchen counter, stirring the pancake batter, laying out the breakfast plates) feels mentally and emotionally drained. She will close her eyes, count to ten, mutter to herself the incantation she learned in Relief Society a week ago: "Stop. Relax. Drop your shoulders and roll your head. God will not overprogram you . . . God will not overprogram . . ."

All day Rachel stays close to the big bay window, keeping an eye out for me. She dutifully feeds her baby dolls from a plastic bottle she painstakingly fills with thousands of tiny circles she has hole-punched from white construction paper. "Milk, Dad! See?" She changes their disposable diapers a dozen times, reads to them from her *Golden Book of Children's Verses,* and takes each for a short walk in her Fisher Price stroller. She's eleven going on five, growing little cone-shaped breasts before she ought to. Her classmates listen to Paula Abdul and Michael Jackson and R.E.M. They go steady with goofy looking boys and brag about going to first, second, and third base. "You play baseball?" Rachel asks. She has one more summer to grow up before starting junior high where the kids hang out in gangs and snort cocaine for breakfast.

Val used to tease Rachel about her babies: "What are you going to be when you grow up? A mommy! A can't-do-anything else so-I'll-be-a-mommy!"

Talk like that always gets a rise out of Natalie. Usually she handles it with humor. "Hey, you in there!" she will holler, slouching into the living room caveman style, shoulders rounded, hands dragging along the sculptured carpeting. Lowering her voice, the dumb football player: "Hey! Who's saying stuff about being a mom? What's wrong with being a mom, hunh?"

She has a bachelor's degree in chemistry and dropped her master's ambitions to marry me and bring three children into the world. Does she regret it? "Don't be silly!" she says, in her sunnier moods. Other times she gestures to the glossy plaque above her chest of drawers, a double-edged birthday gift from her mother, Mrs. Johnston with a T: I COULD HAVE BEEN A BRAIN SURGEON.

Natalie won't miss me today. I've been so snarly that my absence will be a reprieve. Even J. J., Jon, Jr., my grinning little miniature, has noticed: "Dad, how come you always act like the Grouchy Bug?" The Grouchy Ladybug! I bought him the picture book about that irascible insect to cure *his* temper tantrums!

"Look, just because I'm on the bishopric doesn't mean I don't have my ups and downs and in-betweens. People think you walk on water. They think you can't swear once in a while or snitch a sandwich on Fast Sunday or yell some poor fool's head off."

*

"One night when you were a little baby, I had this funny feeling something was wrong. I couldn't go to sleep. I finally got up and went into your room. The blanket was over your head and your face was all blue. If the Spirit hadn't warned me . . . "

"How do you know that was the Holy Ghost? How do you know it wasn't a psychic prompting?"

"The Holy Ghost *is* a psychic prompting!"

*

Natalie can't understand why no one asked Val to the homecoming dance. She's tall, slender, long legs like a model. Classic California. Like her mom.

"Well, would you want to go out with an ice pick?"

"A what?"

It's a foolhardy thing to say, and I invent an instant edit: "With a nice kid?"

Sister Myers tells Val and the other young women that they are special chosen spirits sent to Earth at a special chosen time for a special chosen purpose. They are the most valiant of Heavenly Father's spirit children, reserved for these latter days . . .

Val rolls her eyes and groans. Her arrogance is almost as intimidating as her I.Q. "The glory of God is intelligence," she says. "Just don't ever use it."

A week ago I committed an unpardonable and sneaked into her room—just curious, prowling for nothing in particular, just clues to get inside that busy little brain of hers. I did not see the leather-bound scriptures we bought her for her twelfth birthday; no framed poster featuring Young Women's Values; no *New Era* Mormonads; no certificates of church achievement. Instead, Linda Goodman's *Sun Signs* and Cheiro's *Language of the Hand*. Books on astrology and handwriting analysis. I saw knickknacks on the walls; a poster of Magic Johnson slam-dunking a full moon below a fluorescent red caption: THE MAGIC KINGDOM; box games (Risk, chess, backgammon, Othello); a picture of a tiger stalking through the snow; the masks of comedy and tragedy, the former turned upside down, making a dour duo.

And one more: a black-light poster featuring a young woman, slender and blond, in a flowing white gown, sitting at the foot of a glittering waterfall in some fantasyland. She is gazing longingly at the horizon where a little family of white unicorns is sipping from a bubbling stream. She holds a bouquet of pink flowers. No caption, no title.

Then I noticed a corner of her spiral-bound journal protruding from underneath her bed. I opened and read: "Love is an ice pick. It is a poem which is a process, which is the kid genius, the would-be god/prophet you must be willing to follow blindfolded through the rough and dark and slippery parts. You must sometimes follow the snake into its hole. Are you with me? Are you? Or against? Then get out of your sweet skin and think for a change. Go blow your beautiful brains to kingdom come all ye weary and benighted etceteras unto me—" I heard footsteps, shut it fast, and slipped out just in time. But suspicious eyes passed me coming up the stairs.

Later that night Val confronted me. "Why did you quit writing?"

Natalie looked up from her *People* magazine. "He didn't quit. He never quit!"

I smiled. "I'm a no-talent bum. A has-been-who-never-was."

Val quietly folded up her music. It suddenly occurred to me that (a) for some peculiar reason she had deigned to practice her cello downstairs, in the living room, amidst "us," and (b) she had interrupted her intense practice just to ask me, out of the apparent blue, this question.

"I'm going to be a scriptwriter," she announced resolutely. "I'm going to write screenplays. I'm going to be famous."

I could have told her all about backups and safety nets. Instead, I smiled. Winked. Whispered, "Go for it, kid." She almost smiled back.

Later, Natalie reminded me she was failing three classes. No hope for a college scholarship. She was burning all her bridges. Mentally I reviewed worst case scenarios: She lives at home and goes to a junior college. Or gets a job waiting tables in a bar. Or gets pregnant and jumps off a twenty-five foot bridge. Or a rock. There's always a more worse case scenario.

*

I'm up late again, in the living room, 2:30 a.m. For the third straight night I have been prowling the 2,000-square-foot confines of our home in search of sleep. Eventually I will succumb from sheer exhaustion. Experience has taught me that. Sometimes it takes two or three nights, other times a week or more. In the meantime I drag around like a waterlogged zombie, dozing off at work, in the car, during Bishop Finley's diatribes. But the worry cycle starts. Gotta gotta gotta get some zzzzz's because this other, it does funny things to you, it scrambles your brain and your body until it's not really you saying whatever it was you said, throwing whatever it was you threw.

I try to blame the obvious, but I'd been wrestling with Morpheus long before the incident, months before Bishop Finley's midnight call.

"Do you know a Robert Johnson?"

"Robbie? Sure. He's in my fifth-hour class."

"Can you come over right away?"

"What's up? Is there some kind of problem?"

"Well, yes—yes there's a problem."

Tonight I honestly thought I would win for a change. I'd done everything the doctor ordered: warm bath, yoga stretches, deep-breathing exercises, mental imaging, prayer, calcium in horse pill proportions. But I'm up again, drifting from room to room, covetous of my children's perfect sleep and a little resentful of Natalie's. I feel so absolutely alone in the house, disconnected, as if Natalie and the children have moved on to a different realm without me. Like a lone man in the Garden of Eden. I look across the valley where the streetlights are glowing in the fog like an underwater city, a dream world I have become trapped in. I want to sneak back upstairs and hug my children, make sure they are still there. Instead I crawl back into bed where Natalie has long since entered the land I've been banned from. Is this, in microcosm, the agony of Spirit Prison? Being the one left behind? I place my hand on her soft thigh, press my front to her backside, and try to join her, but I'm denied entry again. My brain resumes its high-speed chase to nowhere.

*

"Can God change his mind?"

"Of course he can—he's God. He can do anything."

"If he knows everything, why would he ever want to change his mind?"

*

I used to teach. Up until a year ago. Now I write grants for the Santa Vista Public Schools. It was part of the so-called deal the attorney for the teachers union cut with the administration. In their view I got off easy. My view? I work long and late and I hate it.

"Well, at least now you get to use your writing talents," Natalie offers. She means well but she knows better.

"Grant writing isn't writing!" I holler during a volcanic moment. "It's nothing but a lot of logical left-brain bullshhh—!"

To which Natalie reminds me, curtly: "It's also a paycheck."

My students were the ones who called it "Dumbbell English." The first day of class I used to hand out 3x5 cards and tell them to write their name and one interesting or unusual thing about themselves. "I'm Tom and I'm stupid." It was depressing how many cards I'd get like that. When I'd ask about their responses, they would shrug: "Everybody says so."

"Who's everybody?"

"My old man, his girlfriend, my friends . . . everybody."

Later I told them to write their name and one good thing about themselves. They would scratch their heads, make jokes, snort, grunt, guffaw, but eventually, with some self-probing, they would mine very very deep and come up with a sparkling bit of something. "I'm Tom and I fix transmissions."

I miss those kids, although in the beginning I never thought I would. In the beginning it seemed like a jail sentence: five years, remedial English. But after earning tenure I refused to move up. My department chair thought I was nuts. "American Lit, Creative Writing, Advanced Comp, A.P. English—take your pick! You've served your time."

Now I know the real thing. Monday through Friday I descend into the basement of the school district's administration building and lock myself in a concrete office that my higher-ups refer to as "The Dungeon." It is dark when I leave for work in the morning and darker still when I return home at night.

Whenever I start feeling too sorry for myself, I detour past the transient camps where ragged family silhouettes huddle over trash can fires like *Grapes of Wrath* effigies. I know I should stop and do something. I know I ought to go down to those camps like Sherry Smith, Santa Vista Third Ward's resident radical, and hand out canned food and blankets. Common sense, safety, are my excuses. How do you know which ones are sincere sufferers and which ones will bludgeon you the moment your back is turned?

And time. Work, church, family, more work. Who has time to feed the hungry and homeless? I fully realize the irony of this statement. On the other hand, what good is a man if he gains the whole world but can't make it to his kid's soccer game?

I wasn't being a very good Samaritan lately. I wasn't being much of anything. At Welfare meeting two weeks ago Sunday, Sister Sherry Smith topped the agenda. She wanted fast offering money to pay her rent again. The discussion went back and forth in a gentlemanly manner until I finally slammed my loose-leaf binder shut in disgust: "How long are we going to keep dishing it out and dishing it out? We don't have to put up with this shit!"

Brother Dover with the Ken-doll countenance stared at me, shell-shocked, while old Brother Roberts, the cowboy-booted executive secretary, popped out of his padded red chair like an angry jack-in-the-box: "What kind of language is that!" Bishop Finley shifted his portly body in his swivel chair, his sanguine cheeks suddenly ten shades redder, embarrassed on my behalf. Normally he would have defused the incident with one of his clever quips. Instead, he dismissed the meeting without a closing prayer.

"Could you stay a minute, Brother Reeves?" It was more than my profanity. I'd always been the one who had gone to bat for the Sherry Smiths in our ward. "Brother Reeves," Bishop Finley had chuckled after one heated welfare session, "you're the champion of the underdog!" Lately I had been the dog under.

Bishop Finley asked how life was treating me? Fine. Fine. Just a little pressure right now. A mess of deadlines all at once. I was sorry, truly sorry. "It just slipped out."

Well, was there any particular problem he could maybe help me with? Problem? No—no problem.

*

3:07. Fed up, desperate, I throw on my paint-stained sweat pants and t-shirt and go running through the neighborhood searching for lighted windows, the silhouettes of fellow insomniacs. But every home seems at rest, a ship peacefully harbored for the night. Nearing the cul-de-sac, I see another demon from my dreams, ghost-like in the early morning mist: a two-legged centaur in shiny blue gym trunks galloping away from me. I break into a wild sprint, sucking in the salty Pacific air, my floppy K-Mart sneakers clapping across the pavement, my eyes boring into his big blue behind. It is a futile chase, yet I run beyond exhaustion to oblivion. I run until my lungs cave in and my legs buckle and snap. I'm a broken pretzel on the blacktop, knees and elbows stinging. I look up at a rainbow-ringed streetlight. I blink once and it's a big white egg in an iridescent nest, twice and it's the moon. I close my eyes, press my palms flat against the cool pavement, and beg God to please grant me sleep.

*

Kneeling on the living room floor, I sense another presence in the room. I say a hasty amen and turn to find my genius daughter watching in her nightgown. She is wearing the most peculiar expression, like the time twelve years ago when she caught Natalie and me sneaking carefully-wrapped gifts under the lighted Christmas tree. It was not a look of shock or betrayal, but the omniscient smirk of Nancy Von Kleinsmid.

"Dad?"

I smile, rise to my feet awkwardly, as if I am trying to stand up in a rowboat, a little self-consciously and self-conscious of my self-consciousness.

She tilts her head at an odd angle. "Dad, I have a question."

"Shoot," I say, dusting off my knees as if I have been kneeling in the dirt rather than on soft white carpeting.

She gestures to the Book of Mormon lying open face-down on the floor, an arm's length from my feet. "Dad, can an intelligent, educated person like you really believe all that mumbo jumbo?"

It worries me that I have to summon up all my earthly courage to look her squarely in the eye and answer, "Yes." For a good half minute she stares at me as if I am an odd piece of furniture she's not sure what to do with. Smiling, she disappears.

*

"Jon?"

When I finally look up, I see Natalie peering around the corner. The clock reads 5:27 a.m. "Are you still going?" It takes a moment: going? "Well?"

I glance at the yellow pad on my lap. The top page is covered with incomprehensible scribble a seer couldn't decipher. "Yes," I say, rising from the sofa. "Sure—I'm going." Trailing her through the kitchen to the back door, I notice that on the FAMILIES CAN BE TOGETHER

FOREVER sign taped to the refrigerator someone has penciled in a subscript: DO THEY HAVE TO BE? I shake my head. Val.

"Have you got everything?" Sack lunch, swim trunks rolled up inside a beach towel like a terry cloth cigar . . . "Don't you want to change out of your sweats?"

"Why? I'm not going to the junior prom?" She shrugs: suit yourself. A month ago we were butting heads over this trip. Now she almost seems to be shoving me out the door.

With a deft two-fingered movement, I hit the light switch and the remote below it and the garage door shudders briefly as it rolls open like a big slow eyelid. It is still dark out and the shadows and silhouettes of the suburban plants look grimly Congo-esque. The lights in the valley are twinkling like a fallen Milky Way. I'm awed by the simple beauty of the scene and diminished by the infinity of it.

Natalie gives me a peck on the cheek like a mother sending her little boy off to his first day of school. She reminds me that J. J. has to give a talk in Primary tomorrow.

"Ah!" I hit my palm against my forehead—a token gesture. I haven't forgotten, really. I've simply run out of time again. "Look, tell him I'll help him when I get home. And don't you go and do it. I said I would and I will."

She smiles knowingly. "Then should we expect you for dinner?"

"Maybe."

A hand goes to her hip. "That helps."

"Okay: no."

As I tuck my six-three frame inside our old Toyota Corolla, she leans casually against the doorway, long and lovely in her magenta houserobe: domestic cheesecake. A loose strand of chestnut hair droops seductively over one eye. She waves her fingers, as if sprinkling fairy dust, and says, without malice or sarcasm, "Have a nice day!" Waving back, I'm overcome by a sudden sadness as if I were leaving on a journey of indefinite dimensions, to the moon and back.

She smiles and says something I can't hear over the high-pitched squeal of the V-belts which sounds like a mass orgy of rats. I remind myself it's time for a tuneup. And a new transmission. And new tires. And and and. I glance at the odometer: 159,876. New car?

I push in the clutch and carefully pull the stick back into reverse, wincing in anticipation of the inevitable grinding of the gearbox, mentally crossing my fingers that it won't, knowing full well that it will. I mutter sweet-good-for-nothings to the cracked vinyl dash as the stick slips into gear without protest only to be betrayed by a belated garbage disposal grind and growl. "Damn!"

Natalie is still talking, saying things I cannot hear. I roll down the window, poke my head out, jab a finger at my ear. "When you get back," she says, "I have a little surprise for you."

"*What?*"

"A surprise."

I switch off the ignition and start to get out, a bit irritated, but she stops me with a little headshake that whisks a loose strand of hair flirtatiously across her face. "When you get back," she mouths, and disappears inside.

CHAPTER 12

The drive up was picturesque but uneventful. Three hundred miles of pastoral poetry come to life. By 10:30 I had left behind the lush farmlands of the Sacramento Valley and was beginning the ascent. Buckskin brown hummocks, matted with chaparral and sagebrush, gave way to scrub pine and billowing oaks, here and there a dead one petrified in a panic-stricken pose. Soon the first patches of brick red earth appeared, like skin grafts, marking the beginning of a brush and timber land still haunted by the ghosts of gold-hungry '49ers as well as by more familiar spirits. The redness spread until the whole ridge looked as if it had been badly scalded. Ambivalent feelings clashed within me—a childlike euphoria versus the knee-rattling anxiety I used to suffer before each opening kick-off: hot chills. Both fought, neither prevailed. I bore down on the accelerator. My Corolla lunged into passing gear. Another five miles and I was greeted by a small wooden sign suspended from two pine poles lashed together in an inverted "L": WELCOME TO PONDEROSA! The real welcome, though, was the sudden appearance of those wonderfully tall oddball evergreens for which the town had been named. Slowing down to twenty, I switched off the air-conditioning (which had served a token function only), rolled down the window, and inhaled the delectable scent of sun-baked pine needles. I was home.

I didn't want to drive through town, though. That wasn't why I had come. To avoid it I turned right on Honeysuckle Lane and backstreeted towards the River via the south side. Although this wasn't my part of town, I'd always felt an affinity for the little brick and stucco cottages crowding the gravel streets. Maybe it was the fastidious flower and vegetable gardens decorating each yard, or the towering elm trees that draped them in maternal shade, creating a cool refuge from hot August afternoons and pre-summer scorchers like today. A quarter-past-eleven and already I could see black eels writhing in the road. The sun had licked up the last onion-skin bit of moon as well as the chalkdust clouds. The sky was beautifully blue.

Another hundred yards and I was passing through a cool channel of air, a phenomena I'd always associated with the pines although more likely it was due to some perpetual autumn magic brewing in Kiley's apple orchard. Twenty-two years hadn't changed the sensation. Another good sign.

Kitty-corner to Kiley's orchard I noticed an old woman in a baggy blue dress and a straw sun hat watering her yard. She smiled at me and raised her hose in salute. Mrs. Koeppsel? Why, she hadn't aged a day since her much-heralded seventy-fifth birthday my sophomore year of high school. Somehow she attained a state as permanent and unchanging as that of the five porcelain ducklings frozen in mid-waddle in the far corner of her lawn. I smiled and waved back, wondering if she was mistaking me for a younger version of my father.

I don't know what, if anything, Mrs. Koeppsel's unanticipated presence had to do with it, but at that instant I made an impulsive decision I sensed I might regret later. I turned left on Bluejay and detoured past the home of my old friend Keith Bernhard.

There was a FOR SALE sign out front. Were Keith's parents still the occupants, hoping to move out? I didn't stop to knock and find out. I wanted to preserve the memory of Clate in his easy chair rattling the evening paper as he grumbled about phantom taxes and soaring interest rates while June quietly mollified him with one of her blue ribbon rhubarb pies. Nevertheless I slowed down for a closer look at the board-and-batten home with the white picket fence, badly in need of paint, the old screen porch, the oak tree from which a tire swing had hung. A frayed piece of rope still dangled from a big branch that stuck out like a gladiator's arm. During our make-believe days, in the guise of pirates, outlaws, Vikings, Civil War spies, Keith and I had stashed secret codes and precious treasure inside the hollow trunk.

Reflecting, I had to smile. Cool Keith. The Monday after the Orland Trojans blew us away 24-0 our junior year, Keith had come to the team meeting wearing a jockstrap like a muzzle over his face and holding a sign: WHAT, ME WORRY? Even tight-lipped Coach Ramirez cracked a grin. That was the same year Paul Newman and Robert Redford starred in *Butch Cassidy and the Sundance Kid*, and Keith and I were instantly dubbed "Butch" and "Sundance." Thanks to the inventive minds of our class raconteurs, our misadventures were elevated to folklore status.

"Remember the time Reeves and Bernhard . . ." sabotaged the senior class graduation . . . dumped an outhouse on Mrs. Barsumian's lawn . . .

My personal favorite was the time Keith and I tried to get an "overall" tan at Blue Lake. We had stripped and spread our naked bodies on the sparkling white sands of a secluded little beach, and everything was fine until an old fisherman and his wife rounded the point in a rowboat. Keith and I promptly ducked behind a piñon tree and waited for the boat to pass. But the old fellow liked the look of our cove and proceeded to cast his line. Keith looked at me and I looked at him. Not a word passed between us, only that silent telepathy that is the mark of true friendship. We each grabbed a hefty piñon stick and charged down the beach, swinging our clubs and hollering like wild Indians, our sunburned scrotums slapping against our naked thighs. The old man was so flustered his pole popped out of his hands and into the lake. His sun-bonnetted wife screamed: "Haaaaaar-veeeey!" Keith and I high-stepped into the water, tossed our clubs aside, and began stroking towards the rowboat. We were halfway there before the old guy caught on. "Damn fool kids!" he yelled, shaking his fist. Keith and I laughed so hard we almost went under.

Cool Keith. After each football game and track meet we would sneak into the private room behind Ramirez's office and plunge into the whirlpool bath, a big silver tub reserved for the coaches and injured players. I could still see Keith's skinny, freckled body turning lobster red in the hot, frothing water, the single corkscrew of hair, like a lone token of manhood, going limp on his bald chest, the goofy smile on his Huck Finn face, his elephant ears.

"I'm proud of my tool!" he would shout, standing at the open window taunting overprotective mothers and their bouncy young daughters passing by. Then he would launch into his "Creature from the Black Lagoon" routine, shrieking as he sloshed around in the metal tub, gargling the epsom waters, reaching a contorted claw over the lip. "The Creature! Heeeeelp! The Creeee-tuuuure!"

Where was he now? Still in town, most likely. And was he still holding me responsible for that? We hadn't parted on good terms. He had blamed Nancy, but she was just a convenient scapegoat. The real rift had occurred several months before she entered the picture, the night of the Corning game.

The local papers had billed it "The Game of the Decade." Both teams undefeated, untied. Corning, the perennial champs, versus Ponderosa, hungry for its first title ever. The Warriors boasted a grueling ground game led by 220-pound Ralph Matousak. We lived (or died) by the pass: Bernhard-to-Reeves. Corning had beef and brawn. We preached speed and finesse. We also (according to the gridiron gurus) didn't have a prayer to beat the Corning Warriors.

I loved football. I loved the lights, the band, the cheerleaders turning cartwheels in their skimpy skirts. I loved how the two teams, armored and helmeted, lined up like warriors for battle. And I loved the magic of the ball spiraling through the lights like a mystical bird in flight. Plucking it out of the night and juking through a swarm of defenders was simply orgiastic. "Hey, Reeves, how many jockstraps you going to steal tonight?" Coach Ramirez would ask me before each game. I was a ham, a prima donna. Back then I lived for Friday nights.

But the night of the Corning game I felt sick to my stomach. I tried to blame it on the lasagna I'd tried to force down for dinner, but I knew better: I was suffering an attack of nerves. Stage fright. Suiting up in the locker room, my hands were so shaky I had to ask the waterboy to tie my shoelaces. That may sound comical, but the pressure was very real to me at the time. I felt as if I were carrying the hopes and dreams of the whole town on my shoulders.

To make matters worse, ten minutes before kickoff Coach Ramirez called me and Keith aside. There was a Stanford scout in the stands, Ramirez said. He'd pulled some strings—a friend of a friend of a friend. Not trying to add any more pressure, but "I think it's only fair you know."

Keith's brown eyes bugged. "Stanford! Sundance!" It was his ticket out of the town he called a "pine tree prison." For me it simply meant more pressure. Now I was carrying his future on my shoulders as well. BYU had already contacted me about a football scholarship. If that didn't materialize, I still had the grades and money for college. Football was Keith's only hope. My feelings must have shown on my face. "Sundance? You okay?"

Our playing field sat like a bowl in a natural amphitheater of pines.

At that point I hastily excused myself and dashed into the nearby woods where I promptly discharged my lasagna dinner. Then I dropped to my knees and prayed as I never had before. But I prayed for all the wrong things. I prayed for speed, agility, stamina, quickness, cunning. I prayed for sure-hands and a cool head. I prayed for luck.

Thunder rumbled in the distance, cautioning me against vain repetitions, as dark clouds squeezed to death the few surviving stars. I prayed on, reminding God that I had never smoked a cigarette or taken tea or coffee, that alcohol had touched my lips only once, when I was a gullible freshman among big shot upperclassmen egging me on. "One sip of spanada was all. Just one."

Lightning flashed, throwing acid in my cheating eyes. I could hear trumpets blaring and war drums beating. I fingered the gold sweat band I wore around my left wrist for luck, testing the elastic. Suddenly the forearms I had pumped up so massively with Joe Weider weights seemed small and shriveled, a little boy's. The thick coils of golden hair evaporated before my eyes. Would the rest of me vanish also? It was like an out-of-body experience except I was a cartoon character being erased one piece at a time.

The first half of the game was a personal nightmare. I fumbled the opening kickoff. The Warriors recovered on our five and quickly put seven points on the board. Keith returned the ensuing kickoff safely to our twenty-seven. We ran two good-for-nothing plays off-tackle to test their defense, then Keith rolled right and hit me on a down-and-out. It was a perfect pass, right on the numbers, but my hands were flippers that slapped the ball into the unsuspecting hands of a Corning linebacker who rumbled into the end zone like a Sherman tank. The point after was good, padding Corning's lead to fourteen. I glanced at the sidelines just in time to see Coach Ramirez break his clipboard on the Igloo cooler. The home fans began booing. Even the natives were restless. In the huddle: "Wait-a-rip, Golden Boy! You got money on Corning or what?" But here Keith took charge, grabbing loudmouthed Palmer by the facemask and pulling him in close: "Shut your face and let's play ball!"

I didn't drop any passes after that, but Keith didn't throw me any either. He couldn't: the Corning rush was on him like a swarm of locusts and I was being double-teamed. A gangly cornerback would chicken-fight with me off the line until I broke free, and then I was instantly picked up by a tough little Chicano free safety who had it out for me personally. Before each snap he aimed a finger at me like a smoking pistol and flashed his mouthguard, a skeleton's wicked grin. On his arm pad he had drawn in black ink a tombstone with my number, 19, and R.I.P. He wore number 24, but his white jersey looked as if it had shrunk two sizes, revealing a six inch strip of belly, a taut washboard covered with mossy black hair. He had an uncanny knack for knowing exactly when the referees weren't looking. He grabbed me and clawed me and bit me on the calf during one pile up, talking trash through the ear hole in my helmet. His special assignment that night was to stick to me like glue and intimidate the hell out of me, and he did so. It was a long first half for me.

Our quick, gang-tackling defense managed to keep Ralph Matousak in check. But with less than a minute on the clock, the Warrior band began playing "The Death March." There was a feeling of controlled panic in our huddle. No one said so, but we all knew that if we didn't score before the gun we were finished. With a two touchdown lead and their masticating ground game, the Warriors could easily eat up the clock in the second half. So on a Corning fourth-and-long from their own thirty, Ramirez sent me and Keith, the two fleetest Pumas, deep for the return, hoping for a big play.

It was a good punt, a wobbly spiral arching high into Keith's airspace, but nothing spectacular so I yelled for him to take it. But the damn thing just seemed to hang there—two, three, four seconds, forever it seemed. "Come on, drop—drop!" I muttered, but it hovered in the lights. I looked at Keith—knees bent, hands waiting, his frosted breath puffing through his face mask—and then at the herd of red-and-white jerseys stampeding towards him.

"Fair catch! Fair catch!" I screamed, racing over. But I was too late. The ball dropped like a bomb and the instant it touched his hands I heard the awful explosion of pads and helmets. I remember watching Keith's head go one way and his body the other with his eyes gyrating somewhere in between. At that point fate or luck or something answered my misguided prayer. The ball squirted out from under the pile of human shrapnell, rolled four yards in my direction, and then, as if it had been carefully instructed to do so, hopped up into my arms.

I looked downfield and saw nothing but a clear expressway of green. So I tucked the ball away and ran like a mad man. The crowd roared and the Puma band boomed and rolls of green and gold toilet paper unraveled in the air. As my teammates mobbed me in the end zone my best friend Keith Bernhard was carried off the field on a stretcher.

In the locker room Coach Ramirez was all business: "Steve, you've got to read and fill, read and fill . . . Box that tight end, George. If Matousak turns the corner on us, it's curtains."

We had a new quarterback now. Keith had been rushed to the emergency room. No word yet. That was all Ramirez said. But as my teammates charged out of the locker room, cleats clapping the concrete, Coach Ramirez took me aside. His nicotine breath was strong, noxious. Bits of sweat glistened on his prickly silver hair. "Keep your head in the game, Johnny! There's nothing you can do about it now except go out and win this game—win it for Keith!" I knew the injury was serious when Coach addressed me in the diminutive.

The second half was simply bizarre. We traded touchdowns early in the third period, keeping our deficit at seven. Then, late in the quarter, the heavens bellowed and the clouds that had been amassing all night burst. In seconds the field was a mud swamp and you couldn't tell a Puma from a Warrior. The fourth quarter looked like a scene from *All Quiet on the Western Front*: blood-muddied trench warfare, going nowhere.

Keith's backup, Max Lyons, was a scrappy little sophomore with no arm whatsoever. Ramirez had ordered him to play it safe, keep the ball on the ground, but time was running out. When we got the ball on our own twenty with less than a minute remaining, Ramirez ran a finger across his throat. Do or die time. Go for broke. Max answered by hitting me on two quick look-ins for ten yards apiece. Then he floated one to the sidelines, apparently into the hands of the cornerback, but I managed to jump in front and snatch the ball away from him. I tightroped fifteen yards down the chalkline before number 24 wrapped his arms around my neck like a steer wrestler and hurled me helmet first out-of-bounds.

By now all heaven and hell had broken loose. You couldn't hear the mountain thunder for the screaming fans. The rain was slanting down like silver bullets as lightning roller-coastered up and down the horizon. It looked like the end of the world or a prelim for the Second Coming.

With 00:39 on the clock, Max hit me on a down-and-out at the twelve. Number 24 was waiting, plastic fangs flashing. I threw him an arm this way and a leg that way and did a quick little spin and dance that left him sprawling in the mud. But then I made a crucial mistake. Instead of shooting for the end zone, I wagged a finger at my fallen nemesis. The gesture cost me a split-second, just long enough for a linebacker to spear me from behind. It was a good, hard hit to the kidneys that left my right side numb and ringing. I was lucky to hold onto the football.

I couldn't get out of bounds, though, and with no time outs we wasted twenty precious seconds lining up for our next—and final—play. The crowd was so loud and the rain was pelleting my helmet so hard I couldn't hear Max's audible, and I doubt if anyone else could either. It was just as well because when our guards pulled right, Max sprinted left. The Warrior linebackers and corners followed the flow, allowing Max to scamper untouched into the end zone. Warriors 14, Pumas 13.

Decision time. We could kick the P.A.T. and come away co-champs, or we could go for broke. We knew what the fans wanted. "Two! Two! Two!" they chanted. We knew what we wanted as well, no sister-kissing ties. We looked at Coach Ramirez on the sidelines. He bowed his head and held up two fingers.

All I remember of the huddle was Max saying, "Ready . . . break!" clapping his hands and quickly crossing himself. My heart felt like a big scared bird flapping madly in a tiny cage. The cold rain had turned my fingers into brittle sticks.

The sky exploded as we lined up on the ball, but the crowd grew dead quiet. I looked down the line at Max whose oversized jersey was hanging to mid-thigh like a miniskirt. Number 24 was alternately throwing invisible daggers at me and scratching the wet grass with his foot, like a bull getting ready to charge. I blew on my cold fingers to warm them.

Max took the snap and rolled right, looking for me in the corner. But I'd been triple-teamed and the end zone was jammed up like the L.A. freeway. The Warriors blitzed through our line and swarmed all over Max. He stiff-armed one but two others grabbed him from behind. Somehow, going down, he managed to flip the ball away.

Four pair of hands went up, and four bodies came tumbling down, mine among them.

I have absolutely no recollection of that football ever touching my hands. But when the official finally unstacked the heap, there it was, cradled in my arms as if it had been magically placed there. I peered up at the referee through the two plugs of mud that had lodged in my face mask to make sure. His arms reached for the rainy sky. Like a stick-up.

Then jubilant chaos. Fans poured out of the bleachers like a dam bursting. They made short work of the goal posts and then came after me. The Puma cheerleaders, heedless of their sketchy green outfits and their reputations, randomly hugged and kissed the muddied players. The Ponderosa band pounded out the alma mater as Puma fans thrust the forked fingers of Victory into the drizzly night air. Across the field the defeated Warriors gathered up their gear and hobbled home as lightning continued to celebrate on the horizon.

If I was guilty of one sin in particular, it was being so caught up in the locker room euphoria that I didn't protest more fervidly when my teammates ushered me off to the post-game festivities. "What about Keith?" I said. "Keith? Tough break, hunh? I mean, if it was really serious, they'd tell us about it, right? Come on, Sundance! This is your big night!" My other sin was believing them.

At Rocky Jordan's house the music was loud (the Beatles's *White Album*) and the conversation spirited and boastful. The booze flowed freely as well, in Mr. and Mrs. Jordan's absence. The big sofa chair in the living room had been reserved for me, and I occupied it like a conquering king, toasting the crowd with a tall glass of cherry Coke. My smile was false, though, or half false, and not because I had found out that the Stanford scout had left long before halftime. A lovely young lady had latched onto my arm as I listened to several hyperbolic accounts of my miracle catch, "The Catch." I do not remember that young lady's name or the details of any of those stories or who told them. But I do remember the loud commotion that drew us all outside shortly after midnight and the tall, gawky figure hollering down at us from Rocky Jordan's rooftop:

"On Dasher! On Prancer! On Vixen! Ho! Ho! Ho! Meeeeerry Christmas! Ho! Ho! Ho!"

"Look! Up there!" someone said, pointing.

"It's a bird!"

"It's a plane!"

"It's . . . Keith Bernhard?"

And so it was: his right arm in a full-length cast, from wrist to shoulder. In his good hand he clutched a big brown bottle. "Hail the victors!" he cried. "Hail the heroes!" He tilted the bottle above his head, anointing himself with beer, then christened the chimney. Gripping the TV antenna he began running circles around it, singing, "On Wis-con-sin! On Wis-con-sin!"

Then he collapsed. He was lucky he didn't roll off the roof and break his neck. With the help of my teammates we got him safely down and into my Corvette. It would take weeks to fully purge the interior of the stench from his multiple-vomiting. Mr. Bernhard answered the door. The husky lumberman shot me an accusing glare, mumbled, "Thanks," and took Keith inside.

Monday morning Keith was back at school, cast and all, slapping me on the back like old times. "Great game, Sundance! Helluva game! We showed those hay-balers, didn't we?"

Did we? I think we both tried to carry on as before, but everything had changed now. The childhood dream we had shared of playing college and pro ball together was dead. In a few short months I would leave for college and he would stay behind, most likely to work in the lumber mill like his father. By the time Nancy arrived on the scene in March, Keith and I were seeing each other at track practice only—no more wild escapades, no more jaunts to the River, no more Butch and Sundance. But no ugly name-calling incidents, either. It was a surprisingly un-dramatic split.

Until the league track finals in May. I still have dreams about that race—call them nightmares. The mile relay, the last event of the league finals, trailing Las Plumas by two points, winner take all. All day a big black shot-putter from Las Plumas had been messing with my mind: "Harry's gonna run up your butt and out your eyeballs, white boy! Up your butt and out your eye balls!"

Not quite. Charging into the final turn shoulder-to-shoulder, my legs gobbling up ground as I edged ahead, the brief jetrocket joy down the straight when I was so close I thought I could reach out and grab the tape with my hand. Then out of nowhere the roar of the River which was the sound of a distant locomotive which was her voice, that loud, low, horsey laugh. And then the invisible water smothering me, pushing me back, back, as my arms and legs churned in furious slow-motion as if trapped in taffy. Flashbulbs, cheers, Harry's big blue behind hoisted onto the shoulders of his teammates. Then silence. The empty stands.

Except for her. So present even in her absence. "Damn you! Damn you *and* Harry the Horse!"

In the locker room Keith was merciless. Reeves this, Reeves that. We would have won for sure if Reeves hadn't been out screwing Von Kleinsmid every night! He wouldn't shut up. Maybe he just couldn't.

Maybe he thought I had dressed and left early. When I rounded the corner to his locker, my hair still wet from a shower, my shirt half buttoned, he looked startled. He was wearing a little white towel around his waist and beads of water clung to his freckled shoulders. "If you've got something to say, Keith, say it to my face."

And he did. " . . . if you hadn't been out screwing that Albino Watusi, lousy rotten whore—"

The fight was brief—fifteen seconds. Maybe I had righteous anger on my side because I got in four solid hits before he returned a meek blow to my shoulder. Then my fist kissed him squarely in the nose. There was a muted crack, like a knock on wood, then ribbons of blood trickling from both nostrils. He covered his face and turned away, sobbing. But I knew it wasn't the blow—he was as tough as nails. I gave my teammates a dirty look and ducked out into the warm night where I wept for both of us.

CHAPTER 13

They still hadn't paved the road to the River and I was glad. So what if the rocks and potholes tortured my shocks and the billowing dust dyed my beige Corolla desert red? I'd always dreaded the day blacktop would open that evergreen Eden to the general public. Even so, rounding each hairpin turn, I feared a head-on with some visored young entrepreneur with a money pouch grinning underneath psychedelic neon: RIVER RESORT, PARKING $3.50.

But there were no Golden Arches or toll booths. I parked in the oak tree shade near a beat-up VW bug and a one-eyed Chevy pickup with WASH ME finger-printed on the dust-coated rear windshield. River vehicles. My war-torn Toyota fit right in. A ponytailed young man and his girlfriend were sitting in the pickup, sipping cans of beer, so I did a quick-change act inside my car. At such moments I gained a lot of empathy for Superman. Houdini, too, with his straight-jacket escapes. Contorting my body like a circus geek, I wrestled out of my sweat pants, t-shirt, and priesthood garments and wriggled into my swim trunks— flower-spotted, fake-flannel things that drooped unflatteringly to my knees, a joke gift from Natalie and the kids: HAPPY PAPPY'S DAY!

I'd forgotten to bring sunscreen, a consequence my buttermilk skin would pay for if I weren't careful. Weaving through the branch and bristle towards the roar of crashing waters, I experienced those same pre-game, pre-race chills I had earlier. These feelings were aborted, however, by the sudden appearance of a young woman on a granite tabletop a few yards from the trail. She had assumed the classic pose of sun-worshippers. One leg was slightly bent, eyes closed, lips passionately puckered. The zipper on her white cut-off jeans was lowered to half-mast, and her black bikini top lay neatly at her side, as if secretly housing the twin sisters of her naked breasts. They were big, soft gourds, thickly buttered with a coconut cream that hyper-sweetened the air. I looked a little longer than I should have and thought a bit longer than that. She sat up suddenly, smiling at me as if we shared an intimate secret (which, in a way, we did). I nodded and hurried on my way.

Moments later I was standing on a rocky ledge gazing down at white water leaping dolphin-like over toad-colored stones and fallen timber. Mentally I'd prepared myself for a letdown. The enchanted playgrounds of youth rarely live up to the adult billings in our mind. But this time my memory hadn't betrayed me. A jungle of mountain shrubs spilled onto the loamy banks. Flowered vines climbed the granite walls and dripped from muscle-bound limbs of Michelangelan dimensions. Sunlight added a touch of lemon to the canopy of green. When a breeze came up, the leaves fluttered like flocks of tropical birds. The River hadn't changed.

I took a side trail that meandered lazily down to a sandy white beach glittering with fool's gold. I was lucky. Aside from a small shrine of beer bottles stacked by a fire pit, the beach was empty. The other guests had moved up- or downstream.

As a boy, first thing I would do was throw myself recklessly into the cool green waters. Today I did not. It didn't feel right. Ghosts. I was standing less than fifty yards from where they had found Nancy Von Kleinsmid's broken body wedged between the twin boulders at the foot of the Rock. The *Ponderosa Daily* called it "a tragic accident." The local rumor mill had reported differently.

I looked upstream at the Rock. Split in half by the column of falling water, it looked big, totemic, schizoid, a double face composed of a thousand smaller ones: long-suffering El Greco looks, screaming gargoyles, laughing stallions. Some faces appeared anciently wise, with long green Confucian beards. Others were sad victims. Moaning masks. Shrunken heads. Several beckoned to me. I smiled and wagged my finger at them. Oh no you don't! I've been there! They scoffed, laughed, spit at me. Sweet cool spray.

I pictured myself on top, forty-one years old, soft in the middle, blindingly white, in flowered swim trunks. A comic figure flirting with tragedy. I spread my wings Icarus-like and leaped, wondering if I would soar heavenward, as in my dreams, or fall head-first to destruction? More déja vu: twenty-four years ago I had stood on this little beach cheering with my other classmates as Steve Valkenburg scaled the granite face and with a six-pack of courage in his gut leaped to his broken neck, vegetable existence. The night before he had kicked a forty-five-yard field goal to give Ponderosa a last second win over unbeaten Willows. The whole town had stormed the field and chaired him to the showers. Fourteen hours later he was lying in the Ponderosa Hospital, mummified in straps and bandages.

I would not dwell on such thoughts today. They were contrary to my purpose. I hadn't come here to relive gridiron glory or drag skeletons out of long-locked closets or contemplate weighty life and career decisions. Today I had one objective: to shamelessly and guiltlessly lollygag in the sun. Wife, kids, church, work, other stuff . . . For one whole day I was determined to leave all my precious baggage behind.

Wife, kids? Baggage?

Precious. One whole day.

I stood on the hot sand with my back to the sun, savoring its warmth, quietly taking inventory. Along the opposite bank, rippled reflections flickered on the overhanging rocks like liquid fire. A brook trout browsed around a skull-shaped stone, ringed with algae, a friar's tonsured head. A watersnake, no thicker than a shoelace, signed its autograph across the slick green surface. Little stones carpeted the river bottom. In the filtered sunlight they sparkled like gold doubloons.

I spread my body belly-flat on my beach towel but I couldn't seem to relax. I finally resorted to a technique I'd learned at a mandatory stress management seminar. At the time I'd damned the thing as New Age hokum, contemporary snake oil. Later, though, desperate, I'd tried the technique to combat sleeplessness. Would daylight prove more accommodating? I closed my eyes and, listening to the authentic echoes of the River instead of the fake macaws and babbling brooks of the relaxation tape, tried to assume a state of total weightlessness. Beginning at my toes and spreading slowly up the length of my body, like piecemeal anesthesia, I sought nirvana. But the instant I was about to drift off—a gnat, a mosquito, a tiny something, buzzed inside my ear. Then a little itch, right between my shoulder blades where I couldn't reach. And suddenly all hell broke loose all over my body.

I sat up, angry, frustrated, then laughed, or half-laughed, confessing to myself: I couldn't even relax anymore. I'd forgotten how.

Baggage.

I checked my watch: 1:16. The kids had finished their Saturday chores by now. Natalie made sure of that. Natalie and her eternal checklists.

What was J. J. doing? Probably at Matt's playing Nintendo or Super Mario Brothers II. Or Zelda the Conqueror. He used to be my bit of calm within the storm. I took delight in the way he hid his toy soldiers, tanks, and dive bombers throughout the house, slipping a sniper between the slanted walls of the *World Book Encyclopedia* or dangling a paratrooper from the ceiling fan. I loved to watch him don his green Teenage Mutant Ninja Turtle pajamas and karate kick his bumper cushion. Loved to wrestle with him on the living room floor. Loved racing him on mountain bikes around the cul-de-sac. That was when there was time, which there seemed to be less and less of now. Instead of a joy he was becoming a little nuisance, laying guilt traps everywhere I stepped. "Hey, Dad, wanna play Ghosts in the Graveyard?" "I'd love to buddy, but . . ."

His face would scrunch up painfully, as if he had been shot with a poison arrow. "Oh, *Daaaaad*!" I used to humor him. "Hey, cheer up! You get the night off without your grouchy old man!"

Now I get angry and defensive. Not at him so much as the situation. Life. The wicked paradox. "Look, you wanna eat, don't you? Money doesn't grow on trees." Killing him with clichés. The proverbs of my father.

Now he asks timidly, wincing: "Don't get mad. Just asking."

Who's getting mad?

He was becoming a stranger, and I think we both felt guilty about it. Last Saturday when I had a little free time: "Hey, J. J., wanna play Army guys? Desert Storm?" His square little head twisted uncomfortably. "Well . . ." Glancing outside where Matt and Trevor were skating down the street on roller blades. "Well . . ." A better offer? Take it, kid! No hard feelings! Losing him at eight-and-a-half!

"We'll play Hero Quest later, okay Dad?" Later I'd be at a bishopric meeting. "Sure, J. J."

I should have brought him with me. Such a beautiful place—perfect for a picnic. He would have loved the waterfall. Rachel, Natalie. They all would. Even Val, if I could have somehow coaxed her along. My little island unto herself. Who needs college? Hollywood, here she comes! "Shoot for the stars!" Robert Browning said. Someone's got to write the Great American Screenplay, why not her?

Hollywood! Why encourage her? You're just setting her up for a Humpty Dumpty fall.

I repent, go back to the drawing board. Go to college, kid . . . just in case.

You don't think I'm going to make it, do you? You don't think—

I didn't say that.

You implied it.

No, not even implied.

You think I'm going to end up just like you—a frustrated writer-turned-school teacher-turned whatever it is you've turned into. That's what you think, isn't it?

Oh gosh, let's holy hope not!

Very funny, Dad. I don't appreciate your sarcasm.

Well, join the country club, because I don't appreciate very much of anything these days. I'm tiring of this, quite frankly. Look. A butcher, a baker, a candlestickmaker, a scriptwriter—what's the diff? Relax, kid. It's only mortality. The twinkling of an eye.

Val was most profound in the world of philosophical discourse. Art, Truth, Beauty. When she entered the social/political arena, she became trite, banal, typically teenage. "AIDS, Dad! Think! People—young people like me—could *die* if something isn't done! And don't say abstinence. That's a totally unrealistic solution."

"What's so unrealistic? Just tell the boys to keep it in their pants!"

"Right, Dad. Like you did?" Didn't I?

More damn history. A campfire on this very beach, the golden flames swaying like seven Salomes. Sitting beside me, in a fluorescent green bikini, the voluptuous Annette Plikta. Reaching back into her mini-cooler, removing two cans, pulling the flip-lid on one, swallowing hard, offering me the other. "Jonathan, come—have a beer with me!" That accent—a touch of Zsa Zsa Gabor. Cosmopolitan. The woman in charge.

Glancing at her wet round thighs still glistening from our midnight swim. Smiling stupidly. "No thanks."

"Then smoke a joint with me!"

"No thanks."

"No thanks?"

"I can't."

"Can't or won't?"

"Neither, I guess."

"I don't get it. You don't drink, you don't turn on. What do you do, besides lift weights and read The Good Book?" I stared into the fire at the marshmallow shriveling to a black nugget on the end of my stick. Annette stood and sauntered down to the water, calling out in a husky, hushed voice, "Jonathan!"

I looked over my shoulder. She was facing the River, back to me, her golden loins glowing in the firelight. "Do you do this?"

Something dropped to the sand. She turned around and I found myself in a stare-down with her bare breasts. I had seen them before in art history books, the Venus de Milo. When she stepped forward, they responded with a healthy little bounce. Somewhere in my roiling brain Brother Crumb cried out: "Don't abdicate your eternal throne for a few moments of fleeting pleasure!"

Wasn't I being tempted beyond my capacity to resist? Maybe, but didn't you ask for it? Accepting her invitation to the River, flaunting your virility without jeopardizing your virginity? Another voice, from another part of my head: "Get your brains out of your crotch!"

Annette smiled. She took another step, another bountiful bounce. "Jonathan?"

"No," I said, stabbing my marshmallow-tipped stick into the red hot coals. "I don't do that either."

She laughed—a loud, mocking laugh. And I read her mind. You big phoney, Reeves! You're an even bigger phoney than me!

"Go for it!" cried a voice that was neither still nor small. "Go for it!"

I looked up, shrugging the mantle of warmth off my back, and saw a group of high school kids wading upstream. They were led by two beefy young men with broad shoulders and compact thighs. One was wearing green gym shorts with P.H.S. FOOTBALL lettered across the hem. He was carrying a black cassette player the size of a suitcase that tried to outshout the River. The other young man, in brown cutoffs, wore a cast on his left forearm and a cellophane bag secured with adhesive tape over the cast.

"Las Plumas kicked our butt!" said one. "Las Plumas kicked *every-*

body's butt!" replied another. "Yeah, but they kicked ours hardest!" voiced the third. Las Plumas? Then times hadn't changed.

Following several yards behind were three young men and four young women. Boys, girls. Kids. Tall and gawky, the boys sloshed through the water like long-limbed neanderthals, swinging their gorilla arms and snapping their heads back to keep their stringy, wet hair out of their eyes. Soft boys trying to appear hard.

The girls I couldn't say. Three of them wore bikinis: a busty little blond, an anemic brunette who kept looking nervously over her shoulder as if being chased by bloodhounds, and a short, plump girl with fluffy black hair and Mexican skin. The fourth girl strided ahead of the others in a scarlet tank-suit, skin-tight, and a pair of baggy gold gym shorts that left her loins a half-secret. She had long, thick hair like Natalie's, chestnut brown, and Natalie's high cheekbones and haughty tilt of chin. Her dancer's thighs sent sensual messages as she swaggered upriver, jesting at sexual scars that never felt a wound.

Or had she? Who could say anymore? At Santa Vista High they hung full-color posters of scantily-clad Amazons admonishing: BE A MAN, WEAR A CONDOM! Before I was banished to the dungeon, every morning Linda Finklestein would take a seat in the front row, her denim skirt rising from mid-thigh to her upper echelons as she crossed her nubile thighs. As a teacher, caretaker, the father of a daughter her age, I would tsk-tsk, shake my head, pity the poor deluded soul. But as a man, I couldn't deny the sexuality that slithered every time her round little buttocks rumbaed into class. I feel sorry for her. I have seen too many who appear used at age fifteen. They wear streetwalker's scowls and chomp fat wads of gum like the lovely girl in the scarlet tank-suit. But who was I to judge these young people? Physician, heal thyself!

They had gathered on a sunny sandbar on the opposite side of the River. Two of the gawky boys tossed a frisbee back and forth while the third intermittently snapped a towel at them. The skinny brunette began wringing out her soaked t-shirt. The busty little blond sneaked a hand across her chest as she stooped down to remove a pebble from her sneaker while the Mexican girl spread her flamboyant beach towel on the sparkling sand. Thrusting his hips to a heavy rap beat, the boy with the cast gestured crudely to his football buddy who raised his whiskered chin and laughed. The girl in scarlet stifled a yawn.

Then everything seemed to freeze in time. The boy quit snapping his towel. The music stopped. The frisbee died in mid-flight. I soon knew why. One of the gawky boys had stroked across the River and, using the hand and toe holds nature had provided, was monkeying up the granite wall, the sun taking snapshots of the muscles in his arms and shoulders.

"Go for it, Dave!" yelled one of his friends. Then another: "Show us some gusto!" Dave stepped boldly out onto the ledge and beat his chest like Tarzan. He shared the cocksure look of Steve Valkenburg, blond and feisty, that is until he looked down at the twin Medusas waiting below, at which point his face turned to stone and he took an awkward step backwards.

"Come on, Dave!" shouted the boy whose pimple-pitted face looked like a pineapple. "Show us some gusto!" said his second. He was wearing a Garth Brooks t-shirt.

Jumping was fairly safe, really. There was ample room between the two boulders if you aimed yourself reasonably well, and even if you missed a bit your sneakers could absorb the more brutal part of the blow. But I hadn't forgotten the view from on top. Every foot seemed like ten looking down. And the River always seemed to roar louder, like an angry god cautioning against blasphemy. You had to have hair on your butt, as Keith used to say.

"Go for it!" yelled Pineapple Face. "Show us some gusto!" "Come on, you woman!" "Come on, Dave!" said the bikinied blonde. Dave looked down and faked a laugh.

I fully understood the ritual, the need, but through adult eyes it seemed juvenile, vain, and just plain stupid. Risking life, limb, mobility— for what? A cheap thrill? A pretty girl's eye? A flash of fame? All of which vanished the moment some dumber, more daring fool triples your double-gainer. You're dust in the wind. And not even that.

There was no need to worry, though. There were no divers here, only jumpers. You could always tell. "You want an engraved invitation?" hollered Garth Brooks.

Suddenly Dave's head went down, as if ducking a punch. His arm swung at the empty air. "What's up, Dave?" Pineapple Face yelled. "It's

Mike Tyson!" teased the boy with the cast. The others laughed. "A bee!" Dave yelled, taking another swing. Pineapple Face shook his head, a little amused, a little disgusted. "Look at this guy! Afraid of a bee!"

The chorus commenced: "Jump! Jump! Jump!" "A bee!" the blonde tittered. "He's scared of a bee!" "Come on, Dave!" Pineapple Face pleaded. "Shut up!" Dave said, backing away from the ledge. Pineapple Face groaned.

Then something happened that completely changed the dynamics of the ritual. The girl in scarlet stepped out onto the ledge. She had taken the back route to the top while Dave was hedging. She looked ridiculously pose-conscious. She put her right foot forward, muscled thighs barely crossing, a hand draped casually around the thick limb of an overhanging oak. Like an ad for Calvin Klein, the Jungle Queen wearily caressing the trunk of her pet elephant. She also wore that bored-to-tears look that was *de rigueur* among the young. Chewing her fat wad of gum, blowing a lazy pink bubble, holding it a moment before sucking it back in.

The boy with the cast hopped up on a tortoise-shaped rock, his beer belly sparkling with sun-bleached hairs. "Go for it, Cindy!" The other boys joined in: "Go for it!" "Come on, Cindy!" The bikinied girls remained silent.

The suspense was unnecessary. Cindy's type never scratched. She nonchalantly stepped off the ledge, dropping straight as a pike between the two boulders. Her face reappeared instantly, cool, unperturbed. Ice.

The boy raised his cast approvingly. "All right, Cindy!" The other boys cheered while the bikinied girls gazed nervously downstream, as if anticipating unwelcome guests. Chest-deep in the water, Cindy tilted her head back and submerged it so her dark, glossy hair lay on her back like Count Dracula's cape.

All eyes returned to Dave who had reappeared on the ledge. There was absolutely no honorable out now. With a banshee scream he threw himself from the ledge, whipping his legs together and crossing his arms over his chest like a mummy. There was some fidgeting on shore, some mental counting maybe—one one thousand, two one thousand, three— until he burst out of the swirling waters with a triumphant fist puncturing the blue air: "Yessssss!"

"It's about time!" Pineapple Face said as Dave dragged himself melodramatically onto the beach. He was playing the shipwrecked sailor, the survivor of a horrendous ordeal. The boy with the cast shook his head. "Gimme a break!" Dave plucked his towel off the sand and began patting himself dry. His chest was still heaving.

The ritual was over. Fine. No casualties. Kid's stuff. As they gathered up their towels and t-shirts I resettled myself on my beach towel, the needling warmth of the sand seeping up through the soft terry cloth and into my chest and stomach, an electric blanket effect. I might have dozed off at that point, but when I looked again, the little Mexican girl was poised on the ledge, fingers fluttering nervously as she tried to psyche herself up. Short and chunky, with fat little sausage legs . . . I knew her type too.

"Don't!" I yelled. "Stop!" I was on my feet. She glanced at me, then looked downstream where the others had paused to watch. "Hey, look at Laura!" one of them said.

I tried humor. "I hope you've got collision insurance!" It was her face, flinching in a way the others' hadn't, like something waiting to be re-broken. The others were pointing and gesturing at me. Who was this nosey old fart in funky flowered underwear?

"Did you always want to be a vegetable, or is this a sudden impulse?" She glared down at me as if I were a psychopath. Her eyes grew colossal; her fingers went to her lips. She appeared to be chewing them.

The voices of the others carried upstream. "That girl from Walnut Creek, she jumped from the top!" crowed Pineapple Face. "That girl from Walnut Creek had gusto!" said Dave. "That girl from Walnut Creek had something else, too!" The rap music pounded like a sledgehammer.

I tried one more appeal, but she was already falling in a wild flurry of arms and legs. I dashed into the water, knee-deep, ready to pick up the shattered pieces, but she popped up like a buoy. Her wet brown face was shining like a newly minted coin as she turned to her friends for applause. When she saw them laughing and snapping towels fifty oblivious yards downstream, her face tightened in a look of self-hate and anguish I had seen too many times before. It was the face of Nancy Von Kleinsmid in the pole vault pit the night of the Preference Dance, and of my daughter Rachel every day of her life.

CHAPTER 14

The night before she went in for brain surgery, Rachel and I had a little talk. It started out innocently enough. How was school today? Do you like Mrs. Mickelson? Did you make any new friends? Then I smoothed the covers on her bed and told her a story. It was about an Indian boy who is ostracized by the rest of the village because he talks with an incomprehensible lisp. But one day by accident the villagers discover his peculiar words have power. Magic. When a famine strikes the village, the elders seek the boy out.

But that night Rachel was on to me. Halfway through she pulled the covers up to her nose, like a veiled Arab, and asked, "Dad, am I going to die?"

At first I tried to laugh it off. "Oh, no! Of course not!" But her big blue eyes rebutted me. Don't lie, Dad.

"I don't know, sweetheart," I said, and I fumbled under the covers to find her hidden hand. I turned my head aside and when I looked back she had aged twenty years. "It's all right, Daddy," she said, stroking my brown hair which was growing thinner by the day. "You gave me a blessing, remember?" In fact I'd given her three priesthood blessings, the most recent one an hour ago. My body was limp from the fast Natalie and I would not break until late afternoon tomorrow.

As I wiped my tears with my fists and fingers, she calmly handed me the box of Kleenex on her nightstand. "Here, Dad."

"Thanks, Raych," I said, sniffling, blowing, apologizing, reminding myself to be strong, tough, set an example.

"What's it like, Dad?"

"What's what like?" I said, still playing the fool.

She got a little cross with me. "Dying, Dad!" she seethed through gritted teeth.

I got a little angry back at her. "I don't know! It's not like I've done it before!" Her upper lip twitched, a clever smile. I smiled back, stroking her ash blond bangs.

"Do you think it hurts?" she asked.

"No," I said, a little too slowly, cautiously. Then, with more conviction:

"Oh no no no! I'm sure it doesn't hurt at all! I think it's probably like—well, it's probably like falling asleep and waking up somewhere else."

"Will there be people? I mean, besides Jesus?"

"Oh, sure. Lots and lots of people."

"Strangers?"

"No, not all strangers."

"How do you know, Dad?"

"Because . . ." She lowered the covers below her chin, her eyes demanding the truth again. No lies. "Because my mother will be waiting there to greet you."

"Grandma!" She popped up in bed, bouncing brightly. I'd told her all about my mother who had wanted nothing more than a houseful of children and grandchildren.

"Yes, Grandma will be there," I said. "First in line, I'll bet!" At that moment I did not feel guilt or deception or compromise, nothing but a sweet, warm relief flowing from top to bottom, inside and out. At that moment I knew this simple truth as surely as I knew my own name.

But late that night I sneaked into the backyard and dropped to my knees again. The dew on the dichondra quickly bled through my Levis as the salty ocean air nibbled at my ears. The moon was a frothy face through cheesecloth clouds. Vague and distant. Non-negotiable.

I have since told no one, not even Natalie, about the promises I made that night. Promises I can't afford to break for fear he may renege on his. It could happen anytime. Sitting on the velour sofa with a *Boxcar Twins Mystery* open in her lap, her eyes will suddenly glaze over as if she is leaving us again. I snap my fingers like a hypnotist rescuing his client from Neverland. "Hey, kid! You okay?" I smile extra wide, to show I'm only joking, and she smiles back, as slowly as a sunset, and as final.

So you worship out of fear?

No, because I believe. But my belief is founded partly in fear.

Then you have doubts?

Everyone has doubts.

I don't believe. I never have.

Someday you may need to.

That stuff never works, you know. Except on TV.

My other daughter the cynic at age sixteen.

I remember Rachel sitting in her high chair in the dumpy little rental trailer we would be leaving soon for good. Our days of graduate poverty were finally over. Earlier that afternoon I'd received a phone call offering me a position teaching high school English in Santa Vista, a mini-metropolis on the northern California coast. My contract, the pleasant voice informed me, was in the mail. To celebrate, I'd bought two deep-pan pizzas and a tub of spaghetti. Red sauce from that splurge was smeared all over Rachel's mouth. "Hey, Raych looks like a vampire!" little Valerie squealed. We were in high spirits, Natalie, Val, and I, laughing, joking. "What a great Dad!" Natalie said, genuinely pleased. "Well, Mom," Val gasped between bites, "you're the one who picked him!" I was a hero in my little home.

Then something happened that would change everything. Rachel's blue eyes fogged up. Her lower lip rolled out like a second tongue, and her head started tilting sideways like a ship slowly going down. At first I thought she was joking—she had always been such a happy little kidder. "Poor baby," Natalie said. "She's falling asleep. Let her down, Jon." I did, and she staggered into the living room like a drunkard. More clowning? "Raych?" Natalie sprang out of her chair. "Rachel!" I ran over. She looked as blue as Baby Smurf.

The hospital was only a few blocks away, so I scooped her up and rushed out to the car. "Val! Dial 911—tell them we're on our way!" Val was only five but a gifted five. I drove like fury while Natalie sat in back giving Rachel mouth-to-mouth. By the time we reached the emergency room Rachel's lips were pink again. Winter had abandoned her face. Much ado about nada? We had hoped so, but as the young doctor poked and probed her little body, her eyes fogged up again and she tilted off to sleep.

Then the awful part started. They stuck an I.V. in her chubby little arm and shoved a needle up her spine. She was so tired and confused she hardly winced. I was less courageous. As I watched the syringe fill up with thick green fluid that looked like a slimy salad oil, there was a sudden flash, then everything went black. When my eyes opened, I was staring at two intersecting scratches, like the crosshairs on a rifle sight, on the pale linoleum floor.

Natalie made excuses for me. I hadn't eaten since noon almost. Hypoglycemia. Low blood sugar. I knew better.

It wasn't meningitis—that was the good news. What then? They weren't sure. More tests, observations.

We flipped a coin, literally, and Natalie went home to look after Val while I stayed with Rachel. They put her in an oxygen tent, a plastic see-through jail of swirling white gas. "Daddy! Daddy!" she screamed all through the night. "Daddy—oh, Daddy! Please! Help me, Daddy! Help!" It looked as if she were evaporating before my eyes. She was passing through the veil and I was powerless to stop her. I tried to mollify her with funny clown faces that had always gotten a big laugh at home. Tears streamed down her face like a spring thaw. When I couldn't stand it anymore, shirking doctor's orders, I lifted the hem of the plastic sheet, slipped my arm inside, and gripped my baby's desperate little hand. "Oh Daddy! Daddy, please!"

Tests, observations. Three days, two nights, revealing nothing. No news is good news? Yes and no. More probing, to make sure. More complex and expensive probing. More bucks I didn't have. At the time you don't quibble about cost. But for every needle, every chart, every meal on a plastic tray, the cash register rings double ex post facto.

You also play the *if* game: *if* Rachel's first seizure had occurred a week earlier, the medical bills would have been covered by the university's student dependent insurance plan. Or a week later, by the Santa Vista Public Schools. Was it dumb Fortune? Coincidence? Or God issuing more adversity to make up for my pampered youth? Was this punishment for past sins? Other possibilities: Whom the Lord loves, he chastens. The rain falls on good and evil alike. Crap happens.

But that was only the beginning. The neurologist, an austere young woman with the whittled look of a Russian gymnast, ran Rachel through another torture chamber of tests, including one where they put her in a giant capsule, stuck a lance in her arm, and injected her veins with blue dye. Later, showing us the X-ray, we saw two black, blurry hemispheres with an irregular split in the middle. "Epilepsy," she said, tapping the clipboard with her forefinger.

"Are you sure? Absolutely?"

She looked appalled. Insulted. "I beg your pardon?" They put her on phenobarbital, an awful red syrup that looked like fluorescent blood, and after that she was never again our happy-go-lucky little girl. Groggy, lethargic, dopey-eyed, she would sit on the heater vent clutching her little Kathy doll, blubbering uncontrollably.

So you fast and pray and give her another blessing. "Rachel Ann Reeves, in the name of Jesus Christ, by the authority of the Melchizedek priesthood . . ." You summon all your spiritual reserves and hope you've got the strength and faith and heart to make a miracle, to defy the brilliant young bifocaled doctor with the Dorothy Hamill hair who warns that this could be it permanently. But you have the power of 600 plus prayers, the whole Santa Vista congregation and more, so you take her off the pheno-freako stuff and look! One two three four five weeks. See? You kneel and thank God. Singing praises you embrace your wife and weep and then one day when you least expect it, with no apparent cause, while she is opening the refrigerator to get an apple or something you hear a tell-tale thump! and—"Raych?" And she's lying on the floor like a little blue-faced druid. "Raych!"

This time you get a second opinion. More tests, more debt, more indentured eternities to the hospital. Digging deeper pits. But the new doctor, the older grandfatherly fellow, he's not so sure. Epilepsy? See this big dark blur right here between the two hemispheres? Oh, don't tell me. Don't. We can cut. There's a risk, of course. A huge risk. Or we can leave her on the pheno . . .

So you fast again, pray again, call upon the multitudes. You haven't begged this fervently since—well, not since the night you pleaded for your mother's life a month too soon and your father's a phone call too late; not since the title game with Corning when you pleaded for all the wrong things. Wish granted. Did you blow your quota prematurely? This time you pray for the right things, leaving an escape clause: Thy will be done. But make my will thy will. Please?

The night before surgery, she looks you in the eye and asks if she is going to die. But there is no tumor. No ugly black blot in her brain. Only the miracle. Dr. Bridges shaking his silvered head. He has the most peculiar news. So strange. When we cut—I don't know quite how to explain this—there was no aberration. Whatsoever. None.

You mean? Yes. Exactly. You leap up and scream sweet hosannahs to the highest heavens. If you live to be a thousand, you will never again experience such unmitigated joy.

She will never fit in like the others, and she knows it. Still cuddling her Cabbage Patch doll—fat doughboy cheeks and little green decals staring pathetically back at you. Dimpled legs and arms, a scrawny mouth, begging kisses. Rope hair. A deformed little thing she mothers clandestinely so her classmates won't know, won't tell and tease.

But she is already spotting her bed. I discover this one morning stripping the sheets while Natalie is out saving the planet, or at least attempting to feed a small portion of it doing weekend volunteer work at the soup kitchen. Her other baby. At night Rachel relaxes in bed against her corduroy bumper cushion, reading more Boxcar Mysteries as she releases megadoses of intestinal gas. When I slip inside to kiss her goodnight, she shuts the book and looks up guiltily. "Sorry, Dad."

"It's okay, sweetheart."

"I hold it in at school all day long so the other kids won't laugh at me."

"It's all right." I shrug. Okay. "Hell, if you can't fart in the privacy of your own bedroom, where can you?"

She smiles. A good sign. Like her playclothes, her pink nightgown smells like rancid vegetable soup. I want to tell her to take a bath, wear deodorant, but Natalie already has. "About a hundred thousand times is all. What are we going to do? It's in one ear and out the other . . ."

She has talked to her about the other thing, too. She even shows me the note as evidence. DEAR MOM, COULDN'T I JUST WEAR A TAMPON SINCE THE PADS ARE SO UNCOMFORTABLE? LOVE, RACHEL. She is only eleven but already the little spikes in her chest are swelling into mounds. Camel humps. When I lean over to kiss her goodnight, I am extra careful not to press or rub against them in any way.

"Good night, Dad. I love you," she says. But there is fear in her voice now. Always.

She is the gentle one, but temperamental in a way unlike her older sister the genius. A hairtrigger temper. Little things pop her cork. Math. Can't do math at all. Still counts with her fingers. One two three four. When I try to help her, it's a mental wrestling match. "The hypotenuse, Raych. The *longest* side of the triangle." Her eyes wander. "Raych?

Hello? Earth-to-Raych?" She clears the table with a sweep of her arm and shouts, "Dad! This is soooo dumb!" It's been a long hard rotten day for both of us, and I'm beat. Between work and church I've been dragged through six knotholes and three meat lockers. "Look!" I yell. "Just *do* it!" I'm a teacher, for pity's sake. Or was at one time. I know better. But I'm hollering at my kid because she can't get the hang of the Pythagorean Theorem. "Just do it! Just listen for once!" She scrapes her chair back and starts to leave. I grab her plump little arm. "Oh no you don't! You get back here!" She yanks her arm free and screams, "That's child abuse!" "Child ab—" I'm shocked and insulted. That dirty word. "Why, you little—I'll show you child abuse . . ." No. No, I won't. "You get back here! Do you hear me?" "No!" she screams. "I hate math! I hate school! I hate everybody because everybody hates me! I hate you too! You think I'm stupid because I play with babies and teddy bears and think they're *real* and just because you don't and you hate me and everybody at school hates me this whole family hates me—"

"You get back here!" I yell. "You're not going to run off crying like that! Not this time!"

Her face is a giant fist, all folds and wrinkles. Ninety-nine years old. She starts sobbing lugubriously. I've blown it. I'm angry at myself for letting it happen and furious at her for—what? Making it happen? Bringing me to this boiling point again? Is it Rachel or life generally I have a quarrel with? All day it seems I put out, put out, like a white collar whore to all these hundred others I don't give half a damn for but when I finally get home to my own I feel so sapped and shriveled . . . Damn! Hell!

Then I lose it totally. I grab her by the back of the neck and start shaking her. There is terror in her blue eyes as they gyrate in their sockets. I tell myself to stop, stop it right now, are you nuts or something? Put her down. Let go you big stupid cowardly idiot. Let go! But I can't. I'm over the edge, or tilting dangerously over it. But just as I am about to fall to my destruction I hear an old voice. A whisper. Stop, Jon. Stop now.

I do. I let her down. She is ghost-white, staring at me like I'm a hatchet murderer. "Raych?" Rushing forward, she throws her arms around me and stuffs her face into my belly. "I'm sorry, Daddy!" she sobs. "I'm sorry I was bad again."

I tell her no no no a thousand times it's my fault, please understand that, please?

But she doesn't. Later I hear her muffled whimpering in the downstairs bathroom. Damage control, Dad. Doooo something! Quick!

I knock gently. "Raych? Hey, kid?" It takes a while, but eventually she unlocks the door and hastens back into the corner where she curls up by the toilet with her Kathy doll and her "Booey," the ragged remains of her receiving blanket which she refuses, vehemently, to discard.

I squeeze into the corner, put my arm around her. "Sweetheart—hey, kid." I tell her I'm sorry. I shouldn't have lost my temper like that. Tough day. Yeah. Dads have them too. It's universal, kid. My precious little slow one, my beloved little turtle.

I tell her again that it was my fault, all mine, I'm sorry kid, sorry I blew a gasket, but she's still crucifying herself. So I try another tack.

I tell her, little girls her age, or about her age, they start changing. She's changing. Her little body is. Maybe you've noticed, haven't you? I wonder: Has Natalie had this little talk with her yet? Am I jumping the gun? Stealing her rice bowl? "Sweetheart, you're changing. Like a caterpillar that becomes a beautiful butterfly."

"I'm going to be a butterfly?" Her rosebud lips widen. She is intrigued and delighted, it seems, by this possibility. A butterfly, an ant, a grasshopper, anything except what she is now. Scrap the metaphors.

"Like a butterfly, sweetheart. You're changing. From a little girl into a young woman." She looks me straight in the eye, waiting. Yes? yes?

"When that happens, this change, it does things to you. It makes you act weird sometimes—" Oh, Natalie would love this. If she could only hear. What pit am I digging myself deeper and deeper into? "It makes you feel moody sometimes. Sometimes you feel like yelling or screaming or crying and you can't understand why. You can't help it."

"Like when I had the medicine?"

The medicine! The pheno-freako stuff! "Yes! Yes, like that!"

She nods. "Oh."

"I'm telling you this because it helps me—so when you have an episode and call me names and say you hate everybody, I can remind myself:

Hey, Rachel's just having a little moment here. And you can know that too. I think it'll help you, don't you think?" She nods. Strokes her Kathy doll's ratty rope hair.

"And one more thing, sweetheart. Some people just don't work well together. It's got nothing to do with them, or being right or wrong. They just don't work well together. Maybe you and I are like that. Maybe next time Mom or someone else should help you with your math—"

But here she turns and locks me in a desperate bear hug. "Oh, Daddy," she cries, "I want to work with you, please? I know I can work with you, Dad!" Sobbing. Pleading. Stuttering. "I-I-I'm s-sorry, D-daddy. I d-don't deserve to go to J-J B's or have good p-parents like you and m-m-mommy. I d-d-don't deserve good schools or to g-go to college or a nice h-home or anything." It's always like this. After the scream and storm, ultra-penitence.

More damage control. I give her a little pep talk. I tell her about our older brother, Jesus, how he knew we'd make mistakes. I tell her sinning is like footprints in the sand, and repentance is the sea washing the footprints away, as if they'd never been there. Not like a nail in a board, where you remove the nail and putty and paint over the hole but the scar remains. Not like that at all. I tell her when we say bad things about ourselves, like I'm no good I'm dumb I'm stupid everybody hates me I hate myself, it's really Satan talking. He's whispering in our ear, trying to make us hate ourselves because he hates himself and misery loves company. But he's lying. Jesus loves us. Otherwise he wouldn't have suffered all that pain, bleeding from every pore. He loves you. I love you. Your mother loves you. Everybody loves you.

Telling her this, I remind myself to practice what I preach. I tell myself to listen up: what's sauce for the goose is for the gander too, whatever that means. I tell myself to listen up and learn. And hope she is better at it than I am.

"Jesus paid for all our sins?" She looks a little dazed. She has heard about the Atonement countless times in Primary and Family Home Evening, but this time she seems to truly grasp the magnitude of that phenomenon. Her face glows with wonder and delight.

"Yes," I say, "All of them."

"Even the really really really bad kind?"

I wonder what she has in mind, by really really really bad? She's much too young to really really really know. For her sake, or mine, or simplicity, I reply, "Yes, even those."

But Val, who has ears that stretch to China, chimes in from the hallway. "Oh? And what about denying the Holy Ghost?" Eavesdropper! Rachel's head jerks my way, awaiting my rejoinder.

"That's an exception," I qualify, patting Rachel's bare knee.

She smiles, content, her little world uprighted, and hollers through the door: "That's an exemption, Valerie!"

"And what about murder?" Val counters, unwittingly touching a sore spot. A personally puttied and painted hole. A scar.

"Even murder," I say, "under certain conditions."

"Certain conditions," Val sneers cynically. "So it's never automatic."

"No. It's conditional—repentance is always conditional. A broken heart, a contrite spirit. None of this phoney baloney sorrow of the damned stuff."

"Then God forgives and forgets? Abracadabra? Presto?"

"That's my understanding."

"Then how does he know whether or not we're repeat offenders? Because if he's forgotten, he's no longer omniscient, which means he's no longer God. But if he says he forgets but in fact doesn't, he's lying, which makes him imperfect which makes him ungodly."

Val can be very exasperating. "I think you always remember. You'd have to. How could you possibly forget if say you had an abortion or something like that? And how could you learn from the experience if you completely forget about it? But the sting goes away when you've truly repented. The agony's put to rest."

"Agony. I've never felt agony for any sins."

"Then count your blessings. Count your lucky stars."

"Then there are things—sins—you never forget?"

"Never. You can't."

"Have you ever done anything you wish you could totally forget?"

"Yes."

"What?"

"I can't remember."

"Very funny."

"It's personal."

"How personal?"

"Too personal to share."

"What you're really saying is everything's relative."

"Relatively speaking?"

"No, absolutely speaking."

"Yes."

"Figuratively—or yes, absolutely?"

"Absolutely. Jesus atoned for the world's sins. He either did or he didn't. Is there anything relative about that?"

"I'll think of something."

"I'm sure you will."

I have completely lost Rachel during this exchange. I put my arm around her; she turns and crushes her soft round body against mine. But just when I think I have done my paternal duty, have truly penetrated her little mind, she looks at me and asks, "Dad? What's a pore?"

Later, I feel an urge to slip into her room to check on her. She is the fragile one who in a fit of post-craziness might throw herself from her second story window.

Her light is out, her bed empty. I spot her kneeling by the closet wrapping her Kathy doll in a blanket for the night and bedding her down in, of all things, the ice chest she has sneaked out of the garage. She sees me, starts. I smile. "Putting Kathy to bed?" She nods, a little guiltily. "I took the ice chest," she confesses. "Is that okay?"

"Sure. It makes a terrific crib."

She smiles back. "Don't tell Mommy, okay?"

I split my lips with my forefinger. "Our little secret."

The day I lost my teaching job I left work early. I didn't go home, though. I didn't want to tell Natalie yet. So I drove by Rachel's elementary school instead. I think my idea was to call her out of class and take her to JB's for lunch and for an ice cream. I had no plans to tell her what had happened, although I thought that somehow, intuitively, she would know but would not care, would not judge, would just be happy to see me period, job or no job: "Oh, Daddy! Oh boy oh boy oh boy!"

It was morning recess when I arrived, so I parked on the street outside the chain link fence and watched for awhile. The sun had burned through the coastal fog, and the wet green hills were glistening like scoops of lime sherbet. All across the playground little people in designer jeans were running and jumping and swinging and climbing and chasing around in gleeful packs. I envied their free-spirited frolic and the reckless energy with which they whirled around like mini cyclones. For a moment my spirit soared.

Then I spotted Rachel. She was sitting in an old swing in the far corner of the field, head down, hands half-heartedly gripping the metal chain, staring sullenly at her feet. From the street I recognized her red "Annie" shoes. She looked so sad and lonely, as if her Kathy doll had died. I wanted to go over and comfort her but was afraid I'd break down in the process which would have made things worse for both of us.

So I waited, hoping she would heave her head back and her legs forward and with a good old-fashioned kid scream launch herself as high as the damn suspension chains would permit. Or else spring free from that rubber strap and gallop maddog into the many-colored mob. But she retained her sullen position in the swing, as if she had been strapped there without a fight or had long ago given up. Surrendered.

The bell rang. As the other children scattered like antelope, my daughter obediently rose from her swing and marched robot-like into the open mouth of the school building.

I didn't come right out and tell Natalie. I was bitching about peripherals—not the core issue. Church meetings. Meetings meetings meetings! Sacrament meeting, Primary, Sunday school, Relief Society, bishopric meeting, P.E.C. meeting, Correlation Council, Scout Troop Committee meeting. We get meeting-ed to death! We leave our families to attend meetings where they tell us to spend more time with our families. They call meetings to tell us to cut down on meetings.

So what's your point?

My point? What's *their* point! All of this fasting and praying and handshaking and right-hand-raising and scripture searching, tithe-paying, pew-sitting, head-nodding, yes Bishop Finley, no Bishop Finley . . . We do all these things, but it doesn't do any good—doesn't do me any good.

All right, what happened? What's the matter?

You don't want to know.

Yes, I do! Now what's going on!

Okay, this! This is going on! This is the matter! I walk into class the first day of the new semester and give an assignment—write about someone who's made an impression on you. Mom, Dad, Michael Jackson. Anyone. One paragraph. Moan! Groan! Grunt! Growl! Reluctantly, paper is ripped from spiral notebooks. More moans, more groans, but eventually, begrudgingly, they start scribbling. All except three kids. One's a blond with eight-inch eyelashes, another's a chubby albino in combat fatigues, and the third's a wiry clean-cut boy with a face off the Wheaties box. I confront them, nicely: "Why aren't you doing the assignment?" They smile. Beautiful smiles! Nice kids. Polite. The chubby albino speaks for the threesome: "We already know we're going to flunk. The only reason we're even here is it was this or jail." The other two nod. Smile. Then another boy saunters in, a punk rocker—half-Mohawk, half-sputnik cut, and one of those heavy metal t-shirts, black with a screaming skull and a dripping red dagger. He's wearing headphones, shaking his head to the taped trash banging his brain. A Pepsi in one hand, spitting out pistachio shells. I tell him to lose the Pepsi, please, the pistachios, the headphones. He sneers and jabs his thumb in the air: "Up yours!" I tell him to step outside a moment. He flips me off. I send him to Morgan's office with a note. Five minutes later he's back, sitting in the rear, yelling—I mean really screaming it—"War! Inside my head! War! Inside my head!" Shocked? Alarmed? Not at all. He's a little more the exception than the rule, but not much.

I try to work with him one-on-one. "Jason, tell me something you like. Anything." I help him analyze some heavy metal lyrics. "Okay, this is a metaphor . . . This is a simile . . ." He looks at me kind of funny. "I get it." Progress. But I turn my back for two seconds and he's out of his seat, drifting, taking the framed photograph off my desk. "These your kids?" he asks. Another ray of hope! We're getting personal here, human. "Yes," I say. "Yes—all three." "How old's this one?" he says, and he's not pointing to my tall, blond seventeen-year-old but to little Rachel with the timid don't-hurt-me eyes. Then he gets this ugly, wicked grin. "I'll get her!" he sneers. "When you least expect it, I'm going to ram it right up her till—"

I lost it, Nat. I just lost it. I grabbed him by the collar and shook him till his eyes were spinning like a slot machine. "Don't you *ever* do that again! Not in my class! Not anywhere!" Then I hit him. Not just once. I tore into him like a wild man. Three of my football students had to pull me off.

Next thing I'm in Morgan's office. The parents are there, with their attorney. Morgan's sweating bullets, smelling a lawsuit. He's motioning to me. He wants an apology, but I'm not cooperating. Jason's there, wearing his ignorant smirk. The last thing I hear before Morgan shuts the door is the white-collar father bellowing, "I want that sonuvabitch out of the classroom! He's got no business being in a classroom!"

They can't blame that all on you.

Oh no? It's a crash-and-burn profession. Especially in the remedial ranks. By the time those kids hit high school, they're lost. One in a hundred you can really help—one in a thousand! It's depressing. You either turn off your feelings totally, or you go bonkers.

I thought you liked—

I don't. I hate it.

But you can help the one. Like that story about the starfish—it makes a big difference to the one who's thrown back in the sea.

I should have gone to med school, Nat. I had the grades. I even had the money if I'd humbled myself one iota and asked my father. But no! I had to be a writer! A high and mighty cre-a-tor! I fell for all that sacred Priesthood of Art stuff. James Joyce. Matthew Arnold. Percy Shelley. I'm nothing but a sucker—a dumb, broke sucker scraping to pay bills.

Jon—

I should at least have kept going and gotten my doctorate, when I had the momentum. I should have finished.

Why? You don't need a doctorate to write. You said so yourself. I thought we discussed all that.

I need time is what I flipping need!

But why a doctorate?

It's a ticket.

To where?

I don't know. Somewhere. Any place but where I'm at. I'm glad they fired me. It was a damn blessing in disguise. I used to spend six hours a day standing on my head trying to get those whiny brats to write. I'd cut off my right arm for an hour a day.

You're a good teacher, Jon.

Were.

Are!

I've got to get out of this business.

No, Jon. Not because some foul-mouthed kid—

No, not that. I don't regret that at all.

What then?

I killed a boy, Natalie. I killed one of my students.

Jon . . .

CHAPTER 15

Mac's Foster Freeze was still there. So was the Chamber of Commerce depot across the street. Its digital message board read a blistering 102. Pressed against the vinyl bucket seat, my sunburned back felt as if it was being clawed by a lion.

Frankly, I was surprised to find that Mac's was still on the map, considering the other changes. The little clusters of homes sprinkling the woods had grown larger and more numerous, and you had to drive farther to find pure forest now. More FOR SALE signs sagged in front of abandoned homes with waist-high weeds and shingled rooftops that looked like stacks of poorly shuffled cards. The B.P.O.E. Elks Club survived, and Mel's A-frame barber shop, the candy-cane-striped pole in need of paint. But instead of ponderosa pines, the adjacent lots sprouted rows of tin homes where old couples sat on screened porches surrounded by astro-turf.

I parked outside Mac's in the sketchy shade of a gambel oak. A tall, bearded man intercepted me at the glass entry. Faded blue jeans with frayed hems, a ragged work shirt, and long, stringy hair, he looked like a fugitive from the transient camps of Santa Vista. WILL WORK FOR FOOD read the crudely lettered cardboard sign leaning against his Army surplus duffel bag. He held up a wad of paper towels and a plastic spray bottle of clear blue fluid. I listened patiently as he begged to wash my windows for fifty cents. He was trying to get to Houston, he said, his speech slow and slurred. Houston? Via Ponderosa? His sun-bronzed cheeks were shining like hot-stropped leather. It appeared as if any moment his aqua eyes would fade away, leaving two empty holes in his face.

Recent events had taught me something about the fragility of life. Any day I could be walking in this fellow's moccasins. So the only real debate was how much I could spare. I checked my wallet: two fives and two ones. Figure five for dinner. I had a little under half a tank of gas, but the drive home was more downhill than up so I could probably make it without refueling if I drove like an old lady. However, just in case. . . I gave him a five and headed into Mac's.

"Oh, thank you, sir!" he said in an ingratiating Texas drawl. "I'll. . . I'll wash these windows real good!" As he squirted my dust-coated windshield, his dirt-smudged forearm sweeping back and forth across the glass, I called out to him: "What's your name!"

He turned and smiled. "Roger!" Two of his front teeth were missing; the others were crooked and decayed, like rotting fenceposts.

"What's in Houston?" I asked.

He shrugged. "Work maybe. I don't know."

"Well, good luck to you, Roger."

"Good luck to you, sir! And God bless you! God bless—"

The interior provided little relief from the heat. Penurious Max had refused to install air conditioning. The tinted glass helped some, and the venetians, shut tight on the east side, but the token ceiling fan could only stir up a weak sirocco breeze that barely reached the corners of the cramped dining area. A glossy poster on the north wall announced: MID-VALLEY LEAGUE TRACK FINALS/SATURDAY/PONDEROSA HIGH SCHOOL ATHLETIC FIELD.

Ghosts. I was the only customer, yet the young man at the grill was frantically flipping hamburger patties as if preparing to feed the five thousand. Periodically yellow flames shot up through the iron grate like hellfire and the cook wiped the sweat and grease mix from his pimple-pitted face. I empathized. My sweat-drenched priesthood garments stuck to me like flypaper. I was disappointed to see that the old menu board was gone. In my time enticing names like "The Monster Burger," "The Even-Meaner Burger," and "The Monster Burger That Ate Marysville" were hand-printed in ghoulish green letters on a slab of plywood suspended by rusted baling wire. This was replaced by a slick white panel with stick-on letters that now spelled out a catalog of ho-hum snacks: Burger Deluxe, Cheeseburger Deluxe, Double-Cheeseburger Deluxe. . . It made me wonder if Mac had been replaced as well.

I ordered a greaseburger deluxe, for old time's sake, and a jumbo Dr. Pepper to quench my thirst, then claimed the little round table by the north window-wall, exactly where Nancy Von Kleinsmid and I had spent so many enlightening afternoons together.

Except for Natalie's brown bag lunch, I hadn't eaten all day. I stripped the crisp paper from the burger and took a mammoth bite, the sweet grease going straight to the pit of my stomach. Peeling the plastic lid off the Dr. Pepper, I guzzled like a Cossack, then took another giant bite of greaseburger, and another, trying to block out the echoes from the past:

"Well, Golden Boy, are you going to disgrace God, school, country, and the sweet little girl next door, or are you going to beat that Blunder Butt from Las Plumas this time?"

"Look, I wouldn't know Lance Alworth from Lancelot, but if that's what you really want—then do it, Jon! Do it! And be the best!"

What goes around comes around. It occurred to me that Mac's had been my choice for dinner the night of the Preference Dance.

"Nothing doing, Jon! For once we're going to mingle with the eeee-leeeet!"

More echoes. More voices.

So how was it?

How was what?

The River, what else?

Fine.

Only fine?

I don't know. How was it supposed to be?

You tell me.

I did. It was fine.

What gives? I ask a simple question, you give me the run-around.

You asked, I answered.

Then why didn't you go in?

I did.

No you didn't! You stood on the shore like dowdy old Prufrock.

I went in!

To your ankles, maybe. To your rattling little knees.

Okay, to my ankles. To my knees. So what? It doesn't mean a thing.

It means everything.

Not anymore.

You should have gone in.

I should have done a lot of things.

Shouldn't have, too.

You don't want to get into that now, do you?

I'd spent a full day at the River, yet I wasn't feeling one bit rested or relaxed. I tried to think about Natalie, the kids, the simple joys of family life: beach trips, picnics, the Shakespeare Festival in Ashland. Hoisting J.J. onto my shoulders, waistdeep in the Pacific: "Dad, you want me to do a street flip or a Ninja flip?" "Oh, a Ninja flip, of course!" Dipping underwater, bobbing, one, two, three, and—umpf!—flinging him up and out, a human cannonball exploding in salty surf. Rachel chasing me across the front lawn at dark. "Ghost in the graveyard! Ghost in the graveyard!" Val rummaging through the cupboards late at night, creating culinary novelties: peanut butter and banana chips on toasted French bread. Her midnight talks. "Dad, are you a revisionist, or do you really believe that golden plates nonsense?"

Curling up on the sofa with Natalie, hot chocolate and an old Tracy/Hepburn movie, fingertip kisses, the rain on the skylights like a million little drummers, soft hands that can't touch . . .

I tried to bring these scenes into focus, but they were obscured by the image of that concrete bunker they had stuck me in Monday through Friday from dawn until dark. This is what happened: after some haggling and politicking with the teachers' union, the administration offered me the following: I could write grants for the school district on a commission basis. I would earn 3 percent of the direct costs budget for any of my proposals that was funded, the grant total not to exceed my present annual salary. "Three percent? I write a grant for thirty thousand, I take home nine hundred?"

"Less taxes. Take it or leave it, Reeves." At least it didn't go to court. I suppose I was grateful for that.

As soon as he found out, Hadley Williams, my department chair, stormed into Frank Morgan's office cursing a Mississippi bluestreak. Hadley with the wooly white Uncle Remus hair and the deep Darth Vader voice, who could quote whole scenes from Aeschylus and Shakespeare, pounded Morgan's desk and roared: "You can't get rid of Reeves! He's the only guy we've got who gives a good goddamn about those kids!" He threatened to sue, to resign, to burn the friggin' school down.

To his credit, Morgan didn't knuckle under. A fiery young man who slicked his blond hair straight back and dressed for Wall Street, he had had it in for me ever since I refused to serve on an after-school curriculum committee, claiming "remedial asylum." Morgan had forced the issue. I filed a grievance through the teacher's union, and in this case won, which didn't exactly endear me to Morgan. He called me a slacker and accused me of teaching for a paycheck, putting in time. The day I attacked Jason in class was manna from heaven in Morgan's mind. Cosmic justice.

There were no strikes, no lawsuits or resignations on my behalf. Hadley slipped quietly into my classroom as I was packing up my personal books and belongings. I think he wanted to talk, and maybe I should have. Opened up, I mean. I'd known him eight, nine years. We used to eat lunch together, talked sports, politics, shared war stories.

"You've got to fight this," he said. I was down on one knee, perfunctorily stuffing a box with paperbacks. I could sense his big, dark body looming behind me. "You can't just roll over and play dead." He kept feeding me lines, teasers. I didn't bite. I quietly folded the cardboard flaps, ripped duct tape off the roll, and sealed the box shut. His hand gripped my shoulder. "We're gonna miss you, buddy." My silence told me how alone I was in all of this, how much I had distanced myself over the years. I hadn't even told Natalie the real truth yet.

I stuffed the paper napkin in my empty Dr. Pepper cup and looked outside where the sun had crashed and splattered on the piney horizon. The late afternoon shadows were creeping across the street like a gambler's hands. Coming here was crazy. Every little thing seemed to resurrect some grim memory. Driving past the old clinic where my father had spent half his life bringing babies into the world, I recalled the time my sophomore year at BYU he mailed me a $100 check with a note: LOVE, YOUR FATHER. Instead of accepting his gift, I'd sniffed around for ulterior motives. YOUR FATHER. What kind of sign off was that? Did he think he could buy me off? Bridge a bitter gap with his billfold? His answer to everything. I sent the check back. No note, no explanation. Cold. A year later he learned of my engagement through the family grapevine.

I checked my watch: 6:16. Time to go home. Tomorrow was Sunday. "Saturday is a special day it's the day we get ready for . . ." I could hear J.J. singing that lilting Primary tune in the bathroom. Saturday night baths. I used to help when the kids were younger. Now J.J. swatted my hand if I tried to wet down his cowlick. "Daaaaad!" Where had my youth gone—and theirs? First word, first step, first swing and miss at the plate. Who was that grinning little blue-eyed boy with the Beowulf bangs? He loved to sing. Good voice, too. Fast Sunday. My turn to conduct. Bear my testimony. "Brothers and sisters. . ." True confessions? Bishop Finley, suave, sanguine, shaking my hand, that beaming optimism. A professional glad-hander. "How are you, Brother Reeves?" Me? In body, present and accounted for, sir. In spirit? AWOL. Permanently. Climbing the wooden steps to Bruce Weber's house I'd noticed an ashtray full of cigarette butts behind the chaise lounge. My motives were self-serving: If I cast a forgiving eye on others, will God do likewise to me? Not until Finley brought up Bruce's Word of Wisdom problem in Bishopric meeting did I mention the cigarette butts. Oh yeah, by the way.

Finley was miffed. Why didn't I tell him if I'd known all along? "I thought I was your counselor, not the Thought Police. Not the KGB."

"Don't you see? That brings into question everything he's told me. I just gave him a temple recommend!"

"Okay, if you did, you did. If it's a lie, it's his lie, not yours. It'll fall on his head. He's an adult." Finley and I went round and round. Good naturedly, of course. Always with the salesman's smile.

Why had he called me as his counselor? "Punishment, Brother Reeves," he had quipped. "Retribution. Payback time." He was rotund and had a marshmallow jaw. Eleven months ago he had invited me into his office and dropped the bombshell. I was working two jobs, teaching high school all day and adult education classes three nights a week. And trying to rekindle the flame to write. Blowing on dead coals.

"Can I let you know tomorrow?"

"Tomorrow will be fine." I said I needed to talk to Natalie about it, but I already knew I would say yes. I had no choice. I owed God big time. We all do, of course. But I owed him extra. Before laying his hands on my head to set me apart, Bishop Finley whispered, "Frying pan into the fire, Brother Reeves?" Then he blessed me with strength, time, inspiration, and faith. He paused, adding very slowly, cautiously: "For the other very sacred calling you have on Earth." Finley knew nothing of Jon Reeves the would-be-writer. My secret. Another pause. A caution. "Remember, there is a time and a season for everything." My whole body tingled with wonderfully electrifying warmth, as if I'd grabbed hold of a live wire and never wanted to let go.

But that feeling seemed so far away now, a vague memory. Like everything else. "Jon, let's do lunch!" Bishop Finley said, and I would find some lame excuse to bow out. I forfeited everything lately, including my evening classes—ESL, English as a Second Language. Migrant field workers from Mexico mostly. I loved those people, but lately we spent more time speaking Spanish than English. After the incident, I resigned. No objection from the dean of the community college, and my students were saddened. In my last class Señora Aguilar wept and wailed like the grieving Catholic widows of Esperanza. Three teenaged girls, semi-Americanized with painted lips and ratted black hair, sang a farewell song in Spanish while a fourth plucked an out-of-tune guitar. Their parents joined in, singing loudly and unselfconsciously, flashing their picket-fence smiles. Simple, grateful people who had treated me, *el maestro*, with deference reserved for the village priest back home. They had pooled their pennies to buy me a new backpack, in consequence, I'm sure, to a joke I'd made in class about my old denim one splitting at the seams. Dirt poor families that crammed twenty-plus into mangled two and three bedroom trailers, they needed money for food, clothing, survival, yet no way could I refuse their offering. As I gazed at their dark, sheep-eyed faces—at their blue jeans and windbreakers and cheap sneakers and truckers caps—I tried so hard not to cry, to make a little joke so they wouldn't cry either, and almost succeeded.

Returning home late that night, I sat all alone in my living room with the thick carpeting and the mini chandelier and suffered my worst attack of homesickness since returning from Mexico. This was doubly-damning, because I secretly scoffed at people who labeled their mission "the best two years of my life." What did that say about your spouse, your children, and everything after? But during the months that followed, on those dark Monday mornings when the California sun would hide its face in the cobwebbed rafters, I would plunk down in my concrete dungeon, elbows on my knees, fists in my eyes, and drift south twenty years to a hot, dusty day in Esperanza, and a youthful half-pledge I had made to the widow Rodriguez, that someday when I was older and wiser and knew which end was up, I would return and give back a little of what I had taken away with me. "What your village needs," I used to say, "are doctors, dentists, engineers. . ." The Hermana would smile and nod, her face wrinkling with maternal hope or pride.

I wondered how that might work. Maybe I could create a bilingual school, Spanish/English. Start small, pre-school to sixth grade, then gradually expand to include a middle and a high school. (What did they call it down there? The *preparatoria* and the *segundaria*?) With the right help, I could raise up a whole village of little surgeons and Shakespeares. And teachers, to return and share their gifts. "Because I have been given much I too must give . . ." goes the hymn. If I was really serious, I ought to take some night classes—education administration, comparative and international education, curriculum development . . . I ought to find out which end's up first. It would require money. Lots. Maybe I could write a grant and secure some funding from the States? Did the feds finance foreign enterprises like that?

And just when was I to find time to bring this great and marvelous work to pass? Everyday a dozen more requests crossed my desk: Mr. Reeves, I'm looking for some grant money for our after-school latchkey program for the homeless . . . Mr. Reeves, I need some money for our AIDS Awareness program, could you look into possibilities . . . Mr. Reeves, here's an RFP for Title VII projects for language minority kids. Gimme gimme getme. All worthy causes. Time-and-energy-sapping worthy causes.

So I talked myself out of it. Suppose the good people of Esperanza didn't want a school, didn't want a gringo coming in and telling them what they did and didn't need, should and shouldn't learn? Who did I think I was, some mighty white messiah? It was a moot point. Jason's father was right: I didn't belong in a classroom anymore. Pipe dreams, Jon. You can barely keep your head above water as it is. You're drowning in it, buddy! You're drowning!

After I quit teaching my night classes, Natalie got a parttime job as a pharmaceutical clerk to help atone for my subsequent loss of income. This was not to finance a catamaran; it was milk and shoe money, roof over the head stuff. And to help pay off our eternal debt to the medical overlords (chipping away at an iceberg). Of course, Natalie refused to reduce any of her extracurricular goodwill, which means she now runs in ninety different directions at once, instead of sixty.

Even with Natalie's extra paycheck we were still living on pins and needles, so three months ago I started selling water purifying units for SWEET 'N PURE, INC., a dog-eat-dog outfit based on the Amway model. "Environmentally sound," the glossy promotional brochure proclaims, to assuage the collective consciences of buyer and seller. My neighbor Phil Riley talked me into it. Two years ago he was a poor, persecuted P.E. teacher; today he drives a silver BMW and sails his Cal 22 on weekends. He was constantly admonishing me to quit my thankless, penniless profession and join the SWEET 'N PURE family fortune.

Whenever we are strapped for cash, I dust off one of the 2x2x2 foot cardboard boxes stacked five-high in my garage and go door-to-door in the name of service, free enterprise, and environmental correctness. Phil tells me to use telemarketing strategies. The door-to-door approach died with the dinosaurs. I smile, wave, wish him smooth sailing. My lack of ambition worries him. Sometimes it worries me. I know it worries Natalie. Phil is a good guy, a good neighbor. Despite his evangelical zeal, he is sincerely concerned about me. It's okay, Phil. The paint-stained sweats, the holey sneakers, the five o'clock shadow—it's not poverty. Deep down, I'm just a weekend slob. I have no desire to paste a smile on my face and make a small fortune via kiss-ass coercion. Then again, it beats the hell out of grant-writing. Then again, no it doesn't.

7:05. I pitched my trash and stepped outside. Night had cooled the air a little but not much. The smell of dry pine needles was extra potent, as if they had been roasting undercover all day and suddenly the lid had been lifted, releasing a cinnamon scent. I loved that smell. Summer. Dusk. Pre-season football. Running pass patterns at the high school. Keith dropping back, dodging invisible defenders as he hollered the play-by-play. "Bernhard's in trouble . . . he's scrambling. Looking long for Reeves . . . He's got him open on the sideline . . . looking . . . looking . . . Throwing for Reeves . . . He's got it! He's got it! What a grab! Bernhard-to-Reeves! Kiss it sweet six!"

Afterwards we would lounge on the grass, catching our breath as our sweat dried, talking about girls, teachers, football. Then we would drive to Mac's for a chocolate shake. Sometimes we drove to the River for a late night dip. Not too often. Keith had to get up early to dig fenceholes in the Valley. I slept in and puttered around the yard doing a few token chores to appease my mother before heading to the River to perfect my suntan. Life was simple then. Predictably easy. Then Nancy had stepped in and turned everything topsy-turvy.

A light wind stirred my hair but brought no relief. Like a blow dryer: hot air. The melancholy chords of an electric guitar drifted my way from the Silver Buckle, joined by a female voice, a Dolly Parton impersonator, crawling to the high notes. Natalie the soprano would have covered her ears and cringed. Fingernail scrawl to her fine tuning.

Better call Nat: I'm on my way! No pay phones in sight, so I drove to the nearest gas station, an EXXON that used to be "Harvey's Texaco." The skinny attendant was half-buried under the hood of a Chevy Citation. A large sign overhead read: RESTROOMS FOR CUSTOMERS ONLY. Sure! How far we had come! When I was in high school we would stop here en route to the River and old Harvey would drop his dipstick and hobble over, waving and smiling, to inflate our inner tubes. "On the house!" he would say if we offered to pay. Customers only! Any thought of refueling here went out the window. I'd hitchhike home before paying a buck-fifty a gallon for this joker's watered-down unleaded.

"So where's Harv?" I asked.

The attendant pulled his long-haired head out from under the hood and spit out a slug of tobacco—splat! "Who the hell's Harv?"

"Never mind," I said.

I stepped into the phone booth and fed a quarter into its vertical lips, but when the operator answered, I hung up. What was the matter? I felt like the bumper sticker: JUST BECAUSE I'M NOT PARANOID DOESN'T MEAN THEY'RE NOT OUT TO GET ME! She would be worried sick. Thinking the worst. Death. Dismemberment. But as soon as she knew I was safe—va-voom! "Where have you been?" And: "Dinner's been ready since. . ." And: "You could have called earlier . . ." Then the awful pauses, painfully long.

"Hello?"

"Will you accept a collect call from Jon Reeves?"

"Reeves. . . Reeves. . . Jon Reeves you say? Let me think. I used to know a Jon Somebody. . . way back when."

"Nat?"

"*I'm sorry, sir, but your call will not be accepted. . .*"

"Natalie!"

"The Prodigal Daddy!"

"Speaking!"

"*I'm sorry, sir, but I cannot complete your call. . .*"

"I should have called earlier but—"

"*Sir, please deposit two dollars and fifty cents for three minutes.*"

"Two-fifty for three minutes! That's obscene!"

"No, it's inflation. Operator, I'll accept the charges."

"*Thank you.*"

"So how was Paradise Lost?"

"The River? Fine. I mean, great. It was really really great."

"That's good. Oh, before I forget, I've got two things—no, three. Let me get my list."

Natalie was a fiend for lists. Wal-Mart, dry cleaners, Rachel's appointment, scripture study, family prayer. If she did something not on her daily list, she would neatly pencil it in and cross it out. I noticed the attendant had reburied his head under the hood. It looked as if the Chevy was swallowing him piecemeal.

"Okay, first. Bishop Finley called."

"I'm being released!"

"No."

"Excommunicated?"

"Try again."

"Translated?"

"Keep dreaming. No, he just wanted to remind you about correlation meeting tomorrow. It's Fast Sunday, remember?"

My belly would never let me forget. "Number two?"

"Sherry Smith stopped by."

"Don't tell me—a petition to ratify priesthood ordinations for women?"

"No, the American Heart Association. The Relief Society agreed to help solicit donations. Sherry and I were assigned as partners."

"Nice. Is she still trying to grow a mustache?" Natalie laughed, a good sign. She was in good spirits. Like earlier this morning. Did it have something to do with the little surprise awaiting me when I got home?

"We had an interesting talk. She's—she's not what everyone thinks."

I didn't want to talk about Sherry Smith. She always left me feeling guilty for wearing the shirt on my back. "So how are the kids?"

"Fine. J. J.'s doing time in the laundry room for bathroom talk. He was singing that 'Diarrhea' song."

"How about his talk?"

"We're working on it. Now what was I talking about?"

"J. J. in solitary."

"Not that—Sherry Smith. I drove since she doesn't have a car. On the way home we saw this family standing under the freeway overpass. The father was young but looked old—I swear, Jon, he looked like Methuselah. His poor wife and kids were in rags. It was pathetic. I pulled over and told them about the soup kitchen. Sherry wanted to give them some money but she didn't have any except for a little change. So she gave them ten dollars from the money we'd collected. What do you think about that? Isn't it illegal?"

"Probably."

"Well, I told her it was wrong, but she didn't seem to care. 'Let them throw me in jail!' she said. 'I'm not going to drive away and let a family go hungry!' Well, I couldn't let her—aaaah!"

"Nat?"

"Aaaah!"

"Natalie!"

"It's okay. It's just these. . . aaaah! . . . lousy rotten cramps."

"Cramps?"

"Since around six. They come and go. No big deal."

"Are you sure?"

"It's not like I've never had them before. Anyway, I put ten dollars back in to make up the difference—not like we can afford it right now. But it's just so typical! She acts the humanitarian but we end up footing the bill. At first I was really mad, but when I started thinking about it—I mean, how petty can I get? What's more important, right?"

I typically have superior bladder control. But once I reach a certain point, it can be embarrassing. I commenced a stationary Charleston outside the phone booth. "Absolutely."

"Anyway, it reminded me of my Spiritual Living lesson—irony of ironies: don't let the left hand know what the right hand's doing. If you don't have time to do the right thing, you'd better make time. Don't you think?"

"Absolutely."

"So are you all through up there? Did you talk to the birds and the squirrels and get it out of your system? I hope—aaaah!"

"Cramps?"

"Yes, darnit! Well, I'd better let you go. This phone call's going to cost a fortune."

"What about number three? You said three things."

"I said two."

"No, I'm sure you said—"

"It was two, Jon—take my word for it. I've got my list right here."

"All right. Fine. Two, three. Nothing to start a war over."

There was a long pause, broken by an exasperated sigh. "Well, if you've got nothing else to say . . ."

"I didn't say that."

"You implied it."

"No I didn't."

"Your *tone*, Jon."

"What do you mean, *my* tone. What about yours?"

Another pause, another sigh. I could see her look of long-suffering on the other end: my spirit will not always strive with Jonathan.

"So when can we expect you."

"Me?"

"No, the King of Zanzibar. Of course you."

I gazed over at the attendant, who had disappeared completely. The Chevy had finally finished him off. Still dancing in place, I took a closer look at the glass booth. There was a long, diagonal crack on one side. The glass was dirty, freckled with dead insects. I began mentally connecting them, like stars—there was Orion, the Big Dipper, Gemini . . . It was a self-conscious effort. I was stalling. Then I made another one of those proverbial split-second decisions that could have lasting consequences. "Tomorrow," I said and literally held the receiver away from my ear, anticipating a sound something akin to a car skidding to a cliff-hanging halt: "Whaaaat?"

It never came. There was a moment of silence, then her voice, soft but firm. "Do you have any money?"

"A couple bucks. Why?"

"Then put it on VISA."

"What?"

"The mo-tel!"

"I'll sleep in the car."

"No you won't."

I didn't argue. I really didn't want to fold myself in half and sleep in the smelly Toyota. I noticed that the attendant had been resurrected from the jaws of the Chevy and was watching my bizarre dance outside the booth. He shook his mangy head and twirled a finger around his ear. "Okay," I said. "VISA."

"Fine," she said.

I heard a click, then a bee-like buzz entered my ear. "Natalie? Damn!" I muttered, and bolted into the woods to relieve myself.

CHAPTER 16

I checked into a motel on the north side of town, the cheapest, dingiest hole-in-the-wall I could find. "KOZY KABINS" read the blue neon sign. "VACANCY $20." A shriveled old man with a hearing aid ran my VISA card through his machine and gave me a key. "Third cabin on your right." Cabin?

I opened the door; the hinges groaned. Inside it reeked of tobacco. Groping, I found the switch. The wires crackled momentarily before the light clicked on—a bald bulb hanging like a growth from the middle of the ceiling. A foldaway bed, presently unfolded, hogged most of the room. It was covered with an Army blanket, G.I. square. For twenty bucks I hadn't expected air conditioning, but no fan? I tried the window, but it was cemented shut with an ancient layer of putty and paint. I bent my room key trying to pry it open. Damn it was hot! I propped the door open with an old wooden folding chair. Standing in the doorway, I inhaled the pre-summer scent of the pines, deeply. And again. Gradually the warm night air dried my sweat until I felt like a giant saltine cracker. I trudged into the bathroom to freshen up. It was a closet with a toilet and a washbasin, one of those old porcelain models from the Great Depression with two spigots, one for hot, one for cold, and a rubber stopper. When I turned on the cold the pipes rattled like inmates banging on the bars. Something wriggled in the drain. A cockroach. Why not? I shut the water off and let the little guy scurry up the side before turning it back on. Then I splashed cold water on my face. Jeez, it felt good! River fresh, river cool. I stripped down to my garments, dropped them to waist, and slapped cold water all over my belly and chest. (No soap, no washcloth.)

Wet, dripping, I stared at myself in the cracked mirror. I hadn't shaved, so I looked like a whiskery white-collar convict. I pressed my face up close, brushed back my brittle bangs, and briefly studied the weak blond follicles dying along the front line.

I felt bloated, dropsical, from the double-greaseburger, the jumbo Dr. Pepper, the accumulated weight of the day—of forty-one years. Baggage. I dragged myself back into the "bridal suite" as if I was wearing a suit of armor and ripped the Army blanket off the bed. Three cigarette burns stared at me. I spread my body back-flat on the stained bedsheet, too tired to hit the light switch or raise a stink with the manager. The naked bulb stuttered as if a fat moth were trapped inside. Soft night sounds sneaked in through the open door—a distant car like the rush of running water, the pines breathing. No-noise summer lullabies. If nothing else, the KOZY KABINS were secluded.

I closed my eyes and tried to sleep, but my sunburn hurt like hell. I felt as if I'd been cast into the fiery furnace for a few agonizing moments only to be rescued to endure the mortal aftermath. This was no time for self-pity. My suffering was probably minuscule compared to Natalie's. Cramps? Her appendix had probably ruptured! When it came to pain, she was like one of those pioneer women from the handcart era, all spitfire and leather. With J. J. she was in labor for twenty hours and still refused a spinal block: drugs were for sissies; tantamount to defeat in her mind. When it came down to surgery, she begrudgingly submitted to a local: "I want to be awake," she insisted. "I want to see him—her, whatever, I want to be here, not lost in Limboland!" Afterwards, she refused pain shots. "Tylenol, thank you very much." The good nurse tried to persuade her: "The shot'll help get you back on your feet sooner, which will speed up your recovery." Natalie waved her off. "You want motion?" Rolling onto her side, she dropped her bare feet on the cool linoleum floor and snapped to attention. "Care to dance?" she said. Snatching her I.V. pole, she waltzed the silver skeleton across the semi-private room, out the door, and down the carpeted hall like Ginger Rogers.

What if Natalie's present ailment was metaphysically induced? Another attack of the Heebie Jeebies, her phobia of the unknown. "It's a feeling, like you're floating in a great big ocean with a blindfold on—helpless and hopeless, just drifting forever, and there's nothing you can do about it. . . ."

The first time she described her fear to me, shortly before we were married in the Los Angeles temple, I made the mistake of trying to talk her out of it. "It won't be like that. We'll be resurrected. You'll be with your family, with Heavenly Father, with me."

She got angry. "I know that. Don't you think I know that? It's not that, it's. . ."

"What?"

"It's that that's all there is. Only that, forever and ever and ever—" She pressed her palms to her ears and shut her eyes, as if she were trying to block out some ear-piercing pain. When I tried to comfort her, she flicked my hands away: "No—don't! Don't! You can't!"

Fortunately the Heebie Jeebies struck her only once or twice a year, although the torment could last for several hours, like a full-body migraine headache. Once it hit, there was not much she could do except tough it out. Medication didn't help, prayers didn't help, talking didn't help. The only preventative medicine was being engaged in benevolent causes—the soup kitchen, for instance. Technically, the Santa Vista Family Food Center. This was not Natalie's feel-good weekend hobby but her brainchild, her phone calls, her lobbying and petitioning and hounding of local businesses and churches, until her idea became flesh. She had no patience for whiners or slackers. "Get on the train or get out of my way!" Recruiting volunteer cooks and servers, she would pound the pulpit on Fast Sunday, quoting the prophet Mormon to the affluent members of our ward, rattling complacent cages.

Natalie was good at rattling cages. Especially mine. Ours was a rocky courtship from the start. I met her in an American Lit. seminar at school. Gerald Ford was president, or half-president. Paul Harvey on KSL radio was a god with a lower case g. And Natalie Johnston was a letter-of-the-law liberal from the fleshpots of southern California. Painstakingly true to the faith, she nevertheless made it clear (in gypsy print skirts, macrame shawls, knee-high boots) how she felt about BYU as an institution of higher education. When her chemistry professor proclaimed that his class would prepare the young men to go out into the world and the young women to be better wives and mothers, she hit the roof: "I need Chem 421 to mix junior's infant formula?"

I could picture her perfectly in the long winter coat that used to conceal her lovely figure from the world, the October snow lightly frosting her chestnut hair as the bronze statue of Brother Brigham looked grimly on. And her idiosyncratic quirk, the left eyebrow arching up, the right one slanting down: "You really are serious, aren't you?"

"Of course I'm serious! Somebody's got to write the Great American Novel—why not me?"

Three weeks later she was telling me this relationship was going nowhere. By then we were spending our weeknights together studying in the library or beside the crackling fire in the giant grate in the Wilkinson Center Lounge. Weekends we went to the International Cinema or the Varsity Theater, a buck a ticket: no hair over the ears (men), no skirts above the knees, or an inch above (women).

"I mean, we're beating a dead horse, don't you think?" Marriage wasn't in her immediate plans. She had come to school to get an education, not a husband. An Honors student with a 3.96 G.P.A., her sights were set on graduate school. Medical research.

"So who said anything about marriage?"

"I can tell. You R.M.'s are all alike."

"Don't flatter yourself." I had plans of my own, I said. I was going to travel—first to Esperanza, then down to South America—Peru, Bolivia, Brazil.

"Esperanza?"

I told her all about that little desert village where I had buried my past and had put my future on hold. "Mmmmm . . . It sounds romantic!"

"Romantic? You pee in a ditch and carry water in a bucket. You bathe with a rag out of a tin basin. Romantic?"

Her face soured, as if she had just bitten into a raw lemon. I turned my back to her, fully aware of the histrionic potential of the moment. Spinning back around: "It's the most beautiful place on Earth! The people, the sunsets, the simple day-to-day pleasures . . . An ice cold drink on a scorching hot day in the shade."

Her lower lip twitched. I think she smiled. "It really is, isn't it?"

Nodding vigorously: "Yes! Yes yes yes yes!"

Confessions. She wanted a family, eventually. Did and didn't want to be a working mom. Wanted to be home with her children. "I want to raise them, not Mary Moppet Daycare." She enumerated her husband-to-be's job qualifications: sensitive, intelligent, willing to help with the housework, change diapers, etcetera; a father, not just a paycheck. Qualification number one was an unshakable faith. Not like her father who stopped attending church when she was fifteen. "It caused so much turmoil and uncertainty. I don't want that in my home. I want a man whose faith radiates!"

"Try church headquarters in Salt Lake. You don't want a husband, you want a general authority."

It was like that—we were. On again, off again. After our first and only official date we never kissed, never touched, never held hands, although I confess I was sorely tempted to. She was beautiful—six feet tall, covergirl eyes, high chiseled cheekbones—but forbidden. I resented her for that. I dated other girls and she dated other guys, but somehow we always ended up back together, in the library or the Wilkinson Center. Once I coaxed her into my basement apartment to study. Stepping down the dark, narrow stairway smelling of damp concrete, I pushed open the door to my cramped little quarters and announced: "Home sweet home!" She stared coolly at the narrow bed, the pint-sized refrigerator, the tiny hardwood desk with a lamp that produced a stingy circle of light, the hot plate on which I warmed tin can meals. "There's a bathroom too," I said, monitoring her expression, which remained neutral. "In the morning I can smell bacon and eggs drifting down through the vents."

I was grinning, and she called me on it: "You're really proud of this, aren't you?"

I laughed. "How's that?"

"This self-imposed poverty. This 'pit' as you call it."

"You think this is by choice?"

"I know it is," she said. Like that.

January, February, March, April. We were arguing again, Romeo and Juliet. "The greatest love story of all time? Bah! A couple of teenagers afflicted by a bad case of hormones. Love? How do you know if you really love someone? A pitter-patter in the heart? Cupid's arrow? How do you really know until you've slept with the person a thousand times, when they're sick and throwing up and don't smell so great? Until they make a baby together and Death comes and plucks him up, and you save nickels to buy your dream house and some freak spark leaps out of the fireplace and burns it to the ground. Or you lose your job or your hair or your teeth or your eyes or your legs, and your lover's still sitting by your bed, holding your hand. Then talk to me about love. Romeo? Juliet? A couple of kids playing with matches."

I didn't much care what she thought of me anymore. It was a little after midnight, snow falling, cold white smoke puffing from her mouth. We were crossing a concrete basketball court near Helaman Halls, snowflakes swirling in the yellow glow of the streetlight. Suddenly she stopped. I kept walking. "Jon?"

I turned. She was leaning with her back against the basketball pole. "Come here!" she whispered.

I did, but I was still yammering, Romeo this, Juliet that. Something about her eyes at that moment, deliriously green. Her hands sneaked underneath my old trenchcoat, around my waist, under my shirt, rubbing my nylon garments, traveling up my ribcage to my armpits. My heart was like a woodstove crammed full of fast burning aspen. Any second my chest was going to explode. She leaned her six-foot frame into me, her lips pressing against mine, sweet as a ripe, juicy pear, her wet tongue searching the perimeter of my mouth. I closed my eyes and watched two stars collide. I thought I was going to pass out right there in the snow.

When she finally broke away, she asked two questions. Huffing, puffing. Her hands climbing up and down my sides. "When are we going to get married?"

"Soon."

"How will we live? Until you become a big shot world famous writer?"

"Off love," I whispered in her ear.

She broke away again. No. Sorry. It wasn't going to be like that. Run-down trailers. Welfare checks. No way.

"I'll teach," I said, posing what I had supposed to be a temporary solution to a permanent problem.

She looked astonished. "You will?" As if to say, "You'll do that—for me?"

I shrugged. Sure. Absolutely. Drop dreams, drop whatever. For love, anything.

We were married in December. I still cherished those simple days in our little brick apartment, when our banter flowed freely with no offense taken or intended, and student poverty was smothered in other delights: a walk in the park, a Friday night splurge at the Mandarin Gardens, lying in bed after late-night love, her head on my bare chest, purring in my ear: "Why did you marry me?"

Kissing her thick, dark hair; purring back: "Because you're a good editor."

"What!"

"It's true! You're ruthless!"

"Ruthless?" Chuckling in that sex kitten way of hers, "I know why." And she would lift her long, soft, lovely body on top of mine, reaching down where I was most vulnerable.

"Are you trying to raise the dead? Sorry, I think Lazarus is out for the count."

"Call me the Miracle Worker."

And she was. Two years later, while I was working on my master's at the University of Arizona, she gave birth to our first child at the County Hospital in Tucson, in the poor folks maternity ward. It had been raining all day, sticky, humid, monsoon heat, and the air conditioning was down. Mud clots covered the linoleum floor like deer droppings. The room was old and rundown, with puke green walls and fluorescent lights. Mustachioed young fathers in Levis and t-shirts were sitting glumly in the hallway, as if awaiting a death sentence, while their women painted their lips and eyes and flipped through wrinkled copies of TRUE CONFESSIONS. A woman's voice screamed in the adjacent room: "Bastard! Don't you ever come near me! Never!" A flimsy white curtain separated Natalie from the other young mothers in the ward. The environs couldn't have been more depressing, yet at that moment all the ugly sounds and images seemed miles removed from the inner calm of our little cloth cubicle. Sitting up in bed, the blood and gunk barely wiped clean from between her legs, the sweat still moist on her forehead, little Valerie sucking hungrily on her breast, Natalie looked more lovely than a Renaissance Madonna, so happy and proud and pleased.

"Oh, Jon, isn't she. . . isn't—Jon."

I squeezed her hand. "I love you, Nat."

"I'm sorry I yelled at the end. Thanks for helping."

"You were great. Super. Fabulous."

"You think so?"

"Absolutely. Are you hungry?"

"Starved. But the nurse says the kitchen's closed. No food till *mañana.*"

I got up. "What's your pref?"

"No, Jon. Don't. It's against the rules—"

"Animals, vegetables, or minerals?"

"Jon. . ."

The streets were dark, warm, macabre at 3:00 a.m. The pavement reeked of rain, city rain. Acrid, mildewy, industrial. The old brick buildings looked wet and greasy. I could hear sludge and sewage rushing through the underground arteries of the city. I walked a mile before I found a twenty-four-hour Denny's where I ordered a club sandwich, Natalie's favorite. "Make that two clubs, two strawberry shakes, fries—jumbo fries. Yeah. And put a hurry on that, will you? It's for my wife, and she's beautiful!"

Cradling my carry-out order in one arm, I danced all the way back to the hospital through the early morning drizzle, like Gene Kelly. I breezed past winos and alley cats ferreting through tipped trash cans. The greasy streets and screaming sirens didn't faze me. All sounds were sweet melodies that night. I was immune.

But when I reached the hospital the doors were locked. With some James Bond machinations, I managed to sneak past the sleepy matron at the emergency desk and slipped into Natalie's curtained-off quarters. Her night light was off, the whole floor was dark. She lay there like Sleeping Beauty waiting to be kissed, so I obliged. Her eyes opened with a smile. Val was sleeping in the bassinet beside the bed, her tiny nostrils barely moving. Her hands were curled up like delicate little shells.

Natalie looked surprised but happy. There was a new and different sparkle in her eyes. The other mothers and their babies were asleep. Quietly, carefully, we unwrapped our club sandwiches and sipped our milkshakes, whispering in the dark. When we had finished I tossed the wrappers and plastic cups in the wastepaper basket and kissed Natalie one more time, tenderly, on the lips.

"Well, I guess I'll see you tomorrow—first thing."

"It's awfully late," she said. I shrugged.

Then she did something I had never in a million years anticipated from my law-abiding wife. She shifted to the far side of the hospital bed and lifted up her sheet, forming a small cave, and motioned for me to enter. She put her finger to her lips: Shhhhh!

I slipped into the bed and curled up next to my wife, my front to her back, like spoons. She found my hand, resting on her ribcage, and cupped it gently over her breast.

We were like that. Morning breath didn't matter much, and sweat was a lovely lubricant. Funny that even back then I'd had Esperanza on my mind, at least subconsciously. I reconsidered my plan for a bilingual school, how that might work for my family now. Val would go kicking and screaming—or simply wouldn't go. "No, Dad! N-O!" Rachel would do well; she had the right heart for it. I could see her quickly picking up the language and conversing non-stop with the chatty Mexican mothers, tending their little babies, taking them for walks in the plaza. J. J. would be another kicker and screamer. He would have to be weaned away from his neighborhood friends and computer games. But he too would learn Spanish and see the world through different eyes; an education in itself. It would be hard, especially at first, but life is a learning experience, right?

And what about Natalie? How would she respond? She loved our home in Santa Vista. Loved California, being close to her mother and sisters. Loved her church friends, Kathy, Lori, Gayle. At their monthly book club gatherings they swapped stories and roared like drunken barmaids under the auspices of discussing the works of Garrison Keillor and Amy Tan. When it was Natalie's turn to host, I found myself making unscheduled trips past the living room, peeking in: Gayle the colossus, hitching up her sweat pants and squatting down like a sumo wrestler, miming her husband following his hernia operation; Lori's summation of cowboys and country western music: "I mean, what can you say about someone who considers ten seconds a good ride?" Later I would tease Natalie—"Boy, you were shoveling it deep in there tonight!"—but secretly I envied their loud laughter and guffawing camaraderie. Esperanza? Dirt streets? Outhouses?

Crabbing over bread crumbs.

"Well-to-do? We live in a nice home, sure, and I'm grateful for that. But well-to-do? Unh-unh. Sorry. Well-to-do is when you can walk into Payless and buy your kids a pair of shoes without asking if they're on sale or sweating over whether the check's going to bounce. Well-to-do's when you don't have to cringe every time your daughter needs a dollar for a field trip. The *Healeys* are well-to-do."

"So marry a surgeon."

"Oh, here we go again! Jon the martyr! Saint Jon! Just because you were born with a silver spoon in your mouth you think you have to live in a shack and wear rags to make up for it. And anyone else who doesn't is a greedy selfish money-monger. Well, for your information, I do my part. I do what I can to help. I act, Jon. I do! Which is a whole lot more than I can say for most people who just sit around and talk about it."

"I know you do."

"And I think it's pretty rotten of you to try and make me feel guilty just because we have a decent home. It's not lavish. It's not even the nicest home in the neighborhood, not by a long shot."

"No one said you should feel guilty."

"You implied it! 'We're rich! We're filthy profligates!' Well, if you want to live in a shack, go ahead! But don't expect me to go with you! That wasn't the agreement. That wasn't the plan. And if you all of a sudden want to shift gears—"

"No one's talking about shifting gears."

"Then what are you talking about?"

"I hate my job."

"What do you want me to do about that?"

"Nothing. There's nothing you can do. I'm stuck. Trapped."

"Trapped by a mortgage is what you're saying. Trapped by kids. Trapped by me."

"I didn't say that."

"You didn't have to. I told you I could get a job but—no. You want your wife in the home. It would insult your masculinity. You have this patriarchal hangup."

"Go ahead. Get a job. Then we'll both be gone."

"Oh, here we go again!"

"Look, I didn't mean to start a fight. All I said was—"

"Well you sure succeeded! Nice of you to succeed at something!"

"There! That's it!"

"What's it?"

"That! What you said!"

"Oh get off it! You kill me, you know that? You act so holier-than-thou, but you live in this house too, Jon! You sit there with that sour begrudging guilty look as if that changes something, makes you superior. Like you're in this house but not part of it. Like you're trapped here against your will. A prisoner. In jail. Well, if that's the way you really feel, you ought to get out of this marriage! At least have the guts to do that!"

My skin was coated with an amphibious layer of sweat. I got up, dried off with a towel, flopped back on the bed, but was sweating again almost instantly. I was exhausted, physically and mentally, but I couldn't sleep. I didn't try any of my anti-insomnia tricks; it seemed pointless. Instead I closed my eyes and let my thoughts wander where they shouldn't have, down a dark, jungled corridor ending in a pale sphere of light. Waiting there was the whole-Earth woman I had almost stumbled over at the River. She gave her head a shake and her thick Indian hair tumbled down over her suntanned shoulders. I told myself to stop, now, before you get started. It wasn't worth the aftermath—humiliation, confession. I could see Bishop Finley's face, that look of wounded incredulity. But *why*? Your wife—

"That's got nothing to do with it. *Nada nunca nadie*. You reach a point, you know what I mean—well, maybe you don't know. But you reach a point where you finally say to hell with it. You just don't care anymore. I'm not just talking *that*; I'm talking all the other. Do you know what I mean? Why are we here, anyway? No no no! I know the standard answers. Why would I want to become like God? Myriads of beings and so many kids they'd have to wear name tags for me to keep them straight. I can't even handle the three I have. Kingdoms, dominions, worlds without number . . . It sounds like a great big administrative headache."

"But don't you want to live with Heavenly Father?"

"I'm not sure if I even know him anymore. Maybe I never did."

Bishop Finley looked more than troubled; worse than concerned. I'd overstepped the bounds. He was not amused, but he wasn't supposed to be. I was dead serious.

He grilled me. "You say you're depressed a lot. Is there anything that seems to make you happy? Service, for instance. I noticed you were helping out at the soup kitchen."

"Truthfully? No, it doesn't. I know it should. I don't know what's wrong with me."

"But you do it! You pitch in and help!"

"Out of duty, yes. But joy? Maybe this is the real test. Now is the time to find out if we're truly administrative material. Or if we even want to be. Do you understand what I'm saying? If you really don't derive pleasure from that, maybe you'd better re-think the plan. Maybe some people would be more content as ministering angels or paperboys. Maybe we're not all cut out for godhood. Maybe—"

"But what about your family?"

"Do you really think Heavenly Father would split up a family because one member wasn't up to godhood?"

"According to the Doctrine and Covenants he will."

"Well, maybe the Doctrine and Covenants is wrong."

"Jon!"

9:45. I closed my eyes, opened them, saw spots: a leopard look. Buckshot in my brain. My head felt like a giant ice cube in meltdown. Like a bad dream. Voices, night noises traveled to my ears but barely registered. Rachel screaming in the middle of the night: "Daddy! Daddy! Da-dee-ee!"

Rolling out of bed, charging upstairs into her room. "What's wrong, Raych? What's up?" Sitting up in bed, legs crossed like a yogi, head bowed so her ash blond bangs hide the tops of her eyes. Silent, obstinately so. "Raych, what's the matter?"

Clenching her fists, she bares her teeth and snarls.

"Raych, what? Tell me."

"Birds!" she wails.

"Birds? You had a bad dream about birds?"

"Giant birds!" she shrieks. "That shrink people!"

"I see. Well, do you want Dad to say a prayer for you?"

She nods. Meekly now. Sniffling. Kneeling by her bed, I ask Heavenly Father to please look after little Rachel, one of his chosen spirits, reminding her that there is nothing to fear, that her Guardian Angel is ever-present to fend off giant birds that shrink people.

"Voices, Dad!"

"That's just the water heater, Raych. Good night, sleep tight, don't let the bed bugs bite."

"Bed bugs, Dad?"

"Just a joke, Raych. Like knock-knock."

"You're sure, Dad?"

"I promise. Now try to get some sleep. Big day tomorrow, right?"

What was happening to my little family? Even easy-going J. J. seemed uptight and agitated lately. Swearing like a teenager. Playground talk. Bad vacillations. Whirling around angrily, slugging his mother in the rear: "I hate you!" A week ago I came home from work early and found him curled up in the corner of his bedroom, the lights out, the blinds down, clutching the little stuffed polar bear he had buried in a box two years ago. Giant tears crawled down his cheeks.

"What's wrong, kid?"

He looked up, utterly surprised. "I don't know," he whimpered. "I keep crying and I don't know why!"

Don't know why! Join the club, kid! Join the club!

In this case it was his eyeglasses. Just before Christmas his teacher informed us he was always squinting at the chalkboard. An eye exam revealed he was severely myopic. The ophthamologist, who could barely speak English, recommended bifocals since J. J. only needed correction when viewing from afar. Regular lenses would weaken his eyes generally. Dr. Chen's reasoning was sound, but J. J. took a lot of heat at school. A boy named Paul led the chants: "Six eyes, always cries!" "Mr. Magoo! Mr. Magoo!" My son was half a head taller than that cretin and could have pulverized him with one hand, if he'd had a little meanness in him and my okay. Instead I offered fatherly comfort.

"J. J., buddy, hey—no one's born perfect. Some people have bad ears or no arms or bum legs, or no legs at all—how would you like that? No legs at all? Or like me—no hair?" I ran a hand over my balding scalp. He stared glumly at his hands. I noticed a freshly picked scab on the knuckle of his index finger.

I showed him pictures of Kareem Abdul-Jabbar and James Worthy and Reggie Jackson. "See? What are those guys wearing?"

"Glasses," he muttered.

"Darn straight! And I don't see anyone laughing at them, do you?"

I was encouraged by the beginnings of a smile. But then his face turned to grief. "Now I can't be a pilot!" he wailed. "You even said so! Pilots can't wear glasses!"

"Yes," I said, thinking, groping. "Yes, but you can still be a Navy frogman!"

"A frogman?"

"Sure!"

Then I explained how sometimes things just don't work out the way we plan. So you make adjustments. Sometimes that makes you do things you otherwise maybe would never have even thought of.

"Is that good?"

"Yes. Sometimes. It depends."

Sometimes I can still feel that story aching to be written, like a tangible presence moving around inside me. But the moment I put pen to paper the phone rings or a kid screams. By the time I restore order and return to my work, those wonderful thoughts and images have turned to vapor I try to grab out of the air with bare hands. I usually force a few words, on principle, but they are big, awkward, stubborn, lumbering ogres that trip over themselves and bump into one another. What ends up on paper is so ugly and deformed compared to the sleek, winged creatures I conjured in my mind that it hurts to look at them. Every word is torture, like engraving in stone with a toothpick.

I stared at the ceiling, the stuttering light bulb, the gloomy white walls. Above the token table in the corner was an 8x12 picture in a cheap wooden frame, the type you buy at a K-Mart clearance sale. A tiny figure was trudging through the woods in a snowstorm towards the solitary light of a cottage where a thread of smoke was spiraling upward from the rock chimney. It was a comforting or a depressing scene, depending upon whether you, the weary traveler, had at last reached your destination or were grimly plodding by. It reminded me of a picture Rachel had drawn at Christmastime: a cozy hearth of perfectly rectangular red bricks, softly crayoned, with six Christmas stockings hanging above the fire, each neatly lettered: DAD, MOM, VALERIE, RACHEL, J. J., KATHY. Thinking about Rachel with pencil and straight-edge diligently outlining each little brick, her forehead furrowed, her tongue sticking out the corner of her mouth, suddenly I felt so sad and lonely in that stinking, sweaty, smoky, cramped motel room.

I didn't make a habit of sleeping in the nude. I knew the rules. Thou shalt wear thy priesthood garments night and day, regardless. But tonight I quite frankly didn't give a damn. I peeled off my sticky, sweat-soaked garments and re-settled my naked, sun-scalded body on the cigarette-stained sheets. I gave it another half hour, staring at the fractured plaster overhead, re-drawing continents, lifelines, waiting, hoping, before finally rolling out of bed, dropping to my knees, and trying once again: Father in Heaven, I . . . Please protect Nat, the kids, me too . . . Bless . . . Robert Johnson and his family . . . Keith . . . This heat, you know, it drips and sticks like pine sap. The forecast said Bishop Finley said Sunday . . . Robert Johnson with an O. Eeny-meeny-miney-moe . . . Help me help him. Father? Help me help me. Looking out for, lose thy life to find it. Finders keepers, losers weepers. These creases in the sheets like a sad palm waiting to be read. Shhhh! The spirits are about to speak! Help me help. I really really am.

CHAPTER 17

It was early in the school year, less than a week into it, so I didn't know my students that well. But I was going to be bold and daring and remediate them with Shakespeare. We were going to act out a scene from *Romeo and Juliet*. Proceeding on teacher's intuition, I was assigning parts: Capulet, Montague, Romeo, Tybalt the Prince of Cats. I chose the talkers and class clowns for the major roles, the quiet corner kids for the extras. When I got to Mercutio's part, I paused, uninspired. This is the main role, of course, because Mercutio carries the scene with his famous Queen Mab speech.

"Okay," I said, scanning faces. "Who wants to be Mercutio?"

A hand shot up in back. "Me! Me! Me!" He was a handsome kid, lean and muscular and beachy with sun-bleached bangs hanging in his hazel eyes. He flashed me a Hollywood smile. "I'll be Mercutio!" he said. "Let me!"

I eyed him skeptically. "Mercutio's got to be cool, he's got to be cunning, he's got to be sharp."

"I'm cool!" he said.

"You've got to put some real umpf! into it. No mealy mouth."

"No mealy mouth," he assured me.

I still wasn't convinced. "Are you sure you can handle it?"

He flashed me another movie star grin and stroked the air with his hands. "Heeeey! I can handle it. I can handle it!"

He got the part. And he handled it—he man-handled it! He was cool, he was cunning, he was sharp. I remember thinking, when he finished: This one's going places! This is the starfish you give back to the sea!

Bishop Finley called with the news. Did I know a Robert Johnson?

Yes.

Did I know—well, what had transpired?

No, I didn't.

I guess a few hours ago, after dinner, Robert excused himself from the table, went into the living room, and . . .

My God! A hunting rifle? In his mouth?

The mother's LDS, the father's not. Robert was baptized but never went to church much. They're in our stake, in the Second Ward. Normally Bishop Fry would handle it, but—well, the mother didn't know what to do, so she called the stake president. She was pretty hysterical by then. She mentioned you, Jon. I guess Robert had talked a lot about you. In any case, President Stoddard's turned the funeral over to me. Sister Johnson wants you to give the eulogy. Jon? I'm going over now to meet with the family. Can I swing by?

Yes. Please. LDS? I had no idea.

A large section of the plush mauve carpeting had been cut and peeled from the corner, revealing bald boards with pale blue digits, like death camp tattoos. There was a foggy stain on the walls and the ceiling, like a pink shadow you can't erase or the damned spot on Lady Macbeth's palm, or the enormous pink blotch in the Dr. Seuss book, where the more you rub the worse it spreads. I'm sure it was the lighting, some illusory reflection, but the stain seemed to cover the exposed floorboards also, like a pool of methylate. A hyper-sweet Lysol stench permeated everything.

Of course I remembered the buxom mother, round and soft in her luxurious living room, the dark mascara running like mud down her cheeks as she tried to appear composed, nervously sliding her wedding band up and down her finger, like a slide trombone. She gave us the facts: born December 12, 1971, in L.A.; Eagle Scout; two-year letterman in track and cross-country; president of the chess club. A success story on paper.

I listened, nodding sympathetically, trying not to notice the little acne scars that pocked her cheeks or the little brother hiding in the hallway, spooked eyes glowing cat-like in the darkness, appearing as if the world had come to an end or any moment was about to, hugging a stuffed panda bear.

The wiry father sat in a sofa chair quietly flipping through a photo album, his necktie loose, eyes frozen like a dead man's. Periodically he paused, nodding, muttering to himself: "We were going to go fishing this summer. I promised him. We were going to climb Mount Whitney."

When we had finished, Bishop Finley turned to him. "Brother Johnson, is there anything you'd like to add?"

He looked up, shook his head. "No. No, I don't think so." Flipping through more photos. "I told him to always do his best. If you can't do it right, don't do it." He turned towards us, a stoic, chiseled face I could picture under torture never flinching. But suddenly it did, constricting as he sobbed: "He was a beautiful, beautiful little boy."

Bishop Finley dedicated the grave. He told the mourners to remember this day, the fine weather, the blue sky, the green hills. The perfect rolling outline of the hills. The big shade trees and the little dandelion puffs like fairy queens floating on the breeze. Late summer but it could just as well be spring. Flowers blooming, trees reaching higher and mightier into the sky. The Resurrection will emulate this. The re-birth of all things. Bishop Finley did not tell us to remember the mortician in his somber black suit or the stony faces watching as the hydraulic contraption lowered the casket onto the layer of fake turf that, like a magician's tablecloth, would cover it up and make it disappear for good. Or Robert's baby brother peering down into the hole, tugging at his mother's skirt: "What are they going to do to Robert? When is Robert coming home?"

But it wasn't your fault. You've got to stop blaming yourself.

I didn't even know him, Nat. Oh, I joked with him in class, sure, and asked how he was doing in track. But I did that with all my kids. Nothing special.

Well, you obviously said or did something.

What do you mean by that?

Something special, Jon. Jeez, quit acting so paranoid.

Oh, I did something special all right. Remember how I said I'd never seen him eating lunch alone? Mr. Popularity, Mr. Wit, Mr. Funnybone? Laziness, not lack of brains, had landed him in the Imbecile's Graveyard? Not quite true. Here: I'm pulling out of the school parking lot at 3:05 and I notice a kid sitting on the curb all stoop-shouldered and depressed, like Rachel sitting solitary on the swings. It looks as if he's sailing cigarette butts or bits of litter down the gutter, watching each piece disappear before launching the next. It's an ugly day, smoky gray skies and a November drizzle like a fuzzy TV screen. As I drive by, he looks up with this droopy bloodhound face that lasts a split-second of pre-recognition then switches to a Hollywood smile. I'm in a rush, as usual, speeding towards some manic 4:00 p.m. deadline that spawns another that spawns another and doesn't die until I trudge home at 11:00, the

Stranger in a Strange Land. But he makes it too easy for me. With a grand sweeping motion, he shouts, "Hi, Mr. Reeves!" I smile and wave back, timidly, guiltily. The little voice inside is pestering me to stop and talk to him. Take him for an ice cream. But the bigger, louder, bossier voice is bellowing: "Hey, Jack, you've got a class in an hour, and fifty-five minutes of freeway flying to get there! Look, he's okay—oh-*kay!* You saw the smile. You saw the sky-sweeping hand. He's cool. It's cool."

You think one conversation over ice cream would have helped?

It wouldn't have hurt.

But you're talking sixteen years of parents, family, friends, incidents, and who knows what all else to pin it on. Why you? You can't be everything to everybody.

Can I be something to somebody?

You're talking in riddles again.

I never learn, Nat. I never get it right.

What do you mean?

He was sitting on the curb all alone and I didn't stop. That night he went home and blew his brains out.

Okay. That night, the night before, the night after. We're free, like you said. We can do our part to help, but we're all free. You didn't pull the trigger. You didn't even give him the gun.

That's not the point.

Then what is the point?

History.

CHAPTER 18

It was 11:30 by the time I finally checked out of the KOZY KABINS. Half my day shot! Plus it was doomed to be another scorcher. Already I could smell the pine needles frying in the woods. Easing into the hot vinyl seat of my Toyota, I cringed at late afternoon images of myself as a six-foot-three candle melting into a pool of iridescent goo. Still avoiding downtown proper, I took the long route: Cedar Street to Birch, then left down the Skyway five miles to the turnoff. I could have found the place in my sleep.

The gravel road was paved now, and the four mailboxes at the top of the lane were all neat and uniform: little tin boxes, basic black and neatly numbered on each side, attached to wrought iron poles. The pine trees across the highway had been clear-cut; Ray West's lavish ranch house was now a fleet of mobile homes squeezed together so compactly it looked like a penal compound. The towering haystacks that resembled Mayan pyramids were gone; also, the four prize appaloosas, the meadow of mustard greens, the big red barn.

I coasted towards the grove of gambel oaks halfway down the lane, uncertain what to expect on the other side. My only true visit to the Von Kleinsmid home had occurred my first summer back, after hearing of Nancy's death. I'd just turned nineteen, and I looked it: thick blond bangs hung in my eyes, whiskers lightly peppered my cheeks, and awkward condolences stuck to my tongue. Swirls of dust had trailed my Corvette down the road, overtaking it the instant I stopped in front of the rock walkway leading to the front door. Right off I'd noticed something was amiss: no kids, no toys, no Tonka trucks or mudpies. The dirt yard was empty. Deserted.

As I got out of my Corvette, a screen door screeched open and out stepped a woman who I thought couldn't possibly be the mother of tall, lanky, fair-haired Nancy. She was dark, stunted; a gingerbread troll. Her short, greasy black hair reminded me of chopped liver. Her attire suggested a rodeo clown: baggy flannel shirt, baggy blue jeans with red-checkered patches on the knees, big floppy sneakers, and a faded red kerchief around her throat. As I approached the porch, her green eyes lit up like birthday candles, unsettlingly optimistic against the ramshackle backdrop of her home.

"Excuse me," I said. "I'm looking for Mrs. Von Kleinsmid?"

"You're starin' her right in the eye!" she said, showing off a gap-toothed smile that lacked a front incisor.

"Hello," I said, awkwardly extending my hand. She grabbed it and shook it vigorously. Hers was sticky. I stealthily wiped mine on the seat of my corduroy pants. "My name's Jon—Jonathan. Reeves. I was—well . . ." Where to start? What to say? What to do? Why was I really here, anyway? "I was a friend of Nancy's," I stammered. "A good friend. I was away at college when . . . well, you know."

"Come in! Come in!" Mrs. Von K. said cheerfully. The rusted screen door screeched again, and I followed her inside.

Although small and cramped and very old, the front room had a pleasant homeyness, thanks to the smells of fresh-baked bread and peach preserves drifting in from the kitchen. An old scatter rug was the lone covering on the hardwood floor, dulled by a thin film of dust. The only "luxuries" were a tiny black-and-white TV set with a wire clothes hanger fashioned into an antenna and a small aquarium scurrying with little iridescent fish. The water filter gurgled non-stop while an old washing machine chugged away in the kitchen. A mound of laundry stood near the refrigerator, which was one of those antique monsters you have to defrost with an ice pick. A soap opera played on the TV, which Mrs. Von K. turned down low before wiping her hands on her fruit-stained apron and taking a seat in a rocking chair.

"So you knew Nancy," she said, placing her swollen hands on the arm rests and initiating a slow, rocking rhythm. I only half-heard her, recalling Nancy's story "Third Time's Not Hardly A Charm," wondering how closely the present environs matched that depressing closing scene where the fat girl comes home and tries to drown her sorrows in ice cream. "I say, you knew Nancy, did you?"

"Yes," I said. "She used to tutor me. She was . . . she was very—"

The chair stopped rocking. Mrs. Von K. lunged forward, cutting me off. "Then you must know Billy Watson!"

I answered cautiously. "I knew of him. From football. He was a senior when I was a freshman." I was a little irritated by her burst of enthusiasm.

"Ohhh, well, that's too bad you didn't know him any better. Billy, he's a real sweetheart. I was afraid of him at first there—afraid for Nancy—he's so big, you know. But he's just a sweetheart. The first time he came to take Nancy out, he brings along this great big bouquet of carnations. Well, first thing Nancy starts to reach for them, saying, 'Thank you, Billy—how nice.' But Billy, he pulls them right out from her hands and turns to me and bows like old Prince Charming, and he says, 'Mrs. Von Kleinsmid, for you!'"

She flashed her jack-o-lantern smile and eased back into the rocker, resuming her steady rhythm. "Oh, that Billy—he's a real charmer, I'll tell you! You ought to see him with the baby. You couldn't ask for a better daddy! Couldn't ask for a better son-in-law! Why, twice a month now he comes and takes me down to Chico to dinner and a show. It's too bad you never knew Billy any better than what you did."

Were we discussing the same person? Buffalo Billy Watson? Carnations? Shakespeare?

Obviously Mrs. Von K. had never met the "old" Billy, for she continued rambling on about what a wonderful, sweet young man he was, how he took her for a picnic at Bidwell Park, and what a cute couple he and Nancy had been. "Oh, they'd sit there on that sofa right there where you are, with their arms around each other for hours and hours . . . just like two doves," she said.

Two doves? Whenever I had pictured Bill and Nancy as husband and wife, I had seen bulky Bill in overalls trudging into their crackerbox home, stomping his work boots on the ragged rug, dropping his lunch pail on the floor. Nancy's tentative greeting ("Honey?"), his buffalo grunt reply. "Dinner ready?" Another grunt. "Vegetarian beans? *Again?*" Peeling off his work clothes, leaving a dirty trail into the kitchen, grabbing a beer from the refrigerator, collapsing on the sofa in front of the TV. The baby screaming in the background. Beer dribbling down Bill's wooly chest. Gulping down his dinner. More TV. Nancy rocking the baby in the corner, Walt Whitman on her lap. Sneaking off to bed; Bill, sniffing the scent, following. His rough rude body, grunting, sweating, grinding into her while, underneath, she gnashes her teeth in angry compliance. And long after he has dozed off, hog snore in final hibernation, she's lying awake feeling the sweat dry, his sticky leftovers, staring at the moon, a clean white slate, thinking, My God, what have I done? Whatever have I done?

I really didn't want to believe Nancy had been miserable. Not like that. Yet the image of two cuddling doves . . . This was not what I had come to hear either. I realized, shamefully, that I had another purpose: I was looking for a scapegoat. Blame it on Bill. And I was jealous.

A cry from the back room spared me further deification of Buffalo Bill Watson.

"Baby's awake!" Mrs. Von K. said, rising from her rocker. She disappeared down the hall and returned cradling an infant. I wondered if it was Nancy's child but was afraid to ask. I rose from the sofa. I wanted to say something meaningful, something that would comfort Mrs. Von K. and somehow validate Nancy's life, but my mind was all mush and muddle. I muttered a standard, "I'm awfully sorry about Nancy," and said I had to go.

Mrs. Von K. nodded, gently patting the baby's back. I think it was a boy—big saucer eyes and dark, staticky hair that stuck straight out like a monkey's. "Well, drop by again," Mrs. Von K. said.

"We'll see," I said. I was at the bottom of the porch steps when I spun around and shouted back to her: "She was brilliant! A genius!"

Mrs. Von K. smiled, her mouth a jagged line. "Well, she wanted . . ." Her voice caught. "She wanted to go to college, you know."

"She would have done great things! I had high hopes for her—we all did!"

Now Mrs. Von K. looked puzzled. "What was your name again?"

"Jon Reeves," I said, a little hopefully.

Her eyes pinched shut as she searched her mental files. "Nope," she said, shaking her liver-colored head. "I can't remember any Jon Reeves. Sorry." She shrugged. "Well, Nancy never was much of a talker, you know."

Twenty-two years later the Von Kleinsmid home was still standing, albeit with a major make over: a coat of yellow paint brightened the front porch; buttercups and tulips bloomed in red brick troughs; the TV antenna stood as straight as a sentry on the re-shingled rooftop. Thick green grass matted a front yard free of children's debris.

But it remained Nancy's home, with its board-and-batten walls and undersized windows greeting you like a deformed but friendly face. I parked in front and lingered in my car, windows down, listening for the echo of capering children, the screech and slam of the rusty screen door, the clonking of Nancy's oxfords approaching down the rock walkway. I could almost hear her now, lecturing me on T. S. Eliot's objective correlative or the Neoclassical poets.

Shortly two faces appeared in the living room window, one male, the other female. Sour, scowling faces that appeared as surprised and disheartened to see me as I was to see them. The screen door opened and an old man hobbled over and gave the fender of my Toyota a friendly slap, as if it were a pony. "What can I do you for?" he asked. Stooped and stocky, he had a farmer's sun-parched face.

"I'm looking for Mrs. Von Kleinsmid," I said.

He closed his eyes in deep thought, his Budweiser belly distending his bleached overalls. "Nope," he said, reopening his eyes. "Can't seem to place the name. Can't seem to place it."

"She used to live—"

The old man's hand leaped from my fender as if it had suddenly caught fire. "I've always lived here!" he insisted.

"Always?"

"You callin' me a liar?"

"Let's just say that maybe you're mistaken. You see, I used to know someone who—"

"Like I said, I've always lived here."

"Always is an awfully long time."

"Well, since I been married then."

Okay. Two could play his little game. "Is that so? And when was that?"

"Forty-six years next September! September the 15th!"

"Forty-six years?"

His face puckered meanly. "Are you one of Lawson's men?"

"Who on Earth is Law—"

"Because if you are, you can just wriggle your little behind up on out of here. I told you people I don't—"

"What does he want, Ben?" the old woman shouted from inside. "Is he trying to buy us out?"

Ben whirled towards the window, then back towards me. "Are you making an offer? If you want to make an offer, then make an offer, by God! But don't come spying around here no more. I'll call the sheriff!"

I held up my palms—empty, innocent. "I don't think you need to call the sheriff."

"Ha!" he said and took a triumphant swipe at the air. "You don't want to lock horns with old Ben Bowman! No sirree!"

"Absolutely not, sir. And I'm not trying to buy your property. I'm not trying to sell you anything, either. I'm just looking for—"

"You big wheeler dealers from the city think you can just come in here and look and take as you please. Well, I've got news for you—"

"Tell him to go away, Ben!" the old woman yelled. "Tell him to go away!"

Ben waved her off. "Hold it down a minute, Bertha. I'll handle this. I'll handle it!"

"Look, mister," I said, opening the car door to get out and prove to this man, by virtue of my paint-stained sweat pants and faded maroon t-shirt, that I was anything but a big wheeler dealer from the city. But the instant my foot touched the ground, a German shepherd that had been playing possum by the porch darted across the yard, jaws open, fangs flashing. I pulled my foot back in and slammed the door.

"Blazer!" Ben hollered. "Get back there, Blazer!" The animal froze at attention, like an imitation Rin Tin Tin.

"Look, you've made your point," I said. "Now how do I get out of here? This driveway used to circle around the shed there, but it's been blocked off since I was last here. Of course, that was forty-seven years ago . . ."

"Now just hold on a minute, young fella. Just hold on. If you aren't one of Lawson's scum, then who the devil are you?"

"My name's Jon Reeves. I'm a . . ." But here I was stumped. What was I, really? "I teach," I said, to simplify matters.

"Ah! One of them college professors! A Ph.D. I'll bet!"

"Actually, I'm a—"

"I don't suppose I have to tell you what B.S. means, do I?"

"No, I don't suppose you do."

"Well, then, M.S. means 'More of the Same.' And Ph.D. means—"

I mouthed the words along with him: Piled on Higher and Deeper.

"Say! You're learning something over there! You're learning! Now, who's this lady you're looking for?"

"Von Kleinsmid. I don't know her first name."

"Von Kleinsmid. . . Von Kleinsmid. . . Bertha! Say, Bert! Do you know a Mrs. Von Kleinsmid?"

"Sara Von Kleinsmid? She's up at Extended Care."

"She works there?" I asked.

Ben hollered to Bertha. "Does she work there?"

Bertha hollered back. "Work there? She lives there!"

"No!"

CHAPTER 19

The first thing I noticed on entering was the smell. It was a putrid blend of urine, feces, deodorizers, antiseptics, disinfectants, and cafeteria food. I paused in the carpeted foyer, hoping an employee would see me and offer assistance, but the receptionist's desk was deserted. I noticed that the tips of the leaves on the potted Swedish ivy were brown and brittle, and the outdated flyers announcing stress workshops and 10K runs were yellowing on the bulletin board. A little red light was blinking on the phone like an unheeded distress signal.

To my right, through an open doorway, I could see into the dining area where an early supper was being served. The three long tables in the center were empty. Thirty to forty patients—men and women, a few young, mostly old—sat in wheelchairs spread singularly about the room. Three young women in white uniforms marched coolly from patient to patient like begrudging angels, cutting up their food and wiping the slobber from their sagging mouths. Eating in dour silence, the only sounds being the clinking of silverware and Burt Bacharach music on the loudspeakers, they were a depressing contrast to the plate-glass view of mountain meadows fringed with golden poppies and ponderosa pines.

As I edged towards the doorway my eyes met the glare of a hoary old man sitting off by himself in a wheelchair. He was clutching a knife and fork upright in either hand as if preparing to defend himself rather than to cut into his cube steak. Lean and wrinkled, with a gauze patch over one eye, he kept staring at me, his lips moving strangely, as if muttering a warning or a curse, convoluting the divine promise: as you are, I once was; as I am, you may become.

"Aaaarrrggghhhaaarrroooooh!"

I whirled around to fend off whoever or whatever had produced that hideous cry only to find myself face-to-face with an attractive young nurse. She was wearing a tight white outfit and blond hair in a bun. Here was the beauty, but where was the beast?

"Aaaarrrggghhhaaarrroooooh!"

Further down the hall, beyond the double swinging doors. I was safe for the moment.

"May I help you?" the nurse asked.

I relaxed a bit. "I hope so. I'm looking for—"

"Aaaarrrggghhhaaarrroooooh!" from the other side.

The nurse smiled knowingly. "First visit?" She seemed to relish my discomfort, something I found annoyingly ironic under the circumstances. I struck back. "I thought this sort of thing had been eradicated since *One Flew Over the Cuckoo's Nest.*"

She took offense. "I beg your pardon, but the clients here are physically disabled due to age, disease, accident . . . "

She sounded like an answering machine. I noted she had used the term *client* instead of patient. "I'm looking for Sara Von Kleinsmid," I said.

Her pretty face clouded. "Wait right here," she said and disappeared through the swinging doors, her tight round buttocks swiveling like a hula dancer's. When she returned, she planted her five-and-a-half-foot frame resolutely in front of me and drew a deep breath. "May I ask your relationship to the client?"

"I'm a friend."

"Is that all?"

"Isn't that enough?" She glanced back over her shoulder, as if expecting reinforcements. "Look, is something wrong? I mean, is there some kind of rule against visitors—"

"No! Oh, heavens no! It's just that . . ."

"Yes?"

"Well, Mrs. Von Kleinsmid—it's been . . ." She drew another deep breath. "Room 113-A—straight down the hall, then take a left a right and a left."

"Thanks."

"Enjoy your visit."

"Aaaarrrggghhhaaarrroooooh!"

"Right."

Undaunted, I stepped boldly through the double doors. What I saw on the other side made the dining room look like Disney World. Cluttering the hallway were bodies, decrepit, wasted figures, standing or in wheelchairs, looking like the unfortunate survivors of a holocaust. I saw giant heads on pencil necks, skeletons hooked to tubes and catheters. There were breastless, half-bald women; a man on a table missing from the waist down. A nurse mopped up someone's private mess; a man in the showers wailed. And accompanying everything, the septic stench of death.

There were three men in room 113-A—no Mrs. Von K. The oldest, parked a few feet from the doorway in a wheelchair, was shouting enthusiastically to the other two who ignored him. Heavy-set and bare-chested, he looked like a crusty old sea captain cheering on a mute crew. Another man, ascetically thin, slouched in his wheelchair, his slippered feet dangling. His eyes were blank and lifeless. The third fellow, by far the youngest, was sitting up in bed having a stare-down with the TV. His oily hair looked finger-combed, reddish-gray whiskers fringed his swollen jowls, and—wait! Didn't I know that face? Padded with fat now, the beach boy tan long gone from lack of sun—still, wasn't that the face of Steve Valkenburg, the all-conference placekicker and backstroker who had dived from the Rock? His sleek young body had angled through the air with a falcon's grace for two seconds of infallible beauty before striking one boulder head on, crumbling, rebounding off the other, then like a rag doll plunging into the broil of white water.

His girlfriend, Cindy Haines, the shapely, smiling homecoming queen, had pledged her loyalty, devotion, eternal love no matter what. By the end of the school year she was engaged to Jeremy Williams, the student body president. Steve's classmates graduated, married, had babies, car payments, problems of their own. Life went on.

And so had Steve Valkenburg. Chump-faced, obese, mesmerized by a pair of country bumpkins yodeling on the boob tube, he had not been totally forgotten. There was evidence of family or friends, a stack of letters beside a box of See's Candies on the nightstand. Behind him, on the wall, was a computer-printed portrait of him and a construction paper Valentine with a crayoned inscription: YOU TURN ME ON!

Steve didn't know me. I was a lowly freshman when he was re-writing the Ponderosa High record books. Still, I was tempted to shout out, "Steve! Valkenburg! Number 84!" thinking this might awaken him from his living sleep. But it was obvious that long ago he had spit on Coach Ramirez's pet proverb: A winner never quits, a quitter never wins.

Continuing down the hall, past more loitering patients, I sensed my legs growing soft and weak, wavering like Jell-O. I poked my head inside 114-A, 115-A, 116-A. In 117-A I found what appeared to be a scarecrow sitting up in bed, head bowed, legs crossed lotus-style, a paisley shawl over its shoulders. I was about to walk on when suddenly it came to life. "You were the first!" she cried, holding up one finger, a wrinkled earthworm. Her face was a relief map of Rocky Mountains and Grand Canyons.

"Me?"

"No, the Man on the Moon!" She slapped her skinny thigh and cackled. "Of course you! Are you moving in or checking out?"

Did I look like a candidate to move in? And since when was it possible to check out? "Neither," I said.

"You're new here, aren't you?"

"A visitor."

She looked down sadly. "Me too." She flashed me a carious smile. "Oh, you'll get used to it! You'll learn! You have to, you know. That's the only way. Otherwise . . ." She motioned towards the other three beds—empty; metal skeletons with springs. "That one there," she said, pointing to the far corner, "they came and wheeled her out just yesterday. The nurses, they call this room The Morgue." She cackled again, her eyes like little pits in the rough terrain of her face. "I'm not supposed to know that, you know. This is where they put all the ones that's on their way out. Most of them I don't hardly even get to know their names. They just wheel 'em in and wheel 'em out."

She gazed at her hands, cupped in her lap, her eyes sad, tired, closing. Unlike Steve Valkenburg's, her little niche bore no tokens of endearment from family or friends. Her eyes opened slowly, painfully. "How long you suppose I been here?"

"You mean here, in this building?"

"No no! Here at The Morgue!"

"Six months," I said, estimating high.

She clapped her hands triumphantly. "Five years!" she cackled. "Five years!" Eyeing me sternly, "Do you believe in God?"

"God?"

"Yes, God!"

"Yes . . . yes, I do."

"That's good, that's good," she said. "Because I don't! No, I sure don't! So I just keep hangin' on. I don't know what's over there on the other side—Jesus all in white or just nothing at all. Not even darkness. Nothing. Dust maybe. Deserts of human dust. More than ten thousand Saharas full. Don't kid yourself with maybe otherwise. You ever hear dust talk? You ever seen dust make a baby? Dust don't even grow. You, you're a young fellow. Don't waste all that. I was born on the boat coming over from Sweden. Growing up I had plenty of chances, but I was a good girl. I married a good man and give him good children—nine in all. Still had plenty of chances, but I was a good wife. I waited too long. Erik, he died and the kids was gone and my chances too. Growing old is an ugly thing if you let it be. I just wished I hadn't been such a good girl all the time."

She looked at me with doleful eyes begging for understanding. I touched her forearm—tough and leathery; a piece of beef jerky. She looked up, started to say something, stopped. "Oh, here I've gone and talked your ear off again! Don't mind me, don't mind me! I'm just an old lady in dirty skirts! Ha! Ha! Tee hee hee!"

"It's been nice visiting with you," I said.

"Nice visiting with me! Ha! Ha! Tee hee hee!"

In the next room I found Mrs. Von Kleinsmid. She was no longer the dowdy hausfrau with the child-like fascination for the mundane in life. What had happened to her? She couldn't have been over sixty-five, yet she looked like the Ancient of Days on a hunger strike. Her chocolate chip eyes had turned to mud; her surviving threads of hair were white and frizzled, with pink patches shining through. Pale and gaunt, she slouched in a wheelchair in the middle of the room, naked from the waist down, her broomstick legs spread wide open, a white towel draped across her lap. Her mouth sagged sadly. She stared at the linoleum floor, silent, oblivious to me and her two roommates, lying quietly in their beds. Her face was a desert—no joy, no pain, no sorrow. Nothing.

"Mrs. Von Kleinsmid?" I whispered. "Mrs. Von Kleinsmid?" Her eyes remained on the floor.

The smell was exceptionally potent at that end of the building and my stomach was giving in. Fighting off the nausea, I looked through the venetians at the poppied meadow, then back at Mrs. Von K. I was mistaken. Her face was not a desert. It appeared forsaken by something far worse than old age or disease or whatever it was that brought human beings to this place. Her vacant eyes seemed to cry out with a sense of injustice and betrayal: Why me? Or, better: Why her and not *me*? Or was my time shortly coming? Or Natalie's, Val's, Rachel's, J. J.'s . . . I recalled the wizened old prophet in the dining hall: as you are, I once was; as I am, you will become.

"Mrs. Von Kleinsmid!" I shouted, and the old woman in the bed next to hers raised her head and cast me shark eyes. "Mrs. Von Kleinsmid!" I whispered. Slowly her eyes rose from the floor. Her face looked even worse in direct light—a giant wad of white crepe paper. But as she searched my face, her pale eyebrows jerked upwards in comprehension. She held out her bony hand, her fingers hanging like popsicle sticks. I clasped it gently, for fear of damaging the brittle bones. Her mouth opened wide, revealing three teeth. She smiled clownishly, her head bobbing as if fastened to a spring, nodding, mumbling. What? What did she say? Jon? Jonathan? Yes, that's right! That's me!

Her eyes glowed with optimism. I shared her delight until she lunged for me like a drowning person and wailed, "Nancy! Nancy!" Gripping my forearm, she tried to rise from her wheelchair and embrace the man she was mistaking for her daughter. The towel slipped from her lap. I looked away. "Yes," I whispered, patting her fragile little hand, helping her back down. "Nancy . . . Nancy." She was still smiling when I turned and stepped into the hall.

"Are you all right?" It was the pretty, blond nurse, wheeling a cart down the hall.

"Fine," I said, waiting for the dizziness to pass.

"You don't look fine." She disappeared a moment and returned with a glass of water. "Here. Drink it slowly." As I drained the glass, slivers of ice rushed haywire throughout my body. "I said slowly!"

I handed her the empty glass. "Thanks. Now how do I get her the hell out of here?"

"Mrs. Von Kleinsmid?"

"Yes." I felt angry now, or guilty, something. "Where are her kids? There used to be an army of them—all over the front yard—mud pies, whiffle balls, stick arrows—"

"Kids?"

I was speaking in tongues. "Never mind. How do I get her out?"

The nurse looked appalled. "You can't!"

"You bet I can!"

"There are forms, signatures, clearances."

"You get the forms, I'll get the signatures!" She started to rebut but I cut her off.

She whirled around indignantly and shuffled down the hall. She returned with a stack of papers as fat as the L.A. phone directory. "Here," she said, with a touch of sarcasm that made me all the more determined to follow through. But then she whispered an aside that helped me realize that she, too, was subject to the powers that be: "Good luck!"

Emboldened I scrolled the stack of papers like a club and marched forward, determined to clobber anyone or anything that tried to keep me from my purpose. Nearing the first red EXIT arrow, I could already feel my resolve withering. Even if I did succeed in getting Mrs. Von K. released, what was I going to *do* with her? I could just see myself breezing through the front door: Excuse me, Natalie, but guess who's coming to dinner? And breakfast, lunch, and everything after? A very magnanimous gesture, Jon, but who, realistically, is going to spoon-feed this woman and empty her bedpan all day? While you're out grant-writing, selling, bishopricking?

Excuse me, Natalie, but would you mind taking care of the mother of my would-have-been lover; the woman who came within a phone call of being my wife? Please? Then I had a notion, or a vision: this is where you end up if you are left all alone in the world, without friends or companions; if you abandon them or they you.

CHAPTER 20

Sundown. A special time in Ponderosa, when the western skies catch fire as pine shadows stretch and merge into pools of semi-night. There is a sense of winding down: traffic dying, shops closing, old couples rocking on the porch. Rainbirds awaken herbal odors as young lovers walk the canyon rim. Deeper down, the many voices of the River sing their eternal song.

At sundown my father, when he was not out delivering babies, would sit on our redwood deck, his arms folded over his Buddha belly, watching the scorched sky cool, oblivious to the half-eaten lamb chop on his plate and the swimming pool he never used. I would sit nearby, hands cupped reverently, as if in church, honoring the silence that was broken only by the intermittent sucking and slurping of the long-tailed, plastic canister that surveilled the surface of the pool. "Oscar!" my father would shout suddenly. "Hel-loooo, Oscar!" as if expecting the plastic creature to reply. (Sometimes it would, with a soft, intimate "sluuurp!") Back then it had not mattered if he spoke to me. It had been sufficient to sit in his presence. Sometimes he would invent little tales to tease my curiosity.

"Poppa, where do stars come from?"

"There's a great big giant that sits on the edge of the world, and every afternoon when the sun goes down, he starts screwing light bulbs into the sky. That's why the stars don't all appear at once, you know, because he's screwing in the bulbs one at a time. When the sun comes up, or a little before, that's when he starts taking the light bulbs out, one by one by one by one . . ."

"Why doesn't he just use a switch?"

"It's broken. One day the giant got in a fight with his twin brother and the switch broke."

"Why doesn't he fix it?"

"He can't. His brother's the electrician."

"Why doesn't his brother fix it?"

"He got so mad that he left and never came back." And so on.

On cold winter mornings I gazed in wonder at the steam rising from the heated surface of the pool. "Ghosts," my father would say. Or another time: "Indians. They live down at the bottom and build campfires to keep warm."

When I was a boy I believed almost every word he said, especially about God and religion. It was a wonderful world of mystery and magic, and I believed in it as I believed in the sun and the moon and the absolute immortality of my mother and father: they would never die.

About once a year, when he got particularly ambitious, my father cleaned out the garage—old tools and bicycle parts, cardboard boxes of memorabilia, rusted fifty-pound cans of wheat, a big green trunk labeled "U.S. Army/Capt. Reeves." Hidden way in the back, in a long wooden box nailed shut like a coffin, were the "ancient swords," battle relics scavenged in Germany during the war. There were barbed lances, swashbuckler swords, cavalry sabers, curved daggers of Ottoman design, and my personal favorite, a broadsword he nicknamed "Skull-biter."

If he was in a good mood, and not too anxious to finish, he would let me pry off the wooden lid and scrub the rust from each piece, polishing them up bright. Sometimes, when he was preoccupied sorting through boxes, I would sneak into the backyard with "Skull-biter" and slay a dragon or two, or maybe go one-against-one hundred à la Cyrano de Bergerac. Once, when I was nine or ten, I slipped back into the garage to return "Skull-biter" and caught my father standing at attention in full military dress, his back towards me, the big green army trunk propped open. It surprised me because he never talked about the war, even when I pestered him for details. A short little whip was cocked under his armpit, and in one deft movement he tapped it crisply to the brim of his helmet while clicking the heels of his shiny black boots: "General Patton, sir!" he said. "My regiment would be honored to lead the assault on Calais!"

I watched a few moments longer before retreating quietly back out into the sunlight, feeling strange and trembly all at once, as if my little boy's world had suddenly blossomed and crumbled simultaneously.

I wonder about my own son, Jon Jr., through what distorted lens does he interpret me? One night as I was tucking him into bed, he asked, "Dad, what does extraordinary mean?"

"Oh, out of the ordinary. Unusual."

"Like different?"

"Yeah, different."

He gave the matter serious thought, then proclaimed, "You're extraordinary!"

I smiled. Laughed. A little. "Why do you say that?"

"Because you're different—from the other dads."

I didn't know whether to apologize or thank him. I have no idea what aspect of my behavior prompted this observation. I get up, go to work, to church, eat, sleep. I do not run marathons or hunt caribou with bow and arrow or do anything else out of the ordinary. I am, in my eyes, frighteningly plain. Which makes me wonder: will the hearts of the children yearn for their fathers in spite of ourselves? Young men with their bold visions, old men with their broken dreams.

My father died alone in an apartment in Palo Alto owing six months' back rent. After my mother died he had gradually soaked his assets into a Nevada gold mining scheme. On my twenty-ninth birthday, he had called to tell me I could still get into medical school. He had connections. "It's never too late, Jon." I told him thanks but no thanks. By then we were exchanging Christmas cards and an occasional letter. He always sent the children a $5 bill on their birthdays. I never met his wife, Trudy, but my father always spoke fondly of her. They took dancing classes together and were going to go on a mission when she retired from teaching. Then Death played the joker and plucked her one night in her sleep. Payback time: I didn't find out until two months later when my father followed her back home.

At the funeral I peered into his coffin for one last look. His body looked tiny and shriveled, like a piece of dried fruit, or leftovers from Extended Care. I tried to picture him young and virile, dodging sniper fire while dragging a wounded buddy into a foxhole, or catapulting me off his shoulders into our swimming pool. But the prevailing image was of a middle-aged man squeezed inside an army uniform saluting General Patton in the cool darkness of our garage.

That night, clearing out his apartment, in the upper drawer of his rolltop desk I found deeds to not one but three bogus gold mines. Also, a cigar box stuffed with military memorabilia. I dipped my hand into the box and let the ribbons and medals drip through my fingers like precious coins. I took the box, the black alligator bag with his doctoring things, and his army dress uniform, which I keep in my garage. Every year during spring cleaning, Natalie tries to hide the box amidst the pile of junk we drag out to the sidewalk for the garbage truck to haul away. Somehow I always manage to rescue it just in the nick of time. Natalie shakes her head. "Reason not the need!" I say, reverting to the King Lear cop-out.

My father died a stranger fifty miles from my arms.

I could barely see the far edge of the redwood deck from the empty corner lot where I parked across from my old home. There was the hedge of manzanita bushes that had shielded our backyard from Mrs. Shaw's scrutinizing eyes, and the gravel driveway where I had tried in vain to commit euthanasia on a crippled cat, and the double-garage, shut like a tight-lipped mouth, where my father had stored the precious secrets of his life. Red roses had replaced my mother's marigolds, and the slate-gray exterior had been repainted a nauseating puke green. Otherwise, my home looked much as I had maintained it in my mind.

I hadn't come here to take any leisurely strolls down Memory Lane. I didn't have time: the sun was almost gone, and I had one more stop to make. Still, haste didn't prevent my vision from bending around the corner long enough to glimpse the slender woman in the pastel kimono sitting at her easel on the redwood deck, smiling to herself as a little boy's voice called from the frontyard: "Mom! Mommy, come look! Hur-reee!" I switched on the ignition and headed back towards the highway.

Whoever had bought my old home enjoyed far less privacy and forest than my family, for most of the surrounding pines had been leveled in favor of a little city of tract homes. Standing in front of one of them was a man about my age wearing cut-off jeans, thongs, and a fishnet tank-top. He was fairly tall and freckled, with a head of receding, sand-colored hair, a modest beer gut, stocky white calves, and the beefy arms, neck, and shoulders of a construction worker. He was watering his front lawn. The moment I saw him I pulled over and got out of my car.

"Keith?"

He stared at me hard, showing neither shock nor surprise. I pointed to his hose: "Don't shoot! I'm unarmed."

He didn't smile, although he did keep the hose aimed at the grass and not at me. I climbed the little embankment on which he was standing and offered my hand. "Long time no see!"

He gripped it suspiciously. "Jay," he said, addressing me by my old nickname, minus the "Big."

His voice sounded much deeper, much more serious than I had remembered, and much less cheerful; a lethargic baritone. The temperature must have been in the upper nineties, but there was an iciness in the air. We were two strangers in an elevator nervously trying to avoid one another's eyes. The only sound between us was the thick spray of his hose splattering on the lawn.

"So what have you been up to?" I asked awkwardly.

He shrugged. "Workin', payin' bills, goin' broke—same as everybody else."

I looked around for signs of posterity: a tricycle, a red wagon, a foot-tall model of an X-man robot half-buried in a sandbox. What now? Ask about his wife, his kids, the stock market report? His glare could have melted Superman. "Oh hell, Keith! It's been twenty-two years!"

He answered with a snort. He was still carrying that baggage; had been all these years.

"It was a game, Keith. I dropped a lousy pass."

"It wasn't a lousy pass!"

"Okay, so lousy Jonathan dropped Keith's perfect pass so Keith didn't get a scholarship. But I didn't do it on purpose. And I certainly didn't do it to hurt you or make you look bad. If anything, it made *me* look like stone-fingers. And the fair catch—Keith, you had thirty yards of clear running room. But that punt must have hovered in the lights a good six seconds. I swear, it was like someone was up there holding it, counting down, waiting."

Keith snorted again. "Fate, hunh?"

"Fate, bad luck . . . It hovered."

Keith's lumpy, freckled face hardened like putty. The frog-lipped grin I had known growing up had matured into a very adult and cynical sneer. "You always had a one-way ticket out of here."

"What?"

"It never meant a thing to you. The team, the town." His voice gained volume and velocity. "Not even our friendship. I was your stupid sidekick–"

"Keith!"

"Let me finish! I was your dumb sucker sidekick, trailing you around like a puppy dog, wagging my tail, running buck-naked around the track, spiking the punch at the prom, hanging moon's out the bus–anything to make you laugh and pat my head and, 'Goo', boy, Keithy! Goo' dog–'"

"That's not true! Butch Cassidy and the Sundance Kid. Remember? We were a team! I pulled just as many bone-headed stunts as you ever did."

"No, Jay! No! You were always Mr. Cool. The blond giant in his red Corvette. Anything you did automatically had class. Me? I was goofy, the town clown idiot. No one took me seriously until I started throwing touchdown passes."

"So we're back to the Corning game. I dropped a pass and ruined your life."

"Two passes–"

"Aha!"

"It wasn't the stupid Corning game. Will you get that through your thick skull? It's what happened after."

"The mile relay?"

"Mile relay! Are you playing dumb on purpose? I'm talking about Von Kleinsmid! Once you started up with her, you were in another world. I didn't even *know* you anymore. No one did."

"Hold it. Who didn't know who? You're the one who suddenly grew his hair to his butt and started dropping acid after every meal."

"Right! Me and all the rest!" Keith's thumb tightened over the nozzle, forcing out a stiff, hard stream. I noticed a tattoo on his left bicep: a coiled cobra with DA NANG in script underneath. "We all knew we were doomed to this place, but at least we were aware of what was going on. While we were holding war moratoriums and sit-down strikes and flipping off Dick Nixon, you were still strutting around with your All-American smile, la-de-da, hip-hip-hooray for Mr. Touchdown. Blind as hell."

Keith shot the hose across the yard, drenching the tricycle and the red wagon. His next utterance was odd, a cross between a bark and a chuckle. "Did you know I was stoned out of my mind when I ran that leg of the mile relay? Sheez! I could have given you ten yards on old Harry if I could've run a straight line. But those fieldlights looked like *Close Encounters, Star Wars,* and *Invasion of the Body Snatchers* all in one. Flying graham crackers, you know."

"I could have used the ten yards," I said.

Keith's mouth twisted in disgust. "Did you hear what I said?"

"I was kidding, Keith."

"Kidding?"

Half-kidding. "Yes. Is that a sin?"

"Sin. That's sounds pretty heavy. But if you put it that way, yes, one of them."

"You mean there are more?"

"Is the Pope Catholic?"

I smiled, recognizing a line from one of our old routines. "Do chickens have lips?"

A smile sneaked across Keith's face as he fished for his next line. "Do bears squat in the woods?" His smile vanished. "You probably don't even remember," he said, "but once—it was near the end of our senior year—I was sitting on the steps by the locker room, stoned as usual. Track season was over and I was totally out of sports by then. You and Ramirez came walking out together. You two were real buddy-buddy then. I think you were helping him with spring football practice or something. Anyway, Ramirez takes one look at me and says, 'Bernhard! You look like hell!' Okay, Ramirez is my ex-coach. From him I can take it. But then you looked at me and said something like, 'Yeah, and he smells like it too!' I don't know, maybe you think this all sounds stupid and trivial, but it hurt like hell at the time. After all we'd been through together, you may as well have hit me in the face. That was your first out-and-out show of hostility."

"Hostility!"

"There I was, long hair, holey jeans, sandals, looking like a reject from Haight-Ashbury, and my best friend spits on me!"

Now I was getting upset. "Look, Keith—first, I don't remember that ever happening, and, second, if it did, I'm sure it was just a joke. I didn't mean anything—"

"A joke?"

"Keith, I'm sorry if what I said—"

"It did!"

"Okay, and I'm sorry. I really am. But it was a joke, Keith. Stupid, yes. But exactly the kind of thing you would have laughed at three months earlier. That spring you guys may have gained your causes but you lost your sense of humor."

"You think Vietnam was something to laugh about?"

"No, I don't. But you're forgetting something."

"Forgetting what? That you had all your convenient little outs? Sure, you could afford to laugh! Uncle Sam wasn't calling football stars or Mormon missionaries to Saigon!"

"That's not the issue, Keith."

"Oh? Then what is the issue?"

"I don't know. Maybe that's what I'm trying to find out, why you're still so pissed off at me."

Keith threw down the hose and stomped towards his front door. I followed behind, trying to reason with his backside. "Keith? Do you remember Mr. Hudson? U.S. History our junior year? He had a hearing aid. Remember how you'd sit up front answering his questions without saying the words, just mouthing them so no one else could hear, while old Hudson read your lips, nodding and smiling, 'Good, Mr. Bernhard! Very good!' And do you remember the day he finally caught on? He leaned on his little wooden podium and tried to laugh it off, but there were tears, Keith."

"Come on, Jay! That was different! Teachers were fair game. It was open season."

"Maybe. But how about Kenny Lujan?"

Keith turned off the faucet and wiped his wet hands on his fishnet shirt. "Lujan?"

"The squirrelly little nerd who went out for track our senior year. You put tampons in his locker. It was pretty funny until we got word from the hospital. He went nuts, remember?"

"Lujan was always on the edge."

"Maybe so, but we pushed him over."

Keith licked his frog lips, absent the cynical sneer. "We were pretty bad, weren't we?"

"A joke, Keith. A bad joke."

Keith turned his head aside, slowly, almost painfully, as if twisting his neck against its will. Dark blues were bleeding into the pink horizon. The pines darkened to a roller coaster silhouette. Keith crossed his muscular arms, looked down, then up again. "All of us," he said. "Even the Watusi, the way she was always putting you down. How come you never fought back? She was an easy target, with that Gestapo face and her Twiggy body."

"Nancy was a beautiful woman."

Keith threw back his head and guffawed, as in old times.

"She was," I insisted.

"Jay, that's one thing I'll never understand—why you took up with her when you could have had any chick on campus."

"I didn't take up with her—not like that."

"Oh no? Lunch hour, between classes, after school . . . You two were the talk of the town."

"That's ridiculous! We never even held hands!"

"Everyone thought it was a put-on. She was your easy lay."

"Good gads! I'd forgotten what a little Peyton Place this is!"

"It didn't stop after you left, either. People said she was carrying your kid."

"I don't believe it! I don't believe this town!"

"You might if you'd stuck around. Nancy really changed after you left—or maybe we just never knew her that well. In high school she was nothing but an overgrown bookworm. But after she married Bill Watson—well, you remember what a party fiend Buffalo Bill was."

"He must have dragged her along caveman style. That big dumb oaf! He didn't deserve Nancy. He—"

"Easy, Jay. Relax."

"Those parties must have been murder on her. She hated crowds."

"Are you kidding? She *was* the party!"

"Nancy?"

"Yes, the Watusi Woman! One night she stood up and started telling jokes—political jokes, Watergate jokes. Pregnant jokes were her favorite.

'Hello, friends! Meet the broomstick that swallowed the volleyball!' She was a natural stand-up, like Joan Rivers without the Jewish accent. Was she always like that—funny, I mean?"

"Yes and no," I said.

"She was wild. She did totally crazy things. One night she challenged Bill to a drinking contest."

"Nancy never drank."

"That's what she said, too. 'I'll try anything once!' she yelled, and drank Bill under the table."

"Amazing!"

"Sheez, yeah. Things were cool for awhile. I guess Buffalo Bill knew damn well who the father of Nancy's kid was, and no one was telling him any different—not to his face, anyway. But one night at a party Dave Newcomb got plastered and started mouthing off about you—Jon Reeves the football flunky, Jon Reeves the choke, Jon Reeves the loser."

"*The* Dave Newcomb? The little twerp who played trombone in the school band? That two-faced traitor—every time we got behind he'd play 'The Death March.'"

"That's Dave. When Nancy heard, she stopped her monologue and gave him hell."

"What did she say?"

"Sheez, Reeves, what do you think I am, a tape recorder? That was twenty years ago. I can't remember exactly."

"Well, the gist—give me the gist, anyway."

"Something about winners and losers and how the peons are always trying to drag other people down to their level. We were the peons, I guess, and you were the gifted Superhero."

"Nancy said that?"

"She didn't make any friends that night. Everyone thought you two still had something going. Buffalo Billy didn't look too happy. We laughed it off—Jonathan Reeves, Superman! At the next party Newcomb wore a t-shirt with a big red S."

"That schmuck!"

"That's what Nancy called him, too. So what did happen at BYU? I heard something about your knee."

"That was part of it."

There was sincerity in Keith's voice when he said, "Bummer, Jay."

"Not really. It spared me having to quit. I had surgery, could have worked it back into shape, but by then the desire was gone."

"We all had big plans. Especially you. But that doesn't explain why you dumped us."

"I didn't dump you. I didn't dump anyone."

"Then how come you never wrote or called or anything? Everyone thought you went away to college and got a fat head. Suddenly you were too high and mighty to talk to the dumb folks back home."

"Super Reeves, right?"

"You never wrote, never called."

"I didn't have anything to say. I was embarrassed, I guess—flunking out in football."

"You wanted your legend to live on."

"Legend." I had to smile. "Fear. I think a lot of people wanted me to fail. Jon Reeves the doctor's kid gets what he deserves."

"Us? Nah! We were pulling for you, Jay!"

"And if I failed?"

Keith shrugged. "Then you failed. We pulled for each other, remember?"

"I remember."

"So how come you didn't stay in touch?

"I don't know. Maybe I wanted you to remember me the way I was."

"Or you wanted to remember the way we were. The games, the double-dates, the River . . ." There was a note of sadness in his voice, as if he had just summarized the true highlights of his life. For a moment, I had a painful glimpse of his existence since high school: a slow torture of day-to-day endurance anesthetized by the periodic pleasures of booze, babies, and 4th of July fireworks. "Your dad moved," he offered. "That was part of it."

"Part."

"How's he doing by the way?"

"He died eleven years ago."

"I'm sorry."

"So was I." Keith eyed me curiously. "I guess you heard we had a little falling out."

"Really? You were always so close."

"Well, we were and we weren't." I told him about the gold mines and the day I caught my father play-acting in his army uniform in the garage.

Keith was silent and somber. "That's sad," he said. "I guess. Is it sad?"

"I don't know."

"I'm sorry, Jay. Your mother, too." Keith looked around uneasily. "I went to her funeral, you know. You were in Mexico, I guess. They were great people."

"How about your parents? Are they . . . ?"

"Oh, yeah. Still in Ponderosa. Although they moved into a condo last fall. I guess you're married?"

"Eighteen years."

"Sheez! Any kids?"

"Two girls and a little boy. The oldest'll be a senior next year."

"A senior!"

"Hey, you know you're over-the-hill when your kid starts wearing a training bra."

Keith beamed. "I've got three too—two boys and a girl. They're inside. Saturday baths."

"Then I take it you're married?" I winked to show I was joking.

"Second time's a charm. Remember Brenda Taylor?"

"Tootsie Taylor? The girl with the . . ." My hands made a large circular motion in the vicinity of my chest.

"That Smothered Nogales—that's the one!"

I smiled. "So where are you working?"

"The lumber mill. Going on thirteen years." He shrugged. "It's a living. Before that I was with P.G.& E., like everybody and their dog, and before that . . ." He tapped the Da Nang cobra on his bicep. "Fourteen months."

"Did you see much action?"

"Jay, the fact that I'm here today proves I didn't see much action. It was bad." I could tell he didn't want to go into detail. It was his turn to change the subject. "What are you up to these days? Aren't you a brain surgeon or something?"

"A brain surgeon? I'm a teacher," I said, still trying to keep things simple. I was surprised to see his eyes widen in the same kid-like manner they used to whenever he threw an erratic pass and I somehow plucked it out of nowhere.

"A teacher!"

"High school English."

"Hey, that's great. I mean, I'll bet you can really make a difference."

It was strange, hearing that from Keith. I suppose in certain ways I would always see him as the class clown sloshing around naked in the Jacuzzi.

The screen door flew open and out raced a little freckle-faced boy with the tousled, reddish-brown hair of his father twenty years ago. "Dad!" he shouted, holding up a robot version of a tyrannosaurus rex. "Tyrano's laser's broken," he said.

Keith popped a lid on the dinosaur's belly and fiddled with the batteries. A steady, machine-like growl issued from its insides. Then an amber light began blinking in each eye as its dagger-toothed mouth opened wide. The boy smiled. "Thanks, Dad!" Keith rubbed his head. "There you go, buddy!" The boy raced jubilantly back to the trailer.

"Cute kid," I said, feeling another pang for my children.

"Yeah," Keith mused, gazing sentimentally at the empty space his son had occupied only seconds before. Then he unwittingly smacked me with a two-by-four: "The rest is all bullshit, Jay."

There was a brief silence, then Keith clapped his hands. "Hey! Remember that game against Orland? Fourth and goal from our ten and fifty seconds on the clock? We ran that flea-flicker—a five-yard out to you, then you pitched back to me coming around end. . . ."

"You looked like Walter Payton sprinting down the sideline. Crazy Legs Bernhard! Ramirez loved it! We all loved it!"

Keith was grinning a half-moon. "The next night we doubled with Debbie Hobbs and Lillie Jacobs. First we went to that B-flick at the Starlite."

"*Viva Max*! With Jon Astin and a host of nobodies."

"That's right! Afterwards we went to the River. Good times, Jay!"

"Great times."

"The best," he whispered, and I felt sorry for him again. He quickly perked up, though. "Hey, Jay, have you still got it? The magic hands?"

I knew what was coming, but I honestly did not have time right now.

This was not the final stop I had anticipated. "If you've got the arm, I've got the hands!"

He dashed into his trailer, returning seconds later with a football and a pair of sneakers, shouting over his shoulder: "Be back in an hour . . . No, just an old friend." We squeezed into my Toyota.

"You remember the way?" he asked.

"With my eyes closed."

CHAPTER 21

You would have thought it was the Super Bowl the way he stood there, knees slightly bent, back bowed, gripping the ball sideways under the imaginary center's rump, his snake eyes scanning the invisible defenders as he barked out the snap-count: "Set! Ready! Hike!"

As he dropped back into the pocket, I fired out of my three-point stance and sprinted across the upper playing field, rather self-consciously at first: I did not want to be mistaken for some pathetic ex-jock trying to score touchdowns two decades after the gun.

I ran tentatively. Although jogging had kept my legs and heart fit generally, I hadn't summoned my sprinting muscles into action for years. Planting my left foot to cut right, I wondered if my bum knee would bend and buckle. The leg held, but the instant I turned Keith's pass was waiting for me, a brown bullet whose point speared me in the solar plexus, knocking the wind out of me. I bobbled the ball yet managed to hang on, pivoting quickly upfield before Keith could see me wincing. I sucked in several deep breaths, then, clearing my face, trotted back to the line of scrimmage and tossed him the ball underhand. "Nice throw!"

"Nice hands!"

I shrugged. "It's been awhile."

Next he called a quick slant across the middle, a pattern I had always hated because it sent me on a suicide mission into the province of a nail-eating middle linebacker waiting to stonewall me as soon as my hands touched the ball. Keith used to call this play whenever I got too cocky or as revenge for some personal offense I may have committed. Was he making a statement? No matter. In the absence of evil defenders, I was able to run the pattern without fear.

Keith led me a foot too far, but my fingers became prehensile, reaching and wrapping around the ball like eight sticky tongues. I tucked the ball away and began streaking downfield. Impressed, Keith played color commentator: "Reeves with the flypaper hands makes a miracle grab at the fifty . . . still on his feet at the forty-five, the forty, . . ." Like old times.

Then something strange and wonderful happened. I can't say if it was the feel of the ball in the crook of my arm, the smell of the cool grass rising into the hot air, my dormant legs in fast motion, Keith's hysterical commentary, or the cumulative effect of refeeling those old sensations from back when life was defined in simple tangibles—a cold plunge on a scorching day, a doorstep kiss, marshmallows browning over a campfire, the roar of the crowd as your cleats chewed up the turf, an old Beatles song. Whatever the cause, all of my prior apprehensions disappeared. Like a crazy Don Quixote in invisible shoulder pads, I began zig-zagging downfield, stiff-arming and side-stepping would-be tacklers as Keith ranted and raved: "Reeves throws a head fake, spins down to the eight, another head fake, to the five . . . touchdown Pumas!"

Suddenly I felt nothing but cool relief, as if I had finally shaken off the hairshirt of heat I had been wearing for the past two days. Loose, light, free—the least breeze could have swooped me up and carried me over the pines, the peaks, into the twilight tiers of red, blue, and gold. Crossing the imaginary goal line, I did a little entrechat and spiked the ball into the grass. "Bernhard to Reeves for six!" I cried, trotting back to Keith.

"Okay," he said, straightening his face, all business. "A stop-and-go, on set!" As I lined up for the next play, he looked at me and grinned, and in that grin I read his thoughts: Don't kid yourself. You need this just as much as I do. And he was right. "Jay!" he yelled, still smiling. "What would your principal say if he saw you right now? Or your students?"

"Hey, if they want to watch, let 'em pay like everyone else!"

Keith threw his head back and howled. "No freebies!" Then, serious again: "Set!"

I charged ten yards downfield and did a quick button-hook and threw up an arm: "Keith!" He pumped, then dropped back another two yards as I spun around and sprinted downfield. Looking back over my shoulder, I watched the ball leave Keith's hand—a guided missile growing bigger and bigger as it arched through the air, spiraling flawlessly but way overthrown. I turned on my after-burners, dived into the end zone, and somehow managed to tip the ball with one outstretched hand, just high enough to grab it with the other as I went skidding sideways across the grass.

Keith went nuts in the press box. "Did you see that catch, folks? Did you see it? Jon Reeves coming out of nowhere on a broomstick to make the grab! And they say miracles don't happen! I love it! The fans love it! The world loves it! Just listen to that crowd!"

"You've been practicing," I said, panting as I jogged back to the line of scrimmage. "Right on the money."

"Look who's talking!"

"Some things never go. The hair, yes."

Keith waved me off. "Still Mr. Cool! Hey, I play in a flag football league in the fall—helps me stay in shape. You ought to come up and watch. I think you'd recognize a few faces."

"I'll try and do that," I said. My spirit was certainly willing, but my schedule—something would have to be done about my insane schedule! "I'll do that," I corrected.

Keith's face suddenly spasmed. "Jay, you okay?" he asked, pointing.

I checked my forearms, which had been scraped raw by the dry, brittle grass around the endzone. The stinging sensation was just beginning to seep through, almost in unison with the delayed appearance of blood. I also became aware of a mild throbbing in my left leg, ribs, and hip point, my whole left side in fact, where I had slammed onto the turf. All of this would ache savagely when the numbness wore off, but that was tomorrow stuff. For the time being, I honestly did not care.

"Let's go down to the Poppa field!" I said.

Keith agreed. Tossing the ball back and forth, we crossed the upper, then the lower practice fields, talking about old times. Keith was several yards ahead of me, recalling the night we sabotaged the senior class graduation, when he reached the top of the stadium bleachers built into the hill. He lobbed me the ball and started down the steps, then froze.

"Keith?" I trotted over to him and looked down. Submerged in shadow, the oval of grass appeared more like a cold, dark lake, Mother Grendel's lair, than a football field. Although the western sky was still burning on the lower edges, the pines had turned to pitch, as had the bowl around the stadium. It was like peering into a crater.

The field was empty except for a few Coke cups and the accumulated litter of the two-day league track finals. But the old spirits were stirring. There was the pole vault pit, the scene of my Preference Dance fiasco, and the singed scar of the twenty yard stripe where I had yelled for Keith to field a punt. There was the straightaway where in the last meet, and a thousand sleepless nights after, I had hit the wall and died. And there, galloping around the final turn, was the forty-year-old similitude of Harry the Unpassable! In spikes, shorts, and t-shirt, he was clipping through the darkness like a big hungry animal chasing down its evening meal.

"Sonuvabitch!" Keith whispered. "He's a damn machine. Look at him go! Damn!" We watched Harry's ghost blow past the finish line and walk around the infield several minutes, catching his breath, before gathering up his sweats and heading up the other side of the bleachers.

Keith and I did not say a word. Side by side we descended the concrete steps and lined up on the track. The cinders had been replaced by sea-blue tartan with the lanes numbered in bright red. Keith offered me the inside. I declined.

"On three?" I nodded.

He counted. "One . . . Two . . ." and we were off! First thought: Twenty-yard pass patterns are one thing, but a quarter-mile dead-out sprint? Tomorrow Natalie will be pushing me in a wheelchair. Second thought: So what? For me it was like an out-of-body experience, as if my spirit were on the sidelines watching all the rest. I was flying down the track, my legs flashing through the darkness, my feet never touching the ground. Exactly as in my dreams. There was no pain, no burning, no feeling except for the evening breeze like a warm compress on my face.

By the time I hit the first turn Keith was already out of the picture, struggling to keep pace. I could hear him several yards back grunting and snorting like a big, determined animal. I wasn't taking anything for granted, however. Keith had always been a gut runner with a demon kick. The race was far from over.

Or was it? As I started down the backstretch, the clapping of Keith's sneakers grew fainter and fainter until they disappeared altogether. I looked up at the fieldlights, dead gray moons. The real thing appeared above the pines, like a big eavesdropping eye or a full-faced smile. The joke's on whom?

I was so shot full of adrenaline I didn't feel a thing until halfway down the stretch when the cords in my thighs began to slowly twist and tighten. Stay loose. Stay loose now.

I noticed that my fists were clenched, a bad sign, so I made a little circle with each thumb and forefinger, a trick Coach Ramirez had taught me to delay the onset of rigor mortis in my upper limbs. My legs were still moving freely, though, and my lungs were sucking in the clean mountain air like bottled oxygen. Keith, on the other hand, was coughing and wheezing like a chain-smoking asthmatic.

Leaning into the final curve, I closed my eyes and prepared myself for the inevitable collision. But instead of a wall of water shoving me back, this time I was bursting through a paper hoop with my name and number on it. I glanced up into the stands: Harry's silhouette, like a Hitchcock vignette. I aimed a quickfinger at him. He nodded back.

If he waited for the finish, this is what he saw: the leader gradually losing steam as the other, twisting and straining like a runner underwater, slowly gained ground and with a desperate lunge nipped the leader at the finish. Then the two falling exhausted into one another's arms, breaking apart almost on contact, not violently but delicately and self-consciously, like two strangers who had bumped by accident. And if a microphone were thrust in the winner's face . . .

"Sonuvabitch, Jay! Get me a beer! Oh, my aching legs. I'll never walk again. I'll never do anything again. Nice race, Jay. Helluva race! I never thought in a million years . . . I never . . . Harry the Horse! It was a pisser, Big Jay! The whole thing was one big pisser! Hey, let's go to my place and have a beer—I mean a drink. You still a Dr. Pepper man? Sonuvabitch, Jay!"

CHAPTER 22

It was dark when I drove up, but the porchlight cast a pale ring around two boys squaring off in the dirt yard while a third stood by, spindly arms folded, watching. One boy was big and round, with adobe-colored skin, black bangs, and a hefty belly that made his matchstick legs look comical. Despite his size, he clearly did not want to fight, and my sympathy initially leaned towards him.

His freckled opponent had been getting the worst of it so far, for his t-shirt and blue jeans were smothered with red dust. He looked about eleven or twelve, much too young to be Nancy's child, although he shared her tall, willowy features and baby blond hair.

And her obstinacy. Dusting himself off, he lowered his head and charged with flailing arms. The weird lighting made his movements appear swift and choppy. He hissed and growled as his fists wildly searched their target.

If the plump boy appeared tentative in the face, in execution he was a cool matador. He calmly sidestepped the windmilling arms and delivered two deft punches—one to the chest, another to the face—that left the blonde sprawling in the dirt.

A baritone called down from the porch: "Get up, Marty! And next time he lets his guard down like that, let him have it—pow! pow!"

It was Buffalo Bill Watson, observing from on high. Instead of the gruff stubble that had peppered his cheeks, he now wore a stiff Viking beard, and his prickly crew-cut had grown out to a combable length. He still looked as square and solid as a refrigerator, although a little less intimidating now, in Farmer John overalls. "Come on, Marty!" he hollered.

Marty glanced at Bill, sniffled, and wiped away the tears, leaving a four-fingered stain on his cheek.

"It hurt him!" the third boy yelled. He was a short, skinny kid with a whiny voice. Call him Pee Wee. "And he's bigger!"

"I know he's bigger," Bill drawled. "And I know it hurts. But he's gotta learn now or he'll get the snot beat out of him later." Bill smiled as Marty charged again. When he nicked the plump boy's chin, Bill shook his fist. "That's it! That's it! When he drops his hands like that, let him have it in the jaw—pow! pow!"

The plump boy glared at Bill, who was still smiling. The cool matador became a raging bull, charging Marty and punishing him with a barrage of hard, uncompromising blows: face-chest-back-chest-face. Each hit made a sickening thud.

"Come on, Marty!" Bill hollered. "Get up!"

But Marty lay there, sobbing, rubbing his shoulder. Dirt had stuck to the streams of tears, creating a war paint effect. The victor held his fists under his chin and gave them a little jerk. More?

Pee Wee appealed to Bill. "Why don't *you* fight him? You're bigger than *he* is!" Bill ignored Pee Wee.

Marty attacked again, and again the boy decked him with a double-punch. "I hate your guts!" Marty screamed. "I hate everything about you!"

Buffalo Bill ordered Marty to get up, get up and fight, and Marty probably would have if just then the screen door hadn't flown open. A woman in her early thirties stepped onto the porch. She was wearing skin-tight blue jeans and a red-checkered shirt with the tail knotted just below her breasts, exposing a thrifty midriff. Dark haired and dark eyed, she reminded me of those curvaceous hillbilly beauties in Li'l Abner. Except she wasn't smiling. She was clutching a long wooden spoon like a billy club.

"What are they doing?" she snapped.

Bill's massive head rolled reluctantly sideways. "Well, now, hon, they've got a little something going here and—"

"And you're going to stand there and let them fight!" She flicked the spoon at the two boys as if casting an evil spell on them. Bill exhaled deeply, wearily, suppressing something. His hands squeezed the porch railing, his forearms swelling like firehoses.

"Well, I'm going for a nice long walk!" the woman said. The screen door slammed shut; her feet pounded across the floor. The back door screeched—another slam!

Marty was on his feet again, sniffling as he brushed the dust and bits of weeds from his t-shirt and blue jeans. As he prepared himself for another assault, Bill called down: "Okay, Marty, that's enough. Tell your friends to go on home and you come inside and get cleaned up. Tomorrow's a school day, you know."

"I want to kill him!" Marty screamed. "I want to kill him!"

"Yeah, well, you can kill him some other time. Come on in and take a shower."

"I want to kill him!" Marty broke for the plump boy.

"Marty!"

Marty braked, then ambled towards the house, casting vindictive looks at the other boy. "You all right, Ezekiel?" Bill asked. The boy nodded. "Okay, why don't you two go on home." Ezekiel and Pee Wee disappeared down the dirt road, taking turns kicking a stone along the way. The fat full moon was floating up into the night sky like a big white bubble.

My timing was perfectly miserable, I realized, but it wasn't as if I could come back tomorrow or next week. Besides, no time was good for the task at hand. I climbed the four wooden steps to the front door and gave it two soft raps, which were answered by a gruff, "Come in!" Humbly, I poked my head inside.

"What's up?" Bill asked, amiably enough. He was standing in the kitchen forcing a butcher knife through a huge horn of cheese. The blade hit the cutting board with a loud clack!

I introduced myself. "I knew you in high school," I said.

Bill's bulky forehead furrowed. "Nope," he said, popping a thick wedge of cheese into his mouth and chewing it once or twice before gulping it down. "Sorry." He reached into a bag of tortilla chips and scattered several handfuls on a metal tray. He covered the chips with strips of cheese, delicately, almost reverently, as if covering up the dead.

"I think you and I need to talk," I said.

"Why? You selling something?"

"No."

"Buying something? Are you with Lawson?" I shook my head. Lawson again!

He carefully swaddled the horn of cheese in Saranwrap, put it in the refrigerator, and took out a six-pack of Coors. He freed a can from the plastic holder, punched in the press-lid, and took a long swallow. "Look," he said, running his forearm across his bushy upper lip, "you caught me at a real bad time. Some other time, all right?" I didn't have another time. He took another swig.

"I knew Nancy," I said. "I was her friend."

He set the can of beer on the counter, gently. He studied my face several moments, trying to gauge my sincerity and intentions. "Let's go," he said, grabbing the can of beer and the remainder of the six-pack.

I followed him into the living room, which was dark save a faint diffusion of light from the kitchen area. The room stank of cigarettes and the accumulated heat of the day. A tiny table fan chattered incessantly while impotently stirring up the dead, dry air. Down the hall the shower was running—Marty washing his wounds. I envied him the cool, streaming water but not his bumps and bruises, although I could empathize: the ecstasy of my recent football and track heroics had worn off, and now my body felt like a punching bag. Every little move I made sent spears of pain into long forgotten muscles and ligaments. Yesterday's sunburn compounded my misery. I felt as if I'd been skinned alive.

Bill settled his buffalo body in a vinyl easy-chair near the TV. I sat kitty-corner to him, on an old velour sofa. He clicked on a table lamp which lit up the face of a noble-nosed Indian chief on the wall. I noted some western artifacts—a branding iron, deer antlers mounted on a plaque, a little bronze bronco rider. Fanned across the scratched up coffee table were copies of *Field and Stream* and *The National Enquirer*. I saw no sprouts or whole-wheat flour, no books, no James Joyce, no Jane Austin; nothing even remotely reminiscent of Nancy.

Bill punched another press lid and offered me a beer.

"No thanks."

He nodded and raised the can to his lips, sipping slowly this time. "Nancy . . ." he whispered, and the sound of her name was like a weary echo from the bottom of a well. "That was a long time ago," he said. "A real long time ago. I was pretty young then, pretty inexperienced. Pretty stupid, too. I didn't understand women. I still don't, if you know what I mean. They're too damn complicated. They won't just accept things for what they are. They always want to know *why*—always questioning everything, always picking your brain till you just want to scream sometimes. Do you follow what I'm saying?" I nodded.

Reflecting, he smiled. They had met at a dance, he said. She was sitting all alone in the corner, humming to herself. He felt sorry for her—she'd looked so sad. She said she was recuperating. From what? She shrugged: Just recuperating. He asked her to dance. One thing led to another.

"We had some good times! Some real fine times! Our honeymoon at Tahoe. Skiing! You know she'd never even been skiing before? I couldn't believe some of the things she'd never done. It was fine. We skied, we sat around the lodge, we ate steak and played the slots all night. Five days. She said it was the happiest time of her life. We got home. I went back to work at the garage. She took care of the house. She threw up in the morning and laughed about it when I came home at night. She seemed fine, except for a little morning sickness. But the doctor said that was all normal.

"Three months it was like that. Smooth sailing. Then one day she quit eating. Just stopped. She started picking at her food like a Chinaman. I was shoveling down meat and potatoes while she nibbled rabbit food. Carrots, lettuce, celery. Once in awhile she'd have a little yogurt or something. At first I thought it was maybe the morning sickness, but after the fourth month she'd pretty much gotten over that. I was worried. Carrying the baby and all, she couldn't afford to go around starving herself like that. She was skinny enough to begin with—all arms, legs, and that great big stomach. I used to call her 'Spider'—just teasing, you know. Anyway, I think you can see where I was at."

I was trying to listen, not judge. I of all people was in no position to judge. I motioned for him to go on.

"At first I tried to reason with her. 'You're eating for two, you know?' 'If you don't feed the baby, the baby feeds you!' She'd laugh and make a joke out of it. One day I got fed up. I started yelling at her: 'Why can't you just eat like everybody else? Why do you have to be so damn different all the time?'"

"Different? In what way?"

"Everything! Everything she ever did was different from everybody else! She dressed different, she talked different, she cooked and ate different! She even made love different, if you know what I mean." I had to smile. Creative, innovative Nancy!

"She wouldn't talk to the other women, you know. Hell, what could she talk to them about? She never watched the soaps—she hardly ever watched TV at all! She didn't read the magazines. She didn't like sports. In her spare time she was always reading or writing. And the books she read—they weren't the kind normal people read. They were—well, you know what I mean."

"You said she stopped eating and you got fed up?"

"Fed up to here!" Bill posted his hand above his head. "I started yelling at her, but she didn't answer. She never answered when I yelled at her. She'd just sit there and say in this real calm voice, 'You don't have to scream, darling. I can hear you.' Darling. She always called me that whenever she was b.s.-ing around. But she'd never give a straight answer. It bugged the hell out of me."

Civil disobedience, passive resistance. Thoreau and Ghandi. If Bill had only realized . . .

"Anyway, one morning she set a plate of bacon and eggs in front of me and then sat down and began nibbling on a piece of Melba toast. I blew up. 'Look,' I said, 'I'm sick and tired of all this! I'm not going to live like this anymore. Tonight I'm bringing home a couple of steaks and we're going to sit down together and eat 'em, like man and wife. Understand?'

"But she just sat there staring at the table, smiling, nibbling her toast. 'Understand?' I said. Nothing. Just sat there like a deaf mute, smiling, nibbling. So I reached across the table and slapped the cracker out of her hand. I didn't hit her. I never really got physical with her, if you know what I mean. That's the nearest I ever got, slapping that cracker out of her hand. But I said it again—yelled it. '*Understand?*' I was all but begging her to say yes so I wouldn't have to do that anymore, but she just got up and walked away. 'Go to hell!' I yelled. 'Go to hell!' And then I took off for the Silver Buckle.

"When I got home it was way past midnight and she was crying. We made up. Went to Tahoe that weekend. It was like a second honeymoon, except no snow. After that, smooth sailing again. The baby came. We made the usual adjustments—new parents, you know. But overall things were pretty good. I was working, Nancy was taking care of the baby. We weren't rich, but we were happy. Then one day my neighbor Bob calls me at work and says they found Nancy down at the River. 'So what's new? She goes there all the time?' Bob got real quiet. 'You'd better come down,' he says. 'Right away.'"

Bill took another sip of beer and set the can on the end table. Dots of sweat blistered his forehead, which he wiped clear with his forearm. He looked haggard and depleted, as if he had aged during the course of his story. But I also noticed a glint of relief in his eyes, catharsis.

For the first time I actually felt some sympathy for Bill Watson. No, he hadn't understood Nancy, but who had, really? Yes, he had lost patience with her, but Nancy could have brought Job to a roiling boil. Bill seemed less a cause than an accessory, and perhaps an innocent one. He hadn't known any better; I had.

"What about the baby?" I asked.

"Oh, he was fine. He was only about a month old, so he never really knew."

"Marty?" I was fishing.

Bill chuckled. "Noooo. Bill, Junior. He's at Camp Pendleton."

"Marines?"

"You bet! First Infantry Division." Bill opened another can of Coors. "Sure you don't want one?"

"No, thanks."

Bill took a long swig and smacked his lips. The alcohol was beginning to take effect, reddening his eyes, slurring his speech. He held the beer can up to the light, contemplating it. The shower had stopped.

"I'm not exactly a total stranger, you know. I played ball with you in high school."

"Yeah?"

"You don't remember me, but I remember you. Who could forget Buffalo Bill Watson, the greatest linebacker in the history of Ponderosa High?"

"Come off it! You're b.s.-ing me!"

"You were the best! I only wish Ramirez had played you more at fullback. I still say we'd have beat Orland for the championship if he'd let you run that fourth-and-goal."

"Ah, come on!"

"Seriously! I watched you run in practice. Old Earthquake Watson!"

Bill blushed. "Earthquake Watson," he muttered, grinning.

I had more questions. "What about Nancy's mother?"

"Sara?" Bill shook his head pathetically. "That's a sad case. She's up at Extended Care."

"And her kids? There used to be legions of them all over her yard."

Bill nodded painfully. "Yeah. Those were foster kids, you know. The county would leave 'em for a few months and then bring a new bunch and take the others away. Unfit parents, problem homes. Sara was real good with them, and the state paid a couple hundred a head I think. That was her only source of income for a long time."

Temporaries. No permanent connection. That helped a little. "What about Nancy? Was she . . . ?"

"No. She was Sara's. That's why she went off the deep end when she lost her. She tried to carry on, but she wasn't playing with a full deck after that. I did my best to help. Took her places, shopping, to the mall. It was only a matter of time, though. You could tell." Bill looked at me oddly, as if I had just now materialized in the room. "Why the hell am I telling you all this?"

Marty appeared in the hallway, a towel wrapped around his skinny little waist. "I'm done, Dad," he said.

"Okay, go and get dressed for bed."

"Can I get something to eat first?"

"Sure. There's nachos on the counter. Stick 'em in the broiler."

Marty's sullen face brightened. "Nachos!"

The room seemed to be growing hotter. I asked Bill for a drink, and he returned with a glass of ice water. It needled down my throat like Novocaine. "You say Nancy did some writing?"

"*Some*? That's about all she ever did is write!"

"What did she write about?" I was leaning forward now, growing bolder, pushy.

Bill looked surprised. "Stuff," he said.

"*Stuff*? What kind of stuff?" Suddenly I wanted to slap him on the side of the head. My tone had changed to that of a father scolding his negligent son.

He got defensive. "I don't know. Just stuff."

"Stories? Poems? Letters to the editor?"

"Yeah. Stories. Poems. She was writing a book, I think."

"You *think*?" I was angry now, seeing through the glass a little more clearly.

"Yes. A book. She was writing a book."

"What about? Was it about her?"

Bill shifted uneasily in his padded chair. "I don't know. She never let me read it. I asked, but she always said no—not till she was all finished."

I was on my feet. "Have you still got the manuscript?"

"Sure. It's locked up in her trunk, with her other things."

"Can I see it?"

He was about to say yes, just to get me off his back, I think, but balked. "Why the hell should I?"

"I was her friend, Bill. Maybe the only real friend she had in this town . . . before she met you."

I was going to say more, but he waved me off. "Oh, hell, why not? I've already gone and told you everything else, whoever the hell you are."

"Reeves," I said. "Jon."

CHAPTER 23

The trunk was actually an old cedar chest Bill had stored in his unfinished basement, amidst old suitcases, lawn chairs, bicycle parts, Mason jars, and other miscellaneous junk. If the sudden plunge in temperature was refreshing underground, the ambience was not. It was a dark, dank, tomb. The cinderblock walls smelled like leafmold. Spiders had been busy weaving their threadbare nets wherever wooden beams met. A bald bulb dropped a pallid sphere of light in the middle of the room, leaving the corners in darkness.

It took some serious digging, but in time Bill located the chest. Its metal edges scraped the concrete floor as he dragged it out from under the heap. He dropped to one knee, almost reverently, and propped open the lid, releasing the camphorous smell of mothballs. He carefully removed a white lace dress sealed in clear plastic, pondering it briefly before moving aside. "There," he said, and, pressing the dress to his chest, he left me alone. Then I, too, dropped to one knee.

One half of the trunk was stuffed with neatly folded clothing. I recognized Nancy's thick wool skirts and simple cotton blouses. The other half contained spiral notebooks—the journals she had once carried with her everywhere but had never permitted me to read. Did I have the right to read them now? I flipped through the one on top. Each page was filled with brief notes made in a near illegible scribble.

* Every autumn tree a burning bush, every parcel of grass starched and hallowed.

* Not with meanness anymore, but the ethereal lightness of a ballerina we go: touching, feeling, discovering each new dark and secret part.

* All big cities look like cemeteries from on high.

* Remember this end of the day loneliness: this is what Death is like, for the one left behind. Or divorce.

None of the entries was dated, and, judging by the varying colors of ink, no more than a phrase or two was ever recorded at one time. Apparently she had dashed them off in haste—between breast-feedings, late at night, waiting in line at the county health clinic or the laundromat. I should have searched each notebook thoroughly, but I had to get right to the heart of the matter: her book.

It was not a novel but a series of interrelated short stories in the tradition of Sherwood Anderson. Each page was neatly typed, numbered, and arranged in sequence in a black, three-ring binder. As I had suspected, the stories dealt with the relationship between Derek Scott, the All-American golden boy, and the obese but brilliant Sarah Gates. I recognized several stories from earlier drafts. Here were the polished versions and then some.

I did not read the first story, "Third Time's Not Hardly a Charm." The image of Sara fumbling in the lunch line while trying to catch Derek's eye, ultimately fleeing home to the drudgery of dirty dishes and screaming brothers and sisters was still very fresh in my mind.

I also recalled "Fourth Time Maybe," a hilarious reenactment of my initial encounter with Nancy, when she browbeat me in the student tutoring room, and "Close But No Cigar," which detailed our first "date"—the Double-Eagle for sandwiches followed by a visit to the River. I skipped "Love, Ponderosa Style" and "Nothing Risked, Nothing Gained," and continued digging until I found what I think I had been looking for all along: a story titled "The Dance."

Upstairs, in the kitchen, Bill was opening and closing drawers, tinkering with pots, pans, silverware. The succulent smells of nacho cheese and chicken noodle soup were drifting down, teasing my appetite. Suddenly it seemed like days since I had eaten. Bill's voice grew jolly. "Hey, Marty boy! Rub-a-dub-dub, let's get the grub!" In the dim light of the basement, I read quickly, earnestly, yet with the apprehension of a criminal awaiting a long-delayed verdict.

This story was not fiction but pure autobiography. Sara had asked Derek to the Ladies' Choice Dance. Derek drove, since she had no car, but she chose Burton's Mesa for dinner, her treat. The conversation was strained; the dance, loud, sweaty, awkward. They went for a walk down to the football field and ended up on the big foam cushion by the pole vault pit. A sickle moon grinned in the starry night; crickets, the echo of the band, the faucet slowly overflowing. She didn't miss a thing. Derek slipped his arm around her waist.

Then he did what she had been hoping for all these months, weeks, days. All her life, as she knew it. He leaned over and kissed her, an experienced kiss, but brand new to her. Magic.

She waited just a moment, perhaps to collect her thoughts, debate her next move—to do or not to? But in that moment's hesitation she was all over him. Slobbering, her head jerking wildly as her tongue lapped the margins of his lips. She heaved him back onto the foam pad and began pressing her pillowy chest against his, trying desperately, pathetically, to assert herself in that way. Her hands raced up and down his sides as if they were very cold and she were trying to warm them. He looked frightened, disgusted, appalled. He tried to pry himself free, gently at first, but she persisted more fervently, pressing closer, rubbing faster, harder, whispering with a choked passion that to him must have seemed all too real and frightening and flattering but mostly frightening: "I love you, Derek! I've always loved you from the very start. Oh, God, come to me, Derek! Please! Come to me now!"

There was a war poem by Wilfred Owen describing the victim of a mustard gas attack: "the whites of his eyes writhing in his face, his hanging face, like a devil's sick of sin . . ." This was her expression when Derek put his hand over her face and shoved her away. It was a look she would see every morning thereafter, whenever she peered into her mirror, whenever she heard her own silly stupid voice, whenever the crickets sang their sultry song. It was a tortured look of hate—not for him; never for him—but herself. Knowing his utter contempt . . .

No! Wrong, Nancy. Wrong. Fear, yes. Intimidation, frustration, embarrassment, apprehension, even anger at times. But never contempt. Ever. I read on:

Why had he pushed her away? He acted badly but spontaneously, and he knew it. He felt guilty, responsible, and instantly tried to make amends. He blamed his religion. Yes, yes, he'd love to make love to her, but he couldn't because he was Mormon, and—well, Mormon's don't do that. They can't do that. They're not allowed.

She didn't answer. She didn't anything. One thought kept racing through her mind. If it had been Thunder Thighs, the lovely Annette P., offering herself on that foam pad, he would never have pushed her away. If it had been someone else, anyone else. God and religion notwithstanding. Anyone but her.

The chapter ended there. No word as to whether Sara went home and drowned her grief in ice cream, or began contemplating a more permanent solution. I closed the black binder somberly. Over the years I had relived that scene so many times I thought I had at last become anesthetized to it, yet now I found myself hurting anew, hurting for her. Speculating. Little split-second decisions that chart your course for eternity. Suppose I had obliged, or succumbed, or whatever, and she had gotten pregnant. Would we have married, had children—and what kind of life together and for how long? Given her agnosticism, could that union possibly have survived? Without compromising ourselves to the point of mutual destruction? Natalie would be out of the picture. And Val, Rachel, J. J. My precious family. And whose picture would they be in? Don't even think it. You can't. Mustn't. What am I without them? Forty-one years old and what? Would I be a real writer now or a service station attendant at the local EXXON? Reliving my past via flag football games?

Other angles. I put my oldest daughter in Nancy's place and felt nothing but disdain for the callow young man who shoved her away. Next fragile Rachel took her turn on the foam mattress, and I despised that young man even more. But wait. Shouldn't I love him as well? At least respect him, for what he did? Motive was the key. Suppose it had been Annette Plikta? I gave my little boy J. J. ten years and put him in my shoes. What would I have him do differently? Like father like son? What would I tell him after the fact? When all of the old arguments resurfaced?

"Yes, Elder, but it wasn't your fault. Should you have sacrificed your chastity? Committed the second greatest sin?"

"To avoid the even greater one of murder?"

"Elder! You did not murder that girl!"

"That's not the point! None of this titivating over guilt and sin is the point. The result was the point. Nancy was the point. I was the point. We were the point. Damn my stupid chastity. Damn my fake chaste soul!"

I reopened the black binder and read on, searching for answers, clues, redemption. There were no more neatly typed stories, just notes scribbled out in longhand.

Something was growing inside of her and she had to get rid of it. Otherwise it would keep growing bigger and bigger until she finally burst and that would ruin everything.

So she went to his father the doctor although he didn't know her from Eve, no way could he possibly have. But when she told him, he looked angry although he didn't say anything. He walked over to the door, yanked it open fiercely, and said, "Good day." She was desperate so she pleaded with him. He pointed the way out. "But you're a doctor!" she appealed. "I need your help! You have to—"

He glared at her icily. "Where in the Hippocratic Oath does it say anything about murder?"

And she left crying again.

My father? This was pure fiction—it had to be. Nancy's imagination gone wild. Yet I could see my father coldly stiffing her: on principle he had refused that service to anyone. For the next few minutes I stood in the cool, moldy air of the basement trying to think of absolutely nothing, trying, once and for all, to let go. Noises interfered. A baseball game upstairs. The fans roared several hundred miles away and Bill cheered with them. I could hear crickets chanting in the heat.

I searched for more clues. More fragments. Scraps for intended tales. Evidence.

It was five o'clock and she was feeling the jitters again. She put her ear to the door and listened. Yes! Asleep! At last!

She rushed into the kitchen, sat down at the table, and fed a sheet of paper into the typewriter. At first it was like transitional labor, every word a fierce contraction she had to force out, live through. But soon her thoughts were flowing freely, like a river. She could feel her blood rushing to the rhythm of her fingers dancing across the keys. Yes! Yes! Suddenly she stopped. Listened. Oh God! No!

It started as an innocent little gurgling that quickly rose to a full-bellied cry—his greedy evil selfish little cry! She tore the paper from the roller, wadded it into a ball, and hurled it across the room. Dammit all! What was the use? What was the—No. Stop it. You stop it right there now. And she grabbed herself by the wrist to make sure this time. She reminded herself to stay calm, it was only writing, after all. Only. Not the fate of nations, not the birth and death of souls, not the future of a child which was as great—no, far greater than any book. Yes! Absolutely yes!

She glanced at the clock, hopefully. Any moment now he would come home, come home, please pretty please. And his big comforting arm would wrap around her and she could forget for a little while. But the other would come back, always back and burning, the little unborn babies in her, because every time she even thought a little bit at all, she thought of them; and any time she sat down to birth them, thinking this was her time, their time, finally at last hers and their sacred little piece of time, an hour was all she needed, half that even, but every time something, someone, some dumb human thing interrupted, crying, shouting, aborting the little others; selfish screaming human child. Yet it was the little face she attended to, dutifully, obediently answering the call of her sex, the fat dimpled face smiling so cutely up at her, reaching out helplessly to her, suddenly in her arms growing soft, calm, clutching her as if—yes! As if she were a god or savior or, yes, Mother.

And she was. And he was. And then her heart burned fresh but differently. For a short season. Until she thought of the other, and it all came back, the unborn babies, the wriggling little eggs. She felt them squirming deep inside her, like sand crabs burrowing their way out, so anxious to be freed with him always forever down in there eating them up by the handfuls, swallowing them whole. Hundreds, thousands, myriads. She snapped her eyes shut, pressed her ears. They were calling, crying, screaming, "Mother! Mother! Mommy!"

Another fragment on another sheet of paper:

She tried to explain to him this need, this gnawing hunger, to put down in words her thoughts, feelings, images—the little stuff of life that to his eyes seemed silly and trivial. She tried analogy. You know how you love football? Or hunting season? In the fall you get this look in your eyes, you get the bug, the hunger, and you have to go out in the woods and look for deer. And if you don't, if you can't for some reason, you get all cranky and feisty and feel totally trapped inside. You're in jail. Well, this is the same type of hunger, the same escape.

He didn't understand. "What's hunting got to do with writing?" His eyes were ice cubes. Desperately, she did the one thing she most despised: she begged; she cried; she threw herself all over him.

He said he didn't see the parallel but, okay, if it helps, he'd watch the kid for an hour after he got home. Well, after dinner, then, how's that? Just feed him up good. (She was nursing then.)

So she had an hour at night. But after a full day of diapering and feeding and cooking and cleaning and laundering, she had so little left, absolutely nothing of value to give.

So she left. For three whole days. He had the baby and a dozen bottles of frozen breast milk and whatever else his ingenuity could muster. Three days. But the guilt still gnawed at her insides. Every time she sat down to write, she heard the baby crying. Which baby? *Hers*—her baby. Every time she attended to her little ones she saw the other: she saw him at two, ten, sixteen. "Mommy, where are you? Where are you, Mom?" Now he could walk, talk, score touchdowns. Drive a car. A red Corvette. He could begrudge. "Mom? Mommy?" My baby mine.

So she came home, clutching her child preciously, precious precious child. Forgive mommy please forgive never ever again please forgive . . . This was enough, to be a mother, a mommy, I'll be the best ever mom. And that lasted almost a week. And then the gnawing returned, the hunger, the little eggs squirming and screaming in the void that would never be filled. Oh God! Oh God! she whispered. To you, me, anyone. Any ear.

I closed my eyes, pinched the bridge of my nose, and wondered where the standup comic was who had entertained Keith Bernhard and company at post-graduation beer parties? That was fake Nancy. No, she was never false. Protean Nancy. Nancy the actress, the put-on, the impostor. The Mistress of Evasion.

Postpartum blues? Her suffering cut much deeper than that. The artistic crazies took over. Her baby must have been two or three months old at the time. A light sleeper, like Val maybe: loud, demanding, colicky, a screamer. Constantly craving, grabbing, sucking. A nipple perpetually in her mouth. I remember lying on the floor beside Val's crib holding a pacifier in her mouth all night, after she had sucked Natalie dry and was still screaming. But they grow up, Nancy. It does pass, although it doesn't seem like it ever will at the time. Eventually they grow up. Like you said:

they walk, talk, score touchdowns, compose symphonies. Different headaches, different hassles. You did what you did. You had your reasons—you always had ample reasons. But if you could have just looked beyond the moment, maybe your demanding little boy was a kid prodigy, like my Val. Driving you nuts with his genius. Quid pro quo? The Lord taketh vengeance seven-fold! Whatever we give our parents we reap likewise.

Another possibility. Her early efforts, written in high school, had seemed banal and sophomoric. Her later work matured brilliantly, yet she was barely eighteen. Finding her true voice, climbing to a loftier height, had she dived against destiny? The symbolic act, the theatrics! Vintage Nancy. But unlike the river bats, she fatally miscued. An accident, Nancy! An accident!

I continued digging, searching for confirmation or forgiveness. Tucked deep inside the black pocket of the inside cover I found a sheet of paper folded into quarters. It was brittle as an autumn leaf, the edges crumbling on contact, little pieces fluttering to the concrete floor like flakes of yellowed snow. It was a poem.

THE DARK FOREST (for J.R.)

The dark forest awaits us: I'm hungry
to enter and eat.
The crisp bristles crackle
on touch. And suddenly (instantly!)
we are floating through new continents
where snow falls like midnight
covering the jungles with obsidian shine.
You too change colors
and countenance
(here where you can reach through the rooftop
pluck stars and suck them
like sugar berries.) The moon
is a hard candy ornament
waiting for Christmas to die.
It is the skull and the drum
above and below
and the macaws and skinny creatures

shrieking for gold.
The road is a river
eternally flowing, and
we are as slippery as eels.
Yet some tiger fear comes upon us!
Hurtling downward we burn.
Winter breaks out in a tropical sweat.
I reach, touch,
wondering why you are so dry.

It was dated April 1972. My first year at college. Shortly before her death. Perhaps moments before? Was this her farewell letter? I dug deeper into the chest. Clothing, books—dog-eared copies of *Leaves of Grass, A Portrait of the Artist*, Virginia Woolf, Jane Austin. At the very bottom I found the dialogues, hidden in an old file folder labeled TWENTY YEARS LATER. They were prophetic, condemning, reprimanding, mandatory. I stuffed them and the black binder under my t-shirt and trudged back up the stairs. Call it stealing. Call it borrowing. I don't care. I was not going to let her rot and die in that damp, dark, cinderblock tomb.

CHAPTER 24

—You threw that race, Derek.

—I did not.

—You threw it.

—Look who's talking about throwing things, Sarah.

—You quit. Just like you've quit everything else.

—I've got commitments, responsibilities—you know that.

—Name three.

—Wife, kids, job, church—shall I keep going?

—Of course! Your holy cop-outs! Your sacred time-killers: "I could write but first I have to do X, Y, and Z. If only I had time . . ." If if if! But but but! Where does it stop?

—It doesn't, Sarah. Remember what Willa Cather said? Art is the Grand Taskmaster. It doesn't just say, "Thou shalt have no other Gods before me." It says, "Thou shalt have no other Gods, period." Then how can a good Mormon be an artist? You put God and family first, but you have to approach art as number one, a crazy tightrope act. Like the last first, first last paradox. So you wind up being a mediocre Mormon or a mediocre artist. No one can serve two masters.

—Oh, Derek, will you stop acting so damn exclusive! You Mormons are really something else. You think your little conflicts are oh so different. You think you're so way over here and the rest of the world is way over there. You build a wall around yourselves and tell everyone else to dig to China.

—That's not true!

—It is! You're a proud, egocentric people. Well, I've got news for you: not all gentiles steal hubcaps and cheat on their wives. Shhh! Don't tell, but some non-Mormons love their kids, pay their bills, help their neighbors mow the lawn, and generally enjoy life. In contrast, Mormons are the most hassled people I know—especially the women!

—Aha! So this isn't an art thing—to write or not to write. It's religion! As always!

—It's both.

—No, Sarah. Proud, egocentric, exclusive—you've always had it out for us.

—Don't forget paranoid.

—Why does it bother you so much? Why of all the possible things in this crazy universe does that rankle you the most: Derek Scott is Mormon. Why, Sarah? Why can't you just let it be? I'm okay, you're okay. I'm Mormon, you're not.

—Because I hate your church!

—Why!

—It's ruined you. It's taken 200 pounds of brains and brawn and potential and transformed it into a cowering, mechanical idiot.

—Oh diddily doop poop! Talk about the Great White Lie!

—Fact, Derek! Fact! You know, it's not that you believe in your church so deeply. That I could respect; that I could maybe even understand. But you're just plain afraid not to. You can't let go. When you were a crazy blond kid you had spirit and bravado; you had spunk. And a dream. You were going to knock the world on its gluteus maximus. Instead you got knocked on yours and panicked. You thought you couldn't fly solo after all, so now you're grabbing for security.

—That's good, Sarah. Very good. Prometheus Unbound! Long live the anti-hero! But what good is someone if they're no benefit to anyone else?

—Art accepts human sacrifices, Derek. That's your friend Willa speaking. You flinched. Just like that time on the railroad tracks.

—The railroad tracks! That was the most stupid, inane, idiotic . .

—At the last instant you flinched.

—I wised up is what I did!

—You're hiding your light. That's a sin, Derek.

—My what?

—Your gift. You're afraid of your calling.

—You don't sacrifice your wife and kids and sanity to write silly stories destined for the trash.

—All the more hurrah for bowing to the church! Your children need guidance, they need standards, they need Family Home Evening or they'll end up dope addicts. And if you shirk your marital duties you'll be zapped, or end up a lone man in the Garden of Celestial Delights. Face it, Derek: you can't hack the solitude. You're paralyzed by the odds.

You still think, deep in the Mephistophoclean corners of your mind, you'd love to be a real writer, you want nothing more, you'd hang everything to make it happen—but you balk. Fear steps in; the little voice that keeps you forever on a leash: What if I strike out? What if I can't cut it? Then where am I? What have I got? A big fat royal nothing. Better cling to the bird in the hand.

—You're always so big on talk, always so quick to point the finger. The church, the church! But what's your alternative? Live like Sarah? When the fire gets too hot, throw yourself off a cliff?

—You're skirting the issue.

—No, you! You're the one who's always skirting! Why, Sarah? A husband, a kid . . . Don't tell me about quitting!

—And don't use me as your excuse anymore! Poor Derek, so much on his poor li'l ole conscience. No wonder he can't write. No wonder he's so miserable. No wonder he can't love, enjoy, suck the sweet juice of life! Poor Derek, suffering the sins of the world. See? More evidence! If you truly believed in your Christ, you would have washed all that rot away years ago.

—Then it was an accident!

—Two plus two equals five? Your logic, Derek, mystifies me.

—You really were trying to dive, but you didn't clear the rocks.

—Sorry. It's not that simple.

—Sarah! You're always criticizing me, but look at you! You're the most non-committal person I've ever met. Do you believe in God? Communism? Abortion? What *do* you believe in?

—It's all in my stories. Did you read them?

—Of course I did.

—Carefully?

—Yes! Yes! I read them and wept.

—Derek Scott, the Grim Weeper.

—What you did was foolish. It was cowardly. It was . . .

—Impulsive, irrational, adolescent.

—Yes!

—And don't forget hypocritical: me running out on my family like my father ran out on me.

—That too.

—And all these years you've had to live with that: the embryonic literary genius throwing her life away on a whim! Poor Derek! How you suffer!

—Not that again.

—Yes, that again! If it was intentional, you're off the hook, aren't you? Who am I to criticize what anyone else does with their life when I threw mine away? Well, I hate to disappoint you, but you ain't off.

—That's not the reason.

—Then fill me in. But you can't. You're floundering. You're tinking around, stinking around. Frankly I don't know what's holding you back. If I believed all you claim to believe, I'd be drooling to write about it.

—Maybe, but what makes you so sure the world is willing to read about it?

—You don't think people are tired of turning on the Seven O'Clock News and hearing the daily death count? This planet's got a giant bellyache screaming for relief. Think of the possibilities! All those beautiful concepts that have become fossilized by centuries of abuse and overuse that now exist only as provender for scheming preachers—why, you could breathe life into those words! You could give them flesh and blood, bones, bodies, souls. You could resurrect them. Don't you see? We're the real god-makers.

—We?

—Yes, we! So what's holding you back?

—In a word, talent.

—Oh, caca, Derek! Caca! The first time I read your scribble about losing to Harry the Horse I thought, "Hey, this kid's got something I ain't!"

—No.

—Yes!

—If that's true, you hid it well.

—I was jealous.

—That's a bit hard to swallow.

—Well, that's the skeptic in you. And the coward.

—Me? That's funny, Sarah. I'm the coward.

—Truth offends everyone. It spits you in the eye, doesn't it? It insults the proper and pompous and makes them look like the rest of us. We're all in the same boat.

—Sarah . . . I don't know what to say.

—I do. Save my babies, Derek.

—I can't.

—Can't can't can't! Derek, do something!

—Look, just get off my back, will you?

—I'll get off when you get on!

—All right. I'll slay a dragon!

—Slay two: one for me.

CHAPTER 25

Which dragons? This is what was going through my mind as my Toyota twisted around the tight mountain curves en route to my final destination. Night bugs committed suicide on my windshield as my headlights burrowed through steep pine tree corridors that seemed to turn back into themselves like a mad rat's maze leading me nowhere. I was within a few miles of the turnoff when I noticed red and blue lights flashing in my rear-view mirror. I checked my speedometer: a moderate thirty-five. What gives?

I slowed down, looking for a piece of straightaway to pull over. The officer was less particular about safety, giving me a quick shot from his siren. I instantly braked and edged onto the shoulder. My engine was gasping from the long haul up the hill and there was a spooky tapping under the hood, as if someone were trapped inside. Behind me, the patrolman's radio spit static into the night as his car purred like a big hungry cat ready to pounce. I listened for his approach: ominous black boots crunching pine needles and loose gravel.

"What's the problem, officer?"

He shined a flashlight across my face. "Good evening, sir." He was a young man with a look of polite authority—scrawny shoulders, wispy blond mustache, a high-pitched voice he was obviously trying to lower. "May I see your driver's license, please?"

I produced my California license, which he scrutinized under his flashlight. Circling his left wrist was one of those mini-macrame friendship bracelets so popular among my remedial English students. He was quite young.

"You're Jonathan Reeves?"

"I am."

"And you're the owner of this vehicle?"

"Yes."

"Mr. Reeves, I'm afraid there's been an emergency."

"An emer—"

"Mr. Reeves, you need to call this number—"

I snatched the slip of paper from his hand, but the digits were foreign to me. I looked up, confused. The young man's face appeared watery, as if it were slowly melting. The revolving lights splashed pink and blue across my vinyl dash. "What kind of emergency?" I asked.

"I don't know that, Mr. Reeves. I didn't take the call. All I know is I'm supposed to tell you to call that number. Are you all right?"

"Yes. Yes, I'm fine. There's . . . I think there's a gas station . . . a phone booth. Just down the highway."

The officer nodded. "You have a good evening, Mr. Reeves."

"Same to you, officer."

I waited for the crunch and crackle of his boots to fade, then drove to the Exxon station which was blacked out. There were no other buildings in sight, no homes, no light except for the moon which cast the woods in a giant web of criss-crossing shadows.

I fed a quarter into the little metal box and billed the call to my home phone. Waiting, I braced myself for the worst. Rachel. Another episode. Maybe *the* episode? I smacked my forehead with the heel of my hand. My little baby! My precious little girl! I leave home for two lousy days, and this! What timing! What perfectly exquisite messed up timing! But I'd had it coming. This was my punishment. For hubris. Ingratitude. Forever looking beyond the mark. Never being satisfied with what I had. For always smelling the dung heap instead of the rose garden. You you you, Jon Reeves!

The adrenal rush, coupled with the heat, ruptured my sweat glands. My face, chest, and armpits were dripping. To evade the sauna effect, I stepped outside the glass cubicle. Shortly a voice answered: "Santa Vista Hospital . . ."

"I need to speak with Natalie Reeves."

"Is she a patient?"

"No—I mean, I don't know. I'm not sure. I think Rachel Reeves. Natalie's her mother."

"One moment, please."

She put me on hold. Elevator music, hauntingly reminiscent of the oozing melodies that had tried to sedate me a few hours earlier at Extended Care. A minute later a voice interrupted.

"Natalie!"

"Not Natalie, Maternity. Can I help you?"

"Natalie Reeves, please."

"One moment, please."

More elevator music. More run-around. Then another voice, delicately female. "May I help you, sir?"

"I'm trying to get my wife–Natalie Reeves. It's an emergency."

"I'll connect you with the front desk."

"I was just at the front–"

BZZZZZZZZ . . .

". . . desk."

Once more around the mulberry bush. Then, softly, cautiously: "Jon?"

"Nat! How is she? Is she all right?"

There was an uneasy silence. "Oh, she's fine."

"Thank God!"

"They had to clean it out pretty good, though."

"Clean it out? Good gosh, what happened?"

"They gave me a D and C."

For a moment, I made a vague connection. "D and C?" I said, stupidly.

Then she gave me the slap in the face I so badly deserved. "I had a miscarriage, Jon. I lost my baby." There was absolute silence on both ends.

"Are you all right?" I asked.

"I'm fine. . . now. It was pretty bad there for awhile."

Her stomach cramps. Of course. What else could have brought her to the verge of tears on the phone yesterday? I'd been too wrapped up in my own little concerns to deduce the obvious–on both accounts: this must have been her early morning surprise. I waited; so did she.

"How are the kids?"

"They're at home. They're fine. Val's been great." Our absent-minded genius. But she always came through in a pinch.

"I'm sorry, Natalie."

This time there was a short silence followed by a sigh that seemed almost frivolous. Then she laughed. "No you're not!"

"What's that supposed to mean?"

"You didn't even know I was pregnant."

"Of course, I knew!" This was a lie. I was guilty and, hence, defensive in my guilt.

Her voice grew soft, almost inaudible. "You didn't want another baby."

"I wanted one whenever you did—whenever you felt ready." This was a half-lie. If she wanted another one, I would be half-ready. What I didn't want was a baby born out of obligation or resentment or a token monthly roll in the hay. But she was venting. It was her right, and I deserved whatever I got. It was also her baby, not "ours." She made that clear: I lost my baby. That was intentional, not a post-traumatic slip-of-the-tongue.

"I was ready, but you weren't. I could tell." Headlights swept around the bend, momentarily blinding me. I listened to the car fade like the cool breeze I had been hoping for the past two days. Overhead, stars were multiplying around the obese moon.

"You could have told me—that might have helped."

She laughed, a hurt laugh. "Oh? Like I didn't try?"

I was ashamed. I tried to visualize the might-have-been addition to our family. All I could see in my mind was a flesh-colored smear in the fog.

Natalie began sniffling. Natalie never sniffled.

"I'm sorry, Natalie."

"Oh, Jon, it's all my fault!"

"No."

"It is, Jon. God's punishing me."

"Nat, no. God doesn't work that way."

"I know he doesn't, but this time he is. I asked him to. I didn't want the baby. At first I did but once I got it I didn't anymore—I mean, I did and then I didn't and now that I don't I do. Am I making sense?"

"Yes. Of course you are."

Then she roared into my ear: "DON'T! DON'T DO THAT!"

"What? Do what?"

"That! What you're doing!"

"Hey—Nat—Natalie . . ."

She began sobbing. "I'm so screwed up right now. I read my scriptures, I fast, I have Family Home Evening even though it's like pulling teeth to get Val to participate. Even though you're gone all the time . . . Val thinks I'm an airhead, J. J. talks back to me, Rachel's . . . I don't even know *what* Rachel is anymore. And of course we're in the red again. Every time we get just a little bit of breathing room, it's always Rachel's braces or Val's cello or J. J.'s tee-ball. Or the alternator goes out, or the dishwasher. Every time it looks like we might get just a teeny tiny bit ahead, some stupid thing happens. Then I start going crazy trying to balance the blankety-blank checkbook, and the whole time I'm thinking, I've got no right to be acting like this, what am I so mad about? I've got three beautiful children, a good husband, this new house we can hardly pay for. Half the world's eating out of trashbins, and I'm complaining? And every time I go to the soup kitchen and see the old people and the young people and the little children filing through the line saying, 'God bless you, God bless you' because I put a hard roll on their tray, I feel so lucky and depressed at the same time. And now this! Heavenly Father blesses me with a baby, and I don't even want it until he takes it away and gives it to someone else—someone more worthy. That's what he's going to do, Jon."

"No, Nat—Natalie . . ." At that moment I think I wanted more than anything ever in my life to run my fingers three hundred miles through that telephone cable and gently knead the pain and guilt and suffering out of her. "I love you, Natalie."

"I wish you were here."

"I wish I was too."

"Are you sure?"

"What's that supposed to mean?"

Her voice was fading in and out. I stepped back inside the stuffy booth, a vain effort to improve the reception. "You know very well what I mean."

"No, I really don't, Natalie." Another bead of sweat broke loose and trickled down the ridges of my ribcage. I felt exhausted, drained. My legs were melting out from under me. "You act like this is all my fault. Look, I didn't make you have a miscarriage, okay? God didn't cause it, nuclear fallout didn't cause it. It just happened, okay? Naturally. Normally. Miscarriages happen. They happen all the time."

"That's not the problem, Jon."

"Then what is the problem?"

"You want to know the problem? Okay. Here—here's the problem: why was it so absolutely necessary for you to go up there today? Why didn't you come home last night when you knew I was feeling lousy? Why are you always talking to yourself, mumbling and carrying on?" Her voice sharpened. "Just who the hell is Nancy?"

It was as if my throat had been slit. I clutched the receiver, my lips moving but uttering no sound. I looked down but everything below my waist was submerged in darkness. I imagined debris under my feet—cigarette butts, blotches of bubble gum, a crab-shaped smear of chewing tobacco, a crippled ant or two hobbling about.

"She was an old friend," I said.

"Then that explains everything."

"No it doesn't."

"How long, Jon?"

"Natalie—"

"How long?"

"She's dead, Nat. She's been dead for . . . since before my mission." Silence again.

I filled her in, as briefly and concisely as possible. I told as much as I could. I told her about Mrs. Von K.; Natalie was sympathetic. "That poor girl. Why didn't you ever tell me?"

"It's not something I'm particularly proud of."

"I tell you things I'm not proud of."

"Would that have made a difference?"

"Yes. Telling the truth always makes a difference. Being honest. . . . I still can't believe you lied like that."

"I didn't lie."

"You withheld the truth. Same thing."

"Is it?"

"Isn't it?"

"Look, I'm sorry. What else can I say? Nat? Are you there?"

Silence. Eternity. Forever. Then: "Well, we've got to get her out of there."

"What?"

"The mother—you say you got the papers?"

"A whole stack. It looks like enough red tape to crown the Kremlin."

"I'll call Scott."

Her brother the attorney. If there was an in, Scott would find it.

242

"I mean we can't just leave her in there like that. What if it was me or you or my mother?"

"You're beautiful, Nat! I'm on my way!"

"No, Jon. I want you to bury it first. Finish up whatever it is you feel so compelled to do up there. Then come home. Then we'll talk."

"Nat?"

"Bury it!"

CHAPTER 26

Nancy . . .

You once told me something you had read about death and dying. It was a confession of sorts. You had always denied an after-life—poof! We're smoke! Gone! But this . . . After wrestling free from mortality you are greeted by a grandfatherly fellow who smiles and asks one simple question: not how many books have you written or how many orgasms have you had; not how big is your house or did you pay your tithing. But this: *What have you done for someone else?*

Where are you tonight, Nancy? As I drive this mountain road with every slice of moonlight through the pines a staggered flash bringing another fractured face to mind, I wonder, What have I done for someone else? What have I done for a lonely boy in my English class who isn't anymore, an old woman I barely know who is dissipating in a death depot, my wife Natalie who is trying to fill the void in her belly which is a microcosm of my life? What have I done for a brilliant girl I loved deeply and dearly but didn't realize it until it was too late? Are you listening? Because there's more. I feel like quivering old Lear: "I have taken too little care in this!"

Once upon a time you're young and ambitious and you've got a dream. But you meet a pretty girl, fall in love, and get married. It's the way of the world. The great human flux. You still have your dream, but you've got to eat, right? So in the meantime you're going to scrub toilets or sell used cars. You do whatever to keep tortillas on the table. And luck is on your side, it seems. You strike quickly. A story in *The Atlantic* and you're still in graduate school, barely twenty-five. A certified phenomenon.

But things change. Before you can blink, you're twenty-eight, twenty-nine, thirty; one kid, two, three, a house, a mortgage and a motherlode of hospital bills. You're dragging through each day, and the only light at the end of the tunnel is the cyclops eye of an oncoming train. But you carry on. You baptize your kid, read her a story at night, comfort him when his pinewood derby car rolls in dead last, and just pray to God you happen to be there at the right time and place and say the right thing so he doesn't wander off and stick a hunting rifle in his mouth. It's life, what can I say? But the other's no solution. It's just moving up or down a floor. Rearranging furniture. You drag all the old baggage with you.

Do I get the last word this time, Nancy? I miss you. I wish you were here. I wonder how you and my mother and father are getting along these days. Do you have mountains and pine trees over there? Do you have to balance a checkbook? Are you single and alone or spoken for? And how will you receive me when I pass through the veil? With sharpened fingernails or open arms?

Nancy, there's a nail in my head I can't seem to pull out. Am I getting dizzy or is that dashed white line really a giant sidewinder crawling down the middle of the road? And the moon! Look! Climbing the sky like a great white goddess! Half-masked in a scarf-shaped cloud, like a naked woman in a steam bath. No, don't go! Linger awhile, for I love to watch the moon come and go and come and go and—Natalie!

Finally I'm beginning to comprehend your dread not of death but of what comes after. Will there be Pampers in heaven? Stretch marks? Water units to sell? Books to write? Maybe our worries ought to be more basic: Will there be you? Me? Us? Natalie, I hear clocks ticking, fires crackling, see the idiot light flicker on the dash warning me back. Is the sky really moving? Are those black conifers missiles waiting to be launched? Natalie, wherever you are, remember our wedding night in San Diego? After the big Mexican buffet at Tampico's we drove to San Elijo and parked on the overlook. A chilly December, the white caps thrashing like wild manes. The radio was low, the heater high, and we necked in the front seat, you in your orange wrap-around dress, I in my navy-blue suit. I was advancing toward your legal territory when you abruptly removed my hand and stiffened, as if you were still single, corruptible. "Go in the water!" you said.

On our honeymoon, in mid-winter? "What for? In place of a cold shower?"

"You're always saying how much you *love* the ocean, *love* the water, *love* the beach. Here's your chance!"

It was miserably cold and windy out. The red riptide flag stood as stiff as a signpost. Pacific spray dotted the windshield. But you knew I couldn't refuse. You were my bride of eight hours and it was our first night and I still had something to prove. "Jump in? Here? Now?" Your long-fingered hand muffled a giggle. "I can't just run out there in my suit and start swimming around like an idiot! I've got nothing to wear!"

It was your kid's phrasing that did it: "You're chicken!"

Chicken! Remember how I whipped off my coat, pants, wing-tips, garments, and dashed a hundred yards across the cold wet sand and hurled myself into the charging surf? Rising, still numb from the initial shock, I hurdled a rush of water; then performed a medley of high jumping techniques on the ensuing breakers, clearing one with a fine western roll, the next with textbook scissors, and the third with my forte, the Fosbury Flop. Like Novocaine, the cold deadened any discomfort, and I was aware only of the salty cream foaming all around me. Knee-deep in it, I clapped my hands and slapped my thighs, pounded my chest, and carried on like the big crazy high school jock I thought I had left behind. I was laughing, belching, reveling in the dark privacy of Mother Ocean when suddenly my nakedness was showered with light. The horn honked non-stop, alerting any beachside lovers to this outrageous spectacle, the one and only Great Sea Ass, alias Jon Reeves!

Back bowed, tucked low and tight, I sprinted out of the light-zone towards the car where you, my virgin bride, were in the driver's seat laughing hysterically. As I grabbed the door handle, the numbness wore off and, like an elastic suit, the cold sea water contracted my body, erecting papules on my skin and shrinking my scrotum to a walnut. Naturally, you had locked the door.

I pounded on the window. "Open up! Open up!"

Eventually you obliged, but only after watching me suffer in freezing indignation a few minutes longer. "Very funny!" I snarled, plopping down in the passenger seat. Shivering, I groped for the heater switch (which you had turned off).

"Oh, come on, Jon! Where's your sense of humor!"

"Sorry, I left it somewhere in the Pacific!"

"Relax, Jon."

"Relax! While I sit here freezing to death!"

Then you pressed your warm palm to my cheek. Your hand bore a sweet and sour fragrance I would later identify with our intimate encounters. On touch, a special shiver, distinct from all the others, raced from my face to my groin. The shiver grew warm. I relaxed. Wiping the cold from my face, I leaned forward and placed my hands near the heater vent (which you had turned back on). It was then I noticed you were wearing nothing but your long Godiva hair.

Natalie, can you hear me? Then listen, please. I've been running stubbornly contrary: call it stress, call it change, call it knuckling under to the invisible meanness of life. But it's a disease that creeps in slowly. It starts with a little frostbite, and you do it for protection at first, thinking what you don't feel can't hurt you. But it spreads—it spreads and grows into a glacier. Am I making any sense at all? Let me streamline: Natalie, I love you. I love going to bed with you and waking up to you, the smell of your hair in my face. I love your goofy anecdotes, your compassion for the forgotten oddities of the world. In Spandex or flannel pajamas, helping the kids carve a jack-o-lantern or propped up at night with a Patricia Veryan novel or railing on Bishop Finley for slashing the Relief Society budget. I love your laughter at not enough things. Natalie, I'm sorry again (past, present, all blunders to come). But it's time I think to put on the brakes and not get so wrapped-up and brain-boggled in this making a living business that we forget to—ooooops!—live.

You see, there's this place I've told you about before, a little village way down south called Esperanza. "Hope." The people are dirt poor, they don't have shopping malls or swimming pools. They travel by foot or by burro, yet they have smiles on their faces, toothless smiles, and contentment in their hearts. They live simply but when they see the sun rise every morning like a big red hibiscus, they feel it. They sing and dance and don't fret about house payments, but they surely could use a good teacher or two. Am I building pueblos in the sky? All right. Just a fantasy, perhaps a suggestion, maybe a possibility. Natalie, we need to sit down and talk. Sell the house, I think. Hug the kids, I think. For the first time in a long time you tell me 100 percent what your dreams are and I'll ditto the same with you and then . . . We'll go from there. We'll do whatever we need to.

Dear Val, thanks for pinch-hitting in your mother's unexpected absence. You may put up an icy front, but you've got a good heart. Like it or not. In answer to your latest question—Is there dissension in heaven? How can you have art without conflict or dissent? If everyone's the same there's not much slack for creativity. So I think I'm in your camp on this one. Can you surprise God? Maybe. Can you overthrow him? Heavy stuff, kid. But you just keep thinking; the world needs busy minds like yours.

Dear Raych, I don't know if you remember this but a few weeks ago I sneaked into your bedroom late to kiss you goodnight. You were in the bathroom, but your Kathy doll was lying in your place as if she were really truly alive, staring back at me with her innocuous green decal eyes. And it hit me like a brick: someday Kathy will no longer be a baby but a plain ordinary doll—cloth and plastic. That saddened me. I picked up Kathy and sat on the edge of the bed and held her to my chest, chin over my shoulder, patting her back as I used to when you were her age. You barged in and smiled your Rachel smile. "Da-ad!" you said, gently snatching your baby from my arms. "Like *this*!"

Dear J. J., the next time that punk kid calls you six-eyes, deck him! That's right, you've got my twenty-one gun permission! How's that? Karate lessons? We'll look into Tae Kwan Do or something when I get back, we most definitely will. You've got to know how to defend yourself. But don't lay this guy out on a stretcher. We'll talk about it, buddy. We'll talk.

Natalie, I'm going down now. Switchbacking down. Zig-zag, zig-zag. As the Toyota crawls around each turn, I look at the flash of rapids that seem like silver banners fluttering in the wind. The headlights carve a hole into the night. Twigs and branches snap like bones underneath the balding tires. The dust billows like a red fog all around me. What's up? What's wrong? This place I know like the back of my hand suddenly seems so foreign to me. Hit the brakes! STOP! Where's the water buffalo? Where's the accident that was about to happen?

Down. Deeper. Darker. More night bugs splash on the glass. I park under a black canopy of oaks and step outside. Instead of sweathouse heat, cool currents whiffle through the ponderosa pines. The cooked vanilla scent reminds me I'm on friendly soil. Although I know the trail blindfolded, I weave through the coverbrush cautiously, as if thugs are waiting to ambush me. The twisted trunks of the manzanita trees look like forsaken lovers reaching out with anguished arms. Draped in darkness, the familiar trees and shrubs are black sponge prints on silk-screen, an oriental still-life except for the dark flow of water and, a few feet above it, the manic traffic of bats.

Gripping exposed roots and rocks, I shinny down the steep bank to the sandy beach below. The roots are dry and scaly, reptilian, the rocks as round and smooth as bowling balls. The bloated moon has found a peaceful spot on the water. The cliff beyond it looks mean, brilliant, stunning in the moonlight. The thousand faces of the day coalesce into one great pagan mask. The waterfall is a long, silver tongue lapping the River upward.

I picture myself on top, a tall, rangy fourteen-year-old. Impetuous. A little crazy. Impressionable and eager to make an impression. Some well-intentioned cynic has just spray-painted a skull-and-crossbones at the foot of the cliff, in homage to Steve Valkenburg. Down on the beach, my best friend Keith Bernhard is half-baiting, half-cautioning me: "No way, Jay! No-ho-ho way!" Annette Plikta, the black-haired gypsy beauty, is reclining on an air mattress like the Queen of the Nile. Two skinny strips of polyester fig leaves separate her voluptuous body from total nudity. She looks up at me, yawns, then wipes her hand across her cleavage—a calculated gesture, I realize in retrospect—daring me while reminding me of the secret pleasures I will forever be denied if I miss by an inch and wind up in traction. Keith is in full grin now, daring me as well. My ego, my worst enemy, calls their bluff.

Staring down at my future, I whisper a short, vain prayer, then cross myself, mockingly, winning a laugh. But everything goes numb and dark as my feet let go and I become an arrow angling endlessly down. My head rips through the water, followed by a quivering ecstatic nausea that peels off my body as I burst through the surface. Alive. Whole. Tossing my hair back haughtily, I turn casually to the crowd: "No sweat." Even aloof, recondite Annette stands up and cheers.

Three years later at that same spot, you asked me to jump, Nancy, and I refused. A mere jump. Child's play by comparison. Why not, when I had accepted far more idiotic challenges? The jump was nothing. The dive was even less. I hope you can forgive. Not the jump but the other.

Dear God, Father, why can't I ever get it right for once? How many more times until I finally learn for good? Some shame doesn't wash off easily. Do you understand what I'm trying to say here? Of course you do! You know everything! Patience with me, please. Don't call me back until I've made everything right. Am I playing Penelope, unweaving as I weave? Or does it take an eternity to smooth out the rough edges? Then help me tell the real story, the deep truth which too often has to sneak in like a Greek bearing illumination but not always good tidings of great joy. Which is the whole point, the irony, the freedom and the beauty of it. It's a pain in the ass at times, but precious no matter how many shots you take on the chin. But look at me! Swearing in a prayer! That's how low I'm flying. I'm a disgrace, a nuisance, a potsherd. I'm on the verge! I have been, since day one, forever tottering over the edge. That moon, though, it's so bright right now, doubled on sky and water. Gorgeous. Awesome. Glaring down like your holy all-seeing eye. My brain's beginning to wobble. Why can't I say this to your face? Wait. That comes later. After.

I peel off my clothing—t-shirt, sweat pants, sneakers, garments, everything. Don't ask why. It just feels right. I step into the water, my bare feet sinking into the wet sand. Musty African odors rise from the loamy bank. The black water wraps around my ankles like ambiguous hands, squeezing, climbing to my knees, thighs, waist, half-in, half-out, a centaur sensation. Embracing. I take a deep breath, my legs buckle, and I'm under. Buried. The water stings my sunburned back and scratched-up stomach, but the pain quickly passes. I raise my arms to the night, the water clinging to me like a soothing body lotion, the thrill of goosebumps everywhere.

A dozen strokes is all it takes, and I'm climbing the mossy face, my fingers and toes groping for cracks, friction. I pull, reach and pull, my triceps turning to paste. They swell, thicken, burn. I glance down at the white commotion, water exploding on rock. The round moon is a fireman's net too far away to catch me. I'm ten stories high, it seems, but I'm not a third of the way there yet. A dead oak tree is crouching on top, peering down at me like a cynical old man. I can smell and feel algae everywhere, long strands of greasy green hair. The truant spray stipples my skin like a second sweat.

I reach, grab, pull, wondering how this damn cliff has doubled in size overnight. My toes and fingers continue reading braille. As I near the top, the old man extends a bony arm to me. I accept it, tugging, testing, drawing myself up with both hands. I pause to catch my breath, check my bearings. The canyon walls are stacked up to the stars, tilting perilously inward. The longer I look, the more they seem to lean. Any moment they will topple and bury me forever.

I step boldly onto the ledge, like an eagle in waiting, big-chested, full-bellied, arms spread like giant wings. But when I look down the great watershaft, I lose courage. The twin boulders have turned into killer whales awaiting their next meal. All along the upper bank the shadows bulge like bell-shaped monks in mourning. I close my eyes and listen to the roar of aeons. Lions? Atom bombs? Armageddon? No, not the thunder of destruction but a gradual softening; the sweet roar of angels.

So what now? Where now? This damn Rock seems to be growing in stature even as I stand here. I'm in a hot air balloon rising slowly to the moon. The longer I wait, the farther I'll have to fall. A thousand arguments turn me back: It is a mindless, selfish, juvenile trick, signifying *nada*. You're a husband, a father, full of obligations, not Evil Kneivel or some weekend warrior stunt man. The courageous thing is to turn away, resist the sirens. It's a no-win scenario. If you surface clean, who's to tell? Who knows but fifty billion stars, twenty-five billion pair of dice all showing snake eyes?

You will. I will. We. I hear the midnight moaning of my wife who is confused, grieved, and angered. Smell the sweet stink of flowers, see the sad faces of my children replaying the scene long after they are parents with little girls and boys of their own, forever wondering, as I have wondered all these years, Why the hell Why the hell Why the hell?

Hypocrite! Idiot! Selfish to the end! Don't you dare, Jon! Don't you—

I wait a few moments longer, then turn and take the first fatal step home. It is the wise, responsible thing. Somewhere deep in the canyon I hear a moan: the voice of my father, or the last train out of town. I whirl back around. Like a man from a burning building I leap up and out, spreading my wings as in my finest dreams. I become, again, eagle and arrow.

In a moment it is over: the wind screaming past my ears, my scalp prickling just before contact, and this thought: I have done a terrible, wonderful thing. Then up and out with arms waving. Hollering at the moon, the stars, my celestial witnesses: "Sonuvabitch, Keith! Sonuvabitch, Nancy! Sonuvabitch, Natalie! Universe! Sonuvabitch!"

Hustling out of the water, crouching low, I gather up my clothing and begin the long descent home.